THE SICILIAN HOARD

THE SICILIAN HOARD

A Novel

by

David Weimer

Colossus Press
Summit, New Jersey

Grateful acknowledgment is made to Faber & Faber Ltd for permission to reprint as chapter epigraphs certain excerpts from Roger Crosnier's *Fencing with the Sabre*.

Copyright © 1996 by David R. Weimer
All rights reserved under International and Pan-American Copyright Conventions.

Library of Congress Catalog Card Number 95-74724

ISBN 0-964-8186-5-5 (cloth)
ISBN 0-964-8186-6-3 (paper)

This is a work of fiction. Names, characters and incidents spring from the author's imagination or are used fictively. Any resemblance to actual events or persons, living or dead, is wholly coincidental.

Manufactured in the United States of America

Colossus Press
P.O. Box 105
Summit, New Jersey 07902-0105

To, for and with Joan

The Trail

London

Syracuse

Rome

Munich

The Trail Detailed

LONDON

Viewing
Centering
Finding

SYRACUSE

Jugate
Encrustation
Incuse
Flow Lines
The Hoard
Overstruck
Pierced for Suspension
Want List

ROME

Con turbolenza ma non troppo
Piú mosso; scherzevole
Una rivelazione
Con eleganza
Intricarsi
Aspramente
Con piacere e con dolore morale
Un accenno di pericolo
Abbandonandosi
Con sentimento profondo
Con delirio
La cerimonia, la brillantezza, l'esultanza
Irresolutamente
Affannosamente
Una faccenda difficile

Pensierosamente (solo)
Con bocca chiusa
Tenebrosamente
Andante affettuoso — ma con interruzioni
Stanco e contuso
Quasi un pastorale
Inoperosità forzata — poi rubata
Alla turca
Ondeggiante poi tempestoso
Languido e vivace
La tristezza, il terrore, l'eccitazione

MUNICH

To recover quickly
Absence of blade
To distract
Panic
The arm is extended
Balance and footwork
Parries against his will
Offensive actions
To hit and not be hit
Impaled . . .on the point
The *riposte*
A direct attack
Counter-*ripostes*
False attacks
Two or more parries
Quite a common fault

LONDON

"The respect for truth . . . in England is equalled only by the respect for wealth."

Ralph Waldo Emerson,
"Wealth" in *English Traits* (1856)

" 'I always feel doomed when the train is running into London. I feel such a despair, so hopeless, as if it were the end of the world.' "

D. H. Lawrence, *Women in Love* (1920)

"Hunters for gold or pursuers of fame, they had all gone out on that stream, bearing the sword, and often the torch, messengers of the might within the land, bearers of a spark from the sacred fire."

Joseph Conrad, *Heart of Darkness* (1899)

LONDON

Viewing

I entered, stopped, saw the red tables straight ahead first thing.

Quickly I looked away. I wanted to save those for last.

To the left near the wall a security guard, gray and dark-blue uniform. Male, 30s. No weapons, not even a billy, but beefy and alert. To the right, his twin.

I took a step into the room, looking casual. The room was large, maybe thirty by forty feet. Two young men, navy-blue aprons over dress shirts and ties, sat in plastic chairs to the sides of the tables. The porters, there for errands, ready to back up the guards if called on.

Behind me on the rear wall, in the corners near the high ceiling, two small black video cameras slowly sweeping the room. There must have been more than two, hidden somewhere.

Four tall windows on the front wall. Between the windows, high on the front wall, three honorific busts perched on large bookcases. Shakespeare on the right, maybe Voltaire in the middle, Milton on the left. Meant to honor the scene below, instead they merely overlooked it. The enterprise had started as book auctioneers, I'd heard. Even now, hundreds maybe thousands of used books filled shelves to the sides and rear of the room, floor nearly to the ceiling. After two and a half centuries they were still auctioning books. But now they auctioned *everything*. Everything convertible to cash anyway—large sums preferred—anywhere on the globe from London to Hong Kong and on around back to London, they'd auction it if you let them. The trick was not to let them.

Almost ready for the red tables.

Beyond the tables there were the angels all right, five no six of them, some wafting about, some stationary, smiling attentively. All women, in their 30s and 40s, dressed in muted tans and greens, waiting there to carry the thin trays from the low, black, brass-handled wooden cabinets behind them to the prospects seated at the tables. Attractive women, naturally, responsive to something beyond the clients' requests for trays, beckoning beyond the needs of the moment toward the realm of unspoken desires. Whoever first called them 'angels' surely sensed this mission in them. They weren't merely employed, they were chosen. The enterprise could have used men or even grown boys for these simple tasks. Anyone can carry trays, dress neatly, look cheerful.

But the management wisely chose attractive women. Who better than angels to evoke the shimmering ideals behind the worn coins they handled, to link the visible, imperfect forms of money and power to the perfect forms in which we imagine them? Who better than angels to cast an innocently seductive glow over these deep passions?

Ever so delicately seductive, to be sure. Had I been standing near the angels, I was sure I'd have caught the faint scent of lavender.

Almost everyone else in the room was male, only one or two of the seated clients female. The very room itself, the entire enterprise, cried out its maleness, its devotion to money and to power.

Only the angels were delicate, but everything in the room was subdued. Like the dun carpet the colors were all somber, the voices low. Six large white globed lamps hung from the ceiling and three spots shed light over the tables, all so subdued. Even the red felt of the table tops was subdued, I saw as I moved a few steps closer. A dull tomato shade, the felt padded the tables slightly, in case fragile objects were dropped.

"Would you complete this form, sir, please?" The angel's voice startled me, it was so near. A well-shaped hand held out a sheet of paper. I hadn't realized how close to the front I had moved, nearly up against the first row of clients seated at the tables. There were three tables, four or five clients at each.

I took the form from the hand, stepped backward, looked for a place where I could fill it out. The room suddenly felt suffocating.

I looked up at the huge windows, all heavily draped, all closed. I didn't dare ask anyone to open them.

My leg had begun to throb, down the inside where they'd taken the vein out. I had to sit down, try to get that leg elevated. I spotted two adjacent empty chairs at the nearest table, sat down cautiously in one. But I couldn't bring myself to lift that leg onto the other chair. Simply not done here, my good man. The throbbing grew.

"May I have your form, please?" That angelic voice, and yes the scent of lavender. I filled out the form in a mounting daze. Full name, local and permanent addresses, business connections, all that. I had no business connections, put down "Fencing coach," wondering what they would make of that. I handed the form back. "And the lot number, sir? If you please." The number shone so clearly in my head I'd neglected to write it down. I wrote it down. That attentive hand took the form away.

To my right, a middleaged Oriental man was peering through a small magnifier at a tiny coin. I hadn't seen anything as small as an obol in the catalogue. No, it wasn't an obol after all; he simply had enormous chubby hands. He was impeccably dressed in a dark-blue pinstripe. I had on a tweed jacket and dark pants. The jacket was dark too, but it was certainly tweed. To my left, beyond the empty chair, a rosy-cheeked, elderly man held a gold coin off at a diopter's distance, rotating it very slowly. His was a calm, elegant rotation. An Englishman, no doubt.

And then it appeared—the miniature cardboard box, held by the lovely hand. The angel suspended it for a moment near her breast, then hand and box cascaded slowly toward me, descended with agonizing precision in an arc toward the red felt, came to rest inches from my fingers. Lavender filled my nostrils.

I could barely look at it, I'd waited so long to see it. On one side of the small box the lot number was stamped in black.

Inside the box, encased in a clear, plastic envelope, lay a single silver coin. It was about the size of an American quarter, slightly larger.

"May I remove—?" I fumbled.

"The plastic sheath? Yes, of course, sir," she said quietly. "Just leave the coin in full view, sir, if you would. At all times." She smiled. The angel moved a delicate step backward and toward my right. The Oriental man and I appeared to be in her keeping.

I was sweating horribly now. The room felt a hundred degrees. I appealed to the windows, still closed. I was careful not to lean against the table with my chest, but it had started to ache anyway. I didn't know how long I could handle the pain.

Almost reluctantly, I looked at the coin—and gasped. It was stunning, far more beautiful than I had ever imagined.

Trembling, I removed it carefully from the envelope, placed it on the table. Against the dull red background the silver shone with startling luster. On its raised surfaces—the nose, the cheekbones, the thicker strands of hair—the silver was shiny. The flatter surfaces were dark, quite dark, a deep glowing charcoal gray, surfaces much less touched when the coin was in use, the whole not touched at all for well over two thousand years while it lay buried beneath the mounting layers of soil.

But how could this silver jewel have disappeared? How could any Syracusan of the fifth century have let it out of his sight once he had held it in his hand? Or held *her*—for the great luminous presence on the coin was the haunted and haunting face of Arethusa herself. Some parts disappointed: the nose a trifle broad, the eyelids a trifle heavy, the lips almost too thickly sensual. But with those serpentine locks fanning wildly, uncontrollably outward in all directions from her head, with the elegant necklace and earrings, with the embroidered headband, and the famous four dolphins now subordinated, giving depth to her portrait from behind, the effect of the whole on me was—quite physically—thrilling.

And she was facing *me*, or nearly so. Turned a few degrees left of head-on, she gave the impression of being *about* to face me directly, or of having done so just a few moments before. It was as though after a century or more of having been forced by the Greeks to face straight left or right on all those thousands of tetradrachms and decadrachms, with her visible eye shown implausibly full, locked into artists' conventions, imprisoned by the merely human and arbitrary, the nymph had decided to assert her transcendent authority, present herself in her divine fullness and—while the artists slept and the Syracusan tyrants occupied themselves with building palaces and enslaving neighbors—she had taken out the magic key one night, unlocked her cell and gracefully turned around to face *us*.

This was nonsense, of course. It was an artist who had freed her, the very engraver whose first and last initials were inscribed on Arethusa's hair-band.

I reached for the magnifier in my jacket pocket. The guard near me stirred, saw the small instrument, relaxed.

There it was, sharp under the lens. *KN*, *Kimon*. He had signed his own work! The self-assertion behind that signature, a self-aggrandizement coming late in that glorious century of Sicilian coinage, must have been sanctioned by the Greek communities in which the artists worked, much as Renaissance artists throughout Italy two millenia later had been emboldened to sign their names to their work after centuries of medieval anonymity. To be sure, Kimon had also inscribed Arethusa's name on the obverse, in more prominent letters than his own. He could hardly have put his name on a level with Arethusa's. Syracusans of 410 B.C. would never have stood for *that*.

But Kimon must have been proud, ambitious, sly or all of these. I turned the tetradrachm over. On the reverse, between the double lines near the bottom the letters of his name were again to be found, barely visible. What a powerful rock-crystal magnifier he must have worked with, and how damaged his eyesight must eventually have become. Did he think that damage a small price to pay for fame, his initials and even his full name in silver, passed through thousands of hands, some of them the noblest of hands, throughout Syracuse, Gela, Akragas, Selinus and elsewhere on the island, even to Tarentum on the great mainland and beyond that to Athens itself?

Below Kimon's nearly effaced name, in the exergue, the name of Syracuse stood up strongly still. Both names faded, though, beneath the magnificent horses of the quadriga above, racing spiritedly as the charioteer strains forward to rein them in. But he also seems to be lashing them, with a long thin rod. Why rein and lash at the same time? Perhaps there's another dimension here; the horses may be turning at a post, that rod signaling the direction they're to turn. No, the reins are all held in the same way, not two pairs forward and two back for a turn. And the horses' heads surge in four directions, not likely at a turn—nor likely any time during the race itself. The mysteries here are only slightly reduced when we remember that these are after all *Kimon's* horses. They're posing for him, for his silver tetradrachm. They may commemorate some Syracusan's notable victory at Olympia in the Peloponnese; there were many such Sicilian victories. But Kimon engraved them in silver, for the ages, for me today.

The heat in the room was proving intolerable, my leg was going numb. Suddenly an ache like a large hot needle pierced my chest. I felt in my jacket pocket for the codeine, should have thought of it earlier. None in that pocket. Frantically I tried others. None there. My god, I'd forgotten to bring any.

Abruptly I got up, swung away from the table.

"Say there, what do you think—?" A guard rushed over, grabbed my arm. I tried to shake him off. The other guard pitched in, then others, clutching and holding. "Trying to nick a lot—!" one said. They were forcing one hand open. Then I saw it. I was still holding the coin. I let them take it.

"I didn't mean—," I tried to say.

"All right, mate," a guard said grimly, "let's just walk to the door." Hands locked onto my arms on both sides.

Centering

As I struggled up out of sleep I heard Phil say, "Are you okay?"

"Yeah, sure." I wasn't so sure. My chest hurt horribly, my whole body ached. I thought about trying to lift one shoulder, but gave it up.

"You don't look so great, Pop."

He knew how to get me. "Don't call me 'Pop.'" I tried that shoulder again, felt it rise a little, felt Phil's arm behind me, helping. Slowly I made it up half-way. Phil swung my legs off the bed. I was exhausted. "You must have brought codeine," I said.

"I always carry some these days," he said. "How're you doing?" With some effort I opened my eyes, saw his anxious face.

"Better." At least I could keep my eyes open and speak at the same time. Couldn't do that a few weeks ago. "You must have rescued me—how long ago?"

"Three or four hours." He grinned. "Those guards were really tough, all for calling the bobbies. I kept trying to explain how you just had heart surgery and all that, they wouldn't listen. Then finally some guy in a coat and tie came rushing out. He really heard what I was saying and saw what condition you were in, he told someone to call a taxi—and here we are."

"Taxis cost a bundle," I said. I massaged my left leg.

"You'd rather we walked several blocks and then waited for a bus?"

"I know, I'm sorry. You did the right thing." A nineteen-year-old shouldn't need so much stroking. But I'd forgotten what it's like to be nineteen.

"You need protein and carbohydrates. How about scrambled eggs and wholewheat toast?" That was nineteen too, taking charge, showing his competence.

"Great. But just one egg for me, no bacon, no butter—"

"Sure, sure, I know the list." He was studying my face, sizing me up. "You want another codeine? It's been four hours."

"Yes. I've stopped trying to be a hero." Phil brought me the white tablet and water. I looked at him appreciatively. "*You* were the family hero today."

"Well, I probably did keep you out of the clink." He turned to the tiny fridge in the kitchenette, started getting things out. "The guards got the idea you were casing the joint."

Sheepish feeling. "I sort of was. The secret agent in me, the

George Smiley. Measuring everything, sizing up the human beings, checking the exits, alert to danger. Hangover from all those mysteries I've read. Kind of dumb."

"So you cased the joint. Then what happened?"

I paused. "Well, there was the heat—and the pain." It was always hard to explain. "But mostly it was that coin." It was a strain just to talk.

"Yep." He bustled about the kitchenette, satisfied to be doing something, serving both of us. He hadn't been an Eagle Scout for nothing.

"You know I've wanted for years not just to *look* at those magnificent Sicilian coins in catalogs or museums but actually to touch one of them, to hold it in my hand, feel its surface, look at it close up, clench it in my fist the way a Syracusan must have clenched it over two thousand years ago."

"The tetras and decas, the real beauties," he said, falling into the refrain, maybe listening maybe not. Anyway he was scrambling the eggs.

Suddenly I felt drained. I tried to turn sideways on the bed, to get my elbow underneath me so as to lie down.

"Hey, wait!" Phil dashed over to the bed, helped ease me down. "Just take it easy, no talking, okay?"

"Well, you asked me—"

"Sure, I know. Hey, the eggs—!" My eyes closed, I could hear him rush to the burner, curse quietly. I smelled the burned eggs. Worst smell in the world. I heard him scraping the pan, rinsing it out, getting out the margarine, cracking more eggs.

I'd never be able to explain it. More than once Susan had asked how I got so spellbound by those coins. "You get so—so *gripped* by that ancient world," she said after one particularly difficult episode, "you just leave this one. Do you know it sometimes takes hours for you to come back?" She wasn't being critical, just puzzled, concerned. "It's almost like a seizure, a *grand mal* without the convulsions." She lived so entirely in the present that I was never able to find words to convey how I felt in those magical moments.

"I remember Mom used to say you just fell into a kind of trance," Phil said quietly, more to himself than to me. It was startling to have him tracking my thoughts. "You'd sit there with your coin books, just looking at pictures, then all of a sudden—" He didn't grasp it any more than his mother did. Or than I did, for that matter.

"Well, I was excited today too. Just hearing about that coin auction gave me the shivers—you remember?—and when I learned the coins would be on display the very days we stopped over in London—what a miracle!" I paused. Phil seemed to be taking it in, maybe trying to understand it. "There's something else. As a kid I was always told I had a lively imagination. *An athletic imagination* was the way one grownup put it. That's something you remember. 'It's a gift,' a teacher once said to me. Some gifts you'd just as soon not have, right? Sometimes I've wanted—well anyway, I get carried away now and then." Lame finish.

"Okay," he said, clattering plates and forks, "here's another great breakfast—only it's lunch." I opened my eyes. He was sitting next to the bed, already shoveling it in.

"Help me up," I said. Together we got me to sit. Phil handed me a heaping plate, returned to his. Slowly I managed to eat every bite, every crumb of half-burned toast, every slug of congealed egg. Crooking my mouth in what was meant as a grateful smile, I nodded toward the bed, accepted his sturdy help in lying down again, and slept.

Waking, I felt more alert. Phil was standing by the window, looking out. Another overcast day. The room would have looked overcast even on a sunny day. It was a crummy room, muddy wallpaper, dirty rug, shabby curtains, not even a picture on the walls. Plenty of tiny brown ants running up and down the walls, though. Well, London was expensive, and a week in Sicily was going to cost plenty too.

I must have made a sound. Phil turned toward me, looking grim. "Seems to be brightening," he said. Only two days in England and he'd picked up some of the weatherman's lingo. "Are you up to a short walk?"

I hesitated. "Have to try," I said, motioning for help to rise.

Together we got me dressed. It took ages. Phil watched me put on the elastic stockings. "I thought you were done with those," he said.

"That leg's had a lot of strain today." I paused, summoning my forces. "How about going over to the park?"

It was slow going. That collapse at the auctioneer's had left me just enough energy to move my body. My chest still ached horribly, where the wire loops held my bones together, but we made it across Bayswater Road, raging traffic and all, into Kensington Gardens. Phil came briskly to life. After the morning's crisis and the stifling hotel room, a taste of freedom. "Whaddya say, Dad, how about four or five miles?"

His sense of humor. But I was happy to have him cheerful. He glanced at the pedometer on his belt, flipped open its cover. "Reads one-tenth of a mile so far," he said. "Not bad. Let's try to do a mile, okay?"

We entered the park on a broad asphalt walk lined by splendid maples on both sides. It was late afternoon. Shadows lengthened across the walk. Phil's spirits were rising fast. He kept striding ahead of me, then falling back. "I had no idea it would be so big. And what trees! The oaks must be two hundred years old!" He was an oak himself, tall and sturdy, pure hardwood, or mainly.

Except for a few high-rise buildings looming over the trees in the distance, the park seemed limitless. If I'd been feeling better I'd have shared Phil's expansiveness. No, I *was* sharing it, I realized. It *did* feel good to be here in London, really good, the way we'd anticipated back in America when we were planning this trip. Just what my doctor should have ordered. Things were looking up.

"Wow! Why didn't we ever come here before?"

"There are parks like this in Ohio," I said, "well maybe not quite so big."

"Nothing like this. And look at all these people from different cultures." Two years in college had given him words like "cultures." Before that he had talked like a typical American adolescent barbarian. Even better, after years of early-adolescent dogmatism at college he'd learned to say "perhaps." Susan and I had considered that improvement worth the whole cost of tuition. One day, just before she died, she and I made the mistake of telling him how pleased — and amused — we were with this new refinement in him. Phil didn't think it was funny at all.

"It's a whole United Nations," he said, staring at the Moslem women in black gowns, some with black face masks. Phil noticed that others had eye masks of some shiny material like foil, wondered what the difference was. There were large dark-haired families all dressed up, maybe Eastern Europeans. Lively, voluble groups, visibly enjoying themselves, doubtless Italians. A Babel of languages drifting by, snatches of Arabic, Spanish or Portuguese, German, something Oriental, two or three I couldn't identify. "I think I just heard Serbo-Croatian," Phil said. It was a family joke.

Scores of young males and females sprawled on the grass. The afternoon was still warm, the sun was out, and some of them were picturesquely half-naked. In our line of sight there must have been hundreds strolling, lounging in green and white deck chairs and lying down in the park, but the park was so spacious we weren't crowded in the least. "It's a real microcosm," he said, almost reverently. He'd brought home the word "microcosm" at the end of his sophomore year, over a year ago. No telling what his junior year would have given him.

"Phil, you weren't just a hero today, you've been a hero all year."

"Okay, okay. You've said that enough—"

"But it's true." I stopped walking, to face him. He stopped. "You can't imagine how much I've needed you, how grateful I've been—"

"You're supposed to keep walking, right? Get your aerobics up." He started walking on.

I resumed walking. "Let me just say a little more. If you hadn't quit college to help me out last year, I don't know how I could have survived your mother's death, then my surgery—"

We ambled on in silence for a while, my energy surprisingly up, my love for Phil welling up in a great current. I thought of a great round dark-blue pond I had seen as a boy in northern Ohio, its water calm at the surface but ceaselessly pouring out into a stream at the edge even as a powerful underground current pumped fresh water in at the center, silently, invisibly.

"And here we stopped off in London so you could see some of England, and now you're having to take care of me—"

"I'll still get to the Hard Rock Cafe and the other hot spots," he said. "You'll be okay by tomorrow." He seemed to believe that.

"You've got your mother's optimism," I said. He had her practicality too, her tough-mindedness, her empirical bent. There was a lot of Susan in Phil. I looked him over, saw him biting his lip, realized that his mother's death must have affected him in ways that we had somehow never managed to talk about.

"You know," he said, his tone sharply altered, "you and Mom didn't always seem that—well, lovey-dovey." Pigeons rose in the air, battling gusts of wind.

"No, you're right," I said, startled less by his shift of subject than by his having perceived what I hadn't realized he had even observed. "Partly right, anyway. Susan was never very demonstrative—was even a bit—" I hesitated.

"Cold?"

I shuddered at his objectivity. It was a new quality in him. How had I failed to notice its coming on? "It's hard to judge such things. I sometimes thought that—well, if I had been readier to open up—"

We walked on, lost momentarily in our own memories.

"She was remarkably responsible—and generous," I said, wanting to throw something large and solid into the gap threatening to open up before us.

"This trip, for instance," he said.

"Well yes, this trip. That life insurance she'd paid installments on all those years without telling me. She had no idea she'd die first, but just in case—" I hurried on. "She didn't know how I—how we—would spend the money she left, but I'm sure she would have been pleased—"

"With our coming to Europe?"

"You bet. With our going on to Sicily, so I can do my research—"

We had come to a seated marble statue of Queen Victoria. We stopped to inspect it. Victoria's face hadn't been improved by the weather, looked badly pockmarked. Maybe it wasn't marble.

"Let's go back, okay?"

"You sound upset." Phil looked at me searchingly.

I just didn't want to talk about it.

We turned back toward Bayswater Road.

Brilliant red kites swam in the air a hundred feet up. Sheepdogs, Yorkies and a lone Weimaraner trotted past us. A dense swarm of pigeons suddenly rose in front of us, and an elderly woman slashed at them with a cane. I grew angry with her. I knew I was on the edge.

Back at Shab Hotel I lay down, had just enough energy to check Phil's pedometer. It read 2.5 miles. Phil told me that meant I'd accomplished a lot today.

Phil had picked up a phone message. "It's from your friend Massimo, Dad. Says he's delighted we're in London, asks us to meet him at Il Carretto for dinner, says it's not far from here. Eight o'clock. You up to that?"

For Massimo, I'd be up to it.

Finding

The head waiter at Trattoria il Carretto selected a table for us at the rear of his little restaurant, a table for four—Phil, myself, my leg, and Massimo. The waiter's name was Rosario, he told us at once, evidently pleased with his name, his job, the restaurant, or all three. Il Carretto *was* a delight. Chianti bottles everywhere, small mirrors, replicas of Sicilian yellow and red donkey-cart wheels imbedded in the partitions.

Except for being a little tall, Rosario looked the way a Sicilian should look, wiry, black-haired, alert. Judging by what I'd seen of his compatriots, he was also a good deal more cheerful than most Sicilians. Possibly because he was not in Sicily.

When he discovered that I spoke Italian, his friendliness moved another notch higher. "*Lei parla molto molto bene, signore,*" he said, his arms flung wide in wonder. "*Penso di no,*" I said, "*soltanto un poco.*" But I warmed to his warmth. His was partly professional, but like that of nearly every Italian I had ever met, essentially genuine. I was a racist, I realized—or a nationalist?—I loved Italians.

"*Vostro figlio parla italiano?*"

"No, I'm afraid not."

"Well, maybe you'll learn Italian some day, eh?" he said to Phil. "We only speak it in Sicily when talking with foreigners like Italians from the mainland, but it's a good language." He laughed. "Of course, we use it now and then in London, here at the restaurant. Good for the atmosphere."

"Do you know Massimo Bellini?" I asked him.

"Of course I know Massimo," he said exuberantly. "Everybody knows Massimo. He's our favorite smuggler! Oh, *scusate,* I'm being called." He dashed away.

Phil was having a good time. "Is Massimo anything like him?"

"I guess you wouldn't remember. It's been a few years since Massimo came to the States. He's like Rosario only magnified ten times. Much broader"—I gestured outward from my waist—"even livelier and—well, see for yourself, he'll probably be here in an hour."

"Why an hour?"

"If he were pure Italian, he'd be two hours late. But he's spent most of his life in England, so he'll compromise."

I was wrong. Massimo was almost on time.

The clamor preceded him. There was his explosive entrance—cries of *Buona sera, buona sera!* flung into the air simultaneously by Massimo and three or four waiters gathered there—and then an almost palpable turbulence as he churned through the air toward us.

"*Ciao*, Michael," pumping my hand where I sat, and "*Ciao*, Philip!" pumping his. Gazing fixedly at Phil, still holding his hand,

Massimo said, wonderingly, "È *come suo nonno*. I would know you anywhere. You're his grandson without question." Still he held Phil's hand, appeared reluctant to let it go. "I guess you knew him," Phil said, visibly uncomfortable with Massimo's effusiveness.

"Hasn't your father told you the story?" Massimo looked incredulous. Then noticing my hoisted leg, he said quickly, "I'm sorry, Michael, terribly rude of me. How are you feeling?" He sat down. Phil too.

"I'm okay," I said, "eighty percent okay." Hand over heart. "This place on my chest is still tender as hell. I'm glad you didn't try to hug me—"

"You were sitting down or I would have," he beamed.

"And if I move too quickly sometimes I feel the plates in my chest grinding away—"

"Like those tectonic plates under the San Andreas Fault in California," Phil said, not wanting to get left out.

"I saw California when I visited you in the States," Massimo said solemnly to Phil, "but I don't remember the plates."

"You can't see or hear them—" Phil began, but then saw the smile spreading on Massimo's face.

"You're such a *bel giovanotto*, Philip," Massimo said, squeezing Phil's biceps appreciatively. "Your father and mother—" He stopped, embarrassed. "I'm sorry, I forgot for a moment—"

"It's all right," I said.

"Well, they certainly brought you up properly," Massimo continued, "or at least they fed you properly. Which reminds me—" He gestured to Rosario for the menu.

"Have you ever noticed," Massimo asked, "how in an Italian restaurant the first course arrives almost the minute you order? You know why? Italians get truly irritable when they feel hunger. The waiters bring the *antipasti* immediately just to prevent riots." Rosario stood there, holding the menus, appreciating Massimo's performance.

"But you're Sicilian," I said.

"We can get irritable too," he said, waving away the menu from Rosario's outstretched hand. "*Insalata tricolore, per favore,*" he said, "with a little extra mozzarella—and extra avocado—and extra tomato too, while you're at it." His "tomato" sounded like "to-mahto." The English pronunciation should have sat strangely on him, with his rich olive complexion and black hair, but somehow it didn't. He had absorbed England, as his Harris tweed jacket, cashmere sweater and Wallabees showed, without being absorbed by it. No environment would ever fully absorb him, I realized. Even Sicily, notoriously sponge-like, would never have absorbed him had he stayed there. Even now, chatting happily with us here in London, he seemed more Arab than Sicilian, with a mingled gentleness and strength that must have flowed to Sicilian shores on the waves of the great Arab invasions. Those invasions had left a marvelous legacy of architecture, gardens, poetry and language, but if they had left only Massimo Bellini, I reflected, they would have been justified.

As predicted, our orders came swiftly. Massimo was already savaging his *insalata* as he told Phil how we had met. It was, I'm convinced, his favorite story. "Your grandfather, Philip, was a remarkable man. I'm sure your father is too, but I got to know your grandfather—Kurt—extremely well for a short time. You can't imagine how short a time. Only a few minutes." He was eating slowly now, then put down his fork.

"It was nineteen-forty-three. A watershed year for Sicily, though I hadn't an inkling of that at the time, I was only seven years old. I didn't know much of anything at the time, only that my father had been gone a long time, off in the war somewhere, and that my mother and I had all the chores to do." Massimo looked at me keenly, as though wondering whether I could possibly understand what his life was like then. "It was the year Mussolini got kicked out, only the Sicilians didn't know or didn't care about *that* at the time. They had hated or despised Il Duce for *years*, if they thought about him at all. So when he got the boot, they knew it would make no difference whatever to them.

"No, for us it was the year of the great invasion. Two invasions, really. The second was the Americans and the British, landing on the beaches in the south. They'd sailed across from

North Africa, having beaten Rommel. It's not far from Tunisia to Sicily, and everybody expected them to come. But no one knew when.

"The invasion before that was the Germans. Once they sensed that Mussolini was crumbling, they began to move whole divisions down the mainland, hundreds of thousands of troops, and thousands into Sicily as well. As soon as Il Duce was out, they took over Italy completely, treating it like another occupied country, not as badly as Holland or Norway, but very nearly. Then when Eisenhower made a deal with the Italians, an Italian surrender really, the Germans knew an invasion was only a short time away."

Massimo paused, peering back a half-century. "That's when they took over Sicily too. They moved troops, tanks, artillery, planes, the works, onto the island. They shoved the Italian troops aside and put German generals in charge. They built airfields, dug gun emplacements, especially in the south, of course, from Siracusa westward to Gela, Agrigento and on over to Selinunte—all the ancient towns where the Greeks had minted coins, as though the Germans wanted to protect the hoards their friends the Sicilians might dig up there—what a joke, eh? They built tank barriers, underwater obstacles against landing craft, all that. Sicily became a bloody fortress."

"So how did the Americans ever get onto the island?" Phil asked. He was fascinated.

"They almost didn't. It was their first amphibious operation against Europe, and they were nervous. The Yanks and the Brits. Lots of cock-ups to begin with. They bombed their own troops. Paratroops fell miles off course. Landing craft drove up onto the wrong beaches. The Germans mostly made the right moves, pinning them down, knocking them out. Gritty fighters, those Germans. A real nightmare.

"But at last they did get ashore, the Americans and the British. On a narrow front from Gela to Siracusa, and then they just had to battle their way north."

Again he paused. "Montgomery took the British up the east coast, got bogged down. The Americans moved north to the west of them. Tough fighting for days. Then Patton, your General, had this bright idea. He probably had had it long before he landed. He'd back-double, sweep farther west than the Germans would expect and head straight north for Palermo, get a big victory for the Americans and headlines for himself. It was a bad strategy, I learned when I grew up and started to read military history. But spectacular!

"And it puzzled the Germans. If Patton was sending all his tanks north to Palermo, he *must* have some brilliant idea. So the Germans got worried. When Germans start to worry, they're really thorough. The generals got worried, their officers and N.C.O's got worried, every German soldier got worried." Massimo paused again, knowing he had us. Tables nearby were nearly full. Everyone nearby was listening. I had heard the story before, but was entranced too.

"They weren't only worried, of course. They were exhausted. Thirsty all the time and hungry for most of it. It was summer, and summer in Sicily is *hot*. Even in the north, in the mountains, where I lived, the daytime temperatures were over a hundred degrees. When a soldier was wounded, the medics couldn't even take his temperature unless they had a pan of cold water to put the thermometer in first.

"That's where your grandfather came in, Philip, and where I did too. *All* the Germans were tense, on edge, nervous, expecting American tanks round the next farm-house at any minute. A German cut off from his unit would be really jumpy.

"That's what happened to this one. Early one morning he sneaked on to our farm, hungry, thirsty, desperate for anything he could eat or drink. Even a cheese rind would have done. Or dirty water. He looked everywhere, round the barn, behind the haystack. There was practically nothing for *us* to eat, indoors or out, but he didn't know that. All he knew was that he had to eat something or he'd pass out, be captured, possibly tortured by the Americans.

"That's when he came right up to the farm-house, kicked in the door, which wasn't locked, and jumped into the kitchen, saw my mother looking shocked in front of the stove. I was right there, just a few feet away. I saw it all. The German looked wildly around the room, couldn't even see a water tap. There wasn't one. He wasn't sure what to do, but his hunger and thirst drove him. He grabbed my mother by the shoulders, started shaking her, shouted at her in German, shook her and shook her. Mother didn't know what he was saying. She didn't know any German, didn't even know any Italian, she was just a Sicilian peasant.

"But all that didn't matter anyway. The German soldier was so crazed with hunger and thirst—maybe he was crazy even when he wasn't hungry, who knows?—he shook her so hard she couldn't have said a word even if she'd wanted to. Then he dragged her out of the kitchen into the yard. I was terrified. I watched it all from the kitchen window. The German started to slap her face, first one side then the other. He slapped her hard. I was afraid he would kill her. As he might have done." Pause.

"Then this other soldier—an American—came running across the yard, straight toward them. I'd never seen anyone run so fast, don't think I ever have since. He threw himself on that German, hit him in the back, the side, the head, the shoulders, solid punches and wild punches, he seemed as crazy as the German. The German was caught by surprise, he tried to fight back but he was just too surprised. He stepped back from my mother, reached for his gun.

"The American pulled out his revolver. He was so angry that I swear to this day he was going to kill that German. He lifted the gun, aimed it, and even though the German threw up his hands in surrender I swear the American was about to pull the trigger. Even from the kitchen window I could see him trembling with rage."

Massimo looked down at his hands, as though having felt them tremble with the memory. "Then he lowered his gun. He just took the German prisoner, tied him up. Some other American soldiers came up then and took the German away.

"But what the American soldier did next was just as important to me, both then and now. He put his arms round my mother's shoulders, led her gently back into the kitchen, and gave her to me."

The silence around us was profound.

"That American soldier was your grandfather, Philip. So now

you see why I feel that you and your father are a part of my very own family." He said this quietly, movingly, plainly feeling again the shock of that boyhood experience. He laid his hand on Phil's arm.

Gradually the hum from other tables resumed. "We could use a family now," I said to Massimo.

He turned to me. "Yes, I can see that. After that terrible automobile accident to Kurt and your mother—" He stopped, remembering. "Then you wrote to me about your wife's death. I shared some of your pain, though only in the way one can at a distance. But seeing the two of you here now—just the two of you—" He glanced at my leg, seemed oddly thoughtful. It was a Massimo I hadn't seen before. "Look, Michael—" Again he hesitated. "Look, I am going to tell you—but it has to be just between us, all right?" Another hesitation. "I'd like to make you a present, a little gift—and Philip too."

"No need," I said, waiting.

"Ah well," he said, "there's need and there's need." And then abruptly, keeping his voice low, "There's this friend of mine in Siracusa," he started, then veered off on another tack. "You know I pretty much keep clear of Sicily now? Not just personally but clear of their coin trade too. It's Carthage for me. The coins are a little boring, but they're good safe stuff. Mostly, anyway. The odd ceramic piece on the side, to spice it up, to keep myself interested. Just London to Tunis, a short flight, empty suitcase going, full coming back. Perhaps lunch with the American Ambassador. Nothing special, except for his white wines, but a bloody sight tastier than the food here in England. Except at home. My wife's an excellent cook. She cooks like a Bolognese, not a Sicilian. We've a nice little house in Hampstead. I'd love you both to come and see it."

Phil looked as mystified as I felt.

"I still love Sicily, I still have some relatives there, but I'm afraid of it, do you understand? Maybe I'm a bit of a coward. But I still have relatives there, some friends too. One of them is this coin dealer in Siracusa. Actually, now that I think of it, he's decidedly a coward. That's no doubt why he got in touch with me. He doesn't know how to handle it." He stopped.

"It?" I said.

Massimo paused, as though still on the edge of a decision. "The find," he said.

"The find," Phil said.

"The find," Massimo said, delaying interminably. He plunged on. "My friend's name is Luigi. Full name Luigi Crocefisso, believe it or not. You can't imagine how apt that surname is. He runs a small coin business, strictly retail, strictly legit. A tiny business really, almost nothing at all. He has one small smelly room," looking around the restaurant, "*much* smaller than this one, on the island of Ortygia, the old part of Siracusa. It's an odd location for a coin shop, he doesn't make much money at it, just likes old coins, spends hours when no customers come in—which is most of the time—just fingering the old bronzes, must wear them all down to the point where the faces and horses all disappear. No wonder he doesn't do any business, is always on his uppers. He also eats and sleeps in the same small room. Seldom bathes. Must talk to himself all the time, the way solitaries do, develop strange habits." Massimo seemed faintly amused, but also deeply excited.

"The other day—less than a week ago, just five days ago, in fact—some young chap comes to his flat. He was younger than Phil perhaps, though not much. He looks at Luigi's pitiful coins, under the dirty glass in an old counter, and asks Luigi how much this one is, and that one, and so on. Luigi gets a little worried. Siracusa is a low-crime town, but there is *some* crime, and this young chap is acting as if he has something on his mind. Burglary perhaps. Stolen goods. Something dicey.

"Then all of a sudden he pulls a handkerchief out of his pocket, unfolds it and holds it up to Luigi's face."

"Chloroform?" Phil asked.

"A decadrachm," Massimo said. To Phil, "Do you know what that is?"

"A big one," Phil said. "Dad has shown me pictures. About the size of a silver dollar."

"Silver," Massimo said. "Brilliant, shining silver, this one. Apparently mint condition, uncirculated."

"Fifth century?" My heart was pumping fast.

"A Demareteion, Michael, a Demareteion."

"Great Caesar's ghost," I said, helpless before the fact.

"Great Gelon's ghost, you mean," Massimo said. "It was astonishing. Luigi knew enough to be astonished. As a thinker he's not exactly a whippet, but Siracusa is after all where he lives, and as you know, Michael, that's where Gelon's wife, Demarete, inspired those coins." He added, chuckling, "After she'd inspired Gelon, naturally." Massimo was now enjoying himself. "So here's Luigi, who's rarely seen anything fancier than a seventh-century Ionian electrum goat's head, suddenly face to face not just with a Demareteion but with a Demareteion in mint condition."

"And so—?" I could barely force the words out.

"Well, his mamma must have taught him something. Luigi plays it cool, tells the lad he'll have to know where he found the coin, and so on. It turns out the lad trundled a wheelbarrow at an archaeological dig up north in the city, a new dig, just started by archaeologists from Rome. Big stuff. They'd long had digs going over near Dionysius' Ear and other places in the area, but for some reason had held off on the Latomia dei Cappuccini."

"The Cappuccini quarry?"

"Right."

"But that's where—"

"Where all those Greek soldiers died," he said, "or may have. There's still some argument about that, I hear—it may have been over near Dionysius' Ear, in the Latomia del Paradiso, or some other quarry. There were lots of quarries in that part of Siracusa in those days."

"Where all the limestone for the temples came from," I said. "But the Demareteion—?"

"Well, this lad hadn't been on the job more than a day or two, he was somewhere down in the quarry just heaving a barrowful of soil along, shovel on top, beginning to realize what a rotten job it was—I'm telling you what Luigi told me—when he decided to rest.

He put the wheelbarrow down, but he'd only just learned how to handle the thing and it was top-heavy, and he'd put it down on sloping ground, and so the whole bloody thing fell over—what a mess! So as fast as he could—filthy as the job was, he didn't want to lose it—he moved the barrow on to level ground and shoveled the soil back into it at top speed. Only he went too far—" Massimo loved his effects. "He dug into the ground *beneath* the soil he'd spilled—"

"And that's where he found the coin," Phil said, eagerly.

"Exactly," said Massimo. "So Luigi, when he heard the story, couldn't help getting a bit excited. He *tried* to help it, but he couldn't. Luigi wants nothing more than a quiet life. He can't stand surprises. And here he was, faced with the biggest surprise a coin trader could ever have."

"And so—" I prompted.

"Luigi swore the lad to secrecy, promised he'd pay him a nice sum as soon as he sold the coin—and he took the coin—"

"Into his trembling hand," I said.

"You know just how he must have felt," said Massimo. "I'd have felt that way too. I've never had anything like that happen to me, not even with the American Ambassador's help. And the old Carthaginian silvers are no match for the Siracusan. Anyway, late that night, Luigi sneaked up to the quarry. The young fellow had told him how to get through the wire fence, so Luigi opened it up, scrambled down the slope to the place the lad had described to him. He searched everywhere but couldn't find a thing. You have to realize that the quarry is completely overgrown and has been for centuries. So it's almost impossible to tell one place on those slopes from another. The whole quarry is much bigger than a cricket field, mind you. And then there are the sheer walls on three sides. Mostly overgrown too, of course, but still sheer. Luigi didn't have much sense of where to look, or how. He just bumbled around, cursing the grass and the shrubs—and then he remembered the archaeologists' dig. He looked around for a freshly dug area and found it. It was a small pit, only three or four feet deep, the dig had barely begun. Luigi got down into the pit and then—talk of fool's luck—I doubt that Luigi's an *idiot savant*—he kicked at a bulge in the ground, near one side of the pit." Pause. "And he saw it." A longer pause.

I hated Massimo at that moment. "Come on," I said heatedly.

"The skeleton," he said. "Or a bone of it. Enough for him to know that it was a skeleton."

"Human?" Phil asked.

"Luigi must have thought so. He was so bleeding scared he just ran back the way he had come, up the slope, through the fence, ran all the way back to his flat in Ortygia. It took him a while to calm down, to think it over. It took him all night in fact. He says he didn't sleep at all, just kept thinking about the skeleton, wondering who or what it might be, probably some man, but who? He got out his new coin—he'd hidden it away in a small purse under his mattress, as though no one would ever think to look there—he touched the silver surface lightly with his finger, no doubt aquiver with pleasure and fear—"

"Why fear?" asked Phil.

Massimo looked at him for a moment. "Mafia," he said simply. "Siracusa happens to be the one city in Sicily that the families don't seem to care about, I'm not sure why. But if they got word of a big coin like that one—well, Luigi didn't need to be very bright to know what could happen to him. So what he did next was *really* surprising. And brave. He waited till the next evening and went up to the quarry again, by a roundabout path, looking behind him all the time. I can see him doing that, a rather pathetic and ridiculous figure, taking two hours to make the half-hour walk. Under the wire fence, down the slope. He'd almost forgotten where the skeleton was, but finally he found it. This time he'd brought a small trowel. He hadn't wanted to be seen with a big shovel, naturally. He's thick, but not *that* thick. So he set to work with the trowel, digging away all around and under the skeleton. He hated it, he told me. He hates having anything to do with the dead. Also he hates work. Anyway he did it. It took him hours, he said. Not quite sure how many.

"And then he found it. The skeleton lay on its side, as though its owner had gone to sleep or perhaps died in that position. And crooked in one arm, below the other hand, lay a small thick leather bag, in surprisingly good condition. In the bag"—Massimo seemed to open the small bag as we watched—"in the leather bag, soiled and damp from the ground where it had rested for centuries but quite clean and dry inside, Luigi saw what is probably the most remarkable hoard of coins found in this or any other century."

Rosario had detected our silence, swiftly came over. "*Primi?*" he said, pencil poised over pad. His patience, like Rome, seemed eternal. All three of us waved him away.

"More remarkable than the Turkish hoard of '84?" I asked.

"Not nearly as big," Massimo said, "but of more consistently high quality. And of an amazing range. All fifth-century, as far as Luigi could tell, so we can't be sure of it. What he says is that there were not only decadrachms but also tetradrachms from Gelon's time right down to the autographed pieces toward the end of the century."

"You mean," I gasped, "specimens of each main type?"

"I mean just that," he said. "What's more"—Massimo's look here was positively roguish—"there were *two* specimens of each type. Like Noah's ark, wouldn't you say?"

Phil had to ask, "There aren't a male and a female—?"

"No, no. There's almost always a goddess on one side of the coin, yes, but the horses on the other side aren't necessarily stallions."

"Two of each type," I mused, trying to rein in my emotions enough to think. "Sounds like something a collector might do."

"My very thought," said Massimo. "I've never known a collector actually *do* it. Too expensive. But if a wealthy Siracusan had started to pick up some of the most beautiful coins as they fell from the mint, and if he had started early in the century, let's say about the year 480 B.C.—"

"Collecting them for beauty, you mean, rather than their money value—"

"Of course. If he got them as soon as they were issued, their money value would have simply been market value at the time. But what would have caught his attention, starting with those lovely quadrigas and full-size Artemis-Arethusas of the 480s, was their sheer beauty, the new engraver's artistry. I'm thinking of this collector—for that's the only explanation I find plausible—as an aristocrat, someone educated on Greek poetry, Greek architecture, Greek sculpture, not an ordinary merchant."

"But wealthy," Phil said.

"Yes, he had to be. Even at mere market value, a tetradrachm was worth its weight in silver."

"But this aristocrat," I said, "wouldn't have been alive through the whole century—"

"Like Thucydides through the Peloponnesian War, say?" Massimo's knowledge sometimes startled me. He had dropped out of school as a boy. "Our aristocrat could have had children, you know, and passed his collection on to them, and his enthusiasms. I've thought about it hard over the past few days, and I can't find any other explanation for it."

"For the collection, you mean."

"Yes."

"So the skeleton," said Phil, "was maybe the grandson of that first aristocrat."

"Possibly," said Massimo. "Except that no Siracusan aristocrat was likely to find himself down in that quarry with all those Athenian prisoners."

"Maybe he slipped and fell in," Phil said, trying to be helpful.

Massimo refrained from laughing at that notion. "You have to try to picture that quarry at the time."

"Wait a minute," I spoke quickly, "how do we know exactly what time we're talking about?"

"We don't. I admit that. I'm guessing. That's all we can do. I haven't seen all the coins in the hoard either—I wish I had!—so I don't know the date of the youngest coin. That would at least give us something to go on, don't you agree?" I nodded. "So all we can do is speculate. Some guesses are better than others, though. That's one thing I've learned in thirty years as a coin trader. There's a lot of guess-work in my trade, but at its best it's *informed* guess-work. More reliable than practical politics or weather-forecasting, I dare say. My guess is that this hoard is somehow connected with those Athenian soldiers—"

"The seven thousand—." My heart was racing.

"Yes. You know the story better than anyone, Michael. Those poor bastards who got thrown down into the quarry after the Siracusans finally chased them out of the city into the hills and river-beds, killed most of their comrades, brought these poor devils back into the city, no doubt taunting and kicking them and worse along the way. The Athenians had thought Siracusa would be a push-over, you know, and like patriots everywhere when their empire is at its peak the Athenians must have been complacent and arrogant and insufferable." I had never heard Massimo so impassioned. Did he speak as a Sicilian embittered by all those centuries of arrogant invaders?

"That's your war, isn't it, Dad?"

"It's mine, all right," I said, still trying to digest Massimo's stunning news of the coin hoard. "That's what I'm going down there to research."

"The Athenian Expedition of 415 to 413 B.C.," Phil said, a certain self-satisfaction in his voice. So while I rambled on about it back in the States he was sometimes listening after all. "There was more to it," I said, "than just Athenian politicians sitting at home and fantasizing they could take over Siracusa and maybe Catana and Gela and rest of the island as well, without a struggle. To feed their own population they had to import wheat, and Sicily had wheat aplenty. Rather than bargain for it, they decided to own it. And so they put together a huge military force, huge for the time that is, all sorts of ships and troops, but the Siracusans fought back like you wouldn't believe, even won some naval battles against the Athenians, who were about the best combat sailors in the Mediterranean at the time, and finally beat the Athenian troops too."

"It's one of the only times in recorded history," Massimo said, "when Sicilians managed to beat their invaders." He was a patriot all right.

Phil stayed right with it. "So how do you think the hoard got down into the quarry with the prisoners?"

"I just don't know," Massimo said. "If you and your father and

I could have a few *pesce spada* dinners together, and enough Settesoli to wash the *pesce* down, we might be able to figure it out."

I was leaping ahead. "We'd have to see those coins."

"We'd *want* to see those coins, you mean," Massimo said. "I'd love it. The dream of a lifetime. You'd love it. Every coin dealer, numismatist, auctioneer and collector in the world would love it. Even to *see* just one of those coins—better still, one of those pairs!" He closed his eyes, seemed in a kind of ecstasy, caressing those lovely little silver artifacts.

"I'm going to try," I said. I hadn't said it deliberately. The words just came out.

"Try what, Dad?"

"Try to see those coins."

Phil looked amazed.

"Why not?" I felt surer and bolder as I spoke. "We're going to Sicily anyway. Those coins might shed light on my project, you never know. At the very least the skeleton and the coins and all that would dramatize the fate of those prisoners for modern readers. It's a priceless opportunity. Downright Providential, the more I think of it."

"You're not *really* serious, are you, Michael?" Massimo had been looking at me with astonishment. "You can't have considered—" For a change, he fumbled for words.

"Have considered—?"

"Well, the danger," he said, simply.

"Like the Mafia," I said. "You said a few minutes ago that they didn't operate in Siracusa—"

"No," he said forcefully, "but they can get to Siracusa in a few minutes! You're just not being realistic."

"I'm not interested in buying or stealing the damned coins," I said. "I just want to *look* at them."

Massimo exploded. "You think the godfathers are going to know that? You're out of your mind. I know more stories—listen, a small hoard was found three or four years ago, nothing like this one, on the outskirts of Agrigento. Some farmer found it, I think. Within an *hour* of his telling his wife—just one hour, mind you—

half a dozen thugs were there, guarding the site, more semi-automatic weapons than thugs."

"Well, Agrigento has local Mafia, doesn't it?"

"Yes it does. But doesn't an hour strike you as being a bit too bloody soon? And then over at Enna, just last year sometime, there was this tuppenny trader, much like Luigi but more energetic. Who *wasn't* tied in with the local mafiosi. They didn't seem to care, as long as he just made a few lire here and there, buying and selling small stuff. But one day he tried to pull off a big deal, without cutting the godfather in. You know what happened? They ran him over with a truck, broke both his legs. He still can't walk straight." Massimo looked at me hard. "Enna's just a ninety-minute drive from Siracusa."

"I could be in and out of Luigi's shop in an hour," I said. I felt completely serene, knowing I had to go.

Phil's face expressed his uncertainty.

I asked Massimo, "How did this Luigi happen to tell you about the hoard?"

"He's in a complete panic," said Massimo. "He doesn't know anyone in the coin trade he can trust. He hardly knows anyone in the trade at all. He lives right on the bread line, but he actually spent money on a phone call to me here in London. *That's* how panicked he is."

"And you told him—?"

"To sit tight. To bury the coins somewhere, but *not* under his mattress. I'll try to contact someone I can rely on to take the coins off his hands, get them out of Sicily, see that he gets paid."

"Who could do all that?"

"I'm not entirely certain," Massimo said. "As I said, Sicily isn't my territory. But I have good contacts in Rome, to start with. A dealer or two, one wealthy collector who knows the ropes, some others."

"But if they're in Rome—?"

"As it happens, I have to go to Rome tomorrow anyway." He hesitated. "Otherwise, despite everything I've warned you about, I'd be tempted to go along with you and Philip to Siracusa." He had acknowledged his defeat, the triumph of my impulse over his common sense. I loved him at that moment.

"Anyway," Massimo added, "Rome's the place for me. I've got to find couriers to take those coins out of Luigi's hands as quickly as possible. Luigi's such a fool, he could just lose them—or somebody could talk him out of them—or the mafiosi—well, anything could happen."

My mind was awhirl with images of brilliant coins, lurking menace, the flashing Mediterranean, brave deeds—

What Phil was thinking at the moment, I wasn't so sure. The expression on his face was ambiguous enough for me not to ask.

SYRACUSE

"You have all heard of, and most of you have seen, the Syracuse stone-quarries: an immense and splendid piece of work, carried out by the kings and tyrants. The whole thing is a profound excavation in the rock carried down to an astonishing depth by the labours of many stone-cutters; no prison more strongly barred, more completely enclosed, more securely guarded, could be constructed or imagined."

Cicero, The Verrine Oration (70 B.C.)

"The [quarry] gardens had an almost Turkish prolixity and richness."

Lawrence Durrell, Sicilian Carousel (1977)

"Only Sicilians think they are different from the rest of their fellow-countrymen. We in the rest of Italy know that the island is like one of those concave shaving mirrors, in which we see our image pitilessly enlarged, both faults and virtues."

Luigi Barzini, From Caesar to the Mafia (1971)

"[The bus conductor] was from the province of Syracuse and had had little to do with violent death: a soft province, Syracuse."

Leonardo Sciascia, The Day of the Owl (1961)

SYRACUSE

Jugate

To our surprise and relief the Aereo Trasporti Italiani pilot located the runway at Catania. How he did so was baffling, so densely did the pollution hang over the city. He set the plane down on the tarmac with a fine Italian hand.

Getting stiffly out of the plane, we were assaulted by powerful sulfurous fumes. Somewhere I'd read about that sulfur factory in Catania. Reading about it was better. The ferocious heat would have been awful enough without the stench.

Only one car-rental agency was open at the airport, and the agent told us he had only a single car on hand. Phil and I took a look at it. The Fiat was a battered old two-door 126, barely large enough to hold both of us. I protested, suspecting that the agent actually had a larger car around somewhere. Short and cynical, he was made of hard rubber. The time had come for me to be Italian. I unbuttoned my shirt, showed him my thirteen-inch scar, a scarlet red from throat to gut. "Riding in that box will kill me," I said funereally. He shrugged his shoulders.

I looked at the rental agreement. "Two hundred and eighty thousand lire?" I stared at him, incredulous. "I just want to *rent* the car, not buy it!" I knew that I was shouting. "For two days? For that we should get a Lancia or an Alfa Romeo, and new!"

He didn't even bother to shrug this time, just turned back toward his office.

We had no choice, and he knew it. We signed.

Phil and I squeezed into the car. He had a few inches between his chest and the steering wheel, but the extra space I had on the passenger side vanished when I shoved a rolled-up sweater between my chest and the seat belt. The seat was rigid and there was almost no leg room. Even protected from the seat belt, my chest began to ache.

Phil gripped the wheel, looked at me. "You okay?"

"Let's get out and stretch after a half-hour," I said. "That'll help. Anyway it's only sixty kilometers to Siracusa."

We pulled out of the parking lot toward the airport exit some little distance away.

Phil was driving slowly, nursing what horsepower he could from the feeble engine and still trying to find room for his long legs when we pulled up to the big red-and-white STOP sign at the exit. I was still upset by the whole scene at the rental agency, by the cramped car, my physical discomfort. I rolled down the window, anything to feel less sardined.

Wondering why Phil didn't move beyond the sign, I looked out the windshield to see a young man in a black leather jacket seated on a Vespa right in front of our car. He was looking straight at us, grinning.

The glass shattered on Phil's side, glass slivers flying everywhere. Phil fell toward me, arms in front of his face. The rear window shattered with a sound like a gunshot. I ducked, hugging my chest.

Then nothing, except the muffled clatter of Vespa engines, fading. I peered out the windshield. Nothing, no one.

Phil wrenched open his door, leaped out. "They're gone," he said, alarm and anger in his voice. He looked wildly about.

"Phil, are you okay?"

"Just cut a little," picking glass fragments out of his arms. "You?"

"The same." The cuts felt like tiny bee stings, that's all.

We looked over the car. "Must have done it with tire irons," Phil said. "Welcome to Sicily." Then he darted inside the car. "Goddammit—they got my backpack!"

"Passport? Money?"

He felt his armpit. "No, they're here. But my clothes—!" He sounded less enraged than aggrieved.

"Real bastards. You hear stories of these guys in the cities, roaring down the streets, two to a Vespa, snatching purses—but I never expected out here—"

"What about your stuff?"

"You put it in what passes for a trunk, remember?" Suddenly I was annoyed, depressed. "Let's brush off the seats and take this wreck back to that friendly sonofabitch."

Miraculously, in the half-hour we'd been gone the rental agent had found another Fiat, a larger one.

"Just turned in a few minutes ago," he said, answering our unspoken question. He produced a fresh rental agreement, all made out with our names, credit-card numbers and everything.

I looked at him with amazement. "How did you—?" And then I knew. What a louse. I glanced at Phil, saw the light dawning on his face. I'd seldom felt like murdering anyone but I felt it then.

The agent read my mind. He'd had practice.

"*Sei un pezzente,*" I muttered, staring him hard in the eyes. I'd wanted to say *bastardo* or *cornuto* or *filho di putana* or *stronzo* or *pezzo di merda,* but figured one of those could get me murdered in Sicily.

"You want the car, sign here," he said, ignoring the insult.

"*Pezzente,*" I said again, knowing I was going to lose this one too. I reached for the document, looked it over. "Another hundred thousand lire?"

"It's a bigger car," he said. "And you're a high-risk driver now."

I slammed the paper down on the desk, started to leave. "Let's go, Phil."

Phil caught my arm. He was as mad as I was, but saner. "What choice do we have?"

I knuckled under. Again, we signed. Pursuing the hoard had to have better moments than this.

"So it was a scam," Phil said as we approached the airport exit again. This time he didn't even pause at the STOP sign, roared right through. The traffic was heavy and he narrowly missed a car as he spun onto the highway, accelerating fast.

"A double scam," I said. "Both the agent and the bandits make out. They're probably all brothers, or father and sons. A closely knit family."

"If I spot a Vespa ahead of me—"

"Check out the driver's shirt—see whether it's yours?"

Somehow the flim-flam at the airport had already begun to fade into a picturesque incident. "We'll get you new clothes—somewhere." Absentmindedly I picked glass out of my hand. The air rushing in through the open windows was abrasively hot.

The incident had one desirable result. Our struggle against a common enemy had brought Phil and me closer together. During the flight from London to Rome, the layover in Rome and then the flight to Catania he had been aggressively restless. On top of the usual son-father frictions he'd had to stomach my shoving Sicily ahead of London, my insisting that we catch the first plane out the next day so that he didn't have a chance to visit the Hard Rock Cafe or anything else. He didn't complain; that wasn't his style. But he silently let me know all the way from London to Rome to Catania how selfish I'd been. He was right. I hadn't even thought to ask him in London whether he was willing to risk the dangers Massimo had made such a point of. The dangers hadn't truly felt real to *me*, and only on the plane out of London did it occur to me that they might be more real than I had acknowledged, and that I should have been more concerned with Phil's welfare. By then it was too late.

Now, in any case, thanks to those conspirators at the airport, Phil's dissatisfactions seem to have vanished, or at least been driven underground. Even his mother and I had sometimes been brought closer by some common enemy, if only by one of our rapacious landlords.

He held the wheel with one hand, patted it lightly with the other, and looked with pleasure at the climbing needle on the dash. "Speed limit 110 kilometers—how about that?"

"That's only sixty-six miles an hour," I said.

"Yeah, I know, I know," he said.

As we pulled away from Catania the traffic gradually thinned out. The air remained thick, though, and as we drove south the acrid smell of oil refineries and chemical plants soon overpowered the odor of sulfur. In this larger Fiat I could now sit almost sideways in the passenger seat. Easier on my leg. I could even glimpse Mount Etna out the rear window from time to time. I thrilled at the sight of it, from this distance a beautifully formed flattened cone, somehow soothing and menacing. It was a gigantic dinosaur, ten thousand feet high, had probably terrified real dinosaurs seventy million years ago as it had terrified Sicilians in the last few thousand. White smoke drifted languidly skyward from its funnel. Aetna, the Forge of Vulcan, the Forge of Cyclops, Jebel, Mongibello, the Mountain. Pindar and Aeschylus told of its eruption in 475 B. C. Scores or even hundreds of eruptions later, it was now erupting every few years, as though spewing out the wars and other pollutions of the times, purifying the land once again.

"I thought you said Sicily was beautiful," Phil said, eyeing the huge oil plants and the oil tankers anchored offshore.

"Much of it is," I said, "at least the other parts I've seen. Right now we're driving into the biggest mass of chemical plants in Europe, that's all."

"Sounds like the Sicilians got dumped on."

"You bet—by the Italian government and the industrialists. Esso, Montedison, the big multinationals. Yet another foreign invasion."

We drove on silently.

"Massimo never said how you two met," Phil said.

"It was in London, on our first trip abroad, your mother's and mine. About ten years ago. I was a young Assistant Professor at the college, desperately eager to see the Mediterranean world I had read about so many years. I had gotten a research travel grant to visit Italy and Greece, and Susan and I would have been happy to meet Massimo in Sicily—we were going there anyway—but he'd long since emigrated to England.

"He was lucky in having had an aunt who went to London before the war and married a Neapolitan grocer in Soho. She was a sister of Massimo's mother, you understand, the woman my father saved from the German soldier. This aunt and her husband were interned as enemy aliens during the war, but they were nevertheless so grateful to be living in England rather than in Sicily that after the war they kept trying to get Massimo and his young sister to join them there. They also wanted help in the grocery, so that their motives weren't entirely pure. Massimo's mother kept resisting—England must have seemed as far away to her as the moon—and wouldn't let her daughter leave home for another few years, but finally on his eighteenth birthday she gave Massimo her blessing.

"So Massimo had a job in England, a sponsor and just enough English to get by the immigration board. But you can imagine how irksome his life in the grocery would have become to him, once he got used to living in London and saw twelve- and fourteen-hour workdays stretching out indefinitely into his future. So he started picking up jobs in the little Italian restaurants in Soho, washing dishes until his English improved, then waiting tables. He left the grocery, became a waiter fulltime until one day an English coin dealer who frequented the restaurant asked Massimo why he was wasting his life there and invited him to learn the coin trade at his shop over near the British Museum."

"I'll bet Massimo took over the shop," Phil said.

"Eventually, yes. And of course made a great success of it. When he made his first bundle he came to the States and looked me up. I'm sure he would have wanted to see my father, but Kurt had already died."

"Is he really a smuggler?"

"I'm not sure," I said. "I suspect that he does some borderline stuff, if not over the border, but he's never said so and I don't know enough about the coin trade to know whether some deals outside the law may in fact even be inevitable."

"Well, he seems like a terrific guy to me," Phil said.

"He is—," I said, a certain hesitation evident in my voice. Phil glanced at me sharply. "It's not important, really—only a slight sense I've had the few times I've seen him over the years that his attitude toward me, or maybe toward my father, is more complicated than it appears."

I watched the shoreline. "That's the Gulf of Augusta coming up on our left," I said, "beyond that little peninsula. Somewhere around here, probably on the north side of the peninsula, the Athenians anchored their ships before attacking Siracusa. Their logistics base was Catania, back there. In the fifth century it was called Catana."

"Looks like we came to the right place for a classics professor." I searched his face for irony. None visible.

"Ancient history, not classics." God, it was hard not to be a pedant, even with one's own son. "Back home I try hard not to bore you with it. But it's what I make my living at, yes."

"You love it, this ancient stuff, I know that." Would he get rid of the word "stuff" when he was a college senior? "That Greek war you and Massimo talked about. Do you really think it has something to do with the coins?"

"That's just a guess. Or maybe a hope." It was the first time since leaving London that either of us had mentioned the hoard. On the plane I'd thought of nothing else. "Look, I need to stretch. Let's pull off on that little road over there."

Crossing the northbound lane of rocketing traffic was hair-raising, but Phil swung across without seeming to flinch. We drew up near a stand of huge cypresses. The peninsula was nearly flat, but we were on a slight rise of ground and could easily see the Mediterranean close by. What we mainly saw were the tankers and the oil port, but as we climbed out of the car I was already beginning to look beyond them.

"God, it stinks," Phil said, sniffing the air.

The fumes nauseated me too, but somehow they seemed fitting for a place so reeking of blood and battle and hopeless causes. I massaged my bum leg, trying to get the blood circulating again.

We looked east, watching the sea darken from a deep cobalt blue through shades of gray as the earth spun away from the sun behind us. A few clouds caught the final glint of sunlight, then turned as dark as the charcoal sea. The port of Augusta dissolved into a few unblinking lights along the shore. Quickly the tankers offshore lost their third dimension, became black silhouettes. Not a living tableau but a dead one.

Behind that tableau, beyond it, due east, lay Athens.

"That violence back at the airport—," I began. "Nowadays we

think of peace as normal, and violence as an interruption. In ancient Athens the reverse seems to have been true. I doubt that most Athenians actually preferred violence. More likely they had become habituated to it, out of necessity. The Spartans and Persians and others were forever making war on them, or threatening to do so. By the fifth century the Athenians themselves had waged war successfully enough at home and abroad to take their own belligerence for granted as perfectly normal."

"Sounds like some countries today," Phil said.

"The more I've read about the Athenian Expedition, the less surprising it all feels. The Athenians' follies are our follies, their fate probably our fate too, eventually." As I spoke, the triremes and smaller vessels rose up off the horizon, sails filled toward the west. Over the years I had watched that Expedition sail a hundred times. "The orators' debates in the Athens Assembly, the mounting of the military campaign, all sound tiresomely familiar. The great surprise lay in the ending, which was ghastly." A fearful loneliness washed over me. The Athenians' loneliness? That of their soldiers and sailors? My own?

"How big was this armada?"

"The first wave had sixty warships and forty troopships. Close to thirty thousand troops. More ships and more troops were sent later. Not just infantry but archers, slingers, cavalry, marines, other specialties. Not a bunch of raw recruits. Battle-tested veterans. Not all of them actually Athenians. Allies from Rhodes, Crete, other places sent troops too. A great many of them were slaves and mercenaries. Eventually there were about forty thousand fighting men in the Expedition."

"But they *were* beaten."

"Astoundingly, yes, they were. By the Syracusans, who up to that time had fought only small-scale land battles here and there, and had very little experience with sea battles. Not only were the Athenians astounded, the whole Mediterranean world must have been astounded." At this very moment I realized that I wasn't simply researching this doomed Expedition, I was obsessed by it. But obsessed with *what*, exactly? The fact of its doom?

"Sorry for the lecture," I said. Suddenly I remembered Luigi, glanced at my watch. "Phil, let's go. Luigi's supposed to be at the hotel in a half-hour."

I walked back to the car almost briskly. The stretch and the talk had done me good. Hand on the car door, I looked north, toward Mount Etna. In the dark its white vapors were still visible, lofting skyward. Its vast bulk invisible, I knew it was there, sheer mass, at once inert and animate, brooding and indifferent.

Encrustation

The remaining twenty-five kilometers took us only twelve minutes, but they felt agonizingly long. The prospect of seeing and handling those coins now crowded my brain.

Abruptly the dull glow of Syracuse broke into clusters of distinct lights. Below us, the city curved into a beautiful double bay. "Nowadays Siracusa has maybe a hundred thousand people," I said. "In the fifth century B.C. it had a half-million." Phil whistled.

We drove down the hill quickly, got lost repeatedly in the dark streets, finally pulled up at the hotel, tired and impatient.

If our guidebook was to be believed, the old hotel where we were to meet Luigi once charmed Winston Churchill. If so, it must have used up all its energy on that enterprise. The building appeared to list slightly to seaward, rather risky with the harbor so close by. The entrance was in disrepair, the *portiere* was in disrepair.

"Any messages?" I asked him as we entered. From hidden depths somewhere he summoned the strength to shake his head.

Phil carried my suitcase to the elevator. We stopped in front of the black cast-iron cage, saw an antique lift inside, exchanged glances, trudged up the antique stairway instead.

Our room had a black cast-iron bedstead and funereal wallpaper, but it also had an immense bathroom with white marble-facing everywhere.

And there was a balcony. I stepped out on it, barely noticed the cast-iron railing, having seen something else.

"Come here," I called to Phil, "quickly!"

He jumped onto the balcony. "What's wrong?"

I pointed downward.

There it was, in the moonlight all dark green and silvery, with faint touches of bright color here and there. Here and there around the periphery a border of white stone defined the center.

"Looks like a jungle from here," Phil said.

"It's the quarry," I said, trying to absorb the moment, feeling it slip away from me.

"The one where—?"

"Yes. The Latomia dei Cappuccini. Almost certainly the one where the seven thousand spent their last days. Of course, no trees down there *then*, no shrubs, no flowers, no green at all. Just rock. It was a working quarry, sheer depth and sheer walls." I gripped the rail tightly.

Phil peered hard at the dense vegetation. "I was wrong," he said. "It's not a jungle, it's a garden. Some of it looks planted, like those trees there. Those look like lemons. And oranges." Suddenly he seemed all energy and spirit. What had aroused him? "And those cypresses—gigantic vines all over their branches!"

A startling, pungent perfume rose powerfully up from this garden. As though the quarry walls formed an enormous open bottle, containing the scent, directing it upward, toward us. Phil tilted his chin up, inhaling with pleasure.

"Dad, could we go down there?"

I'd had the identical impulse. "Luigi knows the way into the quarry," I said. "I want to get in there too."

"Even before we see the coins?"

"Well, yes. Somehow I feel I've got to go down into that quarry first, visit the place—" I hesitated.

"Where the skeleton was?"

I nodded. "And still is."

Hours later we were still waiting. We had taken turns walking downstairs, checking with the *portiere*, looking around outside the hotel, checking out the streets nearby. No sign of Luigi. I was frustrated, anxious, grim, puzzled, restless, angry.

"You said give Italians two hours," Phil said. "It's been less than that."

"Okay, another half-hour. Then I'm going to find his place downtown. Massimo gave me his address."

But another half-hour and no Luigi.

We locked our room, descended the stairs, left the hotel, started south on the nearest street—and saw him ahead of us, a half-block away.

Incuse

I knew instantly it was Luigi. *Furtive* was the first word that came to mind. Then *scared*, no not scared, *terrified*. He was half-walking, half-scampering in a half-crouch, dodging this way and that along the buildings on one side of the street, glancing ahead and then behind, as though imitating some movie soldier he had seen who was checking for snipers in an enemy town.

Phil and I stood still, watching him. He almost ran into us, jumped back petrified.

"*Va bene, Luigi, va bene,*" I said as calmly and reassuringly as I could. "*Sono Michele e questo ragazzo è mio figlio, Filippo. Gli amici di Massimo.*"

Luigi was trembling violently. A pathetic figure. If I hadn't been so wrought up I would have felt sorry for him. He seemed unable to speak.

I took him gently by the arm, started slowly back toward the hotel. "*Del caffè, forse? Il portiere—*"

"No, no," he said urgently, wrenching free of my grasp. "No porter, no lights—!" His English was scratchy, but distinct.

"Okay," I said. "No porter, no people, no lights. Look, Phil and I want to go down into the quarry—to have a look—"

I thought he would faint. He looked on the edge of collapse.

Phil spoke quietly. "Luigi—it is Luigi, isn't it?—" Phil's voice struck a remarkably soothing tone. Luigi looked at him for a moment, nodded. "Luigi, my father and I just want to take a quick look at the place where the coins were found. It's important to us. We've come a long way, from London, from America, we're very tired. We don't want to stay down in the quarry, just have a look. Then we'll come up, I promise you." I had never seen Phil so tactful.

Possibly it was Phil's tone, possibly a thought that glowed dimly on Luigi's brow, but Luigi seemed to pull himself together somewhat. "Just a fast look, okay?" His voice sounded a trifle stronger. "Okay, I take you down. I'm the only one who knows the way." Except for the wheelbarrow boy who found the first coin, I thought.

Just a hundred yards away, a high chicken-wire fence that ran from one end of the hotel passed near us and wound its way eastward in an immense, irregular circle around the sunken garden. The chicken wire looked fairly new but crumpled here and there at the top or bottom. What had crumpled it? Possibly boys who couldn't resist climbing over or under it into the forbidden. I wondered if any of them would get lost down there, or be injured with no help nearby, and so join the graveyard of skeletons. Besides the skeleton sheltering the bag of coins there must have been a great many others still claiming the rectangle of stone on which they had died, over the centuries gradually shrouded like their patch of stone by the dust, then the leavings of the grass, dirt, shrubs and trees that must have sprung quickly out of the limestone crannies once the quarrying ceased, then the detritus from the quarry walls eroded by the punishing weather. Once the Athenians died, as nearly all seven thousand had, many of their corpses had been dragged out of the quarry, but untold numbers of them had been left where they died, the flesh rotting from their bones. Over the years they had been composted. Or nature tried to compost them, forgetting that bones don't rot. The soil now covering most of these skeletons could easily be fifteen feet thick. No wonder the dead guardian of the hoard hadn't been discovered for over two thousand years, and then only by a fluke.

With a certain lurch to his gait, swung fitfully to leeward by the light wind from the harbor, Luigi led us to the wire fence. Our presence seemed to have restored some of his confidence, or given him some, if he hadn't had any before tonight. He surveyed the quarry greenery as a gardener might who merely pruned its trees but felt proprietorial about the whole. An eccentric fellow, Luigi. He struck off to our right along the fence, away from the hotel. At irregular intervals along the way boldly printed signs on the fence read SCAVI ARCHEOLOGICI – *Vietato L' Accesso ai Non Addetti ai Lavori!*

Soon Luigi stopped, unbound two strips of the wire fencing, opened them wide enough for a person to enter, and motioned to us. Behind us the streets were impenetrably dark. Only a luminous half-moon and dim light from outdoor lamps at the hotel enabled us to identify objects at all. I would have sacrificed a small goat to the gods for a flashlight.

Phil and I passed through the fence, stood on the rock edge. We must have stood at the very top edge of the quarry, though the greenery falling away gradually below us erased any sense of a precipice. That gradual slope puzzled me. Shouldn't there have been a sheer drop-off? To the right and left of us the rock wall did appear to drop off steeply into the darkness.

That potent scent rose to greet us, almost too strong to inhale. "It's Rappaccini's garden," I said.

"Meaning – ?" Phil said.

"There's poison in that perfume."

Luigi closed the fence behind us, knelt in front of us, squinting into the green darkness, beckoned us to follow him. "*Attenzione*," he said importantly, swinging his legs over the rock edge, beginning the descent. He moved cautiously, and so did we. The drop from the top to the ground below was only a few feet, but when I landed I felt the impact in my chest. I clutched my chest with both hands and waited it out.

We had landed on solid earth, surrounded by trees, vines and shrubs. Luigi gestured again and to my surprise we found ourselves on a narrow asphalt walk, sloping downward. It looked as though this section of the quarry, at least, had been banked artificially, to provide easier ingress and egress. When? I wondered. The asphalt would have been laid sometime in the last half-century, but who might have wanted in or out?

"How old do you think these trees are?" I asked Phil in a whisper. He had worked one summer in Ohio as a landscape gardener, gotten really interested in trees and shrubs of all sorts, pulled dozens of books out of the library to read up on them.

"Why are you whispering?" Phil replied, in a voice only slightly louder. "The trees, I don't know. Some look over a hundred years, others younger. Too dark to tell. The stubby ones with irregular branches and silvery green leaves are olives. But the shrubs, look at them—oleanders, yews, lots I can't identify—and the flowers—passion flowers, dozens of other species. They can't get much light, down here under the trees. Look how long-legged everything is." He sounded disapproving. "Anyway, now we know where that perfume comes from."

The Garden of Eden must have smelled like this, looked like this. Except for the presence of Phil and Luigi, I felt achingly alone, enclosed in a densely primordial world, swept back to the very beginning of time, to the moment before time began. For an instant even Phil and Luigi appeared to me wraith-like.

Then they came back into focus. I saw Luigi glancing nervously back at Phil and me. Worrying that we would sandbag him? Heave his corpse into the depths of the quarry? Not a chance. *He* had the hoard. If he was still scared of the skeleton, we'd be there at his side, and anyway we had told him we didn't plan to stay long down here. All his fears really lay outside the quarry. I could only guess what some of them were. Mingling now with the perfume was a sharply different odor. Rotting vegetation. Despite the asphalt walks and some orderliness in the arrangement of some of the trees, it *was* a jungle, a vast compost heap. The mixture of odors, the rotting and the perfume, was disagreeable in the extreme.

Luigi stopped, scanned the trees to his right, dropped to one knee to examine the ground. Another movie pose? American Indian, searching for trail? In any case his was a quite different posture from the one we had first seen. He now appeared sure of himself, or at least not unsure. Perhaps he had unsuspected virtues.

"Not far" was all he said, leading us off the asphalt into the trees and shrubs. I saw a thin white rope strung between low poles. The archaeologists had been here. So *that's* what Luigi had been looking for.

My clothes were drenched, my skin dripping wet. The humidity, which had seemed low if anything outside the quarry, had concentrated in the jungle here. I glanced at Phil, who was wiping his face with the tail of his T-shirt. Surely the Garden of Eden would have had a tolerable humidity.

Luigi had slowed down. "*È qui vicino*," he said, his confident tone faltering. So it was near here, but where? Abruptly he halted. Ahead of us lay what looked like the opening of a small cave. To the right and left of the opening the limestone walls soared straight upward into the darkness, their surfaces chiseled with large, evenly spaced cross-hatched rectangles. Suspended directly over the cave opening, about twenty feet above the ground where we stood, was a huge block of limestone. I knew that it must be part of the solid quarry wall never cut into, except for the superficial chisel marks made by the removal of adjacent blocks, but this great block hung massively in the air as though about to drop at any moment. The dirt forming the cave or grotto beneath might have piled up naturally, protected by the overhanging rock. Then I saw other caverns nearby, some like this one, some apparently carved or worn from the limestone walls. Vines, ivy, grass and flowers covered the dirt surfaces. The effect of the whole was of a gigantic sculpture, whose intimidating scale was softened only by the immense, luxuriant garden that had grown up in its midst.

But for the Athenians, I thought, there had been no garden.

"You go ahead," Luigi said, "not me."

Phil stepped toward the cave opening. I followed. Close up I saw that in front and slightly to the left of the cave was a small, rectangular, freshly dug pit. Footsteps around the top edge, possibly Luigi's and the boy's. Numerous small piles of dirt nearby, possibly the boy's work as he feverishly shoveled the spilled dirt back into the wheelbarrow. Or no, probably Luigi's work with that little hand-trowel. For near these piles was bone, bone-white and startling. Bones, legs and arms, the rib cage, the skull. Almost entirely excavated.

"Curled up like a baby," Phil said quietly.

"Or like a man protecting something," I said.

Luigi had come up behind us. "You seen him," he said, "let's go."

"Not yet," I said. I wasn't sure what I was looking for, but there was something. Some clue to his identity, his motive, the moment of his death. But I didn't even know what to look for. All I could do was stare dumbly, and with a certain awe, at the inert frame, probably an Athenian, probably confined in this hellish quarry for weeks or months, probably dying in great agony of hunger and thirst. In all those weeks or months, surrounded by thousands of men loosed from normal restraints, many of them no doubt vicious at the end, ready or even eager to attack or kill, for any reason or none at all, how did he manage to guard his treasure?

Or maybe he wasn't the one who initially took it down into the quarry. Maybe he was simply the one who had it at the end, possibly after most of the others around him had died, or all of them. Maybe he had simply been the hardiest, or the most vicious, of them all. Maybe the man who took the treasure down into the quarry had been found out early, maybe killed. Maybe the treasure passed from hand to hand, soldier to soldier. They had been a rugged lot, after all, probably some of them ex-cons, released from prison to serve in the triremes, some of them psychopaths, as ready to kill as to scratch themselves.

But who had taken the hoard down into the quarry to begin with? It could have been the man who lay before us now. I stooped to peer at the skull. It was the closest I had ever been to one. Fleshless, the teeth thrust themselves forward from the angular jaw. The nose had carried out its archetypal retreat, as pathetic in death as its protruding cartilage and flesh were absurd in life. No more smelling, poking, prying or meddling there. But it was the eye sockets that held me. They seemed enormous, out of all proportion to the eyes the living creature had had. What had they seen?

A light exploded on the face of the skull. I jerked around and saw Phil poised with his little pocket camera, ready to take another shot of the skeleton,

"No, no!" It was Luigi crying out, as though in pain. "No flash! They see it above." He was almost weeping.

"Sorry," said Phil, continuing to shoot the skeleton, section by section, bone by bone. "Got to use a flash. Done soon."

"For posterity?" I asked.

"For a friend of mine, who's studying physical anthropology." He took one more shot, then turned away. "Maybe he could help identify the guy."

"Signor Michele," Luigi said in a fawning voice, "Signor Michele, enough of this, okay? I got a bad heart." He laid his hands on his chest, Sicilian style, not so much to indicate the location of his heart, I took it, as to assure me of his earnestness.

"I sympathize with your heart, Luigi," I said. No longer so blatantly terrified, he now struck me as less pitiful than insincere and annoying. "All right, let's go back."

I was surprised to find myself reluctant to leave the skeleton. Some link had been established between us, something less than a bond but sturdier than a filament. It was all on my side, of course, all in my imagination. But no less real for that. All unaware I had moored that Athenian to myself with a thread of silk. That he had been an Athenian, not a Rhodian or Corinthian or some other type of Greek, I no longer doubted. For me, he *had* to have been an Athenian, the supreme representative of the entire, doomed Expedition.

Our return to the top was more rapid. Phil stopped now and again to photograph flowers piercing the green shadows with tiny flames. "Just using up the roll," he said, but I could tell that on his own frequency he was as enchanted with this sunken garden as I was.

Luigi's morale appeared to improve the farther we got from the skeleton, but then to sink once again as we neared the top of the quarry. It was impossible to tell for sure what was going on in his mercurial soul.

At the edge of the quarry, Phil climbed that final wall of rock first, then hauled me up after him. Now that our subterranean venture was finished, I realized that I was exhausted. My heart had held up well, the refurbished arteries pumping away as they should, but the rest of my body hadn't yet recovered from the trauma of surgery. I had been aware of that, of course, but hadn't given my body such a brutal test until today.

Phil had also had to haul Luigi up that last stretch of wall. As a physical creature Luigi was almost useless. Or appeared to be. There were moments down in the quarry when he seemed downright agile. Our hour or two with Luigi had shown me a more complicated individual than I had anticipated, or had in any case confused my initial impressions of him.

Now we stood atop the quarry, catching our breath, looking back over the sunken garden we had just left. The lights outside the hotel had mostly disappeared, as had those in the town. In the thick darkness the garden below loomed once again as a jungle, impenetrable.

"On to Luigi's place, Dad?"

Luigi raised a hand, but whether to agree or protest didn't matter. "There's nothing in the world I'd rather do tonight," I said, "but I just can't do it. I'll be lucky to make it back to the hotel." I had some trouble even speaking.

Phil turned to Luigi. "Early in the morning, then?"

Luigi seemed almost surly. "Not early, no. Maybe afternoon."

"Maybe?" I was astonished.

"Afternoon?" Phil too.

Phil had to carry the burden of argument. Argument was what it took. My energy was vanishing fast, my brain with it. All I caught, before stumbling off with Phil toward the hotel, was that we would see Luigi at his apartment around noon the next day. The walk back to the hotel felt like dragging lead boots. I leaned heavily on my son the whole way.

Flow Lines

Only one eye was willing to focus. Sunlight filled the room. It must be morning.

Gradually I recalled last night, the return to the hotel. Over my protest Phil had persuaded me to take a sleeping pill — along with a Percocet, vitamin C, a multi-vitamin, a blood thinner and a cholesterol reducer. Something worked. I had slept nine or ten hours.

A knock on the door. Phil entered, carrying a tray full of dishes and pots, followed by the *portiere*, carrying two cloth napkins. "He said he wasn't strong enough to carry the tray," Phil said, "but I made him carry something. I also made him help fix the breakfast."

For a moment I feared that Phil had fixed scrambled eggs, but the main dish turned out to be pasta.

"I know you need protein," Phil said, happily lifting the lid on the main course.

"There isn't any protein in pasta," I said, then bit my lip. "Or not much," I added. "But I love pasta. Especially for breakfast."

"And real Sicilian olive oil," Phil swept on, "and freshly ground grana cheese. I hadn't ever heard of grana, but the *portiere* said it was the best. Also he had it on hand."

"Wonderful," I said, truly grateful. "And coffee?"

"Yep, cappuccino, how about that, same name as the quarry."

"You're a prince," I said.

We dismissed the *portiere*, fell to on the pasta. Between the kitchen and our room, unfortunately, the pasta had turned cold, and the olive oil had congealed. It could also have used a little seasoning, like poppy or sesame seeds, or even a little salt, but I would never have said so.

"He's not a bad guy, the *portiere*," Phil mumbled, strands of pasta trailing from his mouth. "He's just low on energy, or something. Kind of depressed maybe."

"Did you happen to ask him if he knew Luigi?"

"Yep, he said he didn't. But he says he doesn't know *anyone* in the old town. It's a whole half-hour walk away and he never goes there."

"Our date with Luigi is at noon?" My watch said ten-thirty.

"So he said. He better be there, right? He sure put up a lot of flak last night about seeing us today."

"Don't you find that curious? Massimo must have told him we'd be here, and what for, or Luigi wouldn't have come to the hotel last night."

"He's an odd guy," Phil said, intent on his pasta.

The bath water was tepid but the bathtub was huge, the soap was a mere chip but sudsy, the towel was threadbare but large. I was feeling good and willing to overlook inconveniences.

I dressed quickly, stepped out on the balcony. In the sunlight the jungle was again a garden, parts beautifully cultivated. Lemons now shone crisply here and there, and through the mantle of leaves and vines thousands of flowers gleamed dully. The quarry still unsettled me, in ways I hadn't even begun to fathom, something to do with its very size, for one thing, that gigantic opening into—into what? Into history, of course, but somehow also into something in myself. What that something was, I had very little idea. Something that generated a huge excitement, that's for sure, both thrilling and fearful. I had read about that quarry for years and years, imagined all sorts of grisly scenes there. Now Phil and I had gone down into it, down deep, and returned. And down there, we had had the extraordinary luck of looking on the face of the distant past.

We could have driven down to the old town but decided to walk. The distance was short, maybe only a mile and half, and the cardiologist had insisted that I walk as many miles every day as I could until I was averaging five.

Phil was in really good spirits too. It occurred to me that adolescent energy bore some resemblances to mania, with an occasional lurch into depression. He re-set his pedometer back to zero and checked our bearings on a little compass he always carried with him.

We walked quickly out of the hotel, rounded the quarry fence on our left, turned right onto the road skirting the sea. The road was grandly named the Riviera Dionisio il Grande. The Mediterranean itself was grand, an immense deep-blue sapphire, the road less grand. Clouds of dust swarmed in the air, some of it thrown up by the cars, trucks, bicycles and motor-bikes crowding the road, some conceivably still suspended in the air from the centuries of quarrying. Traffic noise was barbarous, each Fiat and Vespa expressing itself prow and stern, horn and exhaust, as though self-expression were never permitted Sicilian drivers anywhere but on the road. "A Colnago—a Bottecchia—an Atala." Phil was ticking off the bicycle brands he recognized. All I had noticed was that every cyclist somehow managed to sing, shout or otherwise sound off. I hadn't known *opera buffa* to be that strong in Sicily.

Driven by the exhaust fumes behind, pulled by an indistinct image of the glittering hoard ahead, we walked faster and faster. I would have run if I could. Soon we bore left onto the Via dei Arsenale, then the Via Regina Margherita. Less traffic, a little quieter.

"What do you suppose it will look like?"

I knew exactly what he meant. "Can't say for sure, of course. Assuming all of the coins have lain underground for almost twenty-four centuries, they can hardly be in mint condition, even if they were never put into circulation before being buried. On the other hand, if the coins were buried in something tough and durable like a thick leather purse, as Massimo told us, then they might be basically in wonderful condition. A lot depends on the conditions in which they were buried—humidity especially. If they were buried in very dry weather, then even though they were covered by dirt and vegetation afterward, with all that jungle moisture that we felt last night, the coins might have come through remarkably untarnished."

"Like mummies in Egypt."

"Right. And parts of Sicily have fairly low humidity, even if not as low as Egypt or the rest of northern Africa. Here we are today, near the sea, with temperatures moving up into the nineties, but the air doesn't feel very humid, do you think? The jungle down there in the quarry is another thing, but there's a good chance that the quarry in 413 B.C. was dry in the extreme. We know that a lot of the Athenians down there died of thirst, so there must not have been any water standing in the quarry."

We had turned left again, onto the Corso Umberto, which led over the Ponte Nuovo into the old town. The bridge was uncharacteristically restrained, for an Italian bridge, its designers having opted for simple stone arches linking the new town on the mainland to the island. Or they might have started with the ornate but had to settle for the simple, once Mafia contractors had taken their cut. But then the Mafia had never taken hold in Siracusa, I remembered.

We walked across the bridge, the panorama opening beautifully before us. To our left, the smaller of the great double harbors, the Porto Piccolo. A few passenger ships and freighters lay at anchor there. To our right, the Porto Grande, into which the Athenian battle fleet must have sailed. With what terror the Siracusans must have seen those sails fill the harbor! Now the shore of the Porto Grande on the island here was lined with large hotels and other buildings, just visible beyond them the mast-tops of yachts in what was obviously a sizeable marina. Luigi's apartment wasn't likely to be near there.

Over the bridge onto the island of Ortygia, the old town. Lovely trees and shrubs lined a broad new commercial street angling off to the right, through the center of the island. "Oleanders, ficus," Phil was saying. We took the street for a block or two, then struck off into one of the narrow alleys to one side, away from the wealth on the southern shore. The alley lurched this way and that, plainly medieval in its pedestrian quirkiness. Some of the low buildings lining the alley could easily have been medieval too. On another occasion I would have paused to examine them, but not today.

Street markers were erratically located and infrequent. I stopped the next man who looked local. "*Signore, per cortesia—cerco il vicolo Smarrito, numero quindici.*"

Though scowling when we approached him, he broke into a

smile. "*Non è lontano*," he said reassuringly, "*anzi, è qui vicino!*" He was so enthusiastic I suspected this was the high point of his day. "*Venga!*"

He led us around three or four corners, the alleys now still narrower and bounded by shabbier buildings. "*Eccolo!*" he said, pointing to a skinny two-story plain front. I thanked him and he shambled off.

The ground floor of number 15 looked as anonymous as the second floor, but as we got nearer I saw a small tattered card stuck in the window of the door. *Monete Antiche – primo piano*, it read, handwritten.

"He's not announcing it too loud, is he," Phil said.

I knocked on the door, waited. No response. Checked my watch. A few minutes after twelve. Knocked again, more loudly. And again.

One eye and an arc of head glimpsed through the grimy door window. Noise of a bolt shot back. Door opened, but not much.

"All right if we come in?" I asked, pushing firmly on the door. Luigi was leaning against the door on the inside, but gradually allowed me to open it wide enough to enter.

"Anybody seen you?" he asked, that familiar look of fright on his face again.

"No, of course not," I said, trying to sound casual and confident but unable to keep annoyance out of my voice. As he closed the door behind us Luigi looked hard out the dirty window.

The Hoard

Silently he led us up a dark, decrepit staircase, through a bruised old door.

Massimo had been right. It *was* a tiny room, with a single rumpled bed in the rear corner, a straightback wooden chair next to a small wooden table on which sat a wine bottle and the remains of at least one meal, an immense dark wooden crucifix off-center on the wall over the bed but no pictures or anything else, a dark brown oval rug of some indeterminate material askew on the floor. The one unusual object in the room was a waist-high wooden display counter with a glass top, no doubt Luigi's ordinary coin collection. Even this counter looked grungy, as though it had never occurred to Luigi to make anything in his life attractive. The acrid, awful smell of an unwashed body pervaded the room.

This was the individual into whose hands the gods had chosen to place the most magnificent collection of coins ever assembled! It was enough to make one doubt the gods' sanity.

"The coins, Luigi?" I trembled at the prospect of seeing them.

Luigi shuffled over to the display counter, stared irresolutely at the glass top, for what reason I couldn't imagine. Then he shuffled over to the window, squinting ferociously through the dirty pane as though to see through the walls of the buildings across the alley. Then a mincing sequence of steps along one wall, almost a little dance, astonishingly elegant in one so crude, a cause for laughter or alarm. Then he stopped to face the enormous crucifix, giving it a hard look, raised his arms before it, in a gesture of prayer or entreaty. Dropping one arm, he raised the other slightly, touching the wound in Jesus' side, almost thoughtfully.

Then he turned to face Phil and me. "Signor' Michele," he began, placing his hands flat on his chest. The gesture of sincerity should have alerted me. "Signor' Michele—," he tried again. He was standing directly in front of the crucifix, almost a shadow of it. Abruptly he threw his arms out wide, in what might have been a self-conscious imitation of his Savior. "I swear to God—"

"Swear what, Luigi?" I took a step closer to him, torn between revulsion and an impulse to get my hands around his throat. "Swear what?"

Despite his rigid stance any courage he might once have had appeared to have vanished. I could now see his fear, even smell it over the smell of his dirty, unwashed body. But fear of *what*?

"The coins—" Again he halted.

Phil tried his pacifying tone once again. "The coins, yes, Luigi—?"

I felt my usual composure crumple, stepped close to the trembling little man, seized one of his meager arms, still outstretched. "Don't bullshit us, Luigi. What's up?"

He was near collapse. "The coins—I don't got them."

Phil and I looked at one another, then at Luigi. "Why not?" I asked. I could barely speak, rage and grief flooding through me.

"I talked to the boy again—who found the coin—he'd told everybody about it—his family, his friends—I'd told him not to but he did—"

Luigi seemed as grief-stricken as I felt, but I felt no compassion for him at all. "And so—?"

"So maybe the mob already knew about it—"

"And so—?"

"There wasn't time to call Massimo—"

"And—?"

Luigi lowered his one free arm, placed it on his chest. "I did the best I could." We waited. "I told my brother about it—"

"About what?"

"About the boy bringing the coin, about me finding the bag of coins, about me getting killed unless he helped me out—"

"Helped you out how?"

Telling his story had restored him just a little. "Getting the coins off the island."

"How could he do that?" I was astounded at the idea. It had never occurred to me that the hoard wouldn't be right here in Syracuse, waiting for me. What an ass I was.

"Well, he's a fisherman, see? Has his own boat, gas engine and all, fishes the coast all the time, knows tides and currents, all that. Best sailor out of Siracusa." A trickle of pride, all he could muster.

"So he took the coins out of here?" Luigi nodded. "When?"

"Yesterday. Early morning. Before the sun was up. Before anybody could see him."

"But you knew we were coming in last night!" I was ready to weep.

"Yeah, sure. But if the mob got to me first, you wouldnta seen me *or* the coins."

How could he have done this to me? That was all I could think of. "What made you think the mob was after you?"

Luigi snorted. "You don't live here." His servility had shifted to insolence. "I told Massimo you wouldn't know your ass from your elbow around here."

I was stunned. "What do you mean you told Massimo?"

"Massimo said we could trust you but I said Yeah maybe but that wasn't enough—"

I gripped his shoulders as hard as I could, shook him hard. He felt like a rag doll. "Enough for what?" I wanted an answer but I also wanted to hurt him, to avenge my loss. "Trust me for what?"

"Dad, don't—!"

"*No, lascialo continuare, ragazzo,*" a strange voice rasped. "Don't stop him, sonny. He's doing our work for us."

I shoved Luigi away, spun around to face the intruder.

There were two of them—*athletes,* I thought, *discus or javelin throwers* with those shoulders. Then I knew: *mafiosi.* Their good looks and sports clothes had thrown me off. They wore white short-sleeved shirts splashed with bright blues and reds, loud pants, rope belts, rope sandals.

"*Siete inglesi? Americani?*" Gravel-voice spoke an Italian scraped by some dialect or other.

"Look at the shoes," the other man said in a crude English, pointing. "You can always tell by the shoes."

Gravel-voice switched to English, American English, Brooklyn American. "You're right, Pinocchio. Glad I brought you along." The second man did have an extraordinary nose. "What're you guys doing here with this two-bit punk?"

He didn't seem to expect an answer.

At the sound of the intruder's voice I had let go of Luigi. Gravel-voice now took hold of the quivering man by the wrist. "Luigi, you got some coins. We want to look 'em over, maybe buy some."

"No coins," said Luigi, ghost-stricken.

Gravel-voice ignored him, spoke to me. "You—what's your name?"

I finally said "Michael."

"I like Americans, Mike. You can count on 'em — to keep out of the way." This seemed to be a joke he shared with Pinocchio, who grinned crookedly. "I'm counting on *you* to keep out of the way. To get out of here *fast*. Got me?" He moved a step closer to me, pulling Luigi with him. With his free hand he poked me hard on the chest, exactly over the heart, where I was still most sensitive. My chest exploded with pain.

I looked at Luigi, helpless. The hoodlums probably had guns tucked in their belts behind them. Even if they didn't, Phil and I wouldn't stand a chance against them. I looked at Phil, who must have been thinking the same things. He looked at me, resignation glum on his face. We turned toward the door. I could barely walk, felt paralyzed at the heart.

"Don't go, Signor Michele!" Luigi wailed. Gravel-voice still held him by the wrist.

"If you and your boy here want your arms and legs to stay nice and straight," Gravel-voice said, "just keep moving till you get on the next plane in Catania, okay?" His tone was deadly.

With a last look at Luigi, I went haltingly out the door, down the stairs, outside, Phil close behind. I knew the grief-stricken look on Luigi's face would haunt me forever.

Re-tracing our steps down the alley, we stopped at the corner. "We can't just abandon Luigi like this," Phil said in a trembling voice.

"What would you like us to do, call the police? Don't you know that in Sicily nobody ever sees or hears anything where the Mafia's concerned? Haven't you heard of *omertà*? Where have you been all these years?" He didn't deserve my fury. "I'm sorry, Phil. I'm as shaken as you are. I don't think there's anything we can do — except wait for them to leave, then go back."

"He'll be dead!"

It was the cry of a young man who had never before faced the prospect of violent death so close at hand. I hadn't faced it often. "There's a real chance of that," I said evenly, realizing even as I said it that Phil spoke the truth.

"Don't you care, dammit?" Phil struck the wall of the building with both fists. "Don't you care?" He was weeping.

"I care all right." I didn't know what more to say. "Look, let's move around the corner here just a little, keep Luigi's door in sight. The minute they leave, we'll go back." Even as I said it, it didn't sound like a very elevated code of conduct, but I couldn't think of anything better.

Reluctantly, we both turned the corner, stood waiting and watching. I held one hand tightly against my chest, praying for the agony to ease.

Overstruck

A half-hour later, the mobsters left. They turned away from us, Gravel-voice gesturing angrily at Pinocchio as they walked down the alley out of sight. It was a half-hour exactly. I had checked my watch relentlessly every few seconds.

We hurried back, alert to the possibility that the pair might return unexpectedly. They didn't.

The door was closed but not locked. Up the stairs fast, into his room.

Luigi lay full-length on his bed, hands clutching his chest. He might have been asleep, except for his mottled purplish complexion and the look of pain on his face—and except for the coins. A small bronze coin lay on each closed eyelid, or almost. One eyelid had flipped half-open, so that the coin placed there by the hoodlums had slid upward, wedged in the socket, as though on display. I looked more closely, saw half a starfish on the upended coin, the head of Athena on the other. Bronze *litrae*, the cheapest, most ordinary coins of ancient Sicily. Maybe Luigi had nothing better in his collection.

"Looks like a heart attack," I said, finding it difficult to get the words out. "Must have died fast." I didn't try to explain away the look of pain on Luigi's face, or the protruding neck veins. I kept staring at the veins, wanting them to fill with the blood that was no longer flowing.

Then I saw the peculiar angle of one wrist, barely noticeable. Bone broken near the thumb. Phil saw it too. "That's all it took," I said lamely. "The poor guy."

Pierced for Suspension

Of course Luigi had no phone and so we walked down the alley toward the main drag, looking for someone to notify. It was early afternoon, the sun overpowering, the streets abandoned. Three blocks down the main drag we found the *questura*, and I told a *poliziotto* loitering inside the front door that I had a crime to report. Quickly he took us to a large room filled with desks but with only a lone sergeant seated at one of them. Obviously it was the lunch hour. Told of our mission, the sergeant motioned us to chairs, rolled a sheet of paper into his antiquated typewriter. He wasn't satisfied with the margins, pulled the sheet out and slowly rolled it in again, checking the left margin against the right repeatedly.

All of a sudden I realized what we were getting into. As soon as I spoke the word "murder" and gave the sergeant Luigi's address, he'd notify a magistrate, who would come right out to the scene of the crime. When I said "mafia," as I'd have to, he might well send a *squadre mobili* into action. Then Phil and I would have to explain what we were doing at Luigi's apartment, why we were in Sicily at all, why we thought Gravel-voice and Pinocchio were mafiosi, and so on and so on. It might take not just hours but days!

"*Quale delitto?*" he asked, ready to strike the keys.

"Smashing a car windshield," I said. The sergeant's eyebrows went up. "And stealing our clothes."

"Where did this happen?"

"Catania airport," I said.

The sergeant rolled the paper out of the typewriter, laid it flat on the table, tried to press the curvature out of the paper. "That's not our jurisdiction," he said wearily. He looked out of the dirty window.

With apologies for disturbing him, I ushered a perplexed Phil out of the building.

"What's going on?" Phil demanded. "What about Luigi?"

I explained as well as I could, pointing out that he and I would almost certainly have been held as material witnesses for days, even if the police believed our story and eventually let us go, that Gravel-voice and Pinocchio might be waiting for us when we left the police building. I left unsaid my fear that the mafiosi might get the edge on us in the race for the hoard. That was too shameful a motive.

"Are you just going to let Luigi rot there?" I had never seen Phil so enraged.

"As soon as we can find a phone," I said, "I'll call the *questura* and report the murder." Again I felt horribly inadequate in Phil's eyes.

I started down the street, Phil lagging behind. Luckily there was a restaurant in the next block, and while Phil hung around outside, I got *gettoni* from the cashier, asked him for the police number, dialed 113.

We continued on down the street. Neither of us spoke. The street sign said Via Roma.

Finally Phil said, "Do you think they'll pick him up soon?"

"Oh yes," I said. "Italian police are remarkably efficient in mopping-up after a crime. Sicilian police too, from what I've heard, although they rarely catch the criminals."

At the next corner I caught sight of the Duomo to the right, and turned down the street toward it, Phil following. I knew that columns of an immense 5th-century B.C. Temple of Minerva were still visible inside the cathedral and had long dreamed of seeing them, but I was too sick at heart to turn aside for it now.

Another two or three blocks brought us to a wrought-iron fence, waist-high, curving around a large sunken pool far below.

Walking around the pool, we stopped at a second fence. Below us, spread out toward a low-lying strip of land in the distance, lay the lovely blue waters of the Mediterranean. Barely a ripple on the surface, it was so welcome a sight that I almost wept.

Phil's voice startled me. "Back there, when you were shaking Luigi so hard—"

"Yes," I said.

"I kept thinking of what Massimo had told us about that German soldier shaking his mother that way—and about your father rushing up ready to kill him—"

"My God," I said. My heart took another lurch downward. "You were right to try to stop me."

"I'd never seen you like that." His tone wasn't exactly reproachful, closer to surprised and sad. I stared at him, struck dumb by the thought of my father's rage in me.

"Well," he said, "you didn't kill him." Phil sounded detached, but I hadn't a clue as to his real attitude.

"No," I said. "No, I didn't kill him." The sea before us somehow seemed less comforting than it had a few minutes before. I turned around, walked the few feet to the fence surrounding the sunken pool. Several men and women and a large family were strolling around it, or leaning on the fence, gazing at its slowly moving waters thirty feet below. White ducks paddled slowly on its surface, papyrus stalks rose ten feet over them. Water flowed swiftly into the pool from beneath a large arch on one side. Wooden bird houses with outsized entrances hung from the enclosing stone walls. Vines covered most of the wall surface. It all had a curious air of pastoral normality about it, though the whole pool enclosure was anything but ordinary. I felt utterly out of touch with the normal world.

Want List

All of a sudden I knew. "It's the Fountain of Arethusa!" Phil joined me, glancing down. "Is that special?" he asked unenthusiastically.

"Arethusa's is the face you see on the most beautiful Syracusan coins of the fifth century. I handled one of those coins in London." I wanted desperately to talk about beauty.

Phil was helplessly back there in the room with Luigi. "Oh," he said.

I doubted that I could reach him for a while, maybe quite a while. But coming on Arethusa's fountain had lifted my own spirits, if only a hair. If I had believed in signs and wonders, I would have taken this encounter as a sign and wonder. What luck to have stumbled on this pool just when we were so in need of it, and about to leave Syracuse! An omen, perhaps—but of what? Of better luck ahead, of no more horrible deaths like Luigi's, I fervently hoped. Of my catching up with the lost hoard and seeing Arethusa's lovely face again, not just on a single silver coin but on a whole batch of coins, the most elegant batch of ancient silver coins ever assembled on the face of the earth.

Or an omen of worse luck, of no luck at all, of my already having come as close as I would ever come to the hoard, without having touched or even seen one of its fabulous coins? Or of bad luck for everyone, a portent of the hoard's being lost at sea, of that dingy little fishing boat suddenly struck by a storm, swept bow to stern by colossal waves, everything swept before them, deck gear, the pilot house, the fisherman, and yes the small leather bag that had survived two and a half millenia underground with its guardian only to be pitched secretly and ignominiously now into the careless and unconcerned depths, those astonishing coins forever lost?

Worse yet, much much worse, an omen of more death?

"Did Luigi say anything about what direction his brother was headed?"

The hot urgency of my question fell on Phil's cold spirit. "You heard him as well as I did," Phil said.

I was nettled. "Come on, Phil, you're not the only one of us who's heartsick about Luigi. But we've got to get out of here—fast—and we've got to decide what direction to head."

"How about back to Ohio?" His gloom had him by the

temples—but then relaxed a shade. "Or London. We started out this trip to have fun in London, remember?"

I ignored the sarcasm. I absolutely had to stay on track. Not only didn't we know what course Luigi's brother might be sailing—at this very minute—we had never learned exactly *where* Luigi told his brother to take the coins—if indeed he had handed the coins over to his brother, or if he even had a brother, let alone a brother who was an experienced sailor. "Somewhere on the mainland," I said. "It has to be somewhere on the mainland, in Italy. A small fishing boat isn't going to sail to France or Spain. Tunisia isn't far, but there wouldn't be any point in going there. Or Malta, as far as I know. But *where* on the mainland?"

"Naples?" Like a skittish trout Phil's attention had been hooked, however lightly.

"Possible, but Massimo or somebody once told me Naples isn't a big coin center, or a big transshipment point. Rome, on the other hand, is both."

"Isn't Massimo in Rome?"

"Well, he said he would be. He gave me an address there." I paused. "You know, something Luigi said—"

"About trusting you—?"

"Yes. Didn't that strike you as odd?"

"I was too scared at you shaking Luigi to think about it—"

"But think about it now. It must mean, for one thing, that Massimo talked with Luigi *after* we saw him at the restaurant in London. Before that evening Massimo didn't know I was going to Sicily."

"Okay—so—?"

"So Massimo must have told Luigi afterward that I was coming. But why bother to say to Luigi that I could be trusted?"

"Not to steal the coins if he let you take a look at them?"

"Well, maybe. Luigi sure as hell is—was—a scared rabbit. But then Luigi said he told Massimo that wasn't enough—enough for what?"

"Beats me."

"They must have talked about something else, something besides my just taking a look at the hoard."

"I thought we had to scram out of here."

I gave up the trail reluctantly. "You're right." I took a map of Italy out of my pants pocket, unfolded it on one of the stone fence supports. "Look at the distances. That fisherman—let's assume he exists—couldn't possibly sail or motor all the way to Rome. Even if he had enough gas, which isn't likely, he almost certainly couldn't take all that time off from fishing. And the waters from here through the Straits of Messina and north are notoriously rough."

"How do you know?"

"Ancient history. The Straits of Messina had a whirlpool so menacing to sailors that the Greeks called it a sea monster, Charybdis. You've heard of being trapped between Scylla and Charybdis? Scylla's a great rock on the Italian coast. And I've had friends who sailed the Mediterranean around here. They all said they would never do it again." A sharp image of silver decadrachms spinning lazily downward through deep waters startled me with its vividness.

"Okay, so Luigi's brother lands somewhere with the hoard—but where?"

I scanned the lower mainland on the map. "We just don't know. My guess is that he wouldn't go through the Straits at all. He'd go ashore somewhere on the toe, maybe at or near Reggio di Calabria. The Aspromonte mountain range comes down close to the shore there"—I pointed to the faint topographical lines—"but see, there's an airport, there must be some level land. Reggio's a pretty big city, must have dock facilities. Anyway, he'd know his way around. Probably he'd want to land away from the city, now that I think of it."

"And then hitch a ride to Rome."

"Too far, too time-consuming. The Aspromonte range is also full of local gangs, has been for centuries. Some of the worst kidnappings of recent years were based there. Twenty years ago the grandson of J. Paul Getty, the oil billionaire, was kidnapped in Rome and passed on to a band of Calabrian hoods. The kidnappers demanded over three million dollars, got nothing until they cut off young Getty's ear and sent it to a Rome newspaper, along with a photo of the grandson minus the ear. That's just the most famous case."

"So Luigi's brother'd have to hand the hoard over to someone he trusts—"

"Another Sicilian. I've heard incredible stories about how completely trustworthy Sicilians are within their own families. So not just another Sicilian, no. Somebody else, some man, in the family."

"Luigi's family."

"Right. Luigi's family."

"But the whole thing was so rushed—"

"You're wondering how the transfer could have been arranged?"

"Yeah, Luigi didn't even have a phone—"

"I just don't know, Phil. Maybe his brother has done errands like this before. Smuggling of all sorts goes on all the time in and out of Sicily—mainly drugs these days, but other things too. Who better than a fisherman with a little boat of his own? I'd be willing to bet all he had to do was tie up at some usual place near Reggio and walk a short distance to make contact with someone—"

"Who doesn't ask questions, just takes the bag, says 'Sure, I'll see that it gets to Rome.' Sounds good, but—"

"Well, all we can do is guess, right? And hope." I folded the map. "Back to the car?"

Phil hesitated, perhaps reluctant to surrender his rage, or to take leave of Luigi so hastily. He glanced back in the direction of Luigi's bier, then looked at me, then slowly stood erect and followed me.

I still felt dead at the center, but our talk had helped.

Neither of us thought the mafiosi would be following us every step. They had after all turned down the alley *away* from us after leaving Luigi's place. But we took their long-range threat seriously, took off on Route S114 north out of Syracuse, driving fast.

"There's another question in my mind," Phil said, his morale better but his spirits noticeably more subdued than on our drive south.

"How much did Luigi tell the thugs before he died?"

"Yep. If he died right after—"

"They broke his thumb—?"

"Yeah, after that—well then he wouldn't have had time to tell them anything, would he?"

"Could be. But he might have already said just a few words, such as 'my brother—fishing boat,' or even 'my brother took it,' something like that."

"Or he might have said 'Rome.'"

"Or Reggio. We can hope not—but he might have. He was already scared to death just with those thugs in the room. He might have started to tell what he knew the minute you and I left the room. He might have told them everything."

On our right, the Gulf of Augusta. In the daylight it looked tranquil and boring, the last place in the world from which a great military expedition might have shoved off for the attack. All of a sudden I remembered the research I had planned to do in the Syracuse archives. So much for *that*.

"Even if he did," Phil went on, "they'd still have the problem we have, wouldn't they? To figure out where the fishing boat went, and all that."

"Right, except that if Luigi *did* name a destination, Rome or wherever, then the mafiosi know a lot more than we do—and they can get there faster."

"Okay, suppose they do. Suppose it is Rome, and they take a plane there today. Luigi wouldn't have given them Massimo's address, would he?"

"Hard to say. There's a good chance he would have held back on that for a while, or that there wasn't time before he died for him to have given it to them."

"So maybe we're not much worse off than the Mafia guys in finding the loot."

"Or we might even be ahead of them. It *is* a race of sorts, isn't it? Or could be." Of an alarming sort, I thought. My chest ached afresh at the recollection of that brutal poke. They could harm *me*, that's what that stabbing pain meant. They could even *kill* me. I hadn't actually realized it before.

"I guess I'm up to it," Phil said coolly enough, "are you?"

"I'm not sure," I said, looking at him reflectively. "But I'm committed to trying. I haven't been this—this galvanized in a long time."

He shot me an appraising look, returned to his driving.

We kept silently to ourselves the remaining minutes of the trip. At the airport we pulled into the car-robbery agency, parked the car for the head thief to pick up at his convenience and walked to the airline terminal.

At the terminal we bought tickets, chafing at the two-hour wait but relieved that it wasn't longer. I checked out the exits, scrutinized idlers, forced Phil to sit with me near a corner, our backs to the wall, maximum viewing area. Tradecraft I'd often practiced as a game, today in earnest.

We boarded the plane, no enforcers in sight.

As we took off, headed north, Mount Etna loomed dead ahead. In the dusk its great cone looked perfectly black, with enormous billows of white smoke lifting toward the sky. For a moment, just before the plane banked to the west, correcting its course for Rome, it looked as though we were flying straight into the inferno of the volcano.

ROME

" 'What do you think of the opera?' asked our hero. 'What do you think of the Don?'
" 'We all know what Mozart is,' said the marquis; 'our impressions don't date from this evening.' "

Henry James, The American (1877)

"Enzo could arrange to have other museum pieces lifted on order, he said.

TOMMY: *Rembrandt.*
ENZO: *Rembrandt what?*
TOMMY: *Rembrandt, there's a million of 'em. Da Vinci, Van Gogh, ya want me to go down the list? Van Gogh, Da Vinci . . . Y'know what I'm saying?*
ENZO: *V-A-A, G-O-R-A. Van Go?*

"They moved on to musical instruments.

ENZO: *Violins . . . Stradinoff . . .*
TOMMY: *Stradius?*
ENZO: *Stradivar . . . I don't remember the name. Six. They're worth a million dollars.*
TOMMY: *What do they want for two?"*

From taped dinner conversation at expensive New York City restaurant, January 13, 1977, between Vincenzo Napoli ("Enzo"), a Sicilian mafioso, and undercover Detective Douglas Le Vien ("Tommy") of the New York City Police Department

Organized Crime Control Bureau.

Quoted in Claire Sterling,
*Octopus: the Long Reach of the
International Sicilian Mafia* (1990)

"All passes. Art alone
Enduring stays to us;
The bust outlasts the throne —
The coin, Tiberius."

Henry Austin Dobson, *Ars Victrix* (1876)

"Parme . . . knows how to cut fine dolphins, it is true, but for the rest his work displays a moderate talent and a lack of originality."

J. H. Jongkees, *The Kimonian Dekadrachms* (1941)

"Horace . . . a fastidious poet in their classical age . . . told [Romans] not to put antipathies together. The torso of a beast and the feathers of a bird make a monster, he said. But Rome is full of monsters."

Russell Fraser, *The Three Romes* (1985)

"In Rome . . . there was a liberation from the thicket of the self. . . ."

Elizabeth Bowen, *A Time in Rome* (1959)

ROME

Con turbolenza ma non troppo

Even before the plane touched down at Rome I was remembering the excitement of my last trip into the city from the airport. Susan and I had made the twenty-mile trip by bus, thrilled by the first tall umbrella pines we saw from the highway, thrilled by the most ordinary stone farm houses, thrilled even by the flat ploughed fields. I remembered the smell of the hot moist air rushing in the bus windows. I remembered our wonder as suddenly we saw sections of the Great Aurelian Wall, then the ruins of ancient Roman baths, then the fields giving way to scattered buildings, the buildings to the densely built blocks of the metropolis itself. Now I realized that that bus trip into Rome had been one of the happiest hours of our married life.

Why had there been so few?

Jolted back to the present as the wheels thumped the runway, I looked at Phil beside me, wondered whether he felt any of the anxiety I was feeling just now, any of the ache I still felt from the mingled affection and loneliness of those years with Susan. He appeared lost in thought, but lost where I had no idea.

We left the plane, entered the gleaming terminal, all glass, tile and modernity. Leonardo da Vinci Airport indeed! After our rushed flight from Sicily, then the deadening impersonality of the aircraft, all time suspended, abruptly we were back inside time, in the onrush of history. I wasn't sure I could handle that, such a battering Sicily had given my tired frame. And yet battered as I was, I welcomed the human density, counting on Rome to restore my tired spirit, looking forward to the blast of hot moist air through the bus windows.

That was my first surprise. Going quickly through passport control and customs, we learned that buses no longer ran from the airport to the city, that now a high-speed train made the run, a new train every twenty minutes, just twenty minutes into the city. Phil was pleased. He loved the onrush of technology. I was faintly depressed.

We walked out of the terminal, spotted the blue-and-white *Stazione Ferroviaria* sign, entered another building, ascended an escalator, were moved silently along a horizontal ramp, saw from the building window the long steel-and-glass cocoon of the railway terminal, glided to a stop in the cocoon itself. Machines dispensing *Biglietti*, other machines dispensing *Gelati*, still others dispensing plastic combs, plastic statues of the Virgin Mary, doubtless condoms for nonCatholics.

We bought tickets, walked on spotless floors through airconditioned air to the train, boarded and sat down. "I didn't expect a brandnew train," Phil said, gratified. I wished he hadn't said it.

The doors whooshed shut, the train moved out quietly, right on time. Mussolini not needed for that now. I had read somewhere recently that his granddaughter was running for office in Italy, possibly under the mistaken impression that she was needed to keep an eye on the trains. I looked out the window at the landscape rushing past. Stone farmhouses, ploughed fields, somehow not at all the same. Then the Tiber river, crossed by a stark steel bridge, massive clumps of highrise apartment buildings beyond. Where was *my* Rome?

"Here we are, Dad," Phil was saying, tugging at my arm. I must have fallen asleep. "Stazione Ostiense, or however you pronounce it." Passengers were struggling past us out of the train. I sat there, dully. "Come on, Dad. Just a short way to go, isn't it?" I only wished he was the one who knew Rome, could take charge, load me into a taxi, carry me into the hotel, put me to bed between clean cool sheets.

Somehow Phil did manage all that, I never knew how, I was so stupefied. Dimly I sensed that he was nudging me along the station platform, up a ramp to the street outside. I stood there stupidly, looked around, thought I saw a huge pyramid looming nearby. Shouldn't be a pyramid here, I thought. Then Phil was helping me toward a taxi, helping me in, saying something to the driver, holding me upright against the seat with a strong grip on my arm.

The taxi started. I glanced at Phil, who was looking out the window on his side and then on mine, then on his, like a spectator at a tennis match watching the ball in motion. I had just wit enough to be amused, then my wit faded. "It's the Colosseum," I thought I heard him say. He turned to look at me with wonder on his face. Things blurred.

Then we were on the street again, stumbling up a few steps, a strange face looming toward me, then falling into softness—

Più mosso; scherzevole

I awoke to a small room, cloudy light through white curtains, dim traffic noises outside. I was groggy.

"Okay, Pop?" He sounded cheerful.

"No pasta this morning, all right?" I knew that wasn't what I should have said, but my brain felt empty of choices.

"Sure, this *portiere*'s a woman, and she said she knows what to bring us. I'll go tell her you're up."

"I'm not up, just trying to open my eyes," I said, as he opened the door and left. "And if she's female, it's *portiera*," I called weakly after him. I couldn't stand wrong endings on nouns.

The door opened and Phil came in, held the door open for a large woman bearing a huge tray. He was smiling, she was smiling broadly, she set the tray down on a small table. *Buon giorno, signore*, she said. The dishes were covered, but I could tell there wasn't a shred of pasta in any of them. The lusty aroma of dark-roasted Italian coffee hit me. Pure pleasure.

The signora left. Phil was pouring the coffee, handed me a large cup and the sugarbowl.

"Thank the gods, son," I said, "you asked for big cups." I stirred a mound of sugar in, inhaled deeply and took a first slow sip. It tasted Olympian.

"The signora said she knew what Americans like. And look at this." He lifted the napkins from the plates. Fresh oranges, pears, bananas, a mango. Slabs of cheese, two or three kinds, one of them taleggio, a favorite. And a plate heaped with fresh cinnamon pastries, no doubt rushed from a bakery around the corner.

For once I beat Phil to the first bite, but only by a whisker. "We could have had breakfast on the roof," he said, having years before mastered the skill of spitting out words while retaining the food, "but I figured you weren't up to that."

"Where are we anyway?"

"Pensione Suisse," he said, reaching for an Italian pronunciation. "A hundred and twenty-eight thousand lire," he added, watching me over his coffee cup. "Is that too much?"

I glanced around the spacious room, checked out its few pieces of modern furniture, spotted a door ajar. "Bath in the room?" He nodded. "Good work," I said. "How did you hear about the place?"

"You mentioned it when we got on the train."

That wasn't the only thing I'd forgotten, I was sure, or wanted to forget.

"The coin store near the Spanish Steps opens at eleven," he said. "I went down to take a look."

I felt abruptly anxious. There was a world out there beyond those cinnamon pastries. I looked around for my watch.

"It's ten-oh-seven now," Phil said. Of course he had a complex little machine on his wrist, could have given me the time to the hundredths of seconds if I'd asked, or elapsed time, or his pulse rate, anything at all, and done it all underwater.

I rolled over carefully on my side, raised up on an elbow, swung my legs off the bed as I sat up. "That's the best it's felt," I said, testing my chest, my leg. "I just needed to get to Rome, get a good Roman breakfast in me." My energy was up too, the grog had evaporated. "No sleeping pill last night?" I asked.

"You were already asleep when we got in," he said. "We just stuffed you between the sheets."

I moved toward the bathroom, already thinking of the coin shop, Massimo, the hoard. I moved faster.

"Will Massimo be there?" Phil asked.

"Not waiting at the shop, not the minute we arrive," I said, looking at my haggard, unshaven face in the tiny mirror. "But he said the dealer could contact him immediately. Of course, you have to realize what immediately means to Romans."

"Massimo's British, or almost," Phil said, clinking plates and cups in the other room, probably looking for something more to eat or drink.

"You're right," I said, starting to wash my face, "so there's hope. I think he'll come as fast as he can. He wants to see those coins too."

"Wait'll he hears what happened," Phil said, no longer clinking.

I was still slow at everything these days but not as horribly slow as in the first days after surgery. Now I shaved, showered and dressed in something like normal time, even feeling blips of energy.

Quickly we walked down four flights to the ground floor, thanked the *portiera* for her breakfast more hastily than we should have, turned to the right outside the pensione, walked slightly uphill the short stretch of the Via Gregoriana, then left down the Spanish Steps, dodging tourists already lounging there, quickly crossed the Via del Babuino to the right. A minute later we were at the shop. It was three minutes after eleven. I peered through the small glass window in the large metal door. "I'll be damned," I said, "there's someone here."

The someone was Signore Campanella himself. I tapped with a coin on the metal door. Sounds of bolts being shot. Door opening, Signore Campanella appearing.

After *Buon giorno*s on both sides he said, "You're Signore –?"

"Gardner – Michael Gardner, and Philip."

"I'll call Massimo at once," he said, with unexpected dispatch, going to a desk phone nearby. It had automatic re-dialing, I noticed, no doubt a godsend in Rome. He dialed, got a busy signal, pushed the re-dial button, waited. The intermittent ringing clanged from a loudspeaker across the room. "I can't always hear it from the other room," he explained.

Unlike Luigi, he *had* another room, probably didn't sleep in it either. He was well dressed, sported an old Roman coin on a tie clip, shiny old Greek coins on his cuff links, a large French medallion on a gold watch chain across his vest, tiny gold coins on a gold charm bracelet on one wrist, a huge silver coin on a watch fob below his belt, and bright American pennies tucked in his glossy patent-leather loafers. I wondered how he would dress if he switched to selling stamps.

The busy signal stopped, the number connected. "Massimo?" Signore Campanella said, "Massimo there?" He waited, shaking his charm bracelet lightly, appearing to count the coins on it. "Massimo, Tintin here. Yes. Your friends are here, the Americans. They look just fine, yes. Can you come? Thirty minutes then, *subito*. Very well. *Ciao*." I could hear Massimo's receiver slammed down before Tintin replaced his.

"Would you like to look around the shop," he asked, sweeping an arm around expansively to suggest numismatic treasures within the glass cases if only we would look, no doubt greater treasures unlockable from his steel safe if only we said the word. The charms on his bracelet tinkled as his arm circled. His glass display cases were clean and shiny.

"I'd really like to," I said half-truthfully, "but I have to get some brisk walking done before Massimo comes. Doctor's orders." Phil and I started for the door. "We'll be back in thirty minutes — or less. *Ciao*." It was almost rude, by Italian standards. I was wound too tight to manage the courtesies this morning.

Once outside, I struck off to our left down the Via del Babuino. "Would you like a quick tour?" I asked, not waiting for an answer. "Deceptive exteriors here," I said, speaking rapidly, "bland facades, pricey stuff inside — antiquities and coin shops — there's one, there's another — goods invisible from the street — Via dei Greci on left, don't know why named for Greeks—"

"It's great to see you walking this fast," Phil said breathlessly, almost trotting to keep up.

"Piazza del Popolo coming up — note obelisk Romans stole from Egypt — Roman emperors buried here, Nero one of them — careful, dog shit—" — turning sharply left here — "rounding baroque church near-twin on opposite corner—onto worldfamous Il Corso now—straight shoot to Piazza Venezia and Mussolini's balcony—"

"Boy, you know a lot," Phil said, huffing and puffing faster.

"Just showing off," I said, continuing to show off.

"Third-century B.C. Romans called Il Corso the Via Lata—Wide Street—Carnival celebrated here after sixteenth century—if you've read "The Cask of Amontillado" you know Poe has his main character bury another character alive in a *palazzo* catacomb while Romans are celebrating Carnival aboveground—those jeans you're admiring in shop-window there would cost you an arm and a leg—off to right, no time to visit, splendid Altar of Peace, tribute to Emperor Augustus—altar destroyed by barbarians, reconstructed by Fascists in 1930s, almost the only good thing they did besides draining swamps—." I was having a good time, but mainly it helped relieve my anxieties. Why should I be so anxious?

"Left here onto Via Condotti—famous Antico Caffè Greco on left—another Greek puzzle—German Goethe, Russian Gogol, French Baudelaire all had coffee there, whether they liked it not recorded—fashionable shops left and right, most expensive in Rome—crane neck to see members of upper classes inside shops—unknown species in Ohio small towns—"

"If college teaching fails," Phil rasped, now breathing hard, "you can always be a tour guide—"

"Back to Piazza di Spagna," I said, getting winded myself. I was sweating heavily in the midday heat. "Keats-Shelley House ahead to right of steps—coin shop not ours to right of that—no time for that—sharp left at corner—" and in a minute we were back at our coin shop.

Out of breath but invigorated, my chest aching only slightly, I opened the shop door. We entered, stopped. There was Massimo, only a few feet inside the door, waiting for us, his smile a kilometer wide. Tintin stood smiling beside him, looking thin by comparison, his costume coins tinkling faintly.

Massimo spread his arms gigantically like an eagle or an all-embracing father as he came forward to seize both of us together. "Michael!" he roared. "Philip! I am *so* relieved to see you."

"And we you," I said, feeling a surprising rush of relief and gratitude, returning his embrace as heartily as I could.

"Tintin," Massimo said, releasing us and turning to the other man, "my friends and I are going around the corner to the Caffè Greco. We have urgent business to discuss." He was already escorting Phil and me toward the door. "You will excuse us?"

Twinkle-coins had no time to reply. We were out the door in a flash, on our way back around the corner.

Una rivelazione

As we stood inside the door of the coffee shop, waiting for a table, Massimo kept rubbing his hands together, whether eagerly or nervously I couldn't be sure, and searching our faces for signs—of something.

"Babington's, that tea room opposite the shop," he said rather irrelevantly, "charges twelve dollars for a cup of tea. What do you think of that?" I found myself scrutinizing his face too, aware that the folds of flesh above and below his chin made him particularly inscrutable. He must have eaten a lot of pasta up in Hampstead.

At last we were taken to a back room, by a head waiter in black jacket and white pants no less, and seated. A reverse waiter—in white jacket and black pants—approached, took our orders, departed. Normality lifted into the air from the tables around us.

"Well—," Massimo said to us both, inviting a response. I hesitated.

"Luigi's dead," Phil said. He was looking down at his hands, turning one hand outward in a curious way, rotating his thumb.

"My God," Massimo said quietly, the look of pleasant anticipation vanishing from his face. "And the coins—?"

"Gone," I said, still watching his face, for some reason wanting to hurt him. "We never saw them."

"My God," he said, slumping down in his chair. "Have you any idea what happened to them?"

"Luigi told us—," Phil began.

Massimo sat upright. "Then you did see him?"

"For a few minutes," Phil said. I somehow didn't want to fill Massimo in on those events, just wanted to observe his reactions. "He was scared to death," Phil went on, "scared what we would say when we heard the coins were gone—"

"Gone where? Did he say?"

Phil went on, "—scared the Mafia would hear about the coins and come after him—"

"And they did," I said, somehow pleased at the surprise fixed on Massimo's face. "Two mafiosi showed up when we were there. The boy who found the first coin must have spilled the beans—"

"Did they just mention coins or say something about a hoard?" Massimo's question was astute. I hadn't thought of it before.

"They just said they wanted to look over Luigi's coins," Phil said.

"Could you tell where they were from—anything at all about them?"

"Nothing," I said. "Although I did hear one of them say something to the other about Monreale."

"Monreale," Massimo said, nodding slightly, "Well, well."

"That mean something to you?" I asked.

"I'll tell you in a minute," he said. "It may be a coincidence, or it may not." The waiter brought our orders, went away. "How long did you talk to Luigi? What else did he say?"

I gave him the particulars, dwelling on Luigi's anguish.

"So he shipped it out on his brother's boat," Massimo said, his spirits appearing to rise.

"Or so he said," I said.

"Oh, Luigi has—had—a brother, all right, a cool, calm, courageous fisherman. A fearless smuggler. He'll get the hoard to the mainland somehow. You'll see." Massimo seemed almost happy. "Well well, his brother's boat—of course. Luigi's wits were limited, but not his courage!" A second later, "But where on the mainland?"

I told him my speculations.

"You've thought it out brilliantly," Massimo said, seizing my hand and shaking it vigorously. "Of course, it had to be landed near Reggio, picked up by other Sicilians, brought to Rome. There's no good alternative." He was thinking fast. "But in Rome now—who gets the package?"

"We were hoping you'd know," I said, "or could guess."

"Luigi died," Phil reminded us, tonelessly.

"How did it happen?" Massimo asked him, instantly responsive.

"We're not certain," I said. "The thugs forced us to leave, they were there in Luigi's flat only a short time, we saw them leave. We went back, found Luigi laid out on his bed, no overt signs of violence—"

"Except his wrist," Phil said, "bent back—"

"That looked to us like the only violence they committed," I said, as though that were nothing at all. "His face and everything else looked as though he had died of a heart attack."

Massimo did look stricken. "Poor Luigi," he said quietly. "Poor, limited, suffering Luigi." His grief seemed genuine.

But I couldn't allow him to savor whatever grief he felt, not yet anyway. "Before he died, in a moment when he got really angry with me, Luigi said something strange. I've been wanting to ask you about it." Did Massimo look guarded, or did I imagine it? "I remember his words exactly. He said, 'I told Massimo you wouldn't know your ass from your elbow around here.'"

"That doesn't sound like Luigi," Massimo said. "Or me."

"He was frightened and angry. But it's the other thing he said that really puzzled me. 'Massimo said we could trust you but I said Yeah maybe but that wasn't enough—.'"

"Enough for what?" Massimo asked, calmly.

"Exactly my question," I said. "But he never got to answer. So I'll ask you now. What do you think he meant by that?"

I didn't know Massimo extremely well, just well enough to have the distinct impression that he was silently weighing various options. He began, "You recall our long, splendid talk at Il Carretto? That was only three days ago, amazing. We were having an unusually good *conversazione*, the three of us, wouldn't you say? I've met a lot of Englishmen and quite a few Americans, and if you'll forgive me, not very many of them know how to have a real conversation, with opennness and liveliness on both sides, with ideas leading to other ideas, and so on. It's one of the few skills Italians have somehow cultivated, or kept alive, even Italian men. You and Phil are unusual, do you know that? You know how to converse." He was looking straight at me, not visibly calculating. "It warms me. I feel good in your company." Another pause.

"Well, I meant everything I said that evening—how grateful I was to your father, Michael, and therefore how close I felt to you and to Philip. When I said that I wanted to give you both a present, I meant that too. It was a genuine offer." Again he paused.

"What I didn't say—and now I realize there wasn't any very good reason I shouldn't have told you—is that I rather counted on—no, I hoped—that once you heard about the discovery of the hoard you would be eager to see it—"

"Obviously I was."

"—yes, so eager that you would do what you did—decide on an impulse that you would rush down to Sicily to take a look—" Another pause.

"All right," I said impatiently, "and then—?"

"Well, then possibly come up with some ingenious idea for getting the hoard out of Siracusa—keep it out of Mafia hands, you know, with luck get it back to London, or over here to Rome." His voice grew so quiet as he finished this sentence that I barely heard his last words. "After all, you—and Philip—innocent-looking travelers—small suitcases—I was certain that Luigi could help you manage it—" He stopped, embarrassment or guilt surprisingly plain on his experienced face.

"Another set-up," Phil said, eyeing Massimo with disgust, starting to rise from the table. "You kept warning us about the Mafia, saying how dangerous it was—"

"Wait, Philip, please," Massimo said, his hand on Phil's arm. "Listen, please. I *am* your friend, I mean that. Just hear my side of it. Only a few minutes." Reluctantly, Phil sat down.

"That was disingenuous of me—perhaps even a shade dishonest. Looking back now, I suspect the sheer melodrama of the whole situation overwhelmed me. Think of it—the world's greatest coin treasure, a buried treasure no less, Sicily, ancient stone quarries, the lurking Mafia, an intrepid fencer and his adventurous son on an undercover mission! What a prospect! What a challenge!"

"And you as the puppeteer," I said, seething.

"Much grander than that, I as the impresario. To organize the whole enterprise was irresistible. Would either of you have resisted it?" Gesturing majestically, Massimo abruptly dropped his arms, let the vision fade. "Anyway, I didn't resist it, and insofar as I misled you, or any harm came to you, I'm profoundly sorry."

"We weren't harmed," I said.

"But Luigi was, you're thinking," Massimo observed. "What happened to him would have happened whether you went down to Siracusa or not. You see that, don't you?"

"But you lied to us," Phil said.

"Not lied, no," Massimo said to him. "Misled, possibly, but not out of wicked motives. I've tried to explain that."

Phil persisted. "Is there much difference?"

"I think so. We Italians tend to be theatrical, do you know? Sometimes that takes us a trifle over the moral edge—"

"More than a trifle," Phil said, adamant still.

I said to Phil, "I'm on your side." I was emphatically on his side. I felt tricked, badly deceived, nakedly *used*. Accustomed as I was to holding the lid tight on my feelings, I nonetheless knew I was really angry. "Massimo used us all right," I said, still looking at Phil, "for the first and last time." I remembered my fantasies of the hoard, tried to let them drift away, couldn't. "As for the present—"

Massimo grasped the moment gratefully. "Yes, that's all we can deal with now. Let me say again, Phil, I apologize. I want you both to be able to trust me. We want to work together, do we not?"

"On what?" Phil said. His tone was still acerbic, but he stayed in his seat.

"Why, finding the treasure!" Massimo's tone intimated that not trying to find it would be unthinkable.

I hesitated, then felt myself swept out into the onrushing stream again. "You mentioned a coincidence," I said to Massimo.

"A possible coincidence, yes. There's a well-heeled Sicilian coming into Rome today from a village near Monreale. I suspect he's Mafia, though no one has told me that—"

"How do you happen to know he's coming in today?" I asked.

"Through a mutual acquaintance, also a collector."

"Also—?"

"The Sicilian is a collector too, or his father is, I'm not certain which. On a big scale. For a Sicilian, that almost invariably means Mafia, or a Mafia tie-in." He paused, brightening. "I've just had an idea. This Roman acquaintance, an aristocrat, a Marchese, is having a small gathering at his little *palazzo* tonight. I suspect it's because this Sicilian is arriving. Oh, and there may be at least one other guest, a German coin dealer, a truly extraordinary man. I'd like you to meet him. They'll talk coins, but only part of the evening, I'm certain. And the Marchesa will be there—she's bright and charming—and perhaps another female or two." He glanced ever so slightly at Phil. "One of them about twenty or twenty-one, I think. A niece of the Marchesa. A mere Countess, but very attractive, rather unconventional."

I'm sure Phil saw the bait, but it must have been as hard for him to resist as it was for me. We'd both had mainly one another's company for a long time, merely male company at that.

"But even if this Sicilian isn't the one who sent those thugs to Luigi," Massimo went on, "he'd be worth meeting, for you to get the feel of coin trading here. And the Marchese and his German friend are two of the most knowledgeable chaps in Europe regarding coins, above-ground and subterranean, legal and illegal, coin routes, the hottest finds, everything. If our hoard"—I noted the 'our'—"comes into Rome, as we hope, this pair will know about it as quickly as anyone. Of course," he wound up, "you two should definitely be there! I'll speak to the Marchese."

Phil and I looked at one another. He shrugged his shoulders

slightly. I felt more definite about it. I wanted to meet the son of a bitch who might have set his boys on Luigi. "We'll come," I said. "Where's the *palazzo?*"

"I'll draw you a map," Massimo said, very likely pleased that our discussion hadn't gone worse than it did, whatever lurking disappointment he must have felt at the disappearance of the hoard. "It's a short taxi ride from the flat where you'll be staying," he said, sketching lines on a paper napkin. "I don't want to exaggerate. It's not really a *palazzo*, only a *villino*. Even smaller than a villa, but very choice inside."

"Where are we staying?" I asked, surprised that he had a place for us.

"On the Via Caio Mario," he said, pointing it out on his little map. "In the Prati section, not far from the Vatican, a few minutes' walk past the Tiber. It's a lovely flat, you'll see. Marble floors, rosewood furniture, complete kitchen, a TV. It belongs to my sister, Fiorella. She's a few years younger than I and has a flourishing estate-agent business. I very much want you to meet her. *Il conto*," he called to the waiter.

"You expected us to stay," I said, inconsequentially.

"Oh, you'd have had to do that, whether you brought the hoard or not, wouldn't you? These things always take time, especially in Rome."

"What about our clothes?" Phil, not normally concerned about his garb, looked at his torn jeans.

"The young Countess, the niece, will probably wear jeans, most of the young Romans do, aristocrats or not. As for your father in his tweeds, well, the Marchese will consider him a barbarian anyway, not because he's wearing tweeds but because he's an American — and also because he's not the Marchese."

As we paid the bill and left the coffee shop Massimo added, "None of us could possibly dress like the Marchese, as you'll see. He's a strange fellow — a very shrewd collector, remarkably shrewd, but rather bizarre in other respects. I've often wondered why the Marchesa married him. But then Rome is a very odd city."

Con eleganza

That evening, with rising anticipation—though of what, exactly, neither of us was sure—we left our apartment, found the taxi we had called waiting for us in front of our building, found ourselves driven across one of the pleasanter sections of Rome. I felt unusually passive, ready to engage in adventures only if they forced themselves on me, but otherwise content. It was a lovely late-August evening, the day cooling off after the fierce afternoon heat. I had spent the afternoon in our comfortable apartment, napping, fitfully reading a dreadful mystery chosen by mistake from Fiorella's crowded, miscellaneous book shelves, trying and failing to get a satisfactory handle on Massimo's manipulative behavior, reflecting on Luigi's dreary life and horrible fate, speculating fruitlessly on my own. Phil had braved the heat, once the stores had reopened in mid-afternoon, and walked the few blocks over to Via Cola di Rienzo to buy himself pants and a new shirt. Sized for Italian men, they fit him queerly, but he was pleased with having managed the purchases, he was stimulated by Rome, and after three dishes of ice cream at a nearby *gelateria* and a lengthy hot shower at our apartment, he told me he was looking forward to the party this evening, by which I figured he was mainly looking forward to meeting the Countess. Now, sitting in the taxi, he looked young, healthy and radiant. I envied him all that.

On a short street filled with imposing *villini* we stopped in front of a driveway closed by a handsome, black wrought-iron gate. The taxi left. It was too dark for us to see more than the broad features of the building looming before us, a three- or four-story stucco affair, with a massive square tower near the driveway, a vaguely Renaissance look to the windows and facade. Phil was hunting for a gatebutton to push when the iron gate swung open and a rather oddly dressed servant beckoned us to enter.

The entrance to the villino was odd too. You'd think an affluent Roman aristocrat would have laid down a more formal path to his home than a crushed-stone driveway, along which we now followed the silent servant to the rear of the building. There was a sizeable garden of large trees and small shrubs in the rear, with a round stone birdbath in the middle, on top of which a badly damaged stone Cupid balanced precariously on one foot. The Cupid was in no danger of drowning in case he fell, because there was no water in the stone basin. Possible fracture at worst.

"Looks like they laid out a fortune in plantings," Phil said, "and then never took care of them." The landscaper in him sounded offended.

The villino itself was impressive in the rear, a broad expanse of pedimented windows bracketed by a pair of handsome outside stone staircases. The servant took us up the nearer staircase, which led to a door at the top. As we ascended the steps I heard strains of Renaissance music. On original instruments, I hoped. We passed through the door into a sizeable foyer, with only a hurrying servant or two to ignore us, then into a breath-taking reception room.

Clusters of men and women were standing about, drinking and talking in low voices. They were dwarfed by the room, which was a full two stories high. They were also dwarfed and rendered colorless by the vibrant paintings covering every square inch of the spacious walls and the ceiling too. Gods and goddesses, mostly naked, romped with mostly naked mortals in various implausible scenes. They appeared to be having a better time than the guests did.

As we entered, a perky young woman came forward to greet us. "I'm Gabriella," she said in crisp English, extending a limp hand to me, while unabashedly looking Phil over. "You can only be the Americans," she said, her cultivated voice not entirely screening a certain irony.

"I'm Professor Michael Gardner," I said, taking her hand gingerly and inclining my head slightly, as though to indicate my familiarity with aristocratic manners and my disinclination to use them. Gabriella's faint irony irritated me slightly, not the fact that she was indeed wearing blue jeans. Her dreadful perfume irritated my nostrils. But it was her garish T-shirt that I found particularly offensive. It was white, with short, wide bands of gaudy orange and green splotched conspicuously over one breast, while a small target printed brightly in concentric red and black circles gave the precise location of the nipple on her other breast. I wondered, of how many generations of Roman aristocracy was *she* the product?

Phil, offered her hand in turn, seemed ready to take her on her own terms. "I'm Phil," he said, grasping but then dropping her hand quickly, as though he'd been burned, or was about to be. But he was sizing her up.

"I *thought* you were Phil," Gabriella said, her seductive tone unmistakable. Phil, for one, was in for an interesting time in Rome.

I located the source of the music. A small band of musicians was playing mellifluously in one corner of the room not far from where we stood. The piece sounded like an instrumental version of a Palestrina madrigal. There was a lute, a mandolin, a guitar, a lyre, a bass viol, a viola da gamba, a flute, a piccolo, a trumpet and a clavichord. Original instruments indeed! Pure sixteenth-century. No anachronistic double- or triple-stringed harp *here*. If the Marchese had selected the instruments, and I rather suspected that he had, his tastes were scholarly, antiquarian and frighteningly rigorous.

The instrumental purity ran to costume too. The musicians were all wearing Renaissance doublet and hose, simple in design but brilliant in color, the flaming reds, yellows, greens and blues making of the group as a whole a kind of harlequin figure, startling, comic and somehow strangely menacing. It all seemed curiously out of place in the Rome I had just left outdoors a few minutes before.

Out of place too was the concert-grand Steinway filling another corner of the room. I was getting the feel of the Marchese's tastes and wondered why he allowed so modern an instrument in his villino.

Then, past Gabriella's shoulder, I saw a tall and remarkably attractive woman coming toward us. She was dressed in a simple, elegant, sleeveless white dress. She walked gracefully, along that fine edge between self-consciousness and a natural poise. She spoke to one or two of the other guests on the way but appeared set on a course directly toward me.

Only a short distance separating us now, I saw that her arms were nicely tanned, or naturally light olive-brown, I couldn't be sure which—likewise her shoulders, her neck, her chin and cheeks, her forehead. Her hair was a rich, deep chestnut brown. Now looking straight at me, she suddenly smiled, wonderfully, full of wonders.

She held out her hand. "I'm Adriana," she said, in a vibrant voice that plucked every string in my body.

"Yes," I said, "you are." I looked at her hand, still in mine. It was as beautifully shaped as the rest of her.

"And you are Professor Gardner," she said, her tone seeming to confirm my identity ever so delicately and in the same breath to let me know how welcome I was. Her smile magically persisted.

"Your dress is linen," I said, aware of my idiocy but unable to break out of it. "And your necklace is coral."

"You *are* observant," she said. "And my bracelet?"

"Coral too," I said, utterly helpless now. "And your ear-rings, coral too."

"Do you think we might disengage now?" she asked, her fingers stirring gently in my grip.

"I'm terribly sorry," I exclaimed, opening my hand, flexing my fingers, as though her hand had been crushing mine.

She massaged her freed hand slightly, looked at mine. "That's the hand of a fencer, I would say." Her smile had eased from that of a magical woman to that of an interested hostess.

"Oh, well yes, I fence, or used to." I stared at my hand too, finding it interesting if she thought so.

"Once in the Olympics, Massimo tells me," she said. "My husband will be fascinated to know that, and envious too."

My wits were failing me. "Is he a fencer?"

"He would like to be," she said. "He would like to be—well, everything. You'll meet him soon, I'm sure, and can judge for yourself." Her English had a marginal British intonation, possibly Canadian or otherwise Commonwealth. "May I get you some refreshment?"

"Not any more, no, thanks," I mumbled, "—already refreshed—"

"But you've just arrived—," she started to say.

"It's refreshing just being here," I said, utterly unable to climb out of the hole. I looked around for Phil. He had disappeared.

"Shall I introduce you to my husband?" She inclined her head toward his presumptive location. I nodded. She lightly took my arm, guided me toward the far side of the room, where a small group stood. "I should warn you," she said, "the Marchese pretends to understand only Italian, Tuscan Italian of course. Massimo assures me that you speak it." She spoke to a short man in the center of the group. "This is the American Professor, my dear Gilberto," she said to him, "Professor Michael Gardner"; and to me, "and this is the Marchese Gilberto Franceschini Aristide Caponsacchi."

That the Marchese was several inches shorter than his wife and a full head shorter than I was only my first surprise, and the smallest one. He was dressed like the musicians, but in the severest black velvet, with white and gold trim. His jacket ended just below his waist, finished off with a large flap. His sleeves were puffed and slashed, so that his white shirt showed through the slits and in white frills at the cuffs and at the throat. His black tights had puffed-and-slashed knickers of a piece with his stockings. There was an unobtrusive codpiece. His pointed shoes were also of black velvet or a soft leather. An H-shaped satin design appliqued to the front of his jacket, from his neck to his waist, was finished in gold. A large, squarish gold jewel hung from a gold chain around his neck.

But it was the Marchese's stance as much as his costume that struck me. He could only be said to have been posing, his body turned at an angle toward me, his head unnaturally erect, one hand hidden behind him, the other hand spread-fingered on his hip, the elbow cocked aggressively forward. It appeared to me only an elbow, but the Marchese seemed to think highly of it.

"How do you do," he said, uncocking his elbow and extending his left hand toward me. There was a colossal jeweled ring on his large finger, a duplicate I now saw of the jewel hanging from his neck, a four-cornered gold piece with inset amethysts and a gleaming pearl in the slight curve between each pair of corners, truly a papal jewel. I was unsure whether to shake the hand or kiss the ring. Cautiously, I shook the hand.

Short as he was, seven or eight inches shorter than I, he nevertheless managed to to look down at me. I suddenly remembered seeing a jewel like his in a painting by Pintoricchio. Of course, I thought, the "little painter," and Renaissance at that.

"I've met Americans," he said, somewhat as a hardened birdwatcher might say, "I've seen English sparrows." He added, "But it's good to meet another. Good to keep in touch."

I floundered. "In touch with—?"

"Why, the present age, the New World, all that."

"It's not so very new any more," I replied, trying to hook in somewhere. Had my encounter with Adriana left me so unhinged?

"From *my* perspective, my fine-feathered friend, America is still the New World."

So he *did* see me as an English sparrow, or its American equivalent. "And what *is* your perspective, Marchese?" I was acutely aware that Adriana was still standing there, listening and watching. Others were there too, but they didn't matter.

The Marchese drew himself up to his full height. "The Renaissance, my dear fellow, the Renaissance, didn't you know?"

"I'm sorry not to be better informed, Marchese, but I just arrived from America," I said, increasingly annoyed. "Or from Sicily, I should say."

"Oh, Sicily," he said, with a dismissive wave of his hand. So much for Sicily. I decided to stick with America.

"Professor Gardner is a fencer," Adriana said, "an Olympic fencer."

The Marchese looked at me squarely, seeing me for the first time. He asked, coldly, "What weapon?"

"Saber," I said.

Another dismissive gesture. "Douglas Fairbanks and all that," he said. At least he had seen a movie, if not a very recent one. Or perhaps he had only heard of Douglas Fairbanks. "Foil is the only weapon."

"The only one for—?"

He drew himself up, toweringly. His riposte was meant to be terminal. "For a *gentleman*," he said. He stared at me icily, as though trying to decide whether to continue this insufferable conversation. "Castiglione never mentioned the saber."

"Or the epee either," I said, oddly pleased to have found a hook. But it wasn't odd at all; Adriana was there, listening. "In fact, I don't recall Castiglione's actually specifying *any* weapon. Doesn't he have Count Ludovico simply say, in the First Book, that 'the principal and true profession of the Courtier ought to be that of arms' "?

Though startled, he thawed a degree or two. "You've read Castiglione?"

"My field is ancient Greek and Roman history," I said, "and of course for our understanding of that history—." I left the sentence deliberately unfinished, trusting him to notice the embracing pronoun "our."

"Of course," he said, another few degrees warmer still, if only Fahrenheit rather than Centigrade, "one has to know Castiglione. Really know *The Book of the Courtier*, I mean, not just have read it — or read it in some, some—" the words seemed almost hateful to him—"translation."

"I read it in the original, naturally," I said.

He stared at me afresh. "Yes, well, your Italian's not positively dreadful," he said, grudgingly. "You trill the *r* rather imprecisely, fail to sound a doubled consonant distinctly and tend to slur in a dreadful Roman fashion, but otherwise—." He had graded me; I had received a C-plus.

I pressed on. "Count Ludovico also says, does he not, that the true Courtier should be able to 'handle every sort of weapon well on foot and on horse.' Might that not include weapons other than the foil? Which is of course not really a weapon in any case, merely a descendant of the rapier." The Marchese re-froze. "I'm thinking of the passage where Ludovico speaks of the Courtier's 'bodily frame' and says that it should be 'neither extremely short nor tall.' "

I thought for a moment that the Marchese would faint. Fainting wasn't a novelty for him, it appeared, for he lifted a finger to a servant nearby, who immediately produced a small glass vial, which he held to his nose. I smelled ammonia. "The only *important* idea of that passage," he said after a moment, reviving, "is that the Courtier be 'well built and shapely of limb.' " He held out an arm, palm gracefully upward, and pointed a foot outward, displaying his limbs.

"Ah, I'm delighted that you two have met," said a familiar and friendly voice, Massimo's. "I was about to—"

"The American Professor," the Marchese said with ill-concealed disdain, "delights in quoting the most questionable passages from the good Book—"

"Genesis? Exodus? Leviticus?—" Massimo began, the utmost gravity on his face.

"*The Book of the*—," the Marchese began, furiously, then calmed down when Massimo's little joke registered with him. "We've had a moderately interesting chat, actually," he said calmly to Massimo, "with some reservations. The Professor here professes to be a fencer." He was pleased with his little word-play.

"Perhaps you two would enjoy crossing swords," Adriana said.

"I'm sorry," I said hurriedly, placing a hand over my heart, "I just can't—"

"Oh well, then, if you decline," said the Marchese.

"Professor Gardner," Massimo said in the most funereal voice imaginable, "has recently had triple-bypass heart surgery."

Adriana said quickly, "Oh I'm so sorry—!"

I blossomed. "Thank you, Marchesa, but I'm really just fine now—except for not being able to fence."

The Marchese himself was not interested in heart surgery, anyone else's anyway. "I would have enjoyed a bout. Perhaps some other year, if you happen to return." He flicked an invisible particle from his doublet. "Signore Bellini tells me that you are also an amateur numismatist."

"Just an amateur, yes, Marchese," Massimo said hastily, "not a collector or a dealer."

The Marchese inspected me yet again in this new light. No

distinct letter-grade this time, I suspected, only a pass/fail examination.

"An amateur is welcome," the Marchese said, turning away from me toward his wife. He had presumably exhausted the reserves of his magnanimity. At least I had passed. "Shall we dine, my dear," he said, offering her his lesser elbow.

As the anomalous couple strolled away from us on the way to the dining room, Adriana gave me a rather tender look. Or so I thought. My heart surged.

Massimo whispered to me, "He'll talk coins after dinner, with sherry and cigars."

"He doesn't know about the hoard, does he?" I felt a small panic.

"How could he? The hoard must still be somewhere down around Reggio, remember? In any case, we have to keep him—and everyone else—from knowing about it as long as possible. At the same time trying to learn whether he has got wind of it, which is to say when, how and from whom. Those are the crucial questions."

The dining room was on a more intimate scale than the reception room but comparably decorated. The Marchese's fantasy life appeared to govern everything.

The Marchese seated himself at the head of the long, heavy wooden table. Its legs were elaborately carved, the massive feet resembling lion or bear claws. The table linen looked to be hand-embroidered, the silverware was ornately monogrammed, I assumed with the Marchese's initials, but the most conspicuous table furnishing was the majolicaware, whose lively blues and yellows were familiar enough but whose subtlety was breathtaking. Newly lit tall white candles marched the length of the table, roughly the length of a fencing strip.

Adriana came to my side, said in a low voice, "How delightful. You have been seated next to me." I thrilled, wondering who had made out the seating chart.

As the other guests took their places, a latecomer hurried into the dining room, was seated directly across from me. Black hair, pockmarked face, sturdy physique, early 60s. His business suit had a luster to it, of the material that used to be called sharkskin. He looked Mediterranean rather than German. It must be the Sicilian collector, I decided, not having been introduced to any Sicilian earlier. If Sicilian, then possibly Mafia, possibly Luigi's killer. His eye wandered quickly around the guests, came to rest on me. Important not to draw the wrong inferences, I told myself. I am after all the only one in the room wearing sport clothes. His gaze passed on.

I had never seen so many wine and water glasses at a formal dinner. Two liveried attendants, one on each side of the table, started filling them. The Marchese would probably have called them "servitors." They were dressed in his colors, black and white with gold trim. The red wine glistened, the water glistened, everything glistened.

Adriana sat close enough for me to notice the scent of a lovely, delicate perfume. "Do you find mine a strange marriage?"

Startled, I looked at her quickly. "Do you practice telepathy?"

"Everyone with any candor always edges around to hinting as much," she said, gazing at me with a certain inscrutability, "hinting at the strangeness, I mean."

"Some deep mating of souls below the surfaces?" I said, hoping she would say No.

"No, not at all," she said, "although when we met I suppose both of us thought there could be."

"You met—?"

"Ten years ago," she said, simply, her tone suggesting ten *long* years. "I was twenty-three when we married. Very mature, I thought at the time. Distinctly immature, wrong-headed, silly, I realized afterward. Did I marry him for the title? you're wondering. Or the money? He's fearfully wealthy, and I admit to being taken in by that, by the prospect of no longer having to work at a boring job, of being able to practice the piano every day as many hours as I wanted, to attend as many concerts as I wanted, to have the clothes I'd admired in shop windows, to travel anywhere in the world."

So the piano was for her. "And have you traveled?" I was still having trouble adjusting to her candor.

"Hardly anywhere. Gilberto loves nothing more than to dress in that ridiculous costume he put together from Renaissance paintings, and to spend hours examining the coins in his *marvelous* collection with what must be the world's largest collection of magnifying glasses—three-power, nine-power, infinite power—." Her bitterness lay shimmering. The servants brought the first course.

"Does he wear the costume while examining the coins?"

"How in the world did you guess that? Yes, he does, up there in the tower." She gestured upward. "He made it clear soon after we married that he didn't want me to enter the den up there."

I found myself eating, slowly. Dimly the food registered as delicious, but I was mainly trying to digest this woman's revelations. "If I may ask, why have you stayed married so long?"

"It's not the Italian divorce laws, though God knows they're sticky enough in practice. I'm certain it's my inertia, disbelief, recurrent optimism, my cowardice at the thought of making all of these personal horrors public, facing my relatives, my friends, and then of course the journalists, who would love a juicy scandal like this one."

"Your relatives and friends must already have some idea—"

"I'm certain they do. But I've tried hard to wrestle with the whole mess on my own, rather than spreading complaints all over Rome." Another pause. "You're one of the *very* few individuals I've poured it out on."

I liked that *very*. "I don't feel at all drowned," I said, "not even a little wet. I'm a real sponge."

"Ah well, then," she said, inconsequentially, looking around the table, resting her gaze for a moment on her husband, looking back at me for a long time. "How much could you soak up?"

"I have no way of knowing in advance," I said, sensing a rare moment at hand. I took the plunge. "But I would very much like you to test me."

I had the feeling that she too was poised on the edge, deciding. She sat more erect, moving a few inches away from me, appearing to withdraw a bit, protecting herself, unwilling to venture. I felt let down.

A servant placed a note on the table before her. She read it, glanced down the table at the Marchese, shook her head. Turning back to me, she looked angry. "He wanted me to play a little something on the clavichord," she said. "To entertain *his* guests." Then abruptly, "How would you like to stroll on the Pincio with me one day soon?"

"I would love it," I said, suddenly elated. "I've never strolled on the Pincio."

"We could look out over Rome," she went on, "pretend that our lives were under our control—but then yours probably is, is it not?" Now she was looking searchingly at me.

"I don't feel that it is at all," I said. "Not at this moment."

"We could have tea or coffee somewhere nearby," she said.

"I love Roman coffee," I said.

Intricarsi

The Marchese led the way to his den, Massimo and the sharkskin stranger and I following along a short corridor. The walls of the corridor were hung with small framed etchings and lithographs, all of them scenes of Renaissance court life. Massimo's extraordinary German friend seemed not to have shown up.

We followed the Marchese up two flights of a worn marble staircase into the tower. A few steps beyond the top of the stairs was a heavily carved mahogany door. The Marchese inserted a huge brass key into the lock, swung the door open with a ceremonial air, and preceded us into the den.

The stranger and I had not yet been introduced. Introductions, it seemed, were not the Marchese's business. Obviously he hadn't read Castiglione carefully, or had somehow failed to understand that the ideal courtier was above all civil with everyone. It was as though the Marchese had read Castiglione the way intermediate students often grasp a foreign language, understanding all the words but never the main point.

Cigars indeed, as Massimo had predicted. I was fairly sure the Spaniards hadn't imported them from the Americas until after Castiglione died, and wondered whether the Marchese knew that and smoked them anyway because he liked a good cigar. He opened the lid of a silver cigar box on a table, selected a large cigar for himself, closed the lid, took a silver cigar-trimmer from a pocket somewhere, trimmed the cigar with great concentration. The rest of us watched him. Then Massimo took a step toward the table, picked up the silver box, opened the lid, offered cigars to the other man and myself. The other man took one, I declined. Massimo took one for himself, bit off the end and lit the other man's and his own. I looked at the Marchese, half-expecting him to berate Massimo for his cheek, but he didn't seem to care. He was inspecting the clipped tip of his cigar, microscopically. Massimo volunteered to light the Marchese's cigar, from a fresh match of course, but the Marchese declined. Instead he lit a long taper from the fireplace and applied it to his own well-trimmed cigar.

The sherry was probably not an anachronism. The sherry bottle and glasses stood on a silver tray on a small table nearby, but they weren't introduced either.

In a small glass showcase on one side of the room what looked like a coat of arms in black, white and gold shone against red velvet. I could make out three geometric figures in an inverted triangular pattern on the escutcheon but was too far away to be able to identify them. Surrounding the coat of arms hung medals or medallions of various sizes. No coins were visible anywhere in the room.

The four of us stood around, only the Marchese appearing at his ease, or as much ease as ever came to him. The gathering reminded me of one that a jaded friend of mine once proposed—

bringing a group of narcissists together for a dinner party, then watching to see whether in the course of the evening any one of them ever noticed the presence of the others.

Massimo acted. "Michael, I've just been introduced to Signore Brutto, from Pioppo, near Monreale. Signore Brutto, this is a friend of mine, Professor Gardner from America. The Professor is an amateur enthusiast. He knows some Greek coins well but he has confessed to me that he's too poor ever to buy a coin." To me, "You don't mind my telling the Signore that fact, do you, Michael?" To the Sicilian, "And you, Signore, are you also an amateur?" Massimo was already well under way toward the open sea. Just before leaving the dining room for the den he had said to me privately, "Let me do the talking. They expect me to know about coins, but you're an unknown quantity. Don't show them that you know too much." On another occasion I might have found these instructions irksome, but still giddy from meeting Adriana I was entirely willing to be led.

The Sicilian was now speaking. "I'm not even an amateur, Signore Bellini. I hardly know one coin from another. I just happen to have a little money to invest, family money. I come here to consult with the Marchese about a coin or two he has mentioned to me." His voice was nasal and harsh. "Guttural," I kept thinking as I listened, finding the word somehow apt for Brutto. But I was surprised to find him moderately articulate and polite. What had I expected? Perhaps he wasn't the godfather after all. Nonetheless my nerves jangled.

"My dear Marchese," Massimo said, in his most innocent and engaging manner, "might this coin or two be something of interest to me?"

The Marchese, warming his back side at the fireplace, studied the lengthening ash on his long cigar. "I didn't think you took any interest in anything not—Carthaginian." He spoke the final word as he might have said "Sicilian." He must have known Massimo to be Sicilian, must have held him in some degree of contempt. But why then invite still another Sicilian to his privileged home? And a

Sicilian at that whose spoken Italian was distinctly provincial, not in the least Tuscan.

"Well, you're correct there, my dear Marchese. Tunis to London, London to Tunis, that's the route I travel. But as you know, sometimes I find something truly choice and drop over to Rome to see whether anyone is interested." He added, "And I always enjoy visiting this great museum of a country."

"The Mediterranean," Brutto said, "is the biggest museum anywhere."

"From shipwrecks, you mean," I said.

"Yes," Brutto said, looking at me severely as though still trying to read me.

"Particularly around Sicily, I believe," Massimo said to him, inspecting his own cigar ash before returning his gaze to his compatriot's face.

"All the countries that attacked Sicily," said Brutto, "left ships under the waters offshore. Signore Bellini and I know of that, do we not?" he said, turning an expansive smile on Massimo. He had an engaging side, I saw.

Massimo, though an expatriate most of his life, appeared still sensitive on this issue, or perhaps he simply perceived an opening into the game he wanted to play. "Yes, we do. Many years ago I read a couplet by some minor English poet or other that struck the note really well:

The toad beneath the harrow knows
Exactly where each tooth-point goes."

Signore Brutto nodded, smiling slightly. I found myself hoping that Brutto loved the odor of cigar smoke in the air, as I did, would inhale it deeply and continue to warm toward Massimo. I wanted to learn everything possible about him, and fast. "But Signore Brutto," I said, "is there no way to rescue these treasures from under the water?"

Massimo shot me a warning glance. "My American friend is a

little naive, is he not?" he said quickly. To me, "Have you ever tried to find an object as small as a coin under water only five or ten feet deep? The object is never where you think it is. Multiply that difficulty many times over, and think of the equipment it would take, the cost, the sheer organizational effort—"

"And all the countries would have to agree," Brutto said, "if the wreck is in international waters. No, no, my friend, much better to search for one's treasure on land." The statement hung before us in the air.

"If you don't mind my asking," Massimo said to him, "have you ever done that?" I sucked in my breath at Massimo's boldness.

Brutto looked at Massimo coolly, puffed slowly on his cigar, blew a perfect circle toward the ornate wooden ceiling, watched it rise and gradually dissipate. Finally he said, "What kind of a search did you have in mind?"

"Oh well," Massimo said lightly, "nothing in particular. I suppose I was thinking of the frequency with which small hoards turn up in Sicily, usually nothing very valuable, from what I've heard, but nevertheless exciting to coin enthusiasts like all of us." He now looked to be as absorbed in the fate of the Marchese's cigar as the Marchese was.

Unexpectedly the Marchese spoke. "Signore Brutto does not carry out searches. He consults persons of knowledge." Meaning himself, of course. The Marchese was clearly in the stranger's corner.

"To be sure, Marchese," Brutto said, "to be sure. But now and then a challenge comes along that I can't refuse. A challenge on my native soil, I mean. I take my native soil seriously. I am a true patriot, an old-fashioned patriot. Not of the nation but of the land of my fathers. Family, place, honor—the three of them are bound tightly together." He spoke awkwardly, like a man unaccustomed to making long speeches.

"Admirable sentiments," Massimo said with apparent sincerity. "I remember them well from my childhood."

"But you no longer share them?" the Sicilian asked in a sudden shift. He sounded defensive, suspicious.

"In England, where I have lived for many years," Massimo replied, watchfully, "I value my family above all else. As an immigrant, naturally I cannot value England the way a native could. And as for honor—"

"Yes—?" Brutto said.

"Well, I hope my fellow countryman will not be offended if I say in all honesty that I have drifted away from a belief in the rigorous code of honor that I was taught as a boy."

"And so—" Brutto began, his tone hard-edged.

"I have tried instead," Massimo hurried on, "to live as faithfully as I could according to the Ten Commandments, to take Communion regularly—"

"A good Catholic," the other said. Plainly that was not enough. "Let me ask what you would do, Signore Bellini, if some stranger, some foreigner, came onto your property in England some dark night, dug a hole on your land, found a treasure there and took it away as his own? Would you just say, 'Oh well, this is England, not my concern,' or 'Finders, keepers'?" He sounded deadly serious.

"No, of course not—," said Massimo.

"Of course not," the other said, insistently, "of course not. You would assert your rights to that property, the sacred nature of the place your family inhabited—"

"Well—" Massimo began. But Brutto was not to be interrupted. "You would call on anyone loyal to you, would you not, to hunt down the intruder, reclaim your property and teach him a lesson?" Below that courteous exterior the strength of his ferocity was staggering.

The Marchese was hardly to be counted on to rescue a conversation, but in this instance he did. "As I've just explained," he instructed Massimo, "Signore Brutto does not carry out searches. But he is an impassioned collector."

"Yes, I can see that," Massimo said in a conciliatory tone.

"In answer to your question," the Marchese continued, still addressing Massimo, "no, I do not think you would be interested in the coin or two I have been discussing with Signore Brutto." Or any other coin, his tone suggested. And yet Massimo had spoken of him—loosely perhaps—as a "friend." The two of them had known one another for years, though on what precarious basis I was now beginning to see. Then I understood. The Marchese was dismissing Massimo—and me—for the present, but not indefinitely. He wanted to talk business with the mafioso.

For he *was* a mafioso, of that I was becoming convinced. His voice had the menacing tonelessness that I had heard in Gravel-voice and Pinocchio. I felt cold at the bone. Or was I a victim of all the gangster movies I had seen?

Massimo had taken his cue. "If you'll excuse me, my dear Marchese, I've had an unusually fatiguing day and must rise early tomorrow. And Signore," he continued smoothly, turning to the other, "it has been a great pleasure to meet you. I hope that we shall meet again soon, to continue our conversation."

Brutto's face still looked as threatening as a sky full of the darkest nimbus clouds. Astonishingly he managed to banish every cloud with a rough smile, extending his hand to Massimo, and then to me. "Signore Bellini, Signore Gardner, I count on seeing you both again. And as I see that you two are good friends, I count on seeing you together."

Massimo and I left the room, silently descended the stairs, walked along the corridor toward the reception room. "That last remark—," I said.

"Yes, he noticed much more than I thought he would."

"Or than we hoped. My God, what a shark! I could easily see him giving orders to Gravel-voice and Pinocchio."

"But you have no way of knowing he's the one."

I shook my head.

"By the way," Massimo said, "did you notice the Marchese's coat of arms? Genovese. Pirate lineage."

Then we found ourselves near Adriana, who was bidding goodnight to the other guests.

Massimo paid his respects, went on ahead toward the door. "Might we take that walk tomorrow?" I asked Adriana, lingering once again with her hand in mine.

"Would four o'clock be convenient for you? The shadows over the city lengthen beautifully after that." As my 'Yes' was written all over my face she went on, "Shall we say at the terrace overlooking the Piazza del Popolo, then? American time, not Italian."

"How shall I recognize you?" Anything to prolong this moment.

"I will be wearing something subtle," she said, ever so slowly disengaging her hand.

It was not until Massimo and I had walked some little distance from the villino that I remembered Phil. Surely he could find his way back to our apartment. He had written the address down, and he had a set of keys.

Aspramente

I awoke surprisingly early the next morning, lay in bed for a while trying to remember where I was, then remembered. I opened the shutters on the huge windows, was hit by the Roman sun streaming in. It was delightful, all intermingled as it was with memories of Adriana last evening.

Down the short hall in a second bedroom Phil was asleep, snoring thunderously. The gods only knew how late he had got in, or in what condition. I walked quietly on to the bathroom, then the kitchen, peeled and ate a delicious orange.

Shaving, showering and dressing went quickly. I was eager to see Massimo. The fact surprised me. I had left the cafe yesterday with decidedly mixed feelings about him, but in the course of the evening our common front against the Marchese and Brutto seemed to have restored my simpler, older regard for him.

The coffee bar was just around the corner. Massimo was standing at the crowded counter when I entered, nursing an empty cup. "I can't drink another, I've had three *doppios* already," he said as he started for a table in an adjacent room. Reluctantly he let me order coffee for myself and wait for it at the counter. He seemed not so much impatient as restless, anxious to commence something.

Three young countermen were improvising an intricate piece of choreography in front of the shiny espresso machine. They were all dressed in spotless white, like virgin acolytes before the altar, but one of them was clearly in charge, taking orders at incredible speed from the communicants lined up before him at the counter, filling the small cups at the machine, working the handles, emptying the used grounds, relaying orders to the cashier, joking with the drinkers, noting my arrival as a newcomer.

"I've news for you," Massimo finally said as we sat down in the next room. "I have only three or four contacts in Rome, but I managed to see two of them—"

"This morning already?"

"Of course not," he said. "Romans never get up before ten o'clock. You have to catch them at night, which I did. After you went drunkenly off from the party—"

"I wasn't in the least drunk," I said.

"Not even with the Marchesa?" he said, playfully. "After we parted, I made some phone calls and set up meetings one right after the other with two Sicilians I know well."

"Any word of the hoard?"

"Too soon, Michael, too soon. It still can't be closer than Reggio.

"First, let me tell you about our new acquaintance. He's definitely Mafia. My one contact has not only heard of him, he's had dealings with him, indirectly. And Signore Brutto—Arcangelo Brutto, no less—is one dangerous man. *Ammalato di spirito*, they say here, diseased of mind. He has absolutely no scruples. My Sicilian friend says everyone who knows Brutto agrees on that."

"A psychopath?"

"Something like that. I don't know how much you've heard about Mafia executions—"

"I've read some things—"

"—well, our friend specializes in organizing them, or used to when he was younger. Not just the *lupara* jobs, simple shotgun killings. That never interested Brutto. Stranglings were more his thing, specially if the corpse was then dumped in a tank of acid, or dismembered with the body parts encased in concrete drums. Once many years ago he's supposed to have had one mobster he particularly hated dismembered and then fed to pigs.

"My friend says that of course Brutto never does the dirty work *himself*. Not any more. As the godfather, he just gives orders."

I felt numb. "*Is* Brutto a collector?"

"My friend didn't know. But I know a few wealthy mafiosi who are. I've been to dinner parties in London with some of them now and then. After all, when you're loaded with money you've got to spend it on something. Why not coins? They don't *know* anything about coins. It's just an investment to them, and something to brag about to their dumber friends."

"Brutto didn't strike me as dumb."

"Not dumb, no. Let's say uncultivated. Ninety percent of even the younger mafiosi haven't the faintest idea what civilization is all about. How could they? Some of them in the States, I've heard, are college graduates but still behave like thugs. Anyway, now we know who Brutto is."

"Good for you," I said, realizing how odd that sounded after I'd said it. So Brutto almost certainly *had* sent his boys after Luigi. "Doesn't it strike you as curious that the Marchese should be entertaining a mobster like Brutto?"

"It's not curious, it's amazing! As a rule, Roman aristocrats wouldn't be seen dead talking to a mafioso. It's bizarre even for him to have a Sicilian in his house! I get invited there occasionally because I found a really priceless coin for him some years ago, and also because the Marchesa seems to like me. But the Marchese scorns Sicilians in general, and I can't imagine why he would have Brutto to his *home*—"

"Unless—?"

"Unless—something. I don't know what. But it has to be something really unusual."

"Not the hoard?"

"No, not yet. We know that can't—but wait a minute. It's not out of the question that Brutto may have brought some word of the hoard to the Marchese, for instance his suspicion that one was found at Siracusa."

"Why would he do that?"

"I'm just thinking it through. Possibly to cut the Marchese in on it, if Brutto gets his hands on it, and so use the Marchese as a means of breaking into upper-class Roman society. These Mafia types are social climbers to a man."

"Or possibly Brutto hopes to use the Marchese to help him locate the hoard?"

"That's possible. He'd know that the Marchese has lots of connections in the Rome market and beyond, aboveboard and otherwise."

"Or might the Marchese be short of cash, find himself having to deal with a mafioso whether he wants to or not?"

"Perhaps. The Marchese spends lire the way ordinary Italians drink cheap Chianti, but he wouldn't be the first human being to do that while his bank account was empty." He thought about it. "The more possibilities we open up, the clearer it is—that we're in the dark."

"Except that it looks more and more likely that Brutto and the Marchese are somehow in cahoots—"

"What are cahoots?"

"Some sort of partnership or conspiracy."

"Or that a cahoot is evolving between them—"

"Yes."

"And that both men are dangerous."

"The Marchese too?" I found that hard to believe.

"My dear friend, don't underestimate the Marchese, just because of his silly costume and self-importance. I know him well enough to know that deep down he's full of bitterness and resentments, a real cauldron of rage."

"Over what?"

"I'm really not certain. But I've glimpsed the fires down there. Oh yes, we've got to watch out for him too."

"When will you see next see these informants of yours?"

Massimo smiled for the first time that morning. "You're no more impatient than I am. We could hear something a few hours from now, but it's more likely to be a few days. It all depends on Luigi's brother—whether he had smooth sailing or ran into a storm at sea, whether he contacted someone at Reggio or decided to bring the bag to Rome himself, what route he took, and so on and so on."

"What's the minimum number of days you think it might take him?"

"Three or four days minimum. If Luigi did indeed give the coins to his brother earlier on the day that you met him, probably the earliest they could arrive in Rome would be today or tomorrow. And then the courier would have to locate me or some other dealer, whoever that might be, and that could take time. In any case, Michael, you have to realize—"

"That anything could happen en route."

"Anything at all. Luigi's brother—or whoever he might have handed the bag over to—would know enough to avoid the Calabrian gangs, north of Reggio, but other delays of all sorts could occur in southern Italy." He paused. "And then there's the risk—"

"That the courier might open the bag?"

"Yes. If he did—"

"Who could resist that fortune?"

"He wouldn't have to know anything at all about ancient coins to realize that he had some sort of fortune right there in his hands." We both fell silent, contemplating that disaster. That calamity, that catastrophe. I was indeed thinking of the possible loss of the hoard in just such extreme terms. "We have to be realistic," he said, "and prepare ourselves for that possibility."

"Are you really that objective about it?" I asked.

"No," he said.

Con piacere e con dolore morale

Some minutes before four o'clock I arrived at the Pincio terrace, out of breath from my brisk walk from the apartment and the short climb up the Pincio hill from the piazza below. I turned my back on that celebrated view of Rome from the terrace and scanned the park for Adriana. It was much too early in the day for Romans and tourists to have filled the park, for that matter much too big a park for them *ever* to fill it, but enough of them were strolling along the paths under the pines and poplars to make finding an individual difficult.

Then there she was, a trifle breathless, in a subtle dress and an unsubtle hat with an enormous brim. "Against the sun," she said, embracing me with that smile. A large floppy handbag slung over her arm hung loosely against her hip.

We stood there for a moment, she possibly as uncertain as I. "I understand," I said, "that the view over Rome from here is especially grandiose at dusk."

"You've been reading a guide book," she said.

"How did you know?"

"That word 'grandiose,' " she said.

"I was testing your English," I said.

"I thought so," she said.

We started to walk slowly into the park, away from the grandiose view over the city. She too appeared to be saving the view for later. "Where did you learn your precise English?" I asked.

"In Rio de Janeiro," she said. "Where in North America did you learn yours?"

"In the state of Ohio," I said. "You're Brazilian?"

"Couldn't you tell?" Her tone wasn't exactly arch, or was it?

"I've never met a Brazilian before," I said, "to my knowledge."

"Well, this is what Brazilians are like," she said matter-of-factly.

"I doubt that," I said.

She took it the way I meant it. "The Marchese found me exotic. Do you find me exotic?"

"I do," I confessed, "but hardly in the way he must have."

"What is your way?" she asked, then hurriedly, "Shall we walk over toward the Borghese Gardens?" We turned toward the right, passing a green wooden bench on which an elderly man lay asleep, wholly unaware of the excitement I felt swelling inside me. Marble busts of worthies stood on pedestals along the path. Most of them were missing their noses. We stopped at the bust of one worthy. I laid an index finger on the rough surface where the nose had once been. There flashed through my brain an image of that skull in the quarry.

She asked, "How did you happen to become a professor?"

"Inertia, optimism, cowardice," I said.

She looked at me sharply. "You've a quick memory," she said.

"You were saying memorable things last evening," I said. "For me, inertia was certainly part of it, just moving on in the same direction, with the same velocity, into graduate school, then into the classroom on the other side of the desk. I was bookish, liked languages, loved ancient history. It felt warm and comfortable just to keep snuggled up in those things."

"The sport of fencing hardly looks like snuggling."

"Well but it is, in a way. What you can hit and what you can't are very carefully defined, like the rest of school. You're rewarded for hitting the target, punished for missing it, can't stray off the narrow mat on the floor, have to wear the same uniform as all the other competitors. And fundamentally it's all very safe. No one ever *really* gets killed, or hardly ever."

"But I've heard—"

"Well, there are injuries sometimes," I said. "I've injured a few opponents—"

"At the Olympics?"

"No, not there. One has to be extremely careful there. But in college matches—"

"How did it feel to be in the Olympics?" Her interest sounded genuine.

"It was wonderful," I said, "completely and perfectly wonderful. The high point of my life"—looking at her—"to date."

"You must have won," she said.

"Oh no, I lost every bout. I was lucky even to get on the team. I was the youngest by far and had the least experience. At the last minute one of the other saber men fell ill and I was the alternate who took his place. My teammates were all better fencers than I, but anyway we lost. The Italians came in first. The Hungarians and Italians usually won saber, though the Russians got second place that year." I knew I was rattling on but just couldn't stop. "I still remember the names of my teammates. Paul Apostol, Bob Dow, Jack Keane, Al Morales and—wait a minute, I'll think of it—Alex Orban. And I remember one of the Italians—his name was Montano, big man for a fencer, weighed two hundred pounds. He was so ecstatic when he beat one of the Russians that his teammates had to hold on to his helmet so he wouldn't rip it off before the score was announced."

She was looking off down the path. "I'm sorry," I said, "I'm boring you."

"Oh not in the least," she said, "not at all. I've just been feeling—well, jealousy. Partly because you're a man, you've had such opportunities for excitement—"

"The only American fencers to place in the top seven teams that year were women."

"Well, all right, but I mean in general—"

"In general you're right."

"The Olympics that year—your Olympics—were in Munich, where the Israeli athletes were killed?"

"Yes, that was horrible. I never think of my own joy those days without thinking of that bloodshed." The formality and flatness of the Pincio park was giving way to the winding paths, low hills and soaring umbrella pines of the Borghese Gardens. "I'd rather talk about you and Brazil."

"I thought you would," she said. "All right then, I'm a true cariocan, born in Rio, in a dreadful suburb. I understand that in the United States your suburbs are mainly residential areas for the middle classes—?"

I nodded. "You've never been to the States?"

"No. Well, in Rio the suburbs are where the proletarians live, the industrial workers and others like them. My father was a union leader, we could have afforded better housing, but he insisted we live where his fellow workers lived."

"Sounds admirable," I said.

"The principle was," she said, "but the actuality was awful. Cramped rooms, primitive sanitation, erratic water supply, no relief from the appalling summer heat—"

"Helps explain the Marchese's appeal—?" I began, then bit my tongue.

"Without doubt," she said, not seeming to mind. "Oddly enough, my father's principles explain it too. He was a rugged individual. I'm tempted to say rigid, although nearly every one who knew him admired him enormously."

"But difficult to live with," I said.

"Yes. I loved him—adored him in fact, but home often felt like a prison."

"Your mother—?"

"She cared almost as much for my sister and me as she did for her husband, but she was all too passive. She never once crossed him."

"You think he should have been crossed—"

"At least confronted from time to time. If someone around him had given him more perspective on himself, rather than always admiring or deferring to him, he might not have gotten into such trouble." I looked quizzical. She hesitated a moment. "He was all right under the civilian government, in the early sixties. The industrial unions were the spoiled darlings of Goulart, the President. When prices jumped fifty per cent, the unions got a sixty per cent raise. My father led the union at a big Volkswagen plant. The rank-and-file prospered, my father prospered. He even used some of his wages to send me to the Cultura Inglesa, to learn correct English and some English manners. I begged him to let me have piano lessons, but it didn't take much begging. He paid for those.

"Then the generals took over in a coup. Do you know anything about that?" I shook my head. "Well, I didn't know anything much about it at the time, and I was living in Brazil. I was only five years old in 1964. Much younger than you."

"Only by seven years," I said.

"The first time the military coup meant anything to me—"

She paused, looking out over the lovely park, a little pond, persons of all ages peacefully strolling. We had stopped walking some minutes ago. Four nuns in charcoal-gray dresses and white collars sat crowded together on a bench, sharing a bag of potato chips. "If we want to see shadows falling over Rome," she said, "we should turn back now." We turned back. "The first time was when the soldiers came for my father. Unions were one of the main targets, and my father must have been right at the top of the list." Again she paused.

"The soldiers came—"

"Early one morning. Five or six of them, with submachine-guns, if you can believe that. They herded my mother and sister and me into the bedroom. Through the door I could see them punching and kicking my father—" she faltered—"and then they dragged him out of the house. I heard the engine of their car start up, roar terribly, and then fade."

I took her hand, held it tightly. "I'm all right," she said, looking at me directly. "I've lived through the memories so many times all these years that the pain is just a dull ache somewhere in the bones. They took him off to a prison run by the secret police, the DOPS it was called, and there—they tortured him." I caught my breath. "Torture first, ask questions after, that was their routine. Electric shock, beatings, hanging him upside down with his knees bent over a rod suspended from the ceiling—they called it the parrot's perch—all sorts of sexual violations—"

"How long did that go on?"

"For two or three weeks, as far as he could tell, until they saw they weren't going to get any names out of him or break his spirit, not really break it. And so they tossed him in a cell, left him there for another month or so, then one night they put him in a car, drove him to our house, threw him out on the street."

I was aghast. I had never known anyone involved at first-hand in such cruelties.

"After that we had to leave Brazil, of course. We could have stayed. Once my father recovered physically he *wanted* to stay, to fight the bastards, start a revolution, but friends of his made him see the light. If he got back into the struggle, the police would come for the whole family next. That happened all the time. So finally he gave in. And we returned to Italy."

"Returned?"

"Both my parents had been born here. They emigrated to Brazil as a young married couple after the war. There were lots of Italians there and lots of jobs. So they came back to Italy, not to the Naples area where they had grown up but to Rome, where my father was more likely to find work."

"Which he did?"

"In a factory, yes, repairing windows, painting things, taking a turn on the assembly line doing easy jobs. He couldn't handle hard work any more after what they had done to him. And he didn't have the energy for union work either. He just put in a few hours at the factory, came home, ate pasta and drank wine, sat in front of the television, brooded. Then he died, and then mother."

I could only grip her hand more tightly, whether for her sake or mine I wasn't sure.

"The only thing I've ever held seriously against you Americans," she said, taking her hand away, "is your government's support of vicious regimes around the world like the Brazilian dictatorship."

"Americans are political innocents," I said, "I know that."

"I'm not talking about your innocence," she said with sudden heat, "but your guilt."

A gulf had opened between us. It hurt. I hadn't expected anything like this.

She turned her head away from me, looked off toward a point I couldn't see. Whether she was re-living the horrors of the past or was simply angry now, I had no idea. Slowly she swung her head back toward me. With a start I recognized the moment. It was the moment at Sotheby's in London when the head of Arethusa on the silver tetradrachm had appeared to swing round toward me. A thrill bordering on fear ran through me. Adriana's face was much more finely sculpted than Arethusa's on the coin, and her hair hardly serpentine or wild, but the look on her face—

Adriana must have seen an astonished look on my face.

"What's wrong?" she asked, placing a hand on my arm. I couldn't speak. "Oh, I'm sorry, really sorry. I shouldn't have laid the sins of the Americans on your shoulders."

"No," I said, struggling to find my way back toward the present, the silver image on that coin still radiant in my mind. "No, that was all right. I realize that certain kinds of innocence can amount to guilt."

"But I shouldn't have—," she began, "we were having such a lovely time—"

A few drops of rain hit my face. I looked to the sky, startled again. I hadn't noticed clouds gathering, had expected the day to be entirely sunny.

"I have an umbrella," she said, opening her handbag, "but it's rather small." She pulled out the most compact umbrella I had ever seen. She sprung it open, held it over me. It covered my head, one shoulder and half the other shoulder.

"It's very attractive," I said, pretending to admire the large floral print. The rain was now falling heavily.

"Well, if you don't have one, we'll have to share it, will we not?" She closed the distance between us, slipped her free arm under mine, which then found itself around her back. Our faces were five inches apart, possibly four and a half. Her breast lay snugly against my chest.

"Are you in pain?" she asked, seeing me wince.

"It's just anticipatory," I said. "You're awfully close on that side to a spot that's still tender from the surgery." She started to draw away. I said quickly, "Let's try the other side, shall we?" We switched sides, getting wetter as we did, both starting to laugh.

"How's that?" she said, snuggling in on my right side. I saw the pleasure in her face, saw that she saw it in mine. Our faces were now four inches apart, moving toward three. It felt inevitable: I kissed her. She was utterly responsive, merely adjusting our noses slightly. Still kissing, we put our other arms around one another. The umbrella settled down over our heads. The rain poured down, soaking us both. It was sheer delight.

Somehow we found our way down into the piazza below, holding each other tightly the whole slope downward.

"Do you like Caravaggio?" she asked as we made our way slowly across the piazza. Cars and taxis sped round the obelisk in the center, some headed toward us, honking, then recognizing young lovers when they saw them, veering away at the last minute. "What about that coffee?" I said.

"Art is here," she said, pointing toward the church ahead. "Coffee is farther on."

"Art then," I said. I would have been content with either, so entirely happy was I. Soggy as my clothes were, I barely registered the discomfort.

"It's Santa Maria del Popolo," she said as we passed under the Renaissance facade. "Have you ever been here?" I shook my head. "Good. I'd like to introduce you to some of my favorite things in Rome."

The light beginning to fade outside, in the church there was hardly any. Adriana led me by the hand down the left-hand aisle toward a small chapel at the front. I could see the bold strokes in two paintings high on the chapel wall, but few details. Adriana dropped a coin in a box nearby. Light flared harshly over the paintings. I gasped.

We were standing in front of an immense crucifixion scene. It was Saint Peter, I could tell; he was being crucified upside down. Peter's feet were closer to us than his head, one spike showing through each foot. Clothed only in a white loincloth, Peter looked at the spike driven through his left hand, as though disbelieving, or in too great pain to react. Three laborers, all clothed, were struggling to raise the cross into position. Their physical presence was as promiment in the painting as was Peter, as though the painting were equally about both. "Peter should never have returned to Rome," I murmured.

My remark had a certain flippancy to it, which I instantly regretted. Adriana was staring at the painting, her face stricken. Then I understood. Peter's cross was almost the Brazilian torturer's parrot perch. "I'm sorry, Adriana," I said, putting my arm around her, leading her to the other painting.

"*This* was the Caravaggio I wanted you to see," she said.

There was pain in this one too, but of a momentary sort, and leading to great joy. It was the *Conversion of Saint Paul*, Saul lying face up on the ground, his eyes sightless, his arms stretched upward toward the invisible Lord who had just spoken to him, his unsaddled horse looming gigantically over him, an aide in the background tending the horse. Saul was becoming Paul, about to launch his great proselytizing journeys. Then I remembered the tradition that Paul had, like Peter, eventually been executed at Rome. I glanced at Adriana, whose thoughts appeared to have run a similar course. "This was a mistake," she said, hurrying away toward the front of the church.

I followed her to the door, then outside. The rain had stopped. She was standing near the church, looking aimlessly around the rainswept piazza.

"I regret your anguish in the church," I said, "but nothing else today."

At that her smile returned, that smile full of wonders and life, and she put one hand lightly on my shoulder. "I think I don't regret any of it," she said slowly, "not even the anguish."

Un accenno di pericolo

My befuddlement was evident enough to Massimo at dinner that evening but Phil appeared not to notice. I guessed that he had his own befuddlement, and for a not wholly different reason.

The three of us were dining at a trattoria near Caio Mario. All three of us had in fact arrived at the trattoria with our own preoccupations, so that we had given our orders and started in on our soup before any of us said anything much.

Finally I asked Phil, "Well, how did you like her?"

"She's okay," he said, launching himself on the basket of

bread. His appetite seemed more ravenous than usual, so that I suspected there was in fact a good deal more to say about the Countess, whether he would say it or not.

"Could you tell us just a little more?" I asked.

"Well, she's really okay," he said, finishing the bread and looking around for the waiter.

"I should think," Massimo observed, bestirring himself for the first time, "I should think the little Countess would inspire you to a certain eloquence."

"That's right, she's a Countess," Phil said, more to himself than to us. The recollection seemed to move him to a deeper inwardness.

The waiter brought more bread, and also our pasta dishes. Massimo asked for another bottle of red. He had finished most of the first bottle by himself.

"You seem as lost in thought as my son," I said to Massimo, aware of my own silences too.

"Even without the inspiration of a woman," Massimo said, smiling a little at me.

"Well, I don't—" I began, then stopped, glancing at Phil, who was looking at me, puzzled.

"I'll tell you what I'm thinking about," Massimo said, refilling all of our glasses from the second bottle and downing most of his fresh glass. "I suspect that I'm being followed."

"Who by?" Phil asked.

"The most likely candidates are your friends from Siracusa. I think there are two of them."

"One with a long nose?" Phil asked.

"I really couldn't say," Massimo replied. "They weren't close enough for me to see their faces clearly. They weren't together, in fact, and neither one seemed to be paying all that much attention to me—but just enough, do you know what I mean? One of them spent an unusually long time staring in a shop window, as I walked by, over on Cola di Rienzo. Little things like that."

"Did you notice either of them when you came here tonight?" I asked.

"Well, not certainly," he said, his hesitation plain enough. "I don't want to be melodramatic, but I do think—well, that all of us should exercise some caution from now on here in Rome." Then to Phil, "I understand you'll be leaving us before long."

"In a week, I guess," Phil said, possibly reluctant to acknowledge this prospect, given the Countess. "I have to fly to New York, then on to California a couple of days before classes begin. Say, I almost forgot, I have this roll of film from the quarry—the one I shot over in Sicily, Dad, you remember?" To Massimo, "Do you know where I could get it developed fast? I want to get the prints made before going through those X-ray machines at the airport."

"Why not just give it to your father or me?" Massimo said.

"I know a physical anthropologist back at school," Phil said, now animated, "and I'd like him to look at the prints, see if he could tell us something about that skeleton in the quarry."

Here in Europe I was seeing new sides to Phil, and I liked them all. "I'll get the film developed," I said, taking the roll.

"Sorry I've got to dash," Phil exclaimed, abruptly rising from the table and conspicuously checking his watch, "late already." With a wave of his hand he was out of the trattoria.

"Ah, youthful passion," Massimo said. "I remember it."

"He didn't even get to the main course," I said.

"That's where he's going," Massimo said.

Abbandonandosi

I arrived late. The aged bus seemed to make a pit stop at every telephone pole along the lengthy Via Nomentana. Galumphing and groaning, the bus trembled as with a full and leaky bladder. It was a number 60 but should have been a 90.

Heading northeast in the city, shortly after passing Michelangelo's Porta Pia arch, I saw on the right the street I was looking for, the Via dei Villini, Adriana's street. I wondered if she had left home yet for our rendezvous, realized she must have. After all, she had proposed it. Another ten minutes and we were at the stop for Santa Agnese.

Hurriedly crossing the street I found the convent gate, saw the campanile where we were to meet. She was standing there, looking attractive.

"My apologies—" I began, rushing up to her, taking her by the shoulders, kissing her on both cheeks.

"Don't apologize for that," she said, returning my embrace. "As for lateness, don't you know no one in Rome expects anyone else to be on time?"

"But I very much wanted to be," I said, still holding her.

"It was easier for me," she said, "I live just a few blocks from here."

"Do you now?" I said, for some reason not wanting her to know that I had searched out her street from the bus. I just wanted to take a look at her house by daylight. That seemed a rather silly thing to have done, rather adolescent.

I was softly caressing her shoulders. "You Americans are certainly touchy-feely people, aren't you," she said.

I laughed. "How do you know?"

"I've seen lots of your movies," she said.

"Those movies don't have anything to do with American life," I said, now fondling her upper arms.

"Well, English movies never show Englishmen caressing women's shoulders," she said. "Whereas French movies—." She broke off, glancing at her watch. "The basilica closes at noon. And I do want you to see it—"

"Let's go," I said, releasing those lovely shoulders and taking one arm with the utmost decorum.

"The best preserved catacombs in Rome are here," she said, "but I'd rather not visit those, if you don't mind."

A long staircase of white marble led to the basilica entrance. Outdoors the day had begun to heat up, but inside the church it would stay cool. Once my eyes adjusted to the dim light inside I saw a luminous Byzantine mosaic over the altar in the apse. "It's Saint Agnes between two popes," Adriana said, following my gaze. "Seventh century. Do you like it?"

"I've loved every Byzantine mosaic I've ever seen," I said, my eyes fixed on this one as we walked slowly forward in the empty nave till we stood before the marble balustrade enclosing the altar. Always I imagined the craftsmen on their scaffolds fitting the tesserae and tessellae in place, the dazzling gold and white, the browns and greens and ocher, the shades and tints of radiant blue. Did they love their craft as nineteenth-century sentimentalists like Ruskin said they did, or was it just a job for them, under cramped working conditions at that, their bones and muscles tired every morning and aching fiercely by the evening, setting the little cubes into the mortar, their fingers nicked and bleeding from the sharp edges, the cubes set one by one but then by the score, hundreds and finally thousands until every day the same, tedium and resignation settling in like an unremitting midday August Roman sun, the joy in work reserved solely for the artist who designed the whole mosaic?

Adriana's voice startled me. "You have the intensity, if you don't mind my saying so, of someone who has spent many hours of his life alone."

"Too many, I'm afraid. Very unhealthy." I wanted to tell her everything. "As a student and then as a professor, long hours in the library, or home reading books or writing them. Much solitude. Too much, I've just begun to realize, looking back over all those years—"

"But you were married—"

"Yes. I wasn't alone all the time." I paused, thinking back.

"That's a curious way to put it, if you'll forgive my saying so."

"I'm not sure how to put it exactly. I've just begun to try getting that part of my life in perspective—"

"Since the surgery?"

"Yes, since my wife's death, and then the surgery—that really jolted me out of my inertia. Funny thing, I really felt *safe* the whole time I was in the hospital waiting for surgery. I knew they were going to saw my chest apart, lift my heart out and work on it, but somehow that didn't scare me. I'd never been treated in a hospital before, a real innocent. Afterward I saw the tubes stuck everywhere in my body, learned of the bleeding, the stench of burned flesh everywhere in the operating room, the cooling of my body, the needle jabbed into my artery to stop my heart beating, the electric shock to bring me back to life. If I'd been strong enough when I heard all that, I would have thrown up." I shivered, remembering.

"But the worst aftermath of the surgery"—I had a hard time telling anyone, even Adriana, even now—"was that I felt desperately *alone*." I looked at her squarely. "Until this trip—and meeting you."

"I don't know," she said slowly, returning my gaze, "how much perspective I can offer you on any of that."

"Well, perspective can't be the only thing I'm looking for."

She looked puzzled, or amused. "Do you mean that you're ordinary and human too?"

"Ordinary no doubt, human very likely."

She laughed, lightly touching my wrist. "I think you'd best see what you want to see here, so that we have time for the resting place of Constantine's daughters."

"I wouldn't want to miss Constantine's daughters," I said.

Outside the basilica a short walk brought us to a round building, larger than I expected for a mausoleum. Inside, it was a gem. I had expected a tomb to be dark, but it was filled with light from clerestory windows encircling the chamber, light throwing into varying shadows the striking granite columns arranged in pairs around the perimeter and supporting the large dome overhead. Graceful arches linked the columns, mosaics everywhere, many of them looking as new as centuries before.

It was a luminous moment. With Adriana beside me, in the presence of this great beauty, this beautiful haunting past, I realized that I was happy.

"The sarcophagus is only a copy," Adriana said. "The original, of porphyry, is in the Vatican. Not far from your apartment."

A bit startled, pleased, I asked whether Massimo told her

everything. "Not at all," she said, "there's lots more I want to know, such as where you plan to have lunch."

"No plan," I said.

"Well then, how about a bowl of French onion soup at my place?"

"I don't need time to think that over," I said, taking her hand.

Our walk to her villino took place in that golden haze that only lovers know. Though we weren't lovers, not yet anyway. Or were we? I realized that I had never been a lover, not like this certainly.

I was dimly aware that our walk was leisurely, out of time, sharply aware of Adriana's voice as we walked but too sunk in pleasure to register more than a few words here and there or to respond or even to know whether a response was called for. *Ancient Roman road . . . Villa Torlonia, Mussolini's home until they threw him out . . . Jewish catacombs . . .* A change of tone. "And here's the Piazza Rio de Janeiro. Fitting for me, don't you think? We're nearly there now."

Another short block, around a corner, and there was her villino. I only vaguely remembered the massive wrought-iron gate set in the formidable granite and wrought-iron wall. I stopped, looking over the villino itself. Fortress-like, terra-cotta stucco, post-Renaissance design, probably three and a half centuries old.

Adriana was unlocking the gate, pushing it open, starting through. I hesitated. She looked back. "He's gone for the day," she said, waiting. "To Arezzo. Coins." She paused. "In fact, for three days."

I entered the grounds, Adriana closing the gate behind us. "Who made the soup?" I asked as we mounted the stone steps to the first floor.

"I could have," she said, unlocking the heavy oak door with the Marchese's coat of arms painted on it in black, white and gold. Preceding me into the foyer she added, "but I asked the cook to do it before she left for the day, with the other servants."

So there it was, as I realized that I had hoped.

"Maria, the cook, suggested minestrone, but I said No, I was having a distinguished guest and wanted to surprise him."

"Did you say how he was distinguished?"

We passed through the huge reception room where we had met one another and into an elegant small room that I hadn't seen before. "I didn't, actually," she said. We halted.

I took her in my arms, or found myself in hers, kissing passionately.

Needing air, or whatever it is that prevents ecstatic kisses like those from lasting forever, we separated for a moment, but only from the shoulders up. Then behind her I saw a small table laid out beautifully with place settings for two. "You expected me to come," I said, pleased.

"I hoped that you would come," she said, sidestepping a little. Still we held each other tightly, kissing again, prolonging it this time.

Another short break, our faces hardly apart this time.

"Would you like something to eat?" she asked, barely audible. I looked at her lips. "Or later?" she asked.

"Wouldn't the soup get cold?" I asked.

"Would you mind that?" she asked, leading me out of the little room, through the reception room, through the foyer, up a long flight of white marble steps.

In the bedroom I found myself trembling. Adriana undid my top shirt button.

Then we rushed to undress one another, garments flung in all directions.

The bed was enormous, larger than courtier-size or queen-size, larger even than king-size, truly frightening. As we sank together under the soaring canopy I said, "I'm not sure I'm up to this."

"Because it's been so long?" she asked, caressing my thighs.

"Yes—and because you're a Marchesa."

She laughed, then covered my mouth with her own, enfolding my body into hers, swiftly heating our class differences to the melting point, then ourselves explosively to fusion.

Con sentimento profondo

The next three days found me alternately energized and exhausted, clear-headed and befogged, single-minded and perplexed—but almost uniformly happy. I loved Adriana with an intensity that I had only fantasized before. Everything else in my life faded before the brilliance of that fact—Phil, Massimo, Rome, even the hoard. I felt terribly irresponsible, and terribly blessed.

The mornings of those three days began at the coffee bar, a council of war with Massimo, who brought what word he had from the battlefront—still no solid news, nothing distinct, only renewed hope and vague reports from his scouts. We tried to strengthen one another's purpose, to keep our resolve, our focus on the quest for the hoard, but that was difficult. The hoard still mattered to me, at odd moments mattered achingly, but most hours these days I didn't think of it at all. Now and again I remembered that it might well be arriving in Rome any day now, could have arrived as early as the day Adriana and I first leapt under the canopy, but then even the image of those glistening coins vanished in the radiance of my new life.

Massimo was now certain that he was under surveillance, and that worried us. But as the coins hadn't yet surfaced in Rome we seemed safe enough for the time being. The only reason we could think of for the surveillance was for Brutto to pick up some clue as to the whereabouts of the coins. That at least was encouraging. He didn't know where they were either.

Massimo was beginning to show the strain, for the first time wondering aloud why he was chasing will-o'-the-wisps here in Rome, drinking too much and sleeping alone when he could be drinking just enough and sleeping with his amiable wife back in Hampstead. I realized that I had taken his steadfastness for granted. After all, hadn't he set *me* in motion on this journey? Where did he get off, thinking of pulling out of the enterprise? I also realized that I had very nearly forgiven him for having deceived Phil and me that evening in London. Very nearly, but not entirely. In moments when I remembered that deception I felt a certain caution in his presence. I even wondered whether he *was* in fact being shadowed by anyone, or was giving in once again to his histrionic impulses. I felt subtly manipulated by him, his hinting of a return to London conceivably a part of that manipulation.

Then after these morning coffees, my return to Caio Mario, to shave, shower and daydream of Adriana, easily calling up before me the memory of her hair spread out on the pillow, her eyes looking at mine with love.

Then, after rather sketchy contact with Phil around mid-day, a great rush to Adriana's villa, the buses always maddeningly slow, regardless of the impatient lover urging them on, then wonderful embraces with Adriana, lunch somehow always postponed, then joy and ecstasy unbounded. Then a leisurely lunch, late even by Roman standards, then more rapture under the soaring canopy, then much later an evening meal together at some not too conspicuous restaurant some distance from the villa. I was delighted to find that once we were both careful not to put too much pressure on the center of my chest, I could fling myself into love-making with only the pain of joy to deal with. The blood rushed painlessly through my bypasses, all three of them.

Somewhere between lunch and dinner the second day Adriana played the piano for me, at my request. I was an amateur at music, as I was at everything else, but I could tell a first-rate performer when I heard one, and Adriana was unmistakably first-rate. She and the concert-grand Steinway deserved one another. Willing to play almost anything for me that she knew, she nevertheless drew the line at the year 1700. "Nothing before Haydn and Mozart," she said, in an unusual display of closedmindedness. It took me only a few seconds to guess why. And she preferred a line drawn at 1800 and even later. I couldn't believe that she would reject the Romantics, and she didn't. But she particularly loved everything from the Impressionists on that pointed toward the expressive, heart-rending, dissonant, mournful, lyrical, wrenching music of our own century. That day she played for me a selection from Debussy's *Images*, a Prokofieff sonata, Bartok's Sonatina. Her touch was sure, her keyboard technique precise, but above all her feeling for each piece of music was exceedingly sensitive. I was deeply moved—not least, toward wanting to take all that talent to bed again.

On the first two mornings of these memorable days I had managed to exchange only a few words with Phil. He slept until mid-day, then when he finally got out of bed he was either so sleepy or otherwise hung over with whatever he had been doing the previous night that I found it hard to talk with him. The rest of the truth was that I found myself strangely distant from him, as though the Marchese's party that first evening in Rome had taken Phil off on one road and taken me off on an entirely separate one. I thought that I understood the causes well enough—it looked, quite simply, like the young Countess on the one hand and Adriana on the other—but I was perturbed nonetheless. I had come to value our closeness enormously.

On the third morning he arose earlier than usual, appeared more alert, even initiated a conversation as we sat together in the kitchen. "I have to ask you about something," he said, pausing after only his first bowl of cereal. I saw the bold young Countess looming sharp and clear on the horizon, her seductive grin fixed in place, her breasts neatly targeted. Had we ever talked about birth control? I wondered.

"It's about this woman of yours," he said, still staring into the empty bowl.

I was staggered. How had he learned? What did he know? "Did you think I didn't know?" he said, reading my face.

"Who's the father here and who's the son?" I asked, stalling.

"It's pretty plain, you know," he said. "All that excitement on your face when I get up in the morning, humming in the shower—you never used to do that—combing your hair two or three times, rushing off somewhere as soon as you dress, putting me off with junk about coin dealers in the city, staying out late at night."

"You get in earlier than I do?" I was nettled, caught before and after the act. Phil just looked at me.

"Okay, there *is* a woman," I said. After a considerable pause, "It's Adriana, the Marchesa."

Her identity didn't seem a surprise to him. There weren't after all many candidates. "Isn't that adultery?" he said flatly.

Never had I found the self-righteous candor of the young so infuriating. I was about to retort "Who are you to judge?" when I realized that of course he was right. *He* wasn't committing adultery, so far as I knew, and I was. "It's more complicated than it looks," I said, feeling helpless to explain. Then I saw the look of pain on his face. I was shocked, realizing that I hadn't even considered the possibility of his being hurt.

"I've wanted to tell you about it," I began, not quite truthfully. "But we haven't seen each other much—"

He waited, then said, "Well, it's your life."

Still I floundered. "The Marchesa has had a dreadful marriage," I said, "not really a marriage at all. She's shown a lot of courage in putting up with it all." I wasn't doing too well. "She's a remarkable woman," I ended feebly.

"Well, it's your life," he said again.

"I'd like you to get to know her," I said, feeling the truth of that strongly.

"That would be okay," he said, getting up abruptly from the table and rinsing his bowl in the sink, "but I'm leaving Rome pretty soon and don't really have much time till then." I suddenly realized that he was angry.

"Let's at least have lunch together, the three of us," I said, feeling the urgency. "Maybe tomorrow?"

"Maybe," he said, averting his eyes as he left the kitchen.

Fortunately for my state of mind I couldn't linger in the apartment, had to hurry off to meet Adriana.

I broke the news to her of Phil's having found us out, soft-pedaled his emotional response. She thought that our lunching with him the next day would be a sensible idea, if a little intimidating.

"Sooner or later we'd want you two to get to know one another, wouldn't we," I said, not really having framed that idea distinctly until this moment.

"I've been living so utterly in the moment—," she began, trailing off.

It seemed that we had dropped back unexpectedly into history.

Con delirio

I awoke on the fourth day to a shrill clamor in the apartment. As I came to consciousness the noise resolved itself into a shrill doorbell. I got out of bed, threw on a bathrobe, stumbled to the apartment door, wrestled with the bolts, finally got it open.

No one there. The bell rang insistently. Then I remembered: the doorbell was being pushed outside the door to the building, three flights down. I closed the door, lifted the receiver of the wall phone, pushed one button then the other, heard a voice.

"Massimo here, Michael." He sounded urgent.

"Okay, I'll ring you in." I pushed the button, heard the buzzer through the receiver.

Soon Massimo hammered on the door, rushed in when I opened it. He was out of breath, with his bulk must have taken those three flights of steps very hard.

With his first breath he said, panting, "It's arrived."

My heart soared. "The hoard?"

"One piece of it," he said angrily. "Just one piece. Some bleeding idiot—!"

I was still not awake enough to get my bearings in the day, let alone on an unidentified moving target. "Idiot—?"

"Yes, that bloody fisherman, Luigi's brother—or whoever he sent with the hoard to Rome. We don't even know who brought it!" I had never seen Massimo so unhinged. He seemed distressed, furious, uncertain, really wild, all at once. He paced the floor of the hallway restlessly, peered into the bedroom at my rumpled sheets, peered into the second bedroom at Phil's inert body, into the kitchen, as though searching for something, or vigilant against spies.

"Come on into the living room," I said, trying to take him by the arm.

"This is a catastrophe, can't you see that?" He was shouting, then lowered his voice when I nodded toward Phil's bedroom. But Phil, who could usually sleep through almost anything, had heard him, came sleepily into the hallway. "Phil should hear this too," Massimo raced on, his usual tact utterly gone. "He's come all the way from London—both of you have—from America, and for what?" Exasperation poured out of him.

"What's going on?" Phil muttered.

"Massimo," I said sternly, "tell us what happened."

"Give me a drink of water," he said abruptly.

I brought him a glass, took him into the living room, Phil following, still looking bewildered. We all stood there.

"All right, I'll tell you," Massimo said, "as calmly as I can." His tone seemed to disclaim responsibility if his self-control failed. He sat down, clenching and unclenching his fists. "I got word very late last night from one of my contacts. It was too late to call you. She's a very smart dealer, a woman, a Ph. D., an Italian. She's honest but in touch all the time with the marginal or downright dishonest types who bring coins and artifacts and God knows what into her office. Her name is Carlotta. Her office is on the Via del Babuino, near my coin-jingling friend.

"Carlotta called me about midnight. For her to call me at that hour could only mean an emergency." He paused, sipping the water, staring hard at the glass as though some secret swam there invisibly. "It was an emergency all right. Some bedraggled looking fellow had come to her office late in the evening, long after closing hours, and rapped at the door. It's a thick glass door, bulletproof, heavy, with a steel frame. There was no way for him to break in or shoot her through the glass, anything like that. But she was alone in the office, and she had made the mistake of leaving several lights on, so that when she looked cautiously at a mirror on her rear wall to see who was at the door, this fellow saw her reflection.

"So he knew she was there, and he just kept pounding on the door, not so loud as to rouse the police but loud enough to annoy her, to keep her from getting any work done and frighten her a little. She's a tough bird, but in certain circumstances—. It was a bit thick for her, as you can imagine." Another sip of water. He appeared to be calming down a little.

"Anyway she didn't want to spend the night trapped in her office. She could have phoned the police but that could have led to a two-hour question-and-answer session, and anyway she wasn't really certain that the fellow at the door was a desperado and so she decided to go to the door and see what he wanted."

Phil now looked alert. I certainly was.

"She stood inside the door, made a gesture asking what he wanted. He stopped pounding, drew a parcel of dirty newspaper out of his pocket, carefully unfolded it—and there it was."

Massimo stopped, drank the rest of the water, just sat there, appeared lost to us.

"There what was?" Phil asked.

"A coin," Massimo said, curiously detached for a moment. "One coin—a single coin." Another pause. Suddenly he looked up at me, at Phil. "Don't you see?"

"Not yet, Massimo," I said, a wave of fear swelling within me.

Massimo plunged on. "Carlotta signed to the man to hold the coin up against the glass door. When he did, she almost had a heart attack. It was the most beautiful fifth-century decadrachm she had ever seen. And it looked mint condition. So of course she opened the door, brought the man inside, made him sit down, even gave him some fruit and an old bit of cake. He was famished, it turned out, and exhausted. She took the coin carefully out of his hand, just keeping an eye on him to be sure he wasn't casing the joint. But he seemed quite content to be eating and resting.

"After the first minute or two, she told me, she couldn't take her eyes off the decadrachm. It was in fact in nearly mint condition, only a little tarnish on the surface. Imagine that, Michael! Imagine how Carlotta must have felt!"

"That's exactly what I've been doing," I said. "Did she find out where he got the coin?"

"She asked, of course, and he gave her some cock-and-bull

story about finding it in his father's belongings when his father died."

"Did he say where his father died?"

"He named some village in Sicily that she'd never heard of. But he did seem to be Sicilian."

"How did he happen to come to her shop?"

"He said some friend of his in Sicily had told him to come to Rome, to contact some other friend here. And then as far as Carlotta could make out, this other friend—whoever he was—supposedly told him to take the coin around to any one of the coin dealers on Via del Babuino."

"At midnight?"

"That's just one of the implausibilities here, Michael. You could fill a rubbish bin with them all. Carlotta had a hard time finding out anything at all. These chaps toting coins around to dealers usually have remarkably tight lips and vague memories, as you'd guess. And this chap didn't seem too bright either, or didn't want to."

"I don't suppose," Phil said, "Carlotta found out whether this guy was a fisherman, or came by way of Reggio."

"No, she didn't. There wasn't any reason for her to ask those questions, naturally. But we're losing sight of the main point—"

"The extraordinariness of the coin," I said.

"Precisely. It *must* come from our collection." Again, that proprietary *our*. "A coin like that doesn't show up even once in a century."

"And if it did come from the hoard—?" Fearing the worst, I had to hear what he thought.

"Then it looks as though Luigi's fisherman brother, or someone else somewhere along the route from Syracuse to Rome, decided to break up the hoard, to sell the coins off one by one, rather than keep the collection together."

"Isn't it possible that Carlotta's visitor brought her just the one coin to see whether she'd buy it, and how much she'd pay, but with the idea of telling her about the rest of the hoard once he found those things out?"

"Sure, it's possible. But Carlotta asked him about other coins like the one he'd brought her, and he denied knowing about any others."

Phil, deeply absorbed now: "So what does it matter if the coins get sold off one by one?"

Massimo looked at Phil as though suddenly discovering in him the signs of some astonishing and rare disease. Then he relented. "I'm sorry, Philip. I took for granted you'd know, but of course you wouldn't. A collection like ours—and I'm more and more convinced that it *was* originally a collection, that some Syracusan noble, someone like our rich friend the Marchese here, say, started to collect the most priceless Syracusan coins early in the century—very likely those from the mint in Syracuse, now that I think of it—and then passed it on to his sons or to someone else in the family—well, today this collection would be worth a colossal fortune on the coin market—in Munich or Zurich or the United States—only if it were kept together *as a collection*.

"Each coin by itself would fetch a very good price, no doubt about that. In December 1990, at a Sotheby's auction in New York, a Syracuse decadrachm engraved by Kimon brought four hundred thousand dollars. And that decadrachm was only in good-extremely-fine condition, not mint. Mint condition would have brought much more. I'm talking about a coin, mind you, somewhere in size between an American half-dollar and silver dollar, not larger than that. What matters is the *quality* of the engraving, and the condition of the coin, and its rarity.

"And a *pair* of mint decadrachms would certainly fetch much much more than double what a single one would fetch. Nothing like a duplicate pair of decadrachms has ever been brought to auction, so far as I know, or ever discovered. Just one pair would set numismatists' heads spinning the world over!

"But we're talking about an infinitely greater thing here, a phenomenon so extraordinary it's almost an act of God, like an earthquake or a flood or—"

"Or Mount Aetna erupting," Phil said.

"Or something even more extraordinary—don't think that I

exaggerate—because floods and volcanic eruptions have occurred every so often, somewhere around the world, from the beginning of history to the present. But a coin collection like ours—well, has probably never been seen."

"We haven't exactly seen this one," I said.

"No, but it exists," Massimo said grimly, "I'm sure of it. Or existed until this idiot fisherman or whoever he is got his hands on it. If I could get my hands on him—" Massimo's hands garroted his victim.

"Then you'd treat him the way our Mafia friends would like to treat us," I observed. But much of the steam had escaped from Massimo's fury. He had moved on to despair. "The question is," I said, "what can we do now?"

"Talk with this woman dealer?" Phil said.

"Yes, we have to start there," Massimo said, heavily. "She's our only hope right now."

La cerimonia, la brillantezza, l'esultanza

It took us only twenty minutes to walk to the Via del Babuino, walking fast. Carlotta's coin shop was unremarkable from the street, only a small, polished brass name plate and that thick bulletproof glass door revealing its presence.

Carlotta admitted us. She had come down to the shop early, Massimo having phoned her from Caio Mario.

She was bronze all over, not from the sun, I guessed, so much as from within. She was solidly built, a bit statuesque, her reddish-brown jacket and skirt made of a soft leather, with boots to match. Her brown hair was pulled back in a tight bun, her glasses had metallic brown frames, her eyes were brown. I thought she should trade only in bronze coins, or only in silver and gold.

She was cordial enough but decidedly businesslike. Her doctorate was in Classics, Massimo had told us on the way over, and she might have pursued a career as a university professor had her coin-dealer uncle not died just as she finished her degree and left the business to her in his will. She wasn't exactly happy as a businesswoman, but she was extremely good at it, smart and brassy and enjoying the combat of bargaining. She dealt only with the upper end of the retail trade, leaving the really high-priced coins to the big auctioneers in the big cities and the run-of-the-mill stuff to small-scale retailers scattered here and there in cities and towns everywhere.

Without a word she led us upstairs, motioned us to seats around a small round table. The room was only dimly lit, the sole light a high-intensity lamp suspended over the table. Carlotta slid a large framed mirror on the wall to one side along hidden tracks, began to spin the dials of a wall safe. Her reflection in the mirror spoke of concentration, severity, fatigue.

She pulled the safe-door open, reached inside, brought out a small transparent plastic box, something white showing inside. She could easily have carried the box in one hand to the table but used both hands instead, holding it aloft as a priest carries a chalice to the altar. Setting the box gently down on the dark-green felt surface of the table, she waited a few moments, though she seemed hardly the type for silent prayer, then slowly lifted the lid from the box and took out a piece of folded white velvet cloth, placing it exactly in the center of the table. Unfolding the white cloth, quarter by quarter, she disclosed another piece of folded velvet inside, this one blood-red. Again the ritual—for I saw now that that was what it was— quarter by quarter, the red cloth unfolded. I found myself hating Carlotta's ceremonial urges, hating Carlotta.

Then there it was, its silver surface leaping upward against the rich red velvet, glowing with a preternatural light. Did I hear Phil and Massimo exclaiming, or was it only myself?

It was indeed a decadrachm, the most brilliant coin I had ever seen or seen photographs of, ancient or modern. Arethusa's face lay uppermost, in sharp profile, framed by the Greek letters for Syracuse and the famous four dolphins.

"May I?" Massimo asked, hardly waiting for Carlotta's assent before swiftly lifting the coin by the edge, holding it close to his eyes. "I'm terribly near-sighted," he said, reaching for a pearl-handled magnifier lying on the table. His near-sightedness was news to me.

"Dolphins in pairs, fore and aft," he said. "Rather shallow relief. Arethusa's hair bound in a sphendone but with some locks springing outward. Drop earrings, beaded necklace."

"The engraver Euainetos?" I ventured.

Massimo was absorbed now, slowly rotating the coin, the magnifier still to his eye. Carlotta remained standing, her hands folded together before her, her priestly role sustained. I suspected that normally she was unperturbable, but in the presence of this coin even her eyes glowed.

I was aching to see what Massimo was seeing, close up. "May I see that side," I said, "before you turn it over?"

He took another long look, then passed the coin and magnifier to me.

As I moved the lens into focus, Arethusa's haunting face swam toward me. I caught my breath, not wanting to single out details, only to take it all in, to live in the luminous moment.

"I've never seen a Greek coin in that condition," Carlotta said, a certain wonder audible in her metallic voice. "When are you going to tell me where it was found?"

"May I see it?" Phil asked. Grudgingly, and after a prolonged further look, I handed the coin and lens to him. "Hold it by the edge," I said.

"Sure, sure," he said. "I watched you do it." Getting the coin in focus, he whistled softly. "Boy, if they were all like this one—"

Massimo held out his hand. "It's the other side we're anxious to see," he said, the "we" in this instance clearly not including anyone not already initiated into the mysteries. Phil surrendered the objects to Massimo, who—not at all with Carlotta's ceremonial solemnity but with the grace of a magician—flipped the coin over, the lens quickly before his eye. "In the quadriga," he reported, "tremendous excitement in the horses, heads and bodies turned four different ways. The charioteer straining hard to keep them in line. A large Nike in the sky, carrying—I think it's an *aphlaston*—.

"But wait—," he said. Sounding puzzled, he lowered the magnifier, held the coin off at arm's length for a moment, gradually brought it closer to his face. "I can't make it out—," he said, viewing the obverse side through the magnifier once again.

"The horses," I said urgently. "Tell us more about them."

"The horses can wait," he said, a note of bewildered rapture sounding in his voice. He handed the coin and lens over to me, pointing to the arc at the bottom.

"It's a skull," I said, recognizing the object below the ground line even without the lens.

"Yes, obviously," Massimo said impatiently, "but what's next to it?"

It was a geometric design of some sort, a bit rectangular but with sloping sides, and with faint interior cross-hatching. I lowered the lens, shook my head. "I haven't seen anything like it," I said. But I felt Massimo's agitation too.

"Not exactly a parallelogram," Massimo said, "more like a parallelepiped, but narrower at one end."

"May I look at it?" Phil asked. I gave him the treasure.

"Sea monsters I've seen aplenty," said Massimo, "crammed into that little exergue, and ears of barley, chariot wheels, lions, suits of armor—"

"Grasshoppers, crabs, palm branches, octopi, ship's sterns," I chimed in, trying hard to remember all the exergual designs I had seen photographs of over the years.

"But never a skull," Massimo said, "or a little design like that piece of geometry." Turning to Carlotta, "Have you?"

"No," she said, "but then I'm not in the big leagues."

I was wondering about her tone when Phil interrupted. "It's rocks," he said matter-of-factly, rotating the coin slightly this way and that, then laying it and the magnifier on the table. "Sliced rocks, I mean," he said, "like that overhang we saw at the Cappuccini quarry."

Quickly I picked up the coin, magnified the design. "My God, you're right," I said, adrenalin flooding through me. "And the skull—of course!"

Massimo, impatiently, "Of course what?"

"I can date this coin," I said, rushing ahead. "413 or a bit later."

"The Athenian Expedition," Massimo said, light dawning—"the prisoners in the quarry."

"And that *aphlaston* in Nike's left hand," I said, joy flooding through me, "that warship ornament—"

"Symbol of a naval victory," Massimo said, turning exultantly from one to the other of us. "The Syracusans' victory over the Athenians. It all fits! That late decadrachm style—you're right, Michael, it looks like Euainetos all right—that energy and motion in the horses, everything in three-quarter profile—"

"But it's *not* Euainetos," I said, scrutinizing the quadriga side more closely. It's *ch-o-l*," I said, spelling out the Greek letters. "Nearly invisible in the ground line."

Massimo asked, "Is it his full name or an abbreviation?"

"How can we tell?" I said, irritably.

"Let me see," Massimo said peremptorily, seizing the coin and lens from my hands. Focusing quickly on the ground line, he snapped, "*Chol?*—I've never heard of him."

"We've never seen a skull or a quarry in the exergue either," I said, still feeling triumphant. "I'd think you'd be happy to discover a new engraver."

"I am, I am," Massimo insisted. "It's just—well, perhaps any discoverer feels a certain annoyance with his discovery, don't you suppose? The possibility occurred to me only this moment. When Captain Cook happened on the Sandwich Islands, along with his delight he must have felt a certain irritation that the Sandwich Islands had been there in the Pacific all along for centuries and he hadn't known about them."

"So you agree that it *is* a discovery," I said.

"The coin looks perfectly genuine," he said, picking it up once again, with that magician's deftness, looking it over as though he had yet to make up his mind, "and so yes, it *is* a discovery—a major one." He smiled the grandest smile I had ever seen on his face.

I was joyful beyond words. "A first-rate artist," I said to Phil, as though having to explain the momentousness of a hurricane to children, "a first-rate artist no one has known of for over two thousand years. And a coin no one we know of has ever seen."

"Shouldn't we be drinking champagne or something?" Phil had caught the spirit of the moment, even if he couldn't have known the magnitude of the find.

"I keep a little *aperitivo* on hand for occasions like this," Carlotta said, in a lovely burst of joviality. She went to the wall safe, brought out a bottle.

"Occasions like *this*?" Massimo asked, playfully. "How many have you had?"

"I'll tell you that, Signore," she said, bringing out glasses and pouring the wine, "when you tell me what's going on with this coin."

Massimo and I exchanged glances, paused. For all his impresario skills, Massimo had failed to raise with me the question of Carlotta's involvement in the scheme, and in the rush of the morning I simply hadn't thought of it at all. But what could we do? She now had seen as much of the hoard as we had, knew the significance of this one extraordinary coin. Moreover, she had the coin in her possession — the Sicilian had in fact brought the coin to *her*, not to us — but she had also made the coin available to us, having been alerted by Massimo to the possibility of its arrival in Rome. In short, she was now in on the secret. But was she trustworthy? Massimo had trusted her far enough to ask her to keep an ear cocked for rumors of an interesting coin find, but how much further did he trust her? I looked over at him, found him nodding his head slightly. He had doubtless gone through the same train of thought. I nodded in turn.

Massimo then gave Carlotta a neatly selective account of our quest, touching on only the main points of probable interest to her, omitting the rest. I admired his intelligence afresh, his human competence.

"And so this mafioso Brutto is having you watched?" she asked, once Massimo had finished.

"It looks that way, yes," he said, his eyes on her face. "Does that worry you?"

"Yes, frankly. In this business we often deal with questionable types, as you know perfectly well, but they almost never put their goons on you. And now that I have this decadrachm—"

"Well, you're right to be worried," Massimo said, the first time I had heard him make such an admission. "My American friend here has tended not to take Pinocchio and Gravel-voice seriously enough—" I started to protest, then realized that he might have been right. "—even though he saw in Siracusa how tough they could be," Massimo went on, "but once Brutto gets wind of even this one decadrachm here in Rome—"

"How would he do that," Phil asked, "if Carlotta just keeps it here in her safe?"

"Oh, in any number of ways," Massimo said. "Through the courier who brought the coin here at midnight, to start with. What do we know about him? Almost nothing. Just that he acts dumb and has a large red boil on the left side of his nose, isn't that what you said, Carlotta? And who sent him? Luigi's brother? Or someone in between those two? How many Sicilians and others are involved in bringing the coins from Reggio to this point? We still have absolutely no idea. This is a vessel that could leak at any number of points along the way."

"I didn't realize," I said to him, "that you were so concerned about Brutto."

He waved a hand in the air dismissively. "Well, you know, one day all I can see is a shower of silver coins before my eyes, and the next day all I can see is that bloke following me with his long nose. But now that the hoard has actually begun to arrive—or a piece of it anyway—"

"It's more dangerous," I said. Massimo simply looked off into the depths of the dark room.

"How about putting the coin in some other safe place?" Phil asked.

"Such as where?" Massimo asked. Turning to Carlotta, "Do you know of any other place?"

Carlotta pursed her lips, thought it over, shook her head. "There are only one or two other Romans I would trust with the coin," she said, "and neither of them has a place as secure as this shop with a wall-safe like this one. In any case, you wouldn't want to let still others know about the hoard, would you?"

Our conference ended on that ambiguous note.

Irresolutamente

We left Carlotta's shop, looking cautiously about as we stepped out on the street. I felt exhilarated — and wary. I was glad to see Carlotta locked behind her bulletproof door. We saw no one particularly suspicious in sight but agreed that it would be a good idea from now on to vary the routes we took in the city, trying never to take the same one twice. We turned the corner onto the Via Vittoria and headed toward the river.

Massimo said he would work his Sicilian contacts harder now to get some word on the anonymous bloke who brought the coin to Carlotta, and would shift all their search efforts to the south of Rome, to try picking up the courier's trail from Reggio. The coin had arrived in the minimal time we had estimated, he pointed out, so that it had clearly been sent by the most direct route.

"I'll whip my spies into action," he assured us, stopping by the mound of dirt that was now the only vestige of the Emperor Augustus' mausoleum. "But I'm afraid I won't be able to ride herd on them until my return—"

"Return?" I was taken aback.

"Yes, from London. I wanted to tell you earlier today, but then the coin arrived at Carlotta's shop and we haven't had a minute since—"

"Why go to London?" I asked, panic-stricken at the prospect of losing Massimo just now.

"There's an emergency. I got a call late last night from my assistant in London, a frantic call. My shop downtown was broken into yesterday and a lot of coins stolen. I don't keep a large inventory on hand, but if much of it were stolen I could be in serious trouble, truly serious. He just doesn't know how much was taken. I have to fly back immediately."

"Then you had this on your mind this morning—"

"Along with the Carlotta emergency, yes."

"I'm so sorry, Massimo," I said, once more feeling the futility of even trying to share anyone else's troubles. "Sorry for myself too, I'm ashamed to say."

"I know that Phil's leaving soon too," he said. Turning to Phil, "How soon is it?"

"Two days," Phil said.

"Well, but you have—" Massimo started to say to me, then stopped.

"It isn't a question of loneliness," I said quickly.

"No, I'm aware of that," said Massimo. "This is a crucial time for the hoard—possibly the most crucial time for us—and you must realize how terrible I feel to be abandoning you—"

"You're not abandoning—"

"But I am," he said, laying a hand on my arm. "I have a proposal, though, to put to you. It may not only help you during my absence—I hope to return in a few days—but strengthen our joint enterprise here in Rome enormously."

"And that is—?"

"That we bring my friend the German expert in on a small part of our secret, just a fraction of it—"

"What German expert?"

"The one I hoped you would meet that evening at the Marchese's—"

"That extraordinary German."

"That's the one. He's an amazing individual, positively brilliant. For our purposes, he happens to be one of the most knowledgeable coin specialists in Europe, possibly *the* most knowledgeable. He's certainly the best I've ever met, and he has a rock-solid reputation in the coin trade. Absolutely honest, a man of the greatest integrity, if rather aggressive at times in pursuit of his business interests—"

"That sounds a little contradictory to me."

"Well, he's complex. But I think we can trust him. And in a way I think we almost have to. Frankly, Michael, I'm getting discouraged about the prospects. My contacts here aren't many, and they're rather grotty, hardly a trained cadre of intelligence experts. But Wolfgang has contacts everywhere in western Europe, in Sicily and the rest of Italy as well as up in Germany and Austria—and in Greece and Spain, and in America too, in case the hoard gets dispersed—God forbid!—to other countries. That's part of the point— for us to *prevent* that dispersal. To track down the coins just as rapidly as possible. To get cracking on it today, if we can. I can't tell you how urgent this is—" His voice broke, he seemed close to tears.

"That coin we saw this morning was amazing all right," Phil said, "but it's only a coin, isn't it?"

This voice of normality came from such light-years' distance from his own state of mind that Massimo could only stare at Phil, uncomprehendingly. A small group of Oriental tourists crowded past us at that moment, looking at their guide books and then at the dirt mound nearby. I motioned to Massimo and Phil to walk the short distance to the Ara Pacis, near the river. Again we stopped, looking vaguely at the marble altar inside its glass enclosure.

"I'm committed to this search too," I said to Massimo, "even if in ways different from yours. But it's starting to get out of hand, don't you think? First we had to bring Carlotta in on it this morning, and now, just an hour later—"

"I've given it a lot of thought the past few days, Michael," Massimo burst out, "a lot of thought. Wolfgang isn't someone I just thought of this morning." He was terribly roiled.

"No, I didn't mean that," I said. "I'm sure you've looked at it from all sides. It's just that—"

"Wolfgang has still other virtues for us," Massimo said quickly. "He knows the Marchese and could make use of him for us, but I'm certain that at bottom he's scornful of him and would never confide in him. There's also no one more reputable than Wolfgang to appraise the coins, once they arrive. And no one in a better position to decide how they should be marketed." I couldn't tell whether he was rushing in order to present the entirety of a case to me before I protested, or whether out of some sort of anxiety and panic he was improvising, shoring up his confidence in Wolfgang's merits even as he named them.

"The man sounds like a genius," I said, not without irony.

"He is," Massimo said, "I'm certain of it. I'm also certain that we need him, Michael—desperately."

"And we have to decide today," I said, hoping that we didn't.

"I'm afraid so," he said. "I have an evening flight to catch."

"Is he still in Rome?"

"It so happens that he is. This afternoon he has an appointment at some Eastern European embassy but he could see us briefly after that."

"You've already asked him—"

"Only whether he could take coffee with us."

"Do you know whether he'd be staying on in Rome for awhile?"

"I don't, no. We'd have to find out. But with a temptation like the hoard—or even as little of the hoard as you and I decide to tell him about—"

"That's one thing that bothers me—besides the fact that I don't know him at all. What sort of temptation would the hoard be for him? Would he look at it like the chance of a lifetime to make a great name for himself and a great fortune?"

"Possibly some of each, I don't know," Massimo admitted. "He's an enormously complicated soul, as I've told you. You can't really judge him until you've met him."

"Then shouldn't we meet him?" Phil said to me. Embroiled in my own emotions, not wholly trusting Massimo's either, I heard in Phil's voice the sound of common sense. I agreed to meet this genius in the late afternoon.

Affannosamente

Phil and I returned to Caio Mario to find Adriana standing on the steps outside our building, leaning against the front door, scanning the directory of tenants' names.

Our pleasure at seeing one another was instantaneous, but I sensed something urgent in her.

With a glance at Phil, whom she greeted warmly, she asked whether there was a coffee bar nearby where she and I could talk.

"Oh, I'm just taking off somewhere," Phil said, his tact a little too much in evidence. Then I realized with a start that this was only the second time he had seen Adriana, the first time having been their brief introduction at her party that memorable evening.

"No need," I said quickly, then saw from Adriana's face that there was a need.

"Look, Pop, I'll go to the bar. I wanted an espresso all morning." With a wave to Adriana he strode off to the corner, turned right toward the bar. He never drank espresso.

"I'd like to talk with him one of these days," Adriana said as I let us both into the building.

We started the climb up the marble stairs, holding hands. Some unknown laborer washed them every morning, and they were wet and glistening now.

"He's an appealing young man," she said. "But then he is after all your son."

"My limited experience tells me that genes and other people have a lot more to do with the way kids turn out than most parents would like to think. Anyway, something more pressing is on your mind."

"It is," she said, soberly. "But let's wait till we're in the flat, shall we?"

We took the remaining stairs rapidly, entered the apartment, put our arms around each other in the most satisfying way, sat down in the living room close together on the sofa.

She said gravely, "Gilberto. He knows about us."

My heart should have felt pain, the way the hearts of all the other paramours for thousands of years must have felt on hearing those words, but it didn't. Oddly enough, it felt better, relieved perhaps. I told Adriana so.

"Yes, well, sooner or later it had to happen—but right now it's horrible."

"Tell me," I said, holding her hands tighter.

"I didn't expect him to return from Arezzo until tomorrow, as you know. But as he didn't catch us in the midst of our blazing crime, that's a minor matter. What *does* matter is that within a few minutes of his return this morning, someone—some servant, whoever—had told him about your daily visits, and about our afternoon retreats to the bedroom."

"How did he react?"

"He was furious. He *is* furious. He—well—mainly he seems furious with you—"

"As your seducer—"

"Some such thing, yes. It's so—absurd." She hesitated. "You may as well know. Soon after our marriage Gilberto made it clear that he really wasn't interested in—well, our sleeping together."

My eyebrows lifted.

"He doesn't seem interested in boys, or anything like that," she hurried on. "He's not really a *frocio*. He just seems to be, well, sexually neutral. Before marrying him I didn't have any idea such persons existed. He's not dreadful about sex, anything like that. He's just indifferent. Naturally one thing I've resented is not having been told about that before the wedding."

"But now, despite all those years of sexual distance—"

"Despite the tenor of the whole marriage. He's an utterly conventional person. You must have seen that—"

"Indeed, but—"

"So that despite the actualities of our lives together, he's still gripped by conventional ideas of what they *should* be."

"And by fear of what others would say."

"Of course. It's remarkable, isn't it, all this timidity—and rigidity—in such a fearfully intelligent person. He's so smart about Renaissance history, coins—"

I suddenly remembered. "There goes *that* hope," I said, without thinking.

"What hope?" She looked at me, startled.

I got up and took a turn around the room. "Well, I was going to tell you before long—but today is obviously the day." I gave her as rapid a summary as I could of my search for the great coin hoard, starting with Massimo's disclosures at the Sicilian restaurant in London, ending with our visit to Carlotta's office an hour before. I told her of Luigi's death, the Mafia, everything important I could think of, except for some reason holding off on the news of Massimo's imminent departure and the Wolfgang prospect. "So it seems you've taken up with a boyish adventurer," I concluded, "or a foolish treasure-hunter, or something equally silly."

She had listened to my story attentively, continued to look thoughtfully at me now. "You *are* a deep one," she said.

"Really quite shallow, the way it feels to me," I said. "What grown-up in his right mind would act on impulse the way I did in London, just take off on a harebrained chase, abandon a well-planned scholarly enterprise—?"

"Well, a sensible, self-disciplined, wholly rational adult wouldn't—a really boring person, I mean." I grinned. She asked, "Are you sorry you did it?"

"No," I said.

"Is Phil sorry he did it?"

"Mostly no, I think."

"And didn't this adventure bring us together?"

"You win," I said, moving over to take her hand.

After a while she said, "What did you mean when you said 'There goes *that* hope'?"

"Well, just before you told me of Gilberto's finding out about us, Massimo and I were still hoping to enlist his help in locating the rest of the coins."

"So much for that," she said.

"Alas."

"And now you have his anger to contend with."

"I don't see that as a problem for me, not directly, as long as I stay out of his way. You're the one who—"

"No, no, Michael, you're not aware of some things. He's something of a coward himself, but he's sometimes had dirty work done for him. With all his money he just gets someone to round up a few toughs from Prenestino or Borgata Tor Marancia, or Primavalle."

"Why would an aristocrat get involved—?"

"With thugs? I suspect that his coin dealings occasionally get out of hand. Look at that shark who was at our house that evening. And then Gilberto just has a cruel streak, which he loves to rationalize as a strain of courage that he inherited—in some obscure way—from one of the Florentine Medicis."

"His fantasy life is bizarre," I said.

"Yes. If he just kept it to himself, or lived by himself, then it wouldn't matter. But he doesn't."

"So that I should watch out—"

"Yes."

"—and of course you should—"

"Well, yes, though I don't think he would get any rougher with me than he did this morning. It would be too shameful, if anyone found out."

"How do you mean 'rougher'?"

She looked anxiously around the room, as though searching for an exit. "I didn't plan to tell you. He—slapped me hard two or three times." She touched her cheek, remembering.

I stood there, clenching my fists, feeling furious, wanting desperately to get my hands on Gilberto.

"Did you say you were already being followed?" At first, her question seemed merely distracting, but then I realized it had to do with violence threatened from the other source.

"Yes, we think so. Now if I get beaten up—or Phil does, or Massimo—we can't be sure who did it." I meant to dismiss the danger, but I failed.

Adriana said quickly, "We can't let that happen."

"We could leave Rome," I said. It was the first thing that popped into my mind.

Adriana took it seriously. "Yes," she said thoughtfully, "that would at least reduce Gilberto's chances of getting at you, though in his present mood he might well go after you elsewhere—"

"Elsewhere in Europe, you mean?" She nodded. "But mightn't he cool off after a while?"

"I suppose so," she said, thinking about it, "but he takes a long time to heat up or cool down. Anyway there's also the other threat—"

"From Pinocchio and Gravel-voice," I said.

"You seem to be making light of it."

"Not really," I said, touching my chest where Gravel-voice had jabbed it, "not any more."

"The only way for you to eliminate that threat," she said, watching my face, "is to give up your pursuit of those coins."

I went over to the window, looked out over the rooftops and streets. "I came to Rome," I began, trying once again to think it through, "wanting desperately to see those coins."

"You saw one an hour ago."

"Yes, that made me rejoice—I just realized at this very moment that that's what I did when I saw the decadrachm at Carlotta's, I *rejoiced*—that I had followed the hoard this far—"

"And now—now that you're possibly in danger—?"

I thought it over. "The danger really doesn't affect me very much. Maybe it should. I've lived such a protected, safe life that danger seems almost *welcome*, absurd as that may sound."

Adriana got up from the sofa and came over, putting her arm around me. "Perhaps the main question is how much you would regret not seeing the rest of those coins."

"A lot," I said quickly. "But just seeing—and touching—them isn't the whole of it. I realized that early on." Pieces were falling into place. "When Massimo first told me about the hoard, back in London, what struck me first was the sheer adventure of it. Buried treasure! The most beautiful silver coins ever minted! And discovered on the exact site of a great human tragedy that I was planning to write a book about and was going to Sicily to research. That coincidence was too astounding to ignore.

"But then there was Luigi's death. That changed everything. Here was that pathetic, funny little man, perfectly harmless, who happened to have this treasure put in his hands. I found myself hating the bastards who killed him, and the bastard who'd sent them after him. When I met Brutto, if I could have figured out how to kill *him*, I think I would have." Once again I pictured shoving a broken-off saber blade between his ribs. Absurd, and yet not absurd.

"Then today, when I saw that decadrachm at Carlotta's, I knew that the hoard was almost certainly *closely* linked to the Athenian Expedition. What's more, a great coin engraver had recorded that final imprisonment in the quarries of the Athenians. If that's what happened, if I'm reading that coin correctly, then all sorts of fascinating questions arise as to who that engraver was, how he learned about the prisoners, what made him decide to record their fate, and so on."

I was striding back and forth across the room, gesturing. "You can't imagine how exhilarating that discovery was to me today. And then there are still *other* coins in the hoard that I haven't yet seen! Possibly with *other* revelations!

"And so that's where I am now, sweetheart," I wound up. "I just can't imagine giving up the pursuit." I looked at her squarely, wondering what her reaction might be. She seemed to be turning it all over.

"Unfortunately," I said, "the pursuit may get harder." I told her about Massimo's emergency, his departure later today, Wolfgang. "I'm really worried about this German."

"You can't expect me to advise you on some German," she said abruptly, looking away. "I hate the Germans too much."

Her vehemence startled me. "You mean, because of your Italian background?"

"Something like that," she said, taking her arm from around me and walking a few steps away, stopping with her back toward me. "I had an uncle—the Germans—" She was weeping.

I went over to her, put my arm around her. "Just forget about this German," I said. "I'm not even sure I'll talk to him for more than ten or fifteen minutes."

Una faccenda difficile

Massimo and I were to meet Wolfgang at a new apartment of his in Rome. The apartment building stood on the Aventine Hill, in a cluster of new expensive-looking stonefaced buildings. We paid the taxi driver and stood looking at the facades for a moment. There were no sidewalks, no landscaping, not a single tree or shrub. Massimo had told me on the way over that Wolfgang was having his apartment redone, and yet these buildings looked as though they'd just been finished.

"He has tons of money," Massimo said in answer to my unspoken question as we started up the short path to the entrance, "and is very particular about having everything just right." We stopped at the front door, a rugged-looking piece of custom craftsmanship. "We're to meet him here."

I was finding Massimo difficult to talk to this afternoon and was dreading a long, silent wait for the German. Luckily we had to cool our heels for only a short while until a long black limousine pulled up at the curb. It was sporting a small, colorful embassy flag on one fender. "Bulgarian," Massimo said, a certain interest in his voice.

The chauffeur had opened the rear door for the passenger, who rose out of the car to well over six feet, towering over the chauffeur, whom he appeared to thank with a slight bow. He was dressed in a dark business suit, carried an attache case, walked toward us without a greeting or apparent recognition of Massimo until he stood before us.

"I'm Wolfgang Maximilian," he said to me, holding out his hand, which I shook.

"And I'm Massimo Bellini," said my friend, extending his hand formally and bowing ever so slightly toward the German.

"To be sure," Wolfgang said, clasping the outstretched hand, at last smiling and setting his attache case down to put his other hand on Massimo's shoulder. "It's very good to see you." His English sounded perfect, just a shade British. Glancing at me, "You are Professor Gardner, is that right?" Not waiting for an answer, he put a key in the door, opened it and preceded us into the foyer. Someone had once told me that German men always precede women through doors, even this late in the twentieth century, but until now I hadn't known whether they also preceded other men.

As we waited for the elevator, I had my first good look at Wolfgang. Physically, he and Massimo looked to be an archetypal comic pair, the German tall and spare next to the well-fleshed Italian. They looked about the same age, mid-to-late 50s, Wolfgang's lined face and gray sideburns and temples marking him as a bit the elder. He had the slender physique of a well-heeled man who swims laps or jogs or plays squash or otherwise works out regularly at his club. But it was his lined face that held my attention, furrowed not just the way the faces of men his age are furrowed but like the face of a man who has lived *hard*. So struck was I with those lines, furrows and seams that it took me a few moments to realize that his face was also handsome, or had once been.

Its handsomeness was further marred by a small reddish scar slash on one cheek. It looked like an old dueling scar, but I had read somewhere that the infamous German dueling societies had died out under the Hitler regime.

He led us to the elevator, which took us up soundlessly several floors to the top floor. "You'll have to imagine how this will all look," he said as we walked out into the bare apartment. "The decorator finished months ago, the furniture and rugs and all that are ready to be installed, but the electricians haven't yet got the controls right." He punched several buttons on a small wall panel, shook his head. "I have great respect for your Italian craftsmen," he said to Massimo, giving our Anglo-Sicilian friend a group of compatriots he probably didn't want. "They can design anything, and they can repair anything, none better anywhere in Europe, but they do *not* know how to install electronic controls. To be sure, these are unusually complex units. I designed them myself. They will control everything in a room, not just the television and the burglar alarm but *everything*." People too? I wondered.

It was a large apartment, and Wolfgang walked from room to room, examining the wall panels in every one, lifting one panel out of the wall to examine it. Shaking his head, he returned to us. "I'm sorry not to be able to offer you anything—" He gestured vaguely toward the kitchen.

"That's all right," Massimo said. "Michael and I simply want to bring an interesting matter to your attention, and we know you've not much time—" The three of us stood there in the empty room. I noticed that the floors weren't just marble, which was common enough in Rome, but inlaid marble of unusual colors and textures, forming an abstract design that Wolfgang must have commissioned. The marble gleamed from recent buffing.

Wolfgang checked his watch. "Just forty minutes," he said. "I would have been here sooner but those Eastern Europeans"—I noted his discretion—"wouldn't let me go until I had promised to give them an appraisal as soon as I returned to Munich." He looked out of the window over Rome, possibly in the direction of the embassy he had just left. "It's unbelievable what a sense of legality they lack," he said, "or a sense of tact. These are top-level diplomats, or what passes in their country for top-level. Shortly after their Communist regime collapsed last year they smuggled a huge quantity of gold and silver out of the country to their embassy here, gold they had expropriated decades ago from the monarchy when they came to power. Crown jewels, priceless jewelry of all kinds and a sizeable collection of European coins. Someone gave them my name, and they called me in to put a value on the coins, then and there, just like that, as though I were some tradesman like a plumber. When I pointed out that German law forbids me to make appraisals outside Germany, they simply couldn't believe that I wouldn't do it anyway. Finally I agreed to make an appraisal if they would bring the coins to Munich." He looked back at us, a look of something like resignation on his face. "They will of course send the coins to me through their diplomatic pouch."

Massimo said, "Given the few minutes we have—"

"Oh yes," said Wolfgang, "tell me what you have in mind."

For the second time today Massimo related some of what we knew about the hoard. This was an even more virtuoso performance, however, than that for Carlotta. He omitted all particulars of the Sicilian discovery, not mentioning Luigi or the quarry or the mafiosi, saying only that he had learned by chance of a rumored discovery in southern Italy of an extremely valuable decadrachm, and that as he happened to be coming to Rome anyway he had made inquiries of friends here, and after some time had learned that indeed some such unusual coin had just turned up at a dealer's here in Rome.

"Which dealer?" Wolfgang asked.

Massimo hesitated. "I'm really not at liberty to say, at present. Unusual as this coin is reported to be—"

"Have you seen it?"

"Wolfgang, just let me finish telling you the main points, all right? However unusual this coin, I'm told that there may be at least one other one of its quality—"

"In whose possession?" Wolfgang's impatience was evident.

"That's exactly what I don't—what Michael and I don't know." He then explained the necessity of his having to leave for London quite soon, and the urgency he felt of having some expert taking hold of the search for these magnificent coins, however many there proved to be.

"But you've told me almost nothing," Wolfgang said.

"What we had hoped to learn from you first of all," Massimo said, "was whether you might be willing to join us in this enterprise—and if willing, whether you would be staying on in Rome for a short time, enough to make inquiries of your own—"

"I have a considerable business in Munich, as you know," Wolfgang said, "clients importuning me with requests, promises of great rewards, all the rest, more than I could possibly handle in the next five years. Germans, Swiss. French, English, of course American investors too, now a few Japanese coming into the market—" He said all this without boastfulness, as though these were simply the natural consequences of his business acumen, matters of objective truth. Again he looked out the window over the rooftops of Rome, perhaps envisioning his own empire.

"But very few of these present you with anything truly unusual, do they?" Did Massimo really have to bait the hook this richly, I wondered.

"Unusual, unusual, you keep saying unusual," Wolfgang burst out, checking his watch again. "How unusual?"

Massimo held his course. "If it were extraordinary enough, you might possibly find time—?"

"I might," Wolfgang said.

Massimo looked at me, took a deep breath. "It's fifth-century. About 413–410. Siracusan." He knew how to pause for effect. "Mint condition."

"Interesting," Wolfgang said.

"What's more," Massimo continued, something like pride of ownership in his voice, "the designer is a completely unknown name."

"Or just illegible, you mean?"

"Perfectly legible, perfectly distinct," Massimo said. "The coin was uncirculated, only a breath tarnished." He must have been enjoying a quiet triumph of some sort in this little exchange with the extraordinary German. "The name is easily read under a lens."

Wolfgang asked, "And the name is—"

"Ch-O-L. Just those letters."

"On Arethusa's head-band?"

"On the ground line."

"You've seen the coin," Wolfgang said. "You haven't just been told about it."

Again Massimo paused, glanced at me. I didn't know how far we should be entrusting ourselves to this man, barely shrugged my shoulders. Massimo made the decision. "Yes, we've seen it, Michael and I."

"In Rome?" Massimo nodded. "At a coin dealer's?" Massimo didn't quite nod. "Someone you know and trust?"

"Yes," said Massimo.

"And this person told you there is—or may be—another decadrachm like this one?"

"We've been told that, yes," said Massimo, going carefully.

"And so there's still another party who knows about these coins," Wolfgang said. He spoke more rapidly than anyone I had ever heard. "This isn't exactly a secret then, is it." He sounded either a little triumphant or annoyed, I couldn't tell which.

"I never said that it was," Massimo said, rather testily. "One thing we need to find out is how many know about the coins, and who and where they are. Our guess is, not very many thus far—"

"What makes you think not?"

"Until and unless we learn whether you will come in with us, there are some things—"

Wolfgang was now racing on. "Do you know who delivered the coin to your friend?"

"Some idea, yes—"

"A Turk, possibly?"

"No, not—" Massimo stopped.

"A Greek, then? A Sicilian?"

"You seem interested," I ventured.

Wolfgang turned to face me. "What is your stake in this?" he asked me. "I have to know. Massimo said that you were strictly an amateur."

"That's right," I said. "I'm a university professor of ancient history. My interest springs from that."

"We've been longtime friends," Massimo added. "I just happened to mention the coins to Michael—"

"You said coins, plural. So you knew some time ago—"

"Just a few days," Massimo said.

"—that there was more than one coin." Massimo was silent. "How many more, do you suppose?"

Massimo stood his ground. "We really must know—"

"Whether I'll look into it?" Somewhere along the line Wolfgang had made up his mind. "How could I resist—at the very least, looking at that decadrachm you've already seen?"

Massimo looked at me. "She's to be out of Rome tomorrow,

Michael, but could almost certainly see you the next day. Will you contact her?"

And so it was decided, in that driving, circuitous fashion. I would be taking Wolfgang to see Carlotta—and the coin.

Pensierosamente (solo)

After a deeply reluctant farewell to Massimo, who caught a taxi for the airport, I returned on foot to Caio Mario. It was sometimes hard to read Massimo, but today he struck me as decidedly less reluctant to leave Rome than I was to have him go.

It was a beautiful day, I needed the exercise, and I wanted some time alone just to think. My walk took me along the Tiber, and normally I would have paused at every vestige of the ancient world that I passed, taking a full day's stroll instead of the brisk hour or two I had in mind now. Today I saw the Teatro Marcello and even the magnificent Castel Sant' Angelo only peripherally, and only as buildings, devoid of history.

As I walked along I thought hard about Wolfgang. He *was* in fact extraordinary, in some fashion or other, I wasn't sure exactly how. Formidably intelligent, for sure. A formidable human being. But without Massimo's active involvement in the enterprise, could I work with Wolfgang, or he with me?

And what was his exact relation to Massimo? Simply that of a coin expert whom Massimo respected? I recalled Massimo's having mentioned him the first day we met in Rome, and wondered whether even then Massimo had some reason for wanting me to meet the German, or for bringing him into our pursuit of the hoard. Simply money, at bottom? Massimo earned his living off coins, after all, and he certainly had the monetary value of the Sicilian coins in mind, but I had long thought of him as a larger, more complicated, more admirable person than that. Was I mistaken?

And was I mistaken in chasing after the hoard at all? I'd told Adriana of my helpless fascination with ancient coins, which was true enough, and emphasized to her my noble motives in wanting to keep them out of the wrong hands—but was I kidding myself? Maybe mine were the wrong hands too, and Massimo's, and even those of a museum director to whom I might deliver the hoard intact, an act I had once or twice found flitting across the screen of my imagination.

Brutto's were definitely the wrong hands. And while Gilberto's hands were no doubt cleaner than Brutto's, I hated the thought of Carlotta's silver decadrachm falling into the manicured hands of that Renaissance poseur. Thank heavens Adriana hadn't had those manicured hands laid on her, not much anyway. But they must have been laid on her sometimes, must have been laid on her shoulders, on her arms, on her lovely pianist's hands, until she found out about him anyway, found out not just about his sexual chill but about his rigidities, his snobbery, his profound self-absorption.

Why didn't she leave him? After all, she now had me. I wasn't exactly a first prize, but she loved me, I was sure of that, and we got along awfully well together, not just in the bedroom but in the parlor too, with its grand piano, and out on the streets, and talking over great art together. Of course that was Gilberto's parlor, and even if she somehow managed to take the piano with her, if we eloped, where would we put it? Not in my tiny living room in Ohio, that's for sure. Her piano was as big as my entire living room. For that matter, how would we even get the piano from Rome to Ohio—send it by plane? Do they even make cargo planes that large? No, better send it by ship. It was all absurd, the more I thought of it, but it tickled my fancy. For some little time I toyed with images of workmen laboring to get the piano aboard a plane, aboard a ship, cursing the piano, the pianist, the piano manufacturer, nursing their hernias.

Would she even be willing to live in the States, let alone Ohio, let alone in my house there? How would she spend her time while I prepared classes and taught them, conferred with students, attended committee meetings, wrote scholarly articles? Practice the piano? Give an occasional concert? There were only ten thousand souls in my college town, and I doubted that they could handle many concerts. Perhaps in Cleveland, nearby, with its symphony orchestra, if she were good enough. But how talented was she?

All of a sudden the life of a college teacher felt so *dull*. It couldn't begin to compare in excitement with chasing after coins! Or at least after *these* particular coins. How could I conceivably go back to writing scholarly articles, attending committee meetings, preparing classes yet again, saying familiar and obvious things to a new crop of innocents every year, even coaching fencing?

Turning the corner off Via Germanico onto Caio Mario, I happened to glance behind me. Two sportily dressed men were sauntering along a half-block behind, studiously looking at their feet, at the buildings they passed, at the sky. One unmistakably had a very long nose.

I hurried to my apartment building, had some trouble getting my key in the lock.

Con bocca chiusa

The phone was ringing as I entered the apartment.

"Michael? Massimo here. Thank God I got you. I've been ringing and ringing. Listen. My plane leaves in ten minutes. I got bad news just before leaving for the airport. A contact of mine heard from a *carabiniere* friend of his early this evening that an unidentified corpse was found floating in the Tiber—near the east bank, straight down from Carlotta's shop. Near where we were standing this morning. A lower-class type, rough clothes, throat cut."

"What makes you think—?"

"He had a large red boil on the left side of his nose, Michael. And his mouth was stuffed with a plastic bag full of bronze *litrae*."

My heart lurched.

"Brutto's boys," Massimo said. "Signs of torture on the corpse. Oh, there's the boarding call. I'm terribly sorry, Michael—" He rang off.

I just had to talk this murder over with someone—but with whom? I was not to see Adriana until tomorrow, and even if I was willing to risk Gilberto's anger at my calling his wife at home, I didn't want to dump the news of this murder in her lap this evening.

Carlotta? She was frightened enough, might pull completely out of the enterprise, such as it was, if she heard of the murder.

Phil was out of the apartment, I had no idea where, would certainly return late. I could wake him in the morning, but even so there was only so much help he could give me. He'd have last-minute things to do before his flight to the States the following day, and anyway given his imminent departure he couldn't follow through with me on any consequences of this new development.

There was only Wolfgang.

I was too knocked out by the events of the day to think about any of it any more.

I undressed slowly, brushed my teeth slowly, took my medications. Turning out the lights I walked over to the window, peered out through the curtains down onto the street, looked carefully from one end of the block to the other, saw no one. I wondered if Brutto's boys went to bed when normal people did, wondered whether they would see Phil returning, whenever he did. *Diseased of mind*, Massimo had said of Brutto. *Absolutely no scruples*.

I climbed into bed, closed my eyes. Adriana's face swam into view before me, then her hands and the rest of her. I missed her dreadfully, wanted to be held by her. Clutching a pillow instead, I drifted into sleep.

Somewhere in the night I awoke from a terrifying dream. *I was sitting in the stern of a small boat—I somehow knew it was a fishing boat—the tiller in my hand, the wind blowing the water into enormous swells all around. A ragged sail flapped from the mast, the engine kept coughing, the boat was in great danger. A low cabin sat amidships just forward, and a scruffy sailor stood on the cabin, holding onto the mast with one hand and pointing behind us with the other.*

I turned to look behind and was appalled to see an immense wave swelling gigantically toward us, rapidly overtaking the boat. I tried to call out to the sailor but couldn't.

The sailor now pointed downward, into the waves. An enormous black ray swam silently there beside the boat, just below the surface of the water. Then the ray was a dark face with an odd nose, the nose growing longer and longer, the face menacing, the menace feeling closer and closer—

—the point of a knife against my chest, my ribs opening, the pain unbearable—

I sat up, fully awake, my nerves utterly jangled, my chest aching horribly.

Pressing both hands tightly against my ribs, holding my chest together, easing the pain—it was two or three hours before I could settle down to sleep. I slept badly.

Tenebrosamente

In the morning I looked in on Phil, found him snoring more heavily than usual, decided it would be cruel to wake him.

Willing to risk Gilberto's wrath, I phoned his villino. A maid answered, said she would call Adriana.

"Could you see me this morning? Some place for breakfast?"

"Romans don't believe in breakfast," she said. She sounded remarkably calm.

"What do you believe in?"

"I'm not a Roman, remember? There's a small hotel about midway between us that caters to Englishmen who want big English breakfasts."

"A place to talk?"

"A place to talk."

A half-hour later we were sitting at a small table in the corner of the hotel dining room. The waiter seemed disappointed that with our order of muffins and coffee neither of us wanted a fried egg, four rashers of bacon, a grilled tomato, grilled sausage, fried bread or double-thick English cream.

As soon as we were alone I asked, "How are things with Gilberto?"

"He and I are both walking tightropes," she said, unemotionally. "Two different ones. I'll tell you about it in a minute, but first give me your impressions of the Wolf."

"Okay, briefly. He seems to have been born in overdrive. He drums his fingers, twitches his foot, talks a mile a minute—"

"Not appealing."

"No—but he does seem remarkable, in ways I've only begun to discern. A remarkable brain, finely tuned, astute."

"Still not appealing."

"He designs electronic gadgets, possibly other things—"

"Or has designs on—?"

"Yes, quite possibly, though on what specifically I haven't any idea. He's pleased with the coin empire he's already built."

"Trustworthy?"

"I can't tell yet. Massimo trusts him. We both trusted him enough—or felt we had to—for me to take him to Carlotta's tomorrow to see the coin." Adriana lifted her eyebrows. "It seemed unavoidable if we wanted to enlist him in our enterprise."

"A bit like enlisting a general?"

The waiter, openly sulky, brought our muffins and coffee. He also brought a large dish of marmalade and a large plate of butter, as well as cream for our coffee instead of the milk we had requested. He went away before we could protest. The only Italian waiter I had ever encountered who put his own preferences ahead of the customer's.

"May we talk about *you* now?" I asked.

"Nothing has really changed," she said in an oddly flat voice. "He and I haven't spoken to each other since yesterday. We avoid looking at one another. Mostly he stays up in his tower. Mostly I wander through the other rooms, thinking of you."

"Will you leave him?" The words were out before I thought of them.

Adriana considered. "To do that I would have to speak to

him, wouldn't I, and the prospect of that frightens me. I can sense that he's stretched tight, he feels angry, terribly angry—"

"You sound drained," I said, taking her hand.

"Do I? I suppose I am." She looked down at our hands.

I felt infinitely tender toward her at that moment. "Are you willing to try looking beyond his anger—to the future?" She looked up at me, taking her time. "I know you only a little," she said, "and you know me even less."

"I'd love to learn everything about you," I said.

"No, you wouldn't," she said matter-of-factly, "but you should know more before you make rash statements."

"I admit to being rash now and then," I said, "but I've spent most of my adult life trying to be as rational as possible, calmly weighing the evidence, thinking through all the options, being sensible. Since meeting you I've about decided that's an absurd way to live."

"But a little more evidence and a little more good sense wouldn't hurt, would they? Might even be crucial?"

I hesitated, then said, "All right. Tell me more about yourself."

She looked at me attentively, as though to ascertain whether I was serious. "I get horribly melancholy," she said in a tone of voice suggesting that I might well be unable to bear the weight of that revelation.

"All right," I said.

"I don't know if you have any idea what it's like to live with a melancholy person," she said heatedly.

"Not really," I said, "but I have melancholy friends. The academic world is full of them."

"Are we being serious or not?"

"I'm sorry," I said, regretting my flippancy. "It *is* true about my friends. Many of them have a hard time with life, but mostly they seem to manage."

"That may be your view from outside," she said, "but—"

"And look at what you've lived through," I said, wanting to make amends, "your father's imprisonment in Brazil—"

"That's true, but after years of fending off bouts of melancholy

I've come to realize that they usually appear independently of circumstances. Or at least mine do. They're essentially organic, or genetic, or something of the sort."

"Have you tried drugs?"

"Yes, but those only put me to sleep."

"Okay, so I'd find you gloomy now and then. It's not all the time, I know that."

"No, but it's highly unpredictable. Living with me could be an unsettling experience."

"Gilberto—?" I started to ask.

"He rarely noticed. That's how close we were." Her use of the past tense I found encouraging.

"I'm more concerned with what looks to me—with impressions I've had of a sort of—well, preoccupation with death." I didn't know how to put it less harshly.

She looked truly startled.

"I could be wrong," I said quickly, "could easily be. The thought just occurred to me when you proposed that we meet at Santa Agnese with its mausoleum and catacombs not long after you had taken me to see those Caravaggio paintings of the two Christian martyrs."

"But Rome is *full* of death," she protested. "Tombs and monuments and paintings and statuary to death everywhere. It's a Christian city, remember, and reveres a man who was hanged on a cross alive with spikes driven through his hands and feet. If we weren't willing to face images of death, we wouldn't look at anything in Rome!"

Her vehemence took me by surprise. But then given the history of her father's torture in Brazil and whatever cruelties the Germans had visited on her uncle—. "I suppose you're right," I said. "But I still think your melancholy must have sprung in some measure—"

"Might we change the subject?" she asked, signaling the waiter for more coffee.

"I believe you had suggested we talk about your flaws," I said with some heat, "and I was trying to oblige."

"Don't take it so hard," she said, stroking my hand lightly with hers. "I'm just showing you how mercurial I can be."

It did give me pause.

Only after we said goodbye did I remember the courier's murder. But I wouldn't have wanted to lay that burden on her today.

Andante affettuoso – ma con interruzioni

And then, all of a sudden, it was my last evening with Phil. So crowded had my days in Rome become that I barely noticed how they raced by.

Out of dutifulness, affection or some blend of the two, Phil had proposed that we have a final dinner together. "Our last supper," he called it, though which of us was about to be martyred was unclear.

"I'll miss you a lot," I told him as we settled into our chairs at an old trattoria Massimo had recommended.

"We sure got used to each other this year," he said, which wasn't quite the same as saying he'd miss me. But then he did. "I'll miss you too," he said, looking studiously at his menu.

"But you'll write sometimes," I said.

"Yeah," he said. "I'll be sure to tell you what that anthropologist says about the skeleton." He added, "And find out how you're doing and all that."

The waiter brought a heaping plate of olives, green and black, rolls, took our orders. On an impulse I ordered two bottles of German beer. "To toast our getting together again before too long," I said to Phil. He didn't say anything. The waiter left.

"There's something I'd like to talk over with you," I said, wanting to get to it right away. Phil busied himself with the rolls. "Adriana."

"How's she doing?" he asked. The question was at once so silly and so on target that I fumbled for a reply.

"Well, she's all right, under the circumstances. Gilberto has found out about us—"

"That figures," he said, still chewing, still not looking at me. The waiter brought the beer and another basket of rolls.

"Sooner or later, yes. But Adriana and I had hoped to have more time to make up our minds. This puts the heat on us."

He looked at me. "You going to marry her?"

It was a delicate moment. "That's what I'd like. That's what I want you to know. But she's still uncertain about it—"

"How come?" he said forcefully. "You're a swell guy."

He sounded utterly sincere. The unexpected tribute made me gasp. "She's less impulsive than I am, basicly more sensible." I added, somewhat irrelevantly, "She's had an awful life."

"With the Marchese."

"And long before that," I said. I told him a little about her childhood in Brazil, her father's kidnapping and torture. It seemed to me terribly important that Adriana become real to Phil.

"The two times I've seen her," he said, "she didn't show any signs of all that." He didn't sound skeptical, just bemused.

"No, she's come through it all remarkably intact. She's a rare creature."

"Sorry I didn't get to talk with her more," he said, with apparent genuineness. The jealousy or anger I had sensed in him recently wasn't evident now, though I hardly expected it to have disappeared. "Maybe you'll be bringing her to the States—"

"I'd like to. But first I have to get out of Europe."

"What's keeping you?" he said. "The coins?"

"And Adriana's muddle at home. That's not just something we could walk away from, even if she had made up her mind to come with me."

The waiter brought the pasta, and we ordered two more Lowenbraus.

For a while we ate and drank, silently.

The waiter brought Phil's veal saltimboca, my fish. We ordered two more beers. I had never drunk so much, nor had Phil when he was with me anyway. We took turns going to the toilet.

Later, over espresso, and then Amaretto, we talked about Phil's return to college, his chances of finding a good apartment, what courses he hoped to take this fall, whether he'd feel too rusty after his year off. He expressed optimism about everything, appeared really buoyant at the prospect of returning to college. I had mixed feelings about that.

Signaling the waiter for the bill, I recalled a wonderful story. "This American friend of mine," I said, aware that my speech was slurring, "studied Italian before his first trip to Italy, knew that he hadn't learned everything there was to learn about the language but felt happy about knowing something. He and a friend came to Rome, they had a dinner maybe at this very restaurant, he used a little Italian on the waiters, he'd had a little too much to drink. The time came to call for the check, and feeling good by now he threw his hand up in the air and called out to the waiter, '*Il sconto! il sconto!*' The waiter was mysti-, mysti- —puzzled."

"Why?" Phil was a good straight man, or a straight good man.

"*Conto* means 'check' but *sconto* means 'discount.' You see, in Italian the *s* in front of a word—"

"Okay, pop," Phil said, taking me by the arm once I had paid the waiter. Getting the money out of my pocket and counting it for the waiter somehow took a lot of time. Phil steered me toward the door.

"Wait a minute," I said, stopping at an umbrella stand. "I have to get my umbrella."

"You didn't bring one," Phil said.

"Sure I did," I said. "I always carry one, never know when it'll rain."

"That's a cane you got there," Phil said, as we moved toward the door, "not an umbrella."

I ignored him. Always somebody around like that, carping. I wasn't sure we could both make it through the door, it seemed small, but we did.

Outside, we stood there, staring stupidly at the pitchblack streets. No street lights at all, no lights of any kind. I hadn't the foggiest notion where we were. "Did you bring the map?" I asked my companion.

He scratched his head, said "Nope."

"Open your eyes," I said. I knew decisive action was needed. Leadership. Sound judgment.

"They *are* open," he said. "Yours are the ones that are closed."

I opened them. Still dark. "Do you know where we are?" I asked.

"Ghetto," he said. "We're in some ghetto."

Good man. I remembered now. Restaurant in old Jewish quarter. Massimo told us. "We just need to climb that wall," I said, pointing to the dark mass ahead. Get out of the ghetto.

We walked slowly toward the wall. I was careful not to step on any cracks between the paving stones.

A fierce pain shot through my shoulder, then another down my arm. I dodged aside.

"What the hell—!" I heard, the voice suddenly choked off. My voice.

I whirled around to see a black-bearded man lifting a short club for another blow. Reflexes took over. I lifted the cane high, parried at *quinte*, dropped weapon tip as club fell, slashed him on the beard. Hand to beard, club coming in at *quarte*. Parry—stop-cut to eye—*riposte* hard to cheek. Blackbeard down on one knee, hand to eye. I rubbed my shoulder, trying to ease the pain.

A terrific thud hit my ribs, just missed the heart. Blackbeard ahead, swinging upward. A cut to his face, a cut to his neck. Hurt him, hand to neck. Slash hand, slash neck. Club dropped, kicked it away. Beardface crawling off.

A bull head butted me in the gut. Hurt like hell. Jumped backward, *en garde* automatic. Bull-head karate type. Hands threatening. Cut to right hand, cut to left. Damage there. Weapon spiraling down on head—missed—*remise* cut to his ear. More damage. Cold sober now. Lunge and feint to chest, bull-head parries, slash to cheek. Blood there now. Weapon down hard on skull. Weapon bent. Bull-head down, cursing.

Phil shouting "you bastard!" laying into bull-head, murderous punches. Bull-head rolling away now.

Blackbeard nowhere in sight.

Third *ragazzo* lying groaning on street. Hadn't noticed him.

"Come on, Dad!" Phil pulling me off into darkness.

We stood in the doorway of a building, breathing hard, feeling our wounds.

"There were three of them," Phil said. "One with a beard. All jeans and sneakers. All tattooed, all fat."

"How did you notice all that?"

"Two of them went after you first. I sobered up fast."

"Thanks for the rescue," I said. "I didn't know you were in such good shape."

"I'm not," he said. "They were just in lousy shape."

They must have counted on our being easy targets, I thought.

"Didn't look like mafia types," Phil said.

"No, they came from Primavalle," I said.

It was Phil's turn to be astonished. "How do you – ?" he started to ask.

"I'll tell you later," I said. "Let's get back to Caio Mario, okay? You've got an early plane to catch, and we both need sleep."

We limped off to find a late-evening bus, found one. It was a bright orange color. I was grateful for the bright color. Everything else felt gray, dark gray. I ached unbearably.

Stanco e contuso

The next morning, still aching and badly bruised, I barely managed to climb out of bed and stand around stupidly while Phil finished packing. His plane was to leave at noon, and despite my protests he insisted on going to the airport alone. "I'm on my own in the States," he reminded me. "I ought to be able to get to the airport on my own. Besides," he said, looking me over, "you need more sack time."

Seldom had I felt quite as elderly as that remark made me feel. But he was right. I desperately needed more sleep, could barely keep my eyes open. Regretfully, I gave in.

We said So long, affectionately on both sides. I was gratified to find him genuinely concerned about my bruises. His weren't so bad today, he said indifferently.

Then he opened the door, waved behind him on the way out, and was gone.

I lay down on the bed, broke into tears.

The room felt intolerably hot. I opened my eyes, saw that the shutters were open, the sun, almost vertical, heating everything in its path, including me.

I got to a sitting position, feeling stiff and sore, remembered last night's assault. They must have been Gilberto's toughs, not so tough at that. But they could hurt. I felt my shoulder, my arm. It hadn't done my chest any good either, all that wrenching motion. Tenderly I felt my scar, top to bottom, but nothing along its length felt worse than usual. The pain lay deeper, in the bones or muscles. Could any of that wire spiral have been torn loose? Or the metal staples? Without getting X-rayed, I had no way of knowing. I could only guess what a job it would be to get an X-ray done — and competently read — in Rome. I stood up, swaying a little, and walked to the windows, reaching out to close the shutters. The room darkened considerably.

Toilet, a little wrinkled fruit and stale roll, a shave and shower, the water streaming soothingly over my aching body. I stayed in the shower a long time, finally felt the hot water growing tepid, turned the shower off. Drying carefully, dressing slowly, gradually coming into the day, remembering Adriana, Wolfgang, the rest. Through my bruised body I felt Phil's absence terribly, but not as terribly as the moment he closed the door.

I went to the phone, dialed, got Adriana herself.

"I've been hovering near the phone," she said in a rush, "wondering whether Phil got off all right, how you're feeling, how your dinner went last night—"

"Could you see me now," I asked, "maybe come here?"

She heard something in my voice. "What's wrong, Michael?"

"Nothing basic," I said, trying to be more or less truthful. "I'm just kind of knocked out is all. I'd rather not climb on a bus for a while."

She'd be over as soon as she could find a taxi.

When I opened the door for her, Adriana looked at my face, cried "Oh Michael!" and threw her arms around me before I could stop her. I winced.

We walked to the sofa, she helping me as she would a convalescent patient. I must have looked as bad as I felt, about like the bent cane I saw lying on the floor. "It's good to have the young around," I said, failing to keep a certain edginess out of my voice altogether.

She asked me what had happened and I told her, pointing to the bent cane as evidence. "Gilberto's thugs," she said, grimly. Anguish quivered in her voice.

"Looks like it," I said.

She rose abruptly from the sofa, began striding around the room. "That dreadful man! How could he?" Abruptly she rushed back to me, buried her face in my neck, weeping, held me to the point of pain.

"Well, it clarifies things, wouldn't you say?" I said, gently easing her embrace. "And these bruises will be gone in a few days."

"Stop trying to be cheerful," she said, more sternly than I would have expected. I waited for her to say that she would now break with Gilberto. But she said nothing, only inspected the bruises on my shoulder and arms. For this I had to take off my shirt, which led me to think of still other action we might consider. "You can barely stand," she said, seeing the light in my eyes. "And I'd rather you had your eyes open," she said, pulling my shirt on, "at least now and then." I hadn't realized that they weren't open, resigned myself to her wisdom. She buttoned me up, in more ways than one, led me into the bedroom, helped me lie down, dressed as I was.

"Do you know we now have this apartment to ourselves?" I asked as I drifted off.

She was standing next to the bed when I awoke, setting a small tray on the night table. Fruit, rolls, coffee. "I heard you stirring a few minutes ago," she said. "I slipped out to get some fresh food."

I sat on the edge of the bed, reaching for her, snuggled my head between her breasts as she stood there. "I feel *much* better," I said.

"I can tell," she said, pulling up a chair, sitting down, pouring the coffee.

Half-way through a cup of coffee I remembered. "What time is it?"

"About four," she said. "Why?"

"I'm supposed to meet Wolfgang at five," I said, gulping the coffee, stuffing a roll in my mouth, straining to put on my socks. "At Carlotta's."

"Are you really up to seeing him now?"

"Yes," I said, not certain in what sense her question was meant. In any case, I had to be up to it. Wolfgang was in motion now, and I wanted neither him to slow down nor myself to be left behind.

She walked to the corner with me, put me in a taxi. I sat down heavily, looked back at her standing there, her face gradually losing its anguish in the distance.

Quasi un pastorale

From Carlotta's I returned with Wolfgang to his apartment, where the furniture had begun to arrive. There were now four dining-table chairs, though no table. We sat down in the otherwise bare room.

Even with my dense head I could sense a change in Wolfgang. He seemed to be—well, humming. The sight of Carlotta's decadrachm had made the difference. He was friendlier too. He asked me to call him Wolf. That gave me pause. I knew that his interest in me depended exclusively on my being the magnet that pulled those silver coins out of southern Italy into Rome. And yet I wasn't at all sure that I — or Massimo — still *was* a magnet for the hoard any more. If Massimo was right, that the hoard was now being broken up, then Luigi's couriers or whoever had the hoard might have decided that we were irrelevant. They might already have decided to look around for richer prospects.

Well, Massimo had wanted to hook Wolfgang, and he had hooked him. That decadrachm had.

"You and your friend Massimo were certainly sitting on a great secret," he said, after a rather perfunctory expression of sympathy for my not feeling so lively today. "That must have been very satisfying."

"I think we hadn't yet learned how to feel about it," I said slowly, "or at least I hadn't." The point hadn't actually occurred to me before. "I still haven't. I don't even know what to compare the experience to. There I was, fascinated with coins from the time I was a boy, reading about coin hoards but not really having any idea what they were, having just handled my first precious Greek coin a few days ago — all of a sudden having this amazing hoard placed in my hands, or almost." I hadn't expected to speak so freely, and wasn't sure it was wise.

"Possibly like having seen a beautiful movie actress on the screen many times over the years, and then one day meeting her in person?" He seemed restless, got up to open a window, sat down, looked dissatisfied with the breeze blowing in from the other hills of Rome, got up to close the window. It was though the Aventine was *his* hill, and the others were rivals.

"Something like that," I said, still groping for my own version of the experience.

"I remember a fantasy I often had as a boy in Berlin," he said, "in the last months of the war. Your bombers — American bombers by day, to be more precise, and British bombers by night — were well on their way to destroying the city. In the section where I lived there was hardly a block with an undamaged building. The bombs seemed to be falling all the time, although in fact each bombing raid lasted less than an hour. But the sirens went off at other times, and the fire engines went screaming through the streets and explosions occurred sometimes for hours after the raids themselves, and people were shouting or crying out in pain—" He broke off. Those moments were still tormentingly real to him, I realized with a start.

"How old were you then?"

"In early 1945, about ten." He paused. "That winter, that spring, was by far the worst." Another pause. "Except for the first year after the war. Well, I won't bore you with that—"

"I'm not bored at all—"

"Well, I was starting to tell you about my fantasy those years—which was to be in some beautiful, quiet place—above all, quiet—out in the countryside, with a placid horse or cow standing peacefully about, just chewing on something like a mouthful of hay, with the sky perfectly blue, except for a stray white cloud or two, nothing dark, and bright green grass everywhere in sight—" He appeared lost in the memory. I felt myself drawn to this strange, enigmatic man.

"The bombing must have been horrible," I said, aware of the inadequacy of the words. "Did your fantasy ever materialize?"

"In a way," he said. "When I left Berlin to go to Munich, along the road I sometimes had a glimpse of a bucolic scene very much like that boyhood fantasy." He was re-living that journey. "But the cow or the horse or something else was always missing—" Quickly he returned to the present. "Now then, I have a plan—or as you Americans would say, an idea. Why don't we celebrate our good fortune by having a splendid dinner together tomorrow evening, on my expense account?"

"Which good fortune did you have in mind?" I asked, genuinely uncertain.

"Why, the good fortune of our having met," he said, "and of our having come across that magnificent decadrachm—with every prospect of still more magnificent decadrachms to come!" I was surprised to find myself caught up in his enthuasiasm, and while I would much rather have spent the evening with Adriana, I agreed.

Inoperosità forzata – poi rubata

The next day was of a kind I'd always hated. Nothing attractive in sight, not even anything neutral or negative, like preparing a class or reading student essays. Adriana was leaving her villino early for a trip of several hours to the Ardeatine Caves, to lay a wreath at the tomb of her uncle who'd been murdered by the Nazis, carrying out a longstanding family ritual. She would phone me on her return, but at six in the morning, when I had the misfortune to wake up, that delightful prospect seemed light-years away. Wolfgang and I were to meet for a late dinner, and that prospect had its mixed appeal but seemed even more remote.

I lay in bed for awhile, trying to go back to sleep, but the sunlight and rising street noises made that difficult. Even putting a dark handkerchief over my eyes and relaxing my jaw muscles and every other muscle I was conscious of, as a yoga instructor had once taught me to do, didn't work. I tried visualizing an endless row of bronze *litrae*, the commonest, most boring small coins I could think of, thinking to count them until I dropped off to sleep, but I suddenly remembered that two bronze *litrae* were the very coins Brutto's thugs had placed on Luigi's closed eyelids – and the very coins stuffed into the mouth of the murdered courier. I sat bolt upright and climbed out of bed. I headed for the shower, determined to wash those memories out of my system.

That worked, but the rest of the day still loomed heavy.

The only virtue of an unstructured day was that I could rest when I wanted to, and my bruised body emphatically still wanted to. As I wandered idly around the apartment, sitting down now and then, staring at the characterless modern furniture, the miscellaneous books, the hotel-style framed prints on the walls, I tried to picture my landlady, Massimo's sister, and had to give that up. I doubted that I would ever meet her, and that didn't seem to matter.

To my surprise, by the end of the morning I found that I was mildly enjoying doing nothing. Snacking in the kitchen, lying down now and then, flicking channels on the TV, trying unsuccessfully to follow the Italian of the speakers on the tube, all of whom seemed bent on beating Wolf's record for rapid speech, gradually I realized that this sort of idleness was very much what I wanted. My days in Rome, and before that in Syracuse and London and before that the last months in the States, winding up my semester, undergoing surgery, recuperating and all that, had taken a lot out of me, as well as putting a lot into me, and today I discovered that I needed a rest, and was getting it.

After lunch I napped, then found I managed my idleness quite nicely through the afternoon until the phone rang. It was Adriana. She was unusually subdued but asked how I was feeling, what I had done all day. In turn I asked about her day but without trying to push beyond her rather perfunctory replies. The pilgrimage to her uncle's tomb had plainly dampened her spirits, and I just didn't feel like probing the causes. We agreed to call one another in the morning and rang off. I was left feeling somehow disgruntled. Wolfgang and I were to dine at a fancy restaurant, and I was again aware of the limits of my wardrobe. My tweed jacket would be too warm for the August evening and too sporty for the restaurant, but there it was. In London two weeks ago if I'd stopped for even ten seconds to think how insufferably hot Rome would be in August I would have bought a lightweight jacket, but I hadn't. Yet another gaffe. Did I commit more gaffes than most people, or about the same number? Not fewer, I was sure.

The phone rang.

It was Carlotta, breathing hard. "My shop has been burgled," she said. "The coin is gone."

I was thunderstruck. "The decadrachm?"

"Yes," she said. She sounded utterly leaden.

"Any other coins missing?"

"No, nothing else. They went through all of my coin trays, I could tell. The ones in the counters and the valuable ones in the wall safe. But all they took was the decadrachm. The safe was blown beautifully. Professional job."

"But who would have known—?" The list of candidates was short—unless the Sicilian courier had told his torturers about Carlotta before they killed him.

"You know more about that than I do," she said, distress ringing in her voice.

"I'm terribly sorry, Carlotta," I said. "You weren't there when it happened—?"

"No, thank God. I found the small rear window in the shop smashed when I came in a few minutes ago—normally I don't come in this day of the week, I just happened to today—they'd cut through the steel bars over the window like butter—real pros—"

"So it could have happened anytime today—or last night—?"

"Anytime after I locked up at eight last evening."

Alla turca

Wolf had given me the phone number of an office he used on his business trips to Rome. Despite the late hour, he was there. I told him of Carlotta's call, the blown safe, the stolen coin. I didn't have to try keeping the emotion out of my voice. I had already jammed the emotion down deep somewhere.

He said after a moment, "That sounds like the Turks." His voice was harsh and flat, as though he'd been struck hard in the solar plexus.

"What Turks?"

"I don't suppose you'd know about them," he said, not really asking.

"I don't know anything about crime around here," I said, "but it looked to Carlotta as though the thieves knew exactly what they were searching for, and the only way I can figure that happening is for the mafiosi to have gotten the word on Carlotta and the coin before they killed the courier."

"What courier is that?" Wolfgang asked, audibly surprised.

In the rush of the past two days I'd simply forgotten to tell him of Massimo's message from the airport. On an impulse I said, "Look, could we meet somewhere now?"

He named a coffee bar near the Pantheon. That pleasant dinner of ours was obviously out of the question.

"We'll get that coin back" was the first thing he said as we waited for our coffees at the bar. He looked grim, determined. The lines in his face appeared to have sunk more deeply since I had seen him last, reminding me of those photographs of Abraham Lincoln in the last days of his life, after four years of wartime massacres, the death of his favorite son, the vacuum of his marriage. Wolfgang had *suffered*. Tonight his face made that clear in a way I hadn't perceived before. I wondered what agonies other than his Berlin years lay behind his present good health, his apparent self-confidence, his business success.

As we sat down at a table in a corner I began at once to fill in the particulars of my Sicilian caper. On the way to the bar I had decided to go that far with Wolf. I didn't see what could be lost by doing so, and the information might help him get a fix on the decadrachm thieves. I had no way of getting a fix on them myself. I also told him of having met Brutto at the Marchese's, of what Massimo had learned about Brutto's violent history, of our belief that Brutto had had the courier murdered. "Even without knowing of the courier's murder or of Luigi's death," he said, "I took for granted that the mafiosi would join the pursuit of the hoard at some point. Given Luigi's discovery of the hoard in Syracuse, it would have been almost impossible for some mafia family *not* to have heard of it.

"But you should also be aware," he went on, his usual high-speed delivery slowed only a little by the shock of the theft, "that a struggle is shaping up in Italy between competing strong-arm groups, some of them new. There are the old-style mafiosi of Sicily, the Cosa Nostra. In Campagna there are the Camorra, quite powerful in their own way, in Calabria the 'Ndrangheta. Then over in the Aspromonte, near the place where you think the hoard may have been brought ashore, a number of freewheeling bandit gangs—"

"I know about those," I said.

"Yes, well most of the world knows about those, but in recent years a new underworld power has emerged in Italy—the Turks. Turkish smugglers used to channel their activities along routes from Turkey up through Bulgaria into central Europe. All sorts of ancient artifacts, including coins. But now they have expanded their operations."

"So now there's a Turkish mafia too."

"Yes. As well organized as any of their competitors, with strongarm tactics, ruthlessness, almost certainly a number of murders."

"What makes you think they're in on this robbery?"

"The Turks are heavily into coins, as you Americans say, even more so than most of the Italian groups. And the coin we have had taken from under our very noses was not just rare but a real gem. And it was the *only* coin taken. Someone decidedly expert had charge of this operation."

"The Turks are into coins because so many hoards have been found in Turkey—?"

"Of course. Look, to locate that coin we must be systematic. I know of three things I can do. Call my assistant in Munich, have him put out feelers among the Turks there—" Seeing my quizzical look, he explained, "There are several Turkish coin dealers in Munich. I see them all the time, I have lunch with them, I do business with most of them. They are the elite of the several hundred thousand Turks who live and work in the city. There are more than a million and half Turks in Germany as a whole. That's how the German branches of the Turkish mafia got set up. A great many of those immigrants who came as *Gastarbeiter* stayed to go into business. Smuggling just happens to be one of those businesses. I always keep lines out into these groups, the Greeks and Yugoslavs and others as well.

"Second, I'll call Massimo—"

"I'd rather do that," I said quickly, uncertain why.

"All right. I'll contact a Greek trader I work with here. He has an amazing nose for coins about to appear on the market. I've never learned how he does it. He keeps in touch with Sicilians and all the others who run goods in from the South. He's part coin trader, part sleuth."

"What about Gilberto?"

"The Marchese, of course!" He stared at me for a few seconds, as though sizing me up for the job of pumping Gilberto for information. "Better let me talk to him," he said. "He's evasive and cunning. I've known him for years and know which stops to pull. Yes, I'll talk to him. He knows more about smuggled coins than any other Roman."

I couldn't even have said *Buongiorno* to Gilberto nowadays but was relieved not to have to explain to Wolf why not.

We both fell silent, each thinking the unthinkable. I finally said it. "Is the decadrachm lost?"

"Well, *somebody* has found it," he said, a slight smile deepening the furrows around his mouth. It was the only witticism I had ever heard him deliver. "We have to be hopeful. If the coin had been seized by the Italian bureaucrats, even for something as trifling as customs duties, then it would be lost to us forever, like a piece of mail in the Italian post office. But if it has been stolen by the Turks, as I believe, or possibly the Sicilians, then we have a very good chance of finding it. All we have to do is exercise good sleuthing methods."

"Massimo tried that in Rome and didn't get anywhere," I said glumly.

"No, but that was Massimo," Wolf said, his pride embarrassingly evident.

With that we parted. For a moment I watched Wolfgang striding away from the bar, his shoulders squared, his head upright, resolve manifest in every part of his strong body.

I turned away, feeling no hope at all, sick at heart.

Ondeggiante poi tempestoso

After a weary climb up the three flights to my apartment I found that I hadn't the strength to phone Massimo. My body couldn't have handled it, even if my mind could have. The bruises from last night's pummeling were making themselves felt all through my aching limbs, now that I had no Phil or Adriana or Wolfgang or decadrachm theft to distract me. I dropped onto the bed, fully clothed.

Gradually the jangling phone woke me up.

Adriana's voice came from a great distance, asking how I was, how my fancy dinner with Wolf had gone. I wasn't up to telling her over the phone about last night's disaster and asked whether we could meet somewhere. She proposed coming over to my apartment, and although this morning I wanted desperately to get out of there, I said okay.

I fumbled around the apartment, had trouble getting my bearings, my muscles aching even more than yesterday. Slowly I managed to clean up, change clothes, savage a tired banana. I felt horribly out of sorts, only dimly knew why.

Then I knew why. It was that trip of hers out to the Ardeatine Caves. Her uncle's birthday was an event she never failed to commemorate, Adriana had told me, and she had observed it every year since she first learned about his murder by the Nazis. As a child she had gone with her mother or father out to the caves south of Rome where the Germans had shot him along with three hundred other Italians, and when her parents died she followed the ritual on her own.

How could she continue doing that? She hadn't ever *known* the uncle, and while he was supposedly a remarkable man, a talented musician and painter and the Lord only knows what else, her emotional link couldn't have been with *him* so much as with— what?—with the fact of his murder, the horror of it there in the caves, body piling on body as the Germans methodically gunned down the prisoners. Adriana would have been sensitive first of all to the injustice of his death. The uncle had been rounded up arbitrarily along with the others to fill out Hitler's quota of hostages to be shot in reprisal for a bombing in downtown Rome that none of them had anything to do with. But no one *I* had ever known managed to keep alive for so many years a passion for an idea or for a relative she had never even met! No, Adriana was gripped by something else, and I didn't like the feel of it.

As I turned this whole business over in my mind I found myself circling the apartment, pacing from room to room, feeling a numbing anxiety or whatever it was surging within me.

But when the bell rang and Adriana appeared at the door, I rushed to embrace her.

"How are your bruises?" she asked, touching my shoulder.

"They hurt like hell. But nothing got broken. How's Gilberto? In good health?" I couldn't resist the sarcasm.

"He hasn't shown any signs of remorse at having set those hoodlums on you, if that's what you mean. But then I haven't seen him face to face in the last day or two either."

She looked lugubrious.

"Tell me what's on your mind," I said.

"There were soldiers and priests," she said, looking away, "a butcher, Jews, partisans, farmers, boys in their teens, old men—and my uncle, Raimondo, not quite twenty. A gentle soul." Adriana covered her face with her hands, weeping.

"You have to stop this," I said.

"They were taken out to the caves from the city in trucks, in meat vans, their hands tied behind their backs—"

"Stop it."

"A pig-farmer told later how the prisoners were split up into groups of five, taken into the caves. He heard the shots."

I took hold of her shoulders." Stop it, Adriana."

"These caves were ideal from the Germans' point of view. They were three hundred feet long with high ceilings. Good for muffling sound, lots of room for the corpses. They could be dynamited later, to hide the evidence. The earth in the caves was *pozzolana*, volcanic dust, red—red even before the blood ran—."

Another quarry, I thought, another massacre. Was it *her* obsession that distressed me, or mine? I was shaking her hard now.

"You're hurting me," she said, pushing my arms away. "What's wrong with you?"

"This absorption with the dead," I said, my dread returning. "You have to break out of it."

She looked at me as from a great distance. "That advice might better come," she finally said in a controlled tone, "from someone who isn't himself trapped in the past."

That hurt. "I'm beginning to see what my life has been like," I said. "I don't think you've done that."

"God, and I thought Wolfgang had a monopoly on self-righteousness!" She stalked off a few paces, came back. "Don't you realize how absolutely *possessed* you are by the thought of that quarry? By those Athenians in the quarry? By those—those frigging coins? Don't you realize what that means?"

I was taken aback. "No," I said, "do tell me."

"That—that goddess on your coins, *she's* the one you're in love with. And the horses too, for that matter. Those are the only things I've ever seen you expend real emotion on—"

"How can you say that—?"

"And those conferences with Massimo, and with Wolfgang, who has you simply mesmerized. You're even thrilled to be noticed by a gangster like Brutto."

"And thrilled to be followed by two thugs, I suppose!"

"Yes, I think you are, at some level. You're having *adventures* in your life, for the first time, real adventures. I'm just one of them, isn't that so?"

"Oh come on, Adriana—"

"Face it, Michael. You say *I'm* preoccupied with death. But you absolutely rely on people and things around you to bring you into the present, to bring you to life."

"If you're so plugged into the present," I said, furious now, "why don't you leave Gilberto? There's the dead hand of the past if I ever saw one."

"Do you think that a life with you would necessarily mean life for *me*? I'm coming to doubt it. The prospect of going off with you fills me with dreadful uncertainties—"

"America, Ohio, my tiny living room—?"

She looked puzzled. "No, it's *you*."

"You're reluctant to leave all the security Gilberto gives you—"

"Yes, frankly. He's monstrous, but—"

"And then you grew up in near-poverty—"

"Don't be patronizing," she snapped, and started to walk away.

I caught up with her, took her arm. She shook me off. "I'm sorry," I said, suddenly appalled at our anger with one another. "I'm having a rough time now. Things you don't even know about. I know you're having rough days too." She looked at me strangely.

Then suddenly we had our arms around one another, were murmuring endearments, furiously.

Languido e vivace

It was a violent love-making. Later, exhausted, we heard the doorbell ring. "At least they waited," Adriana said as I slid out of bed to press the buzzer in the hall.

"It's Fiorella," the voice piped up from the street, "your landlady."

"Yes, yes, come up," I said, buzzing her in and racing back to the bedroom for clothes. What a lousy time for her visit.

"I'll join you in a few minutes," Adriana said, snuggling down beneath the covers.

I got my shoelaces tied just in time to greet Fiorella at the door. The word "landlady" had evoked memories of mean old skinflints in the States, so that I was agreeably surprised at the pleasant-looking, well dressed woman in her late forties who stood before me.

"I hope I'm not disturbing you," she said as we went into the living room, her living room.

"No, no, not at all," I lied, still not quite focused on the immediate moment. "Some coffee?"

"I can stay only a minute," she said, sitting down and glancing around, possibly to ascertain the condition of her furniture. She looked vaguely familiar, but not nearly as much like Massimo as I had expected. Had I seen her somewhere in Rome? "I'm sorry not to have come over to meet you before," she said, "but real estate in Rome is booming right now, and when that happens I seldom have an hour to myself." I liked this woman right away, as I remembered liking Massimo the first time I met him.

"Commercial real estate? Private homes?" I had now exhausted my knowledge of the business.

"Both," she said, "and other things too. But we specialize in condominiums these days, my partner and I. That Aventine condo that your German friend Wolfgang owns, we sold that to him."

"How did you—?"

"Oh, Massimo tells me a little about you now and then. He's done that for years." She smiled rather archly, looking me over.

"When did you last speak with him?"

"Do I know about the robbery, you're wondering?"

"How did you—?" I began, quickly stopped.

"That happened four days ago, as you know. He phoned me once he got to London and apologized for not having done so before he left Rome. He's most considerate."

So she had the *London* robbery in mind. "Yes, I've always thought so," I said. "He's a remarkable individual. Vitality pours out of him." Post-coitally, I certainly felt all my own vitality drained out of me.

"Indeed," she said, still looking intently at me. "Much as I love him, I've often found him a little exhausting. Now that German friend of yours—"

"Not so much a friend," I said, "as a—" I paused, not sure quite what Wolfgang was to me.

"Well, acquaintance, companion, business associate, co-conspirator, whatever," Fiorella said, pressing on. "The few times I've met him I found him *truly* exhausting."

"You said Massimo told you something about me now and then—?"

"Oh yes, he's a great admirer of yours. Not just because you're a real *dottore*, rather than one of our Italian fakes, although he *is* inclined to value a university degree, never having had one himself."

"Over-value it, you mean."

"I never had one myself," she said brightly, as though identifying a virtue, "but I did attend classes at the University of Rome for a year or two, so that I have a more realistic notion of what goes on there."

"There's nothing magical about it," I said.

"No, nothing magical," she said, pausing. "But a certain aura of power comes with the degree, here in Italy anyway. And to be a *real* professor—well!" I couldn't tell whether she was speaking for Massimo or herself. "Did you know Wolfgang calls himself 'Doctor'?"

"I didn't," I said, surprised.

"Oh yes, although I don't know whether he does it back in Germany too, where everyone is much more fastidious about titles."

"I noticed that he had what looks like a dueling scar," I said, abandoning some of my usual reserve in her engaging presence.

"Yes, it does look like that, doesn't it," she said, pausing for a moment.

"But of course the dueling societies—"

"Have died out?" she said. "Indeed they have *not*. They're very strong at some German universities."

"But the question is—whether Wolfgang—"

"Yes," she said, "that is the question, isn't it. And as for other reasons why Massimo has told me all about you—well, told me *some* things, I should say—of course you know about your father's having rescued our mother during the war—"

"Yes. Actually I've learned more about that incident from Massimo than I ever heard from my father."

"A modest man, your father?"

There was an appealing directness about Fiorella that made me want to be as truthful with her as possible. Adriana had this quality too, but springing from a rich diapason of sounds, most of which at any given moment one only sensed rather than heard.

Fiorella's directness seemed to arrive by a simpler route. "No, I wouldn't say he was especially modest. Maybe he was modest about that particular act of heroism, or didn't feel it was actually heroism so much as something else, like an outburst of rage, attacking that German soldier furiously the way he did."

Adriana came into the room, fully dressed and looking a trifle languid.

"Adriana," I said, getting to my feet, "this is my landlady, Fiorella. Massimo's sister."

They exchanged greetings, swiftly took each other's measure. "We've been talking," Fiorella said as we all sat down, "about Michael's father's reluctance to tell anyone about his having saved my mother's life."

"Michael has told me of Massimo's having first looked him up in the States because of that rescue," Adriana said, "but I've never heard the details."

"Well, ask Michael to give you the details one day," Fiorella said briskly. She had tactfully finessed even looking the question of why Adriana had shown up so tardily from the direction of the bedroom. "As for Massimo's robbery, he asks me to tell you that it wasn't catastrophic — not serious enough to throw him into bankruptcy — but serious enough. He'll need a few more days in London, then he hopes to rejoin you here in your enterprise, whatever that is."

She leaned hard into the last three words, but I pretended not to have heard. "Good news," I said. "I'll be delighted to have him back."

"Well then," she said, rising, "I have to go. I've an appointment with a Norwegian musician who thinks some Norse god has told him he's fated to live in the Trastevere, and that his musical gifts will shrivel up unless I find him an apartment there."

"I'm a musician," Adriana said with a slight edge to her voice, "and I understand how important one's surroundings are."

"Yes," Fiorella said, taking Adriana in once again, "but you look normal. You should meet this Norwegian." To me, "It was a pleasure to meet you, Michael. Perhaps when Massimo returns, we can all see one another again." She included Adriana in her glance.

After a friendly *Ciao* to Fiorella at the door, I returned to Adriana. "You sounded annoyed," I said.

"I know," she said, toying with a marble ashtray on an end-table. "I'm sorry about that. It's just the detritus of the day." She added, "Of the earlier part of the day."

I gathered her in my arms.

"Oh Michael, Rome feels like such a prison to me. I used to love it, but I've come to think it's really bad for me."

Alas, she didn't enlarge that *me* to *us*, though I held her long enough to give her the opportunity to do so.

La tristezza, il terrore, l'eccitazione

Adriana had to return home for some apppointment or other. I phoned Massimo's London office, bracing myself for his reaction to word of the stolen decadrachm, feeling once again my own shock at hearing the news from Carlotta. But his answering machine said he was out of the office. I hung up, considered phoning him at home, for some reason decided not to, called his office back and left a request with the machine for Massimo to return my call.

Wolfgang was to call me as soon as he talked with Gilberto, probably late this afternoon or early evening, but as I didn't know exactly when they would meet, I felt that I had to hang around the apartment until his call came. He was to have gotten a message to me somehow if he'd *not* been able to arrange a meeting with the Marchese today. And then too Massimo might call.

I wandered into the kitchen, feeling strangely agitated, opened the little refrigerator. A carton of milk stood alone. I smelled it, poured the rancid contents down the drain. I wondered whether the market would still be open after Wolf called. The fruit bowl on the kitchen table held one discouraged looking tangerine. I threw it into the garbage pail, which needed emptying. To empty it I would have had to carry it in a plastic bag down to the street and around the corner to a dumpster, but I might miss Wolf's call, or Massimo's. I emptied the pail into a plastic bag, looked around for a wire twisty, found a large one, twisted the throat of the bag hard enough to keep it from drawing another breath ever.

I got out the cleanser, started to scrub the kitchen sink. I scrubbed the drain board, the counter tops, the formica table top, the refrigerator, the marble window sill. I was starting in on the walls when I halted, asked myself *what* I was doing. I wandered into the second bedroom, the one Phil had used, the cleanser and cleaning cloth still in my hands. An ache for Phil struck me hard, a feeling of love, of loss. How were things going for him this very moment? He would have arrived back in California this morning, would have returned to his school by the afternoon, would already have looked up a friend or two. Was he even remembering Rome, remembering me? Probably not, at the moment. Probably relieved *not* to be thinking of me at all, after his caretaker role of the last year. I wouldn't blame him for that, would expect it of him or any son. Maybe he'd think of me on the weekend, in an idle hour. Fondly, I hoped. Mixed, more likely.

I visited the main bedroom, what used to be called the master bedroom, equipped with what Europeans used to call the marriage bed. Another social premise vacating the premises. Better this way, for some anyway. Try out the bed *before* the marriage, see how it went. If it went well, call for the minister or priest or rabbi. If not, go out for dinner and express regrets. Or skip the dinner. I couldn't put myself in that frame of mind, that pragmatic, disenchanted twentieth-century frame of mind. But I realized that Adriana and I had all unintentionally joined the pragmatists. An error? In any case I didn't see how we could have done otherwise, or would have.

Staring at the bed, I closed my eyes, remembered our morning passion. Vividly, wonderfully. Then an image of our anger slashed across my brain and I opened my eyes, wondering how she and I could be both so loving and so furious with one another, all in the space of a few minutes. Well, I knew that sometimes happened. I hadn't lived thirty-nine years without learning something. Even Susan and I—well, she and I never got out to the extremes, maybe that was the difference. Adriana and I pushed ourselves out to the limits. Did I really like that? Did I really want to live with someone with whom that would continue to happen? Still feeling the misery of our clash, I doubted that I wanted to go through that misery again and again through the years ahead.

My mind slid off to Adriana's rage at the Germans. A safer topic. So now I knew what lay behind that rage. The Germans' brutality with her uncle so strikingly like the Brazilian military's brutality with her father, one reinforcing the other, one always summoning up the other in her mind. And she, with her propensity to suffer, how over the years she must have been battered from one anguished memory to another, relentlessly.

I put down the cleaning materials, lay down on the bed. A disconcerting thought: had her hostility toward the Germans rubbed off on *me*? Did her reluctance to leave Gilberto spring in any way from her awareness that I was after all much more a northern than a southern European, for all my bookish interest in the ancient Mediterranean? Could that have turned her in any fashion away from me, on some subconscious level or another, in some subtle or not so subtle form? *Michael Gardner, Teuton.* It was a chilling thought.

Another chill: suppose I never saw more of the hoard than I'd already seen? Suppose Luigi's Sicilians had simply divvied it up along the way between Reggio and Rome, knowing or not knowing how precious each work of coin art was, knowing or not knowing the money value of each coin. For two thousand years all sorts of vandals the length of the peninsula had stripped the temples of their gleaming marble, had robbed the churches of their precious statuary and paintings. Against that background of pillage, what would a few more looted coins matter?

Or suppose Luigi's couriers *did* manage to get the coins into the hands of a trader like Wolf or Massimo. If the trader sold them for fantastic profits to big investors, no one might ever see them again, no one in my lifetime anwyway, not even the bank clerk who opened the safe-deposit boxes to swallow them. But then Wolf was almost certain to learn about such sales, might even handle them himself, and I trusted him to let me see the coins, at the very least, before sending them off to auction. I had no illusions about his making any special effort to get any of the coins into museum collections, so that the public at large could marvel at these art objects for centuries to come. Wolfgang was no philanthropist. But I sensed a sentimental side to him, whether or not it was the kind of sentimental streak for which Germans had long been famous. Might he not, as a friendly gesture to me, if I asked him, try to see that a major museum somehow got the inside track on bidding for at least some of the coins? Perhaps there was no way to do that, I didn't really know. And even if there was, I didn't really know whether Wolf would be inclined to make the effort.

And who had the stolen decadrachm in his hands at this very moment? The one stolen from Carlotta. It might well have been stolen, and stolen more than once, in the fifth century after it left the hands of the craftsman at the mint who stamped it out of the flat piece of silver.

And that Chol, that brilliant engraver—who was he?

I stood on a sheltered grassy knoll next to the limestone cliff soaring straight up to the sky—the pouch pressed tightly against my ribs—a short distance away, a small menacing group of men—naked, emaciated, looking at me, advancing toward me—I backed up against the rock—they came right up to me, began to crowd me—I tried to run, couldn't lift my feet, looked down, saw concrete pouring slowly heavily down my legs, encasing my feet—looked up to see the pockmarked smiling face of Brutto—

I sat upright, sweating and terrified, only gradually returning to the sunlit world, gradually shoving the nightmare off to the edge of consciousness. But it hovered and swooped there like a giant bat, making me feel its sinister presence.

When the phone rang I realized that I had been pacing the length and breadth of the apartment the way a prisoner paces his cell, first measuring its area roughly and then, as the hours pass with infinite slowness, refining the measurements down to the inch. I was just beginning to commit the measurements to memory when the first ring sounded.

It was Wolfgang. "I have wonderful news," he said almost breathlessly. I had never known him to be short of breath before. "A pair of tetradrachms has shown up in Munich!"

"Ours?"

"Fifth-century, Siracusan, silver—everything perfect. And they're identical twins!"

I felt my blood racing. "Where are they?"

"In my office there. They're in my possession—ours. I'll give you details when we meet."

"Did you learn of this from Gilberto?"

"No, no, of course not. I did see him and will tell you about that later. The exciting news is the pair of tetradrachms. My old Munich assistant, Gustav, phoned me at my office here just a few minutes ago."

"You'll go to Munich?"

"This very evening. I hope that you'll follow on the first plane you can catch."

"I have one or two things to wind up here," I said. "The earliest I could make it would be tomorrow afternoon." I didn't even consider not going.

"You wouldn't even have to book tickets till the morning. There's a choice of flights, and they're rarely full." He sounded *happy*.

As I hung up I realized that I had made the decision to go to Munich without even a thought of Adriana. I felt appalled. How could I have done that?

I dialed her number. A maid answered, then Adriana.

"How would you like a short trip to Munich?"

Silence. I felt my heart sink. "Did you hear me?"

"I've just—come by a small inheritance," she said, her tone impersonal, then suddenly playful. "I was wondering how we might make use of it."

"We?" I said.

"We," she said.

My heart leapt up.

In my joy I nearly forgot about Massimo. I phoned his office again, heard his vibrant voice on the answering machine, decided just to leave a message. "Dreadful news," I said, "Carlotta's deka lifted. Culprit's identity unknown. Sorry I couldn't talk to you in person." As an afterthought, "Oh, I'm off to Munich tomorrow." But so rattled was I that I forgot to tell him about the two new tetradrachms.

MUNICH

"Munich almost killed me—but in five weeks it gave me more of human experience than most people get in five years...."

Thomas Wolfe, in a letter to Aline Bernstein, written in Salzburg, October 4, 1928

"I have never really felt spiritually at home in Munich, to which my brothers and sisters and I were transplanted [from the north] when I was barely out of boyhood."

Thomas Mann, in a letter to Felix Bertaux, March 1, 1923

"...a malignant and a turban'd Turk..."

Shakespeare, *Othello*, V, ii, 354

"The Turk is tenacious to a fault."

Eric Lawlor, *Looking for Osman* (1993)

"...the old Cretan saying: 'Stand still, Turk, while I reload.'"

Callum MacDonald, *The Lost Battle: Crete 1941* (1993)

"A milestone in the history of fencing was the discovery of the lunge in the second half of the 16th century."

From article on "Fencing" in the *Encyclopaedia Britannica*

MUNICH

To recover quickly is a necessity if the sabreur wishes to minimize the degree of his vulnerability.

So abruptly had we decided to leave Rome that the sharp differences around us in the hours since then felt merely like increments of that first abruptness. Adriana felt it too, I thought as I looked happily at her seated there beside me. She had appeared as startled as I at the blondness of the Lufthansa crew when we boarded the plane, at their crisp courtesy, at the orderliness of the passengers, all of whom behaved with a calmness and efficiency seldom seen in an Italian airport, as though they were all perfectly aware that they were leaving the land of anarchy and now had to behave.

Except for a handful of Mediterranean-looking passengers aboard, we had left behind the world of olive complexions, dark hair and Roman noses, and even further behind were all those abrasive street noises, unexpected odors and pushing and shoving in crowded buses. Outside the plane it was ninety degrees Fahrenheit; inside it was sixty-five. The difference was vastly more than thermal.

Two steps inside the plane, I had handed my boarding pass to the stewardess, who glanced at my face and promptly said, "*Guten Abend.*" Addressed as a German? Somewhere in my brain I heard a faint click, as of some tiny object falling into place. But what object?

We were seated in first class, a luxury I had never experienced before. The question I had to raise was hardly the most felicitous with which to launch our first trip together: "Can you really afford this?"

Adriana's smile was distinctly mischievous. "I sold some of his coins," she said.

"Gilberto's?" I said, astonished.

"A little collection of his with portraits of the Emperor Caligula." She busied herself with her seat belt.

I was amazed—and hugely amused. "That Caligula is a nice touch," I finally said.

"I thought you would like it," she said. "I had no idea it would bring so much money."

"So that we could live like royalty in Munich?"

"More like that than you might think," she said, not a little pleased with herself. So I had taken up with a thief, a grand larcenist no less. I liked the idea.

"Okay, I'll ask. What made you do it?"

She considered. "I've thought about the theft a great deal since committing it. I'd never done anything like that before. But when I heard Gilberto and that filthy mafioso talking—"

"When was that?"

"The day you and I had that argument," she said.

And afterward, a wonderful reconciliation, I thought.

"And met Massimo's sister," she said. "I had just come back from the hairdresser's and was on my way upstairs when I heard their voices in the corridor leading to the tower. They hadn't expected me to return so soon and had no idea I was there. I could tell they were angry with each other. Gilberto was being unusually supercilious, and Brutto had an edge like steel to his voice."

"Could you tell what they were talking about?"

She looked concerned. "Those coins of yours. No doubt about it. They weren't arguing over *whether* to track down the coins but about which of them was really in charge, or who ought to defer to whom, something like that."

Suddenly she was indignant. "Can you *imagine* the conversation? Here is a Roman Marchese, for all his decadence still an aristocrat, with centuries of pedigree behind him, stooping to a crass business arrangement with—with a common criminal, a murderer! It had been dreadful enough having that thug in the house that evening—at the dinner party, when I met you—and worse, learning of your encounter with his hoodlums at Luigi's, but here he was again, clearly locked into a scheme with Gilberto—"

She rushed on. "But that wasn't the worst of it. They spoke of the hoard as though it were simply—well, simply a great pile of silver, in motion somewhere on the Italian landscape, the property of whoever could get his hands on it. I thought of the other things that hoard is—great art, history, all the things you've spoken of. And here they were, reducing it all to—" She choked on the outrage.

"But there was more," I said.

"Yes. Listening to them, I was just beginning to glimpse the danger for you when they spelled it out. Brutto said it had been a mistake to let Massimo escape from Rome, and he wanted to pick you up and 'squeeze you like toothpaste.' Those were his exact words. Gilberto said that might give Brutto pleasure but it wasn't at all certain that you knew where all of the treasure was. It was better to keep tailing you until you'd led them to the rest of it. That was the point—"

"He *did* say 'the *rest* of it'?"

"Yes. That was the moment when they started getting angry. Brutto said interrogation was something he knew how to do better than anyone else, and Gilberto said the time hadn't yet come for that. Then they moved out of earshot."

A stewardess had been moving down the aisle, now stopped at our row. She spoke to me. "*Entschuldigen-Sie bitte. Hätten Sie gern einen Rotwein oder einen Weisswein, oder vielleicht ein Glas Sekt?*"

"*Beginnen wir mit einem schönen glas Sekt, bitte,*" Adriana responded.

Surprise after surprise tumbled out of this woman. As the stewardess moved on I said, "I thought you hated everything German."

"I learned German in Munich one year," she said.

"What year was that?"

"Exactly six years after you fenced there. I was nineteen, as you had been. I'll tell you about it sometime."

The plane was being towed backward. Absentmindedly I fastened my selt belt, trying to gauge the dangers posed by the two villains. I couldn't even begin to get my mind around it. All I could manage was to say to Adriana that I had been wondering what made her change her mind about staying with Gilberto.

"I'd long been considering it," she said, "as you must have known. It wasn't an easy decision for me—until that frightful conversation. In a way I was lucky. Decisions rarely get made on such a clear-cut basis, wouldn't you agree?" She took my hand in hers. The plane rushed down the runway, took off, the wheels collapsing quietly into the fuselage.

Perversely, the thought that struck me had nothing to do with the threat to me or Adriana—or to Massimo, when he returned to Rome. If he returned. "Wait till Gilberto finds out about the Caligulas," I said.

The plane headed due north, toward the Alps, toward the land of my Olympic exhilaration, the land of great historians and archaeologists, and of the extermination camps. My emotions were churning in a great maelstrom. I realized that even with my brief visit to Munich as a nineteen-year-old, I now felt that I had never *really* visited Germany before. I had changed enormously in twenty years. And now I would be visiting it with Adriana. And no doubt seeing it through Wolf's eyes.

And with ruthless men at my back.

We were faced with champagne, appetizers, linen, glossy printed menus. We couldn't even think of doing them justice.

The stewardess took our orders. I reclined my seat and found a foot-stool rising to meet my shoes. "I can see why you prefer first-class," I said, trying not to let the irony ring.

She looked off in the distance. "Yes," she said, "I'm afraid I do." An image of her concert-grand piano in my tiny Ohio living room flickered across my brain.

"How long after you overheard those two did you steal the coins?"

"Not long. After that horrible moment I wanted to *hurt* him. I couldn't get at Brutto, but I knew I could somehow get at Gilberto. Doing so wouldn't protect *you* in any way, but I wasn't being rational. Some days before that infamous conversation in the corridor I had already started putting money aside for—well, for us, just in case. My allowance is—was—pretty generous, and I was thinking of pretexts for asking Gilberto to advance me larger sums.

After that conversation, on my way upstairs, I knew absolutely that I would be leaving Gilberto that very day. And in the next instant I realized that I could finance our escape—yes, that's how I thought of it—*and* wound him in one of his most sensitive spots by stealing some of his precious coins!"

"But how did you sell them?"

"By the most amazing coincidence Wolfgang showed up at the house a few minutes after the pair went off somewhere together. He had come over to the villino to see Gilberto—"

"Yes, I knew about that."

"And I was already puzzling about which coins to steal. I hadn't the faintest idea which ones were the most valuable. And then there was Wolf down in the front hall! A religious person might call it Providential. On an impulse I told him what I had in mind—without explaining *why*. Wolf is too much a gentleman to ask. And too experienced a businessman, I suppose. I mentioned a general sum of money I hoped to get—"

"And *he* suggested the Caligulas—?"

"Yes. He even went upstairs to Gilberto's study to pick them out. It took him only a few minutes to decide on the Caligulas, locate the trays, pack up the coins, replace the trays and bring a neat little box downstairs."

"Wolf must have guessed that you were leaving Gilberto—"

"Probably, although I didn't tell him."

"—and may possibly have thought of me as someone you were leaving him for. I don't think I've ever even mentioned your name to him, but he's nothing if not astute in all sorts of ways. You see, I've been wondering just why Wolfgang invited me to Munich." I tried to fit it in. "It was later that same day he learned that two of the hoard coins had just appeared in his Munich office. It may have occurred to him that to invite me to Munich to see the coins might very well mean having you there too—and to have you there would be to have a channel open to Gilberto—"

"But that wouldn't do him any good, don't you see. I had *left* Gilberto."

"No, you're right." I shook my head. "So I'm still not sure why he—"

The food came more quickly than it ever does in Economy class, and was attractively laid out on porcelain plates to boot. More linen napkins, silver plate.

"Is it so surprising after all," she said. "You and Wolf are partners, collaborators or something of the sort, aren't you? And you and Massimo brought *him* into the great pursuit, did you not, not the other way around."

"That's all true, but these two new coins showed up in *his* office, in Munich. He wouldn't have had to tell me about them at all."

"He must have been tempted not to."

"Indeed. He's not trying to locate the hoard in order to raise money for AIDS victims or any other lofty cause. And while he's seemed friendly enough in recent days, he hardly told me about the two tetradrachms out of mere friendship."

"Does he still need you?"

I considered. "There are still a few things about the hoard that I haven't told him, and I suspect that he suspects that. And then there's Massimo. Wolf knows that Massimo and I are good friends, so that if he threw me overboard, he might alienate Massimo—"

"Would that matter?"

"I'm not sure. Massimo is well known in the coin trade, and if Wolf did something outrageous, Massimo could certainly spread word of that around."

"But does Wolf really *need* Massimo in any way?"

"I don't know. Most of the hoard is still missing, and it's entirely possible that Wolf may want to keep his lines open to Massimo's Sicilian contacts, even though they haven't turned up much thus far."

We held hands tightly.

Soon the Alps passed below us, signaling boundaries. My excitement, my nervousness, my sense of foreboding grew.

Sabre fencers are seldom in a state of engagement. They fence, more usually, with absence of blade. The chance of using a pressure, which can only be applied if the blades are in contact, is limited.

I had been on the ground only fifteen minutes and to my surprise had already decided that I liked Germany. Or I liked it with Adriana beside me. But then with Adriana beside me I might have liked Calcutta or even Newark, New Jersey. There was nothing in the new high-tech Munich International Airport per se that thrilled me, although I did like its clean smell and colorful shops. It would doubtless be the newest airport I would ever be in, just having opened a few months before. Aboard the plane the Lufthansa pilot had expressed great pride in it over the loudspeaker, the stewardess had expressed great pride in it up and down the aisle, and now the attendant helping us select tickets for the S-Bahn into the city expressed great pride in it.

En route to the S-Bahn we passed two large, enclosed, glistening glass-and-aluminum kiosks in promiment locations in the terminal. They were promotional agencies, one for Istanbul Airlines, the other for Turkish Airlines.

The train tracks were new, the gravel and sleepers were new, the car in which we seated ourselves was shiny, clean and new. I didn't know whether Adriana was any more passionately devoted to cleanliness or comfort than I was, which was only some, but she appeared pleased with the accommodations. The train sped swiftly and quietly on its appointed way.

And then at the first stop a short, wiry, black-haired, olive-complexioned, unkempt elderly man got on and sat down directly opposite us. "A Turk," I thought, although he could have been any number of Mediterranean nationalities. Wolf's observations on Turks must have registered. This man's hands were gnarled and calloused. Garlic was the first odor that pulsed toward us from him, then sweat and unidentifiable other disagreeable odors. Adriana shielded her nose with one hand.

I looked around the train carriage, saw among the generally

light-skinned passengers three or four other dark-complexioned souls, all dressed in middle-class garb. But I had a feeling that our disreputable-looking neighbor would be the one everyone else in the carriage would be aware of.

It must have shocked a great many Bavarians some years after the war to find thousands of dark-skinned, sweating, smelly immigrant laborers like him in their midst, even though the Germans had invited them in to help rebuild Germany, had in fact been eager to have them, had sent agents to Turkey and Greece and Yugoslavia and Italy to recruit them in huge numbers. But then I hadn't really any idea what the Bavarians thought. I wasn't sure I had ever met any Bavarians.

Outside the train a small woods rushed past, industrial parks, residential areas, wheat and vegetable farms, scattered skyscraper apartment buildings. The big yellow and black sunflowers scattered here and there struck a curiously ordinary note. Were sunflowers waving along the tracks when the first prisoners taken to Dachau passed not far from here?

Swiftly the city surrounded us. At Karlsplatz we took our suitcases off the rack and left the train. Adriana carried mine, which was old and light. I carried hers, which was neither. "Looks familiar," I said as I looked around the well-lit, roomy station. "They built it for *your* Olympics," Adriana said. "Yes, I remember," I said.

We boarded the U4 for Arabellapark. "The name of our hotel," Adriana reminded me. "The Arabella. Named for the Richard Strauss opera. Strauss was born in Munich and spent most of his life here."

"That strikes me as a curious fact for you to know."

"This is where I learned German, in Munich. I've meant to tell you. When I finished secondary school in Rome I was offered a scholarship to study music here at the *Staatliche Hochschule für Musik*. It was a priceless opportunity and I just couldn't turn it down."

"Despite your family feelings about the Germans."

"Yes. The music school here was simply the best in Europe. And once I got to Munich, I met mostly young Germans and realized that *they* weren't responsible for the Nazis. So I guess I carry around both sets of feelings toward Germans."

The end of the line was Arabellapark. As we left the train and headed for the escalator I noted that no music at all was playing over a loudpseaker, neither Strauss's nor anyone else's. Only a few passengers' footsteps broke the welcome quiet of the station. We passed a newsstand, where I noticed the Turkish crescent and star on a newspaper. While I stopped to look it over, Adriana spoke to the newsdealer. "He says the paper you're looking at, the *Hurriyet*," she told me, "is the most popular of the seven Turkish papers he carries." I bought a copy and we walked on toward the escalator, which started up noiselessly as we approached.

Aboveground I told Adriana I was perfectly willing to walk the few blocks to the hotel, but she insisted on a taxi. "Everything first class," she said firmly. "For a while anyway." We found a taxi stand, Adriana spoke to the driver, we rode for exactly four minutes, pulled up to the modern very highrise Arabella. Its light-blue and white slab rose sharply into the clear blue sky.

As we paused at the reception desk, where no fewer than four attractive young female desk clerks dealt with guests in as many languages, the principal countries represented in the lobby appeared to be Arab. Galabeyas everywhere, mostly white, with colorful decoration here and there. Orientals, doubtless Japanese, ranked second, all dressed in Western business suits.

A porter hoisted our two bags, seeming not to notice the impoverished condition of mine, and directed us to the elevator. We rose silently to the top floor, followed the porter to our room. He opened our door with enough flourish to make me wonder why, and then I saw. It was a spacious suite, the bedroom invisible off to one side, the livingroom beautifully furnished. From the door I could see on a table a large basket of polished fruit with a bottle of champagne nestled in a bucket of ice nearby, bold pink napkins arranged neatly around the basket and bucket. "I told them it was our honeymoon," Adriana said, leading me into the room by the hand.

We dismissed the porter, went over to look out the broad

windows. The Munich skyline was nothing unusual, punctuated chiefly by the twin domes of a large church. "The *Frauenkirche*," Adriana said. "A useful landmark, if you're ever lost in Munich."

"I plan to be lost all the time in Munich," I said, pulling her with me ever so gently toward the invisible bedroom.

"But the champagne will get warm" was what Adriana said when I told her that Wolf would be waiting for us in his downtown office. She was sitting up in bed, eating a pear, when I emerged from the bathroom, buttoning my shirt. Reluctantly she climbed out of bed, went off to wash up.

"I can't imagine that you won't enjoy seeing the tetradrachms," I said, unpacking my suitcase and wondering whether she would find them as thrilling as I would. "Beautiful silver little works of art."

"We'll just see, won't we," she said, coming naked out of the bathroom and heading for her suitcase. There was something offputting in her tone that kept me from seizing her in the way I was tempted to do. Instead, I phoned Wolf's office, found him there, told him we were on our way. He sounded cordial in the extreme, said he looked forward to welcoming both of us to his city.

Something must be done to distract the opponent's attention while distance is being gained.

A large yellow sign posted on a glass panel facing our seat in the train said *Rauchverbot* in bold black letters. I was spared the need to ask Adriana what it was that we were forbidden to do by the drawing on the sign of a hirsute young lout standing in a subway station exhaling a huge cloud of black smoke in the face of a woman standing nearby. "I wasn't planning to *rauch* anyway," I said to Adriana, wondering whether a great many other things were forbidden in Germany, as I'd always heard.

We got out at Odeonsplatz, walked along the platform toward

another prescient escalator, passing a family that looked Middleeastern to me, the middleaged mother dressed in a longskirted somber suit with a full black scarf wrapped around her head and neck, the father with a dark somber face and sport clothes, three teenage daughters in three disparate modes of colorful dress, one of them in cutoff jeans with a gigantic gray-and-white cartoon rabbit with a red nose printed on a long black sport shirt. However they might have dressed in the Middle East, if that's where they had come from, they hadn't tried for unity of costume in Germany.

Rising to street level at the Odeonsplatz, we walked off the escalator to find a magnificent triple-arched stone loggia directly ahead of us. "Do you recognize it?" Adriana asked as we walked a few steps toward the structure, then stopped.

"Looks like the Loggia della Signoria in Florence," I said, admiring the graceful arches, the early-Renaissance restraint. A few tourists were busily snapping pictures of the massive stone lions guarding the broad front steps.

"Bavaria lies so close to Italy," she said, "it has long imitated our best things. But what this loggia—it's called the Felderrnhalle—means to most Germans is something quite different. It's the place where Hitler marched for the first time, where he got his first martyrs—"

"Did you know that when you were here as a student?"

"No, I didn't know a *thing* about the Nazis in Munich. I didn't know that Hitler once had an apartment here or that his stormtroopers marched here. I didn't know that the *Hochschule* where I studied music had once been the very office building where Hitler held the infamous meeting with Chamberlain. I was as innocent of German history in those days as you are of Latin American politics now." I had noticed this post-coital tartness in her before.

We strolled past the loggia along a street of shops with elegant clothes and leather goods in the windows. The temperature was delightfully cooler than in Rome, the streets were pleasant, the shoppers were amiable looking, we were in love, and so despite the lure of the silver coins waiting for us in Wolf's office, despite themenace sooner or later thundering our way from Rome, I was in no greater hurry to arrive than Adriana appeared to be. The prosperity of Munich washed over us. I could feel its soothing caress.

We passed a bank with large bright-blue posters of the obverse and reverse of a coin displayed prominently in its windows. *Münzen & Medaillen* read the caption on each poster. "*Münzen* are coins?" I asked Adriana. She nodded. I simply had to buy a pocket German dictionary.

We turned right onto Maffeistrasse, skirted a little park. Art galleries, hotels, banks. Large white letters on a shop we passed proclaimed "*Briefmarken.*" In the shop windows numerous postmarked envelopes were displayed in an orderly fashion. "They do make a big thing of collecting here, don't they," I said.

"Germans collect *everything*," Adriana said.

We turned right along a long, narrow, tree-lined park, Maximiliansplatz. "His office should be right along here somewhere," I said, checking the business card Wolf had given me. We spotted his discreet brass plate on a green marble doorframe: M. *Wolfgang Friedrich, Numismatik.*

We climbed the stairs to the second floor. Wolf's appeared to be the only office there. As we approached the door, two floodlights blinked on and I saw a camera angled down at us. We buzzed, waited. The door opened, we entered, were greeted by an agreeable-looking woman in her forties. "For the lights and camera I apologize," she said, ushering us into a waiting room. "We just can't too careful be."

The waiting room was surprisingly plain. Given Wolf's rumored wealth, I had expected it to be rather ornate, on the model of an American corporate waiting room, with expensive inlaid wooden tables, enormous ficus trees, extravagant tapestries and prints on the walls. This one was utterly unadorned, save for a sizeable black-and-white photograph of a yacht under sail.

She was Herta, she told us, Herr Friedrich's secretary and receptionist. Herr Friedrich was with a client now, he would be with us shortly, would we like some coffee? A little strudel, *viel-*

leicht? I accepted the coffee, Adriana the strudel. Herta's daughter kept making strudel for her, she told us, though she knew it made Herta too round—here she patted her tummy discreetly—and she just couldn't resist the temptation. Would we be staying in Munich long? We said we didn't know.

"Myself I will not be probably here very long," she said, not exactly inviting our response but not exactly talking past us either. "I have worked for Herr Friedrich—a wonderful man, but you I'm sure know that—for many years, but my age I am beginning to feel." She hesitated. "No, that is not quite the truth, I am beginning to feel how so many of these coins are soaked, how drenched they are—in blood."

Startled, I glanced at Adriana, looking startled too.

"That is a strong word, I know," Herta went on, "but it is also the best one. One thing I have in my hours here learned is that no great fortune ever grew without suffering."

"Without the suffering of others," I said, warming to this strangely effusive woman.

"Oh yes," she said. "The man making the fortune rarely suffers."

Behind Herta a gaunt, elderly white-haired man dressed in a business suit sat bent over a small desk. The desk was stacked with coins of various sizes, and he was examining one of them with a loupe. He also seemed aware of Adriana and me, and he smiled and nodded his head courteously when he saw me looking at him. A very large, very plump dachsund lay sleepily next to his desk.

"This is Gustav," said Herta, "Herr Friedrich's chief assistant. A very learned man, a very good man. I shall miss him greatly when I to the country return."

Gustav rose awkwardly from his chair and advanced to greet us. We introduced ourselves, shook hands. I saw that his left arm was missing, the sleeve of his coat folded neatly up. "If you are staying in Munich for only a few days," he said, in a remarkably forceful voice for so frail an old man, "might I urge you to visit the Residenz. Most visitors overlook it, or see only the more obvious, gaudy rooms. I have the impression that both of you would appreciate the Antiquarium, a marvelous room, a room quite filled with delightful statuary and Latin inscriptions. There is one inscription in particular that—"

The door to an inner office opened, and a prosperous-looking man emerged, looking satisfied. After him came Wolf, who smiled broadly when he saw us, said goodbye to his client. "At last!" he said, taking each of us by the arm and steering us into his office. "No calls under any circumstances," he said to Herta, who looked after the three of us with a maternal expression. The look on Gustav's face was harder to read.

Once again my expectations miscarried. Wolf's inner sanctum was if anything more Spartan than the waiting room. The walls were painted cream white, the few pieces of furniture were dark brown. Wolf's desk was large but simple, his chair straightbacked, two chairs for clients only a bit more comfortably designed. The only concession to affluence appeared to be the stained oaken bookcases that filled two walls, crammed with books and periodicals. Every title I saw had to do with coins. Unobtrusively in a corner, on a small square table, stood a delicate bronze crucifix. A long, simple wooden bed with a thin mattress and minimal blanket stood against the rear wall. The room reminded me of a monk's cell at a monastery I had visited in Florence. I thought the better of Wolf for that.

Wolf shook my hand firmly, nodded amiably to Adriana, motioned both of us to the more comfortable chairs. Now that he saw us here together, Wolf was very likely taking satisfaction in having guessed correctly. Would he also be guessing now that Adriana had informed me of his collusion in stealing the Caligulas?

Wolf opened a desk drawer, took out a business envelope, handed it to Adriana. "If you'll just endorse that," he said, "I can give it to Herta, who can have cash ready for you before you leave."

"Minus the sum you advanced me," she said, taking out the check and signing it.

"I've already taken the liberty of deducting that," he said, leaving the office for a moment with the check and returning. "I think it best," he said, seating himself and addressing me, "that the three of us know where we stand with one another. I've done a small favor for the Marchesa, who has often shown me the hospitality of her villino."

Though seated on that uncomfortable chair behind his business desk, he managed to look perfectly at his ease, as though at home in his comfortable armchair, discoursing on Bavarian manners. I realized that I had very little idea what his private life was like, apart from the marble floors and electronic controls of his Aventine apartment in Rome. Everything I had seen of him before today suggested a life conducted with skill and efficiency toward the making of money. But as he sat there today I realized also that he had the looks, intelligence and manner of an aristocrat. His hair, starting to gray but still handsomely full, was perfectly trimmed. His hands were folded on the desk before him, and I saw that his nails were manicured and that he wore gold cufflinks.

And yet there was this monastic sanctum.

"My relations with the Marchese, on the other hand, have always been business only." I wondered whether that business connection would continue once Wolf learned of Gilberto's new alliance with a Sicilian killer.

"But now—?" I began.

"The world of coin specialists is a small world," he said matter-of-factly, "and so sooner or later he will learn that I handled the sale of the Caligulas."

"And you're prepared to accept that."

"Of course—although I'd rather he didn't learn until we locate the rest of the hoard. In the interim, he might prove useful to us yet." Then, reaching into another desk drawer, "I am certain you would both like to see our latest treasure."

He brought out an elegant little wooden box, about four inches by five, beautifully crafted of mother-of-pearl mosaic imbedded in a dark wood like walnut outlined with slender strips of ivory. He placed it before us on the desk, opened the hinged lid and sat back.

Adriana gasped. Somewhat to my surprise I found myself not gasping, but figured that must have been because I had recently seen coins no less astonishing in London and Rome. But I *was* delighted to see that the two coins looked identical.

The twin tetradrachms lay in the box, their silver shining radiantly against the black velvet cushioning them. "Do pick them up," he said to Adriana, "carefully by the edge, if you will. I suppose you have seen many of the Marchese's, though none as perfect as these."

"I never looked at Gilberto's coins," she said, carefully taking one coin from the box. She looked admiringly at one side, then the other.

I picked up the other tetradrachm, looked quickly at the exergue beneath the quadriga. "Nothing below the ground line," I said to Wolf.

"I know that you wouldn't have expected to find a quarry design," he said. "This pair has a much earlier date, of course, probably 450–440 B.C. Quadriga barely moving, Nike crowning horses to right. Reverse shows the hair of Artemis-Arethusa bound in *sakkos* with meander and zig-zag patterns. Four dolphins circling. Looks like number 644 in Boehringer's *Die Münzen von Syrakus*, B.M.C.—that's the British Museum Catalogue—number 2.113."

Adriana's face showed what I thought: what a memory Wolf had! "In my business," Wolf said, watching our expressions, "one has to remember everything."

"So this is Artemis or Arethusa on the one side," Adriana said almost to herself.

"Yes, do you like that profile?" His tone was mildly playful. He was plainly enjoying himself, in possession of a pair of the most astounding coins found anywhere anytime, enjoying showing off as the expert he was. "Look at her drop-type earrings. A decade later those will become spirals. That's one way we can date the coins. The earrings, the hairdo, the simple wire necklace, the face could easily belong to a twentieth-century woman, could they not?"

That profile looked to me strikingly like Adriana's. I wondered whether she—or Wolf—noticed the resemblance. A straight, longish nose, decidedly sensual lips.

"What qualities do we look for in a coin? Striking, centering, relief, style, condition." Wolf was still speaking to Adriana, but might well have been addressing a university class of student numismatists. Given his high-speed delivery, taking notes on his lectures could leave one drained. "The Sicilian tetradrachms you see before you have all these qualities to an exceptional degree. They are well struck—no little crudities of detail. They are as well centered as an ancient coin struck by hand on sometimes imperfect metal ever could be. The relief is admirably high. Style is a more subjective matter, but I find it first-rate. And their condition, their state of preservation, as we say? *Stempelglanz, fior di conio, fleur-de-coin*, mint condition."

"They're indescribably beautiful," Adriana said, still holding the coin, turning it over.

"Once you look more closely at the details," Wolf said, "you may find a slight simplicity in the design. Compared to the decadrachm we examined at Carlotta's, Michael, these coins appear a shade primitive, do they not?"

"Hardly—" I started to say.

"It's a subtle difference," he continued, "due partly to the earlier date of these tetradrachms, partly to the smaller area the engraver had to work with on these smaller coins. They're masterpieces of their kind, in any case.

"And so what do we know of the hoard to date?" He was passing on to point two of his lecture, I noticed with some amusement, even as I was grateful for his orderly mind. What I really wanted to hear was how the tetradrachms had arrived at his office. Who brought them? "Not very much, but something. Four coins thus far. First, the decadrachm delivered to Luigi in Syracuse by the boy. None of us has seen it, but for the time being we have to take Luigi's word, by way of Massimo, that it *was* a Demareteion, although we haven't any notion at all whether Luigi knew the first thing about coins. The Demareteion type was long thought to date about 480 B.C. but was more likely to have been—"

"About 465," I said, not wanting to be left out entirely.

"Yes," Wolf said, giving me an appraising glance. "Our second coin, the decadrachm that we examined at Carlotta's, can probably be dated at 413–410. It would almost certainly have been minted soon after the Syracusan defeat of the Athenians. Thus we have a decadrachm from close to the beginning of the great Sicilian era of coins and another from close to the end. That fact tends to confirm the surmise—was it yours, Michael, or Massimo's?—that the hoard was in fact a collection, probably a private collection, that was built up over a half-century."

"Including the tetradrachms we're looking at from about two decades into that half-century," Adriana observed. She was taking more interest in all this than I had expected.

"Yes," Wolf said, "a further confirmation of the pattern we're laying out. And the fact of their being duplicates strongly confirms Luigi's report that the hoard contained duplicates of every coin. Most extraordinary." Even Wolf appeared lost for a few moments in wonder at the collection we were beginning to piece together.

Adriana asked, "Have there been other hoards at all like this one?"

"Never anything *like* this one," Wolf said, "none anywhere in the world. The Turkish hoard of a decade ago was much larger and may have had more decadrachms, we can't be certain. But if we confine our attention for the moment to Sicily, where some two hundred hoards of Greek coins have been found over the past century, we see nothing that compares in quality to what our hoard is beginning to look like." The possessive pronoun *our* had silently passed, I noted, from Massimo's lips to Wolf's. "Let me give you some examples. Sicilian hoards containing fifth-century coins minted at Syracuse have been recorded in every decade save one beginning in the 1880s to the present. I say 'recorded' rather than 'discovered' because it's indubitable that countless hoards were dug up in the two thousand years *before* responsible archaeologists and others entered the field. The one decade with no reported finds was the 1940s, when as you know there was a war on.

"The 1885 hoard, found at Selinunte, contained twenty-one tetradrachms. It was buried about 409 B.C. A 1910 hoard, found north of Gela, had sixty-one tetradrachms, three didrachms and six drachms. Buried about 475–470 B.C. Closer to the burial date—"

"Were the hoards all deliberately buried, then?" Adriana asked.

" 'Hoard' is a loose term," Wolf replied. "It just means any old artifacts dug up out of the earth. We usually differentiate four types of coin hoards—coins lost accidentally, coins reluctantly abandoned, coins saved for an emergency, and coins deliberately collected."

"And so ours is the fourth type," Adriana said.

"*Nehm' ich an*, so I assume, given Luigi's report. I was going to say that a very small hoard found at Syracuse in 1951 has an estimated burial date of 415 B.C., quite close to that of ours. But it had merely eleven litrae and dozens of other trivial pieces. Quite probably some Syracusan's accidental loss."

"I've read of fifth-century hoards discovered in Sicily in modern times," I said, "that were brought from Greece by the military to pay the troops. Probably reluctantly abandoned in an emergency."

"Oh yes," Wolf said, "there are many of those. One way to recognize that type of hoard is by the large number of coins of the same denomination, often in quite good condition. Another way we infer the nature of any hoard is by the container in which it was found. Earthenware pots are the most common. But there are also ceramic and bronze vases, silver boxes, lead boxes, Greek amphoras—"

"Ours was in a leather bag," I said.

"—and the locations," Wolf went on, "everywhere imaginable! In tombs, under roads, within walls, under house pavements or flooring, on the seashore, on the bottom of the sea—." A shudder passed through me.

"I had no idea so many ancient coins had been discovered," Adriana said. Her eyes were fixed on Wolf's face.

"Laboratory experiments with the bronze dies from which ancient coins were struck—every single coin was struck by hand, of course—these experiments have shown that one such die could strike as many as ten thousand coins. Given the population of ancient Syracuse—possibly a half-million—millions of coins must have been struck for this one city alone. What we see in the hoards we've found, then, is the merest trickle from this vast ancient flood. That's somewhat like deducing from the Neanderthal bones discovered a century ago over near Düsseldorf that great numbers of Neanderthal men once roamed this continent."

"Would you tell us," I broke in, "how these two coins arrived at your office?"

He seemed unperturbed by the interruption. "I was in Rome, as you know, Michael, when Gustav phoned me with the news. All he told me over the phone was that two lower-middleclass Turks had shown up in the office here one day with them. A pair of Turks, a pair of tetradrachms."

"Definitely Turks," I said, "not Italians or—?"

"Gustav knows a Turk when he sees one," Wolf said. "He had never seen either of these particular men before."

"But wouldn't Turkish couriers be likely to deal with Turkish dealers?" I was improvising.

"Ordinarily, yes. But keep in mind that ours is an extraordinary hoard in every respect—beginning with the way in which it was shipped out of Sicily to the mainland. Who knows what happened to it from its presumptive landing point near Reggio to the day the first coin appeared in Rome?"

"How did these two Turks explain where they got the tetradrachms?" I asked.

"Something about having inherited them from a distant Sicilian relative, I think it was," Wolf replied. "Gustav says that he didn't listen too carefully. We pretty much assume that the persons bringing coins to our office exercise their imaginations a good deal. We do our best to demand evidence from them of the origins or sources of the coins—the provenance, it's called—but except in unusual instances it's difficult even for the most honest individuals to know exactly what route the coins followed into their hands."

"And these couriers wanted you to sell the coins for them?"

"Yes."

"They must have left names and addresses where they could be contacted."

"They did, yes," Wolf said, inspecting a note on the top of his desk. "Yahya Bozkurt is one of them, or so he said, and the other one—where *do* they get these ridiculous names?—is Memik Cindoruk. I've already asked Gustav to get what information he can on anyone residing at the address they gave. Meanwhile," he said, rising, "you'll have to excuse me. I would be delighted to take both of you to dinner but will have to do so another day. Tomorrow, perhaps? My absence in Rome produced all sorts of demands on my attention."

As we passed into the waiting room Herta put a fat envelope into Adriana's hands, and Gustav smiled and nodded to us from his desk. "You'll have to forgive my not standing," he said, in that rich deep voice of his, "but it has become a real labor to me these days."

"I'm sorry for that," I said. "I was rather hoping that you could guide the Marchesa and me around the Antiquarium."

"Oh well," he replied, looking pleased, "once I stand I can easily walk. That would be my pleasure."

We agreed to meet at ten o'clock the next morning. As Adriana and I left the office, she told me that she had just asked Herta to join her for lunch the next day. "I have a feeling," she said, "that she is full of interesting things to tell us."

"I had that very feeling," I said, "about Gustav."

The average sabreur's inclination is to panic when he has not found the adversary's blade where he expected it. This is due to the subconscious knowledge that he has a big defensive area to cover.

There is no doubt that the head is the most vulnerable area of the target.

Only on the U-bahn ride from Arabellapark downtown did I realize that it was midnight, and on the ride north from downtown to the Olympic Park I had plenty of time to reflect on why I wanted to visit the site of my youthful fame by myself rather than with Adriana.

Simple jealousy, sexual jealousy, that was obviously the trigger. Over dinner at the hotel she had confessed—no, I had to be honest, she had simply told me, and in a perfectly level-headed and friendly way, that she thought I should know of the "mild flirtation" she and Wolfgang had once had.

"That's all it was?" I couldn't help asking.

"That's all," she said. But there was something in her tone that gave me pause. And now, sitting in this nearly vacant train speeding toward the Olympic Park, I found myself turning over the question of whether Wolf had actually invited me to Munich not because of the hoard but because of Adriana. Guessing that I was the unnamed lover for whom Adriana had wanted Gilberto's coins sold, Wolf might well have seized on the arrival of the tetradrachms in Munich as an occasion to invite *Adriana*, in effect, to his city. If I did in fact prove to be the man accompanying her, well then he could figure out how to deal with me once he had both of us on his home grounds.

I groaned aloud, loudly enough to cause the thick-necked passenger sitting a few seats ahead of me to turn around and look me over. I tried to recall the conversations Adriana and I had had regarding Wolf and could think of nothing that suggested her having any romantic interest in him at all. In our first conversation, as well as I could remember, she seemed not to know anything about him at all, asking for my impressions of him. In fact, I had the impression she hadn't even met him. But that might not have been disingenuous of her, could easily be compatible with her having known him as innocently as she said she had. And I could hardly have expected her to tell me of her flirtation with him the first time we discussed him.

Trying with this cold shower of common sense to cool my heated spirit, I left the train at the Olympiazentrum, walked with quickening pulse toward the Olympic Park. That locale had become mythologized in my life, I realized at once as I passed an ordinary man taking a leak behind a large bush, crossed over a massive ring road with ordinary cars committing ordinary speeding offenses. But then I entered the park and saw the gigantic spiderweb of the acrylic and steel tent suspended over the famous buildings, and I knew that I had only partly mythologized it all. I stopped to take it all in. The glowing crescent of a moon hung over the tent, and while it was only a moon, the crescent was also—great heavens, it was also Artemis, linked to the Arethusa of the hoard coins—and it was Islam, and Turkey! The merely private legend of my Olympic days was now immeasurably enhanced by what I had learned since then, and had experienced, and was experiencing even now. I had not anticipated such illuminations, trembled as they continued to unroll.

I was surprised at how well I remembered details from twenty years before. Dead ahead was the Olympic Hall, where I had fenced my heart out and lost, all the while exulting in those few brief minutes on the fencing strip. Beyond that Hall, I remembered, partly covered by the great acrylic spiderweb, lay the huge stadium, and somewhere to my left stood the apartment building where the Israeli athletes were murdered.

I walked slowly on, knowing that I would soon come to the lake created especially for my Olympics. It *was* my Olympics, in much the same way that the Ardeatine Caves were Adriana's. And what was Wolf's symbolic place? I was sure that he had one. Was I becoming possessed by Wolf? I spent a lot of my thinking time these days thinking about him, no doubt about that, and for quite some time even before I learned about that flirtation with Adriana. He *was* a remarkably commanding figure, not just because of his brains, which were formidable, or his grasp of coin lore, which left me behind at the starting gate. Today he had *meant* to be impressive in that magisterial performance of his at the office, and I was in fact tremendously impressed.

But there was something more to my fascination with him. Halting, I began to see a glimmer of what it was. My father had told me some time that both of his parents had been born in Germany. So that had they not decided to migrate from Germany to the States, I might well have been born in Germany. Wolf could have been an older boy I knew on the block—or my older brother. How old did he say he was? About seventeen years older than I, I think it was, my God nearly old enough to have been my father.

Somehow I preferred thinking of him as an older brother, but why? My own father had been more or less satisfactory, that was one reason. He had always been a stern man, but I hadn't known any other kind of father and didn't revolt against him until my late adolescence. There were the occasional rages, but they didn't seem directed at me so much as the world around him. No, it was time to be honest about him too. Kurt was really authoritarian, and I had grown up with the ambivalence about authority that I carried to this day. He was a smalltown Midwestern banker and everything in life was an investment, even a McDonalds hamburger. On the other hand he and my mother insisted that I get the college education they had never had, and they sent me to a prep school, where I learned to fence, and to summer camp, where I learned to sail.

But I had never had a brother, or a sister either, and I had long wanted one. Too much solitariness in my childhood, my youth, my adult life. Sometimes as a boy I had fantasized having a brother, preferably an older one, who could show me the ropes in a puzzling world and protect me from the hostile kids down the block.

And then I perceived that what I really saw in Wolf was not so much the shadow of an older brother as of—*myself*. Maximilian Wolfgang Friedrich was what *I* might have been had I been born in Germany some years earlier, had lived here through the war, endured whatever it was that Berliners must have endured after the war. I found the thought thrilling, and frightening.

But what was it exactly that Wolf had endured? How exactly and where had he spent the war years? He would have been about four years old when the war broke out in 1939, about ten when it ended. All he had told me about those terrible years was the way the bombing had affected him in Berlin. But it must have been horrible for him as a boy. It would have been horrible for me, I was sure of that.

I had stopped not far from an open-air theater, a Greek theater. Twenty years before I hadn't even known of its existence, or if I had known I wouldn't have cared. But there, in that Theatron, lay my future, all my studies of the ancient world, my teaching life, and now the coins. I found the discrepancy between that young Michael and my present self deeply unsettling. Could I really ever have been so unenlightened? Could I ever have been so incredibly *young*?

Past the Theatron lay the lake, artificially created but now looking entirely natural, and beyond the lake lay low hills, their contours barely visible under the dim moonlight. They had been built of rubble after the war, from the Munich destroyed by bombing. Gracefully landscaped, in the moonlight they appeared at this moment the very image of pastoral serenity.

Exhilarated, shaken, nostalgic, regretful, I walked back to the station, waited for a time, took the next train downtown, another to the Arabella. I needed the traveling time to begin pulling myself together.

Once the arm is extended it must not be bent again.

When Adriana proposed the next morning that we have breakfast at a nearby health-food shop rather than face the cheese, bacon, ham, butter, eggs, cream and pastry of a great Bavarian breakfast at the hotel, I said sure, feeling too tired from my night out to protest, even if I had wanted to. I was not looking forward to our breakfast together, sharply conscious of a rip in the fabric of our relations. It was only when she told me that the German term for health-food shop was *Reform Haus* that I managed a chuckle, and then it felt all right to go out to breakfast with her.

She had discovered last evening that a Reform Haus was to be found only a short block from the hotel, and we walked there in the welcome sunshine of the early morning. Porsches, BMW's and Mercedes lined the curbs of the streets near the hotel, and the sight of them somehow made me feel clean heading for the economy and simplicity of a health-food shop.

The smooth-complexioned young woman behind the counter at the Reform Haus exuded good health and good cheer. I was glad for her health, wished I had some of her cheer. She spoke little English and so Adriana did the ordering for us. I understood *das Joghurt* and thought I understood *kaffeinfrei*, but *das Obst, vollkorn-*

mehl and *die Brötchen* went right by me. We sat on bar stools at a counter.

"You're unusually quiet this morning," Adriana said. "Is it what I told you about Wolf?" I pursed my lips, nodded slightly. "*He's* not what should concern you," she said.

"What should?"

"The size of your living room in Ohio," she said, biting into one of the freshly baked rolls that the healthy young woman had just put before us.

How serious are you? I wanted to ask, knowing the issue was much more important than Adriana had just now treated it. But the wholewheat rolls and yoghurt and freshfruit salad and decaffeinated coffee were piling up on the counter in front of us, and my mind was already sliding off to my meeting with Gustav. I was feeling restless here with Adriana, wanted Gustav to tell me everything he knew about Wolfgang.

Gustav had arrived at the palace before me and stood inside the entrance, chatting with the ticket seller. His fat sausage of a dachsund was by his side, though whether standing or lying down I couldn't tell, given the dog's dimensions. Gustav grasped my hand with an energy that surprised me and led me at once to a door on the far side of the entrance room. "Ordinary tourists flock to the Ancestors' Gallery," he said, "or the State Bedroom or the Porcelain Gallery or the Hall of the Decision or the Inner Presence Chamber, but when Herr Friedrich told me you were a university professor of classical history I knew that you would above all want to see the Antiquarium."

With the dachsund trailing after, we passed into a room whose far wall held a bewildering diversity of niches, pilasters, vaguely Oriental statuary, fountains, cornices, brackets, friezes, urns, stringcourses, cones and other decorative features, almost all constructed of small round stones in greens, blues, creams, oranges, browns and grays, except for the oranges all rather soft and subdued. "Done by Italian artisans, wouldn't you say?" Gustav said as I gaped at the stone grotto. "Sometimes those Italians just don't know when to stop."

I thought I detected an American note in his speech and asked him about it. "American prisoner-of-war camp in 1945," he said, as we stood there contemplating the grotto. "And of course I've met a great many Americans since then, in Berlin and here."

"You were in Berlin about when Wolf was?"

"Oh yes," he said, leading me to an elaborately framed door in the grotto wall. "That's where I met him."

He stood to one side of the door and with a small courtly bow gestured within. The hinged door stood open, and as I moved to the entrance I saw stretching out ahead of me the most astonishing room I had ever seen. The only flat surface I saw was the immense marble floor, beautifully inlaid with large squares of burnt-sienna, cream and a grayish-blue, inside a burnt-sienna border, with diagonally laid vari-colored squares forming another border outside that one, and another narrow burnt-sienna border outside that. Numerous windows pierced the sloping walls on both sides, but the sunlight must have been filtered through clouds outside, so dim was the light in the room. My initial impression was of an enormous vaulted cavern stretching off toward a dark horizon.

We walked a few steps into the room and halted. My eyes adjusted to the dim light and I saw that the room had a farther wall, possibly two hundred feet away. Built into that wall was a large fireplace of some red material. The shape of the room was that of an immense barrel vault, whose ceiling of colorful frescoes seemed suspended along a series of broad arches bending up from narrow bases every fifteen or twenty feet along each of the side walls. Each pair of arches was also paired laterally along these walls, the tops of these lateral arches sloping broadly up toward the ceiling, the dull sunlight from windows set in these huge recesses, filling each of them, so that the room felt organized around this double colonnade of faintly glowing niches.

The room grew brighter. The sun must have emerged from behind clouds. I saw the busts of innumerable ancients lining both side walls, set on pedestals at varying heights, and there were full-length statues too.

I looked at Gustav, whose face showed the pleasure he was taking in mine. "The Renaissance was wonderful, was it not?" he said. "All these pagan Roman and Greek emperors and heroes lined up on their pedestals, interred in a sense, while the Christian Mary floats above them in the sky. An earthly burial vault that is also the vault of heaven."

"You haven't always been a numismatist," I said.

"Oh, I'm not really a numismatist at all," he said, "certainly not an expert. I came down to Munich a few years ago when Wolfie—Wolfgang—phoned me in Berlin and said he needed an assistant he could trust. I had just retired from a humdrum job and was delighted to come. I merely learned a little about coins as I went along."

"Wolfgang must have known you well in Berlin."

"Oh, we saw a lot of each other there after the war."

"Would you tell me more about that?"

"First, let's stroll around the Antiquarium, shall we?" The occasion seemed to have taken twenty years off his age. We walked on into the room, stopping frequently. Each of the large window niches was decorated within a square millimeter of its life with grotesque designs. But I was mainly drawn to the marble busts, some Renaissance some ancient, done in a variety of beautiful shades and types of stone. Alexander the Great, Nero and the more meritorious Caesars, a great many of the eminent public figures of the ancient world.

"The inscriptions," Gustav said, pointing upward toward the arches, "march with Roman regularity around the room, and they also have that imperious and pontifical quality that we Germans have always loved." As he spoke, expanding to the occasion, his voice took on an operatic quality, expressive and musical. He would be a bass-baritone, I judged. "*Abstinentia Mater Sanitatis.* Can you imagine Bavarians paying any attention to that, particularly in the beer halls? With or without beer, Bavarians have always been a little insane, which may be why Hitler liked this part of Germany above all others.

"And look at that one. *Veritas Nihil Erubescit Nisi Abscondi.*"

"Truth blushes at nothing," I said, "unless hidden. Whoever built this palace had a severe moralizing streak."

"Oh yes," Gustav said, "but he was a representative Bavarian Catholic of his age. The irony is that he took his little moral aphorisms from the Romans. But then we Germans have long been the principal modern heirs of the Romans. Not even the English or the French or the Americans match our devotion to order coupled to cruelty."

I couldn't tell how ironic he meant to be. "*You* seem to me much less Roman than—say, Greek."

"Oh well," he said, waving the observation away. "Now take Wolfgang. *There's* a Roman. Or, I should say, a Roman convert. What do you say to lunch?"

I wanted to walk the entire length of this extraordinary room and did so, all the way down to the elaborate red fireplace, which two tourists were admiring, and then returned slowly with Gustav to the entrance door, where I turned for a final look at this remarkable mauseoleum.

Outside, the clouds had largely vanished and the sunshine astonished me with its brightness, a reaction I had often had when returning to the present from some immersion in the past. Gustav offered to select a cafe, and we walked in silence along the crowded streets past the post office, the ornately neo-Gothic city hall, into and through a massive outdoor food market, whose fruit and vegetables glistened as beautifully as the flowers, and on to a quieter street. The dachsund, whose name was Siegfried, kept up with us surprisingly well, though doing so caused him to wheeze like a rusty old boiler.

The cafe was, as I should have guessed, Greek, *Griechische Taverne* boldly announced in white letters on a blue awning. "*Ya sas!*" Gustav said heartily to the two men standing at the door. He and I were the first customers for lunch. Gustav then said something more quietly to the two men and they chuckled together.

"You seem to speak the language," I said to Gustav as we sat down at a sidewalk table. "All I know is *parakalo* and *ephkharisto*."

"Only a little," he said, waving the menu aside offered by the waiter. He ordered in English, perhaps out of courtesy to me. "But you read classical Greek?"

"With a dictionary," I said, ordering meze and spanikopita. I knew what those were. "I only manage to keep the rust off my Latin."

"Ah, I envy you your scholar's life," he said. "To live on intimate terms every day with Thucydides and Cicero, hearing their voices, speaking to them—"

"I'm not sure that's exactly what my days are like," I said.

"Possibly it's different in the United States," he said, amiably. "All I have are impressions from fragmentary conversations with Professors here in Germany. As a youth I dreamed of becoming a Professor—I admired one of my classics Professors at the *gymnasium* enormously—but by the time I might have gone to the university the country was preparing for war and I decided that I would volunteer for the State Labor Service and then get my two years' military service over with. A year later came Poland and I was trapped in the Army for another six years."

"Might you have gone to the university afterward?"

"I might have, but I didn't. I was only twenty-five years old then, but I was tired, horribly tired." He seemed to shrink down into his seat, thinking back. The waiter brought rolls, beer. "That's when I met Wolfgang, or Fritz as he was called then."

"He changed names?" I shouldn't have been surprised, but I was.

"Oh yes," Gustav said, appearing to revive with the food. "I'll tell you a little about him, I can see you're interested, and he still interests me too, still fascinates me in fact, despite things—. But I have to tell you just a little about what happened to me in the war, so that you'll understand my reaction to him—to little Fritz—when I met him. Could you bear to listen?" I nodded, eager to hear.

"My first year or so as a soldier was idyllic. Not long after basic training, which of course no one likes, I was sent to France, luckily not with the advance troops but just behind them. What a paradise France was! The wines and the women indeed, though as for song the German soldiers were the only ones singing. If you find my attitude shocking you must allow for my age and provinciality at the time. I was just twenty, I had never before even been out of my

German village, except for the training camps. All the great issues of the war that we debated later—whether the Poles *actually* had been planning to attack us and so on—I hadn't the faintest awareness of. And the German brutalities on the Russian front and in the camps, all that was yet to come, and many of us hadn't even a whisper of those events till near the end of the war. I was a simple car mechanic, and I just repaired vehicles, drank wine and picked up girls."

"And so France was a pleasure—"

"Completely. But then my unit was sent to the Russian front, where life suddenly got serious. I spent twenty cold, terrifying months there. One day I was trying to help some Russian passengers get off a bombed train when one of the cars moved and pinned my arm against the next car. I'm not trying to present myself as a hero. That's just what happened.

"After that, a few months in the hospital near Berlin, other months trying to recover from the shock of losing an arm." He paused. "I never *have* quite recovered from that shock. All I've gotten accustomed to is managing certain tasks without it. Well, as an amputee I could only serve on the home front, and so I was sent to Berlin and assigned to an army unit made up of boys, old men and derelicts like me. I did various odd jobs like air-raid warden."

I felt the peacefulness of the cafe, normal people having a normal lunch.

"Those last weeks in Berlin were ghastly. Shells exploding everywhere, you could hardly see anything for the dust and smoke, water pouring from burst mains, huge craters in the streets, buildings crumpling all around. You had to duck the electric wires dangling from streetcars." He paused. "But worst of all was the stench of corpses. I've never gotten that smell out of my nostrils." He stopped, lost in those memories.

An image of corpses in a quarry fluttered across my brain.

"Well, what with the loss of my arm and the absolute horrors of those days, all in a cause most of us knew was hopeless, I was in a perpetual state of despair, as most of my comrades were. But what could we do?

"Escape Berlin, that's what. My comrades would have thought me crazy, had they known my intention, and perhaps I was a little crazy. None of *them* tried to get out of Berlin. But as the Russians swarmed over the eastern half of the city, one day I took off over the one remaining bridge to the west and miraculously made it through to the American lines. I spent the next few months in the American POW camp. As a mere enlisted man I wasn't grilled too hard by the Americans about my Nazi past—deep in my heart I knew I hadn't had one—and in the Autumn of 1945 I returned to my village not far from Berlin. I learned later it had been blown off the earth, my parents with it. The only other relative I knew of, an uncle, lived in Berlin, and as his prewar address was in what was now the American zone, I decided to risk going back there.

"I won't bore you with the details, but getting through the Russian lines around Berlin was difficult in the extreme, and by the time I finally made it to the American zone I was exhausted, panicked and almost suicidal. You have to know this in order to understand what effect my meeting little Fritz had on me.

"My Berlin uncle was nowhere to be found, and so I took up quarters in the basement of a bombed-out apartment building, along with fifteen or twenty others already there. Water ankle-deep on the floor, cold all the time. Like almost everyone else in the city, I spent my waking hours organizing food and clothing, 'organizing' being our word for stealing. And then early one morning, as I was returning to the city with a few potatoes that I had organized from a farm during the night, I saw this skinny little ten-year-old boy talking energetically with a couple of American soldiers and I stopped to watch. He was organizing *them*, I had the feeling, or at the very least talking them out of something, cigarettes or chocolate very likely. Something about his manner caught my attention. Boldness, self-possession, something like that. I've thought about it often over the years and still haven't identified precisely what it was about him that so enthralled me. For I *was* enthralled, not sexually or anything like that. I like women and I like them grown up. No, what attracted me to Fritz had something to do with his—well, confidence. That's a paltry word for it, but as I've said I had almost given up on life, and then suddenly that morning on that rubble-filled street I saw this tough little urchin taking on the Americans as though he had as much of a future as *they* did! And when I saw him walk away with several cartons of cigarettes I knew that he *did* have a future, that he would win at whatever he did, and all of a sudden I felt that I wanted to know him, to capture a piece however small of that self-assurance of his. And so I ran after him, and introduced myself. At first he bristled and told me to bug off, but eventually I persuaded him that I was genuinely impressed with his handling of those soldiers, that I wasn't out to steal his cigarettes or anything like that. But he was still wary, the way a raccoon bares his teeth at you out of his centuries-old instinct to survive.

"Over the weeks and months ahead I saw him frequently, sometimes every day. He was always off on some hustle, like trading cigarettes for nylon stockings, and stockings for dollars. Gradually, when he realized that I wasn't out to use him, and was in fact a sort of—well, admirer, Fritz relaxed with me and sometimes let me buy him a beer. I had almost no money, and I came to discover that he was piling up quite a little, but he never offered to buy the beer. He had *me* organized, it seems.

"Well, gradually I learned something of Fritz, never everything. His father had been a soldier and was killed in the very France that I had found so peaceful. His mother lived on in the proletarian section of Berlin where Fritz had been born. She had a string of lovers, not always exercising good judgment, so that Fritz acquired a little sister and brother. He already had two older brothers, both in the armed forces. They survived the war, more or less intact. One left Germany soon after the war and became an eminent medical doctor in the United States. The other emigrated to Brazil, where he seems to have made a small fortune as a businessman in some German community there. It was Fritz's fate to remain in Germany. With little schooling at war's end, with no one to sponsor him abroad, he was left to fend for himself. Never was anyone better equipped to do that, at least by the time he had been on the streets for a few years.

"A year after the war he was deep in the black markets, trading and buying and selling—well, everything." He paused. "There was a rumor—I never heard it verified—that he had done a little trading in—well, human flesh. You have to understand, the hunger in Berlin was extreme—." He trailed off, looked away. "Just before the war ended he had started to hang around an anti-Nazi gang of adolescents—there were many such gangs in Germany then, believe it or not—and he learned how to bamboozle the authorities. He was an extraordinarily smart lad, obviously, and had that unusual blend of charm and toughness that makes for entrepreneurial success."

"What brought him to Munich?"

"The same things that brought thousands of other Berliners, and at about the same time. Three or four years after the war Fritz was making a lot of money. He was only thirteen or fourteen years old, remember, but he was already starting to wear business suits and smoke cigars. But Berlin was a dead city. It had almost no industry and very little business, and the four-power occupation kept it in a straight-jacket. The Germans were starting to rebuild, but not in Berlin. The great new magnet was Munich, and thousands of Germans left Berlin for that city in the late 1940s and early '50s. Fritz was one of those. One day with only the clothes on his back and a knife and gun in his pockets—I've heard him tell the story only once or twice, mainly he says nothing about it—and with I dare say substantial amounts of the new German currency in a money belt, he set off for Munich and has been here ever since."

"Leaving you behind," I said.

"Well, there was never any question of my accompanying him. We weren't really that close, and I was never involved in his business schemes." Gustav signaled for the waiter. "I'm sorry," he said, "but I have to get back to the office." To Fritz's office, he might have said.

"He changed his name in Munich?"

"Yes," Gustav said, rising with difficulty from his chair. "It's the arthritis," he said. "Sitting always makes it worse." We started walking, Siegfried lumbering reluctantly along. "A new city, a new life. Fritz had determined to break out of his past, to leave the horrors of Berlin behind, his lowly origins, his racketeering, all that. He would enter the middle class, become a respectable

German bourgeois. And so when the driver with whom he had hitched a ride set him down not far from here in the business district of Munich, the first street sign he saw was for Maximiliansplatz. He liked the name and one minute later he was no longer Friedrich Fritz Blaschke, he was Maximilian Wolfgang Friedrich. He was also a new person. He pursued his bourgeois goals with the admirable relentlessness that you've perhaps seen in him. He entered the coin business in short order and became the reputable businessman you know."

We walked along in silence. "Wolf became a Catholic?" I asked. "Was that part of his transformation?"

"Oh, no," Gustav said, pausing at the entrance to Wolf's office building. "What makes you think that?"

"That crucifix in his office—"

Gustav chortled. "Oh, that. You have to remember that most Bavarians are Catholics, not the least of whom are the wealthy, many of whom collect coins." With that, still chuckling, he shook my hand vigorously and disappeared with Siegfried into the building.

I walked the few short blocks to the Odeonsplatz underground, had just stepped onto the downward escalator when I saw a familiar, portly figure striding toward the Felderrnhalle a few hundred yards away. His back was toward me, and I caught only a glimpse of him as the escalator quickly carried me below street level, but it looked very much like Massimo. *Here*, in Munich?

The fencer's balance and footwork must always enable him to recover a lost measure immediately.

I was still pondering the implications of that possibility when I arrived at the Arabella, out of breath from my haste. Adriana and I had agreed to meet in the ground-floor coffee shop about two-thirty, and I was decisively late. She was not to be seen in the coffee shop and I hurried up to our room.

"Don't apologize," she said as I started to. "I've been having a delightful chat with Fiorella—you remember, Massimo's sister?—and—"

"Calling from where?"

"Why, from Rome. You'd given her our number here, thank goodness, and she called to give both you and Massimo a message."

"Did she say Massimo was here?"

"Yes, and she sounded surprised that he hadn't contacted you yet. The message was that Gilberto appears to have come into a lot of money recently. Fiorella's realtor friends tell her that he has been investing heavily in Rome real estate—"

"Does that make sense to you?" I heard my own impatience.

"Well, it's surprising that he would invest in real estate. If he came into a large sum of money he'd be more likely to pay off his debts. He has *lots* of those."

"But if the sum of money were *very* large—?"

"Then I suppose he might pay off his debts and *then* buy real estate, yes. As an old-line aristocrat he has always had an agrarian streak, and he does own farm-land here and there, just collecting the rents of course. He would never live anywhere but in a city and it's not out of the question that he would buy property—"

"Did Fiorella spell out what she thought his investments meant?"

"Not in so many words, but the fact that the message was for both you and Massimo suggests, wouldn't you say, that it has something to do with the hoard?"

It meant that Gilberto had latched on to some part of it, yes. Only a very small part, I hoped. But even a single decadrachm from the hoard could bring him a small fortune. Would Brutto have had a hand in his acquiring a coin?

"If he somehow acquired even one of the coins," I said, "I wonder how he would put it on the market."

Adriana and I looked at one another. The only big-time coin-dealer's name we knew of lay heavily in the air between us, unspoken.

"I had coffee brought to the room just before you arrived," Adriana said, going over to a cart on which gleaming coffee-ware stood. She poured me a cup. "I had a fascinating lunch with Herta—"

"Tell me." Things were breaking faster than I could absorb them, but I wanted to have all the pieces in hand.

"She's a delightful woman, a bit kooky, but warm-hearted and really quite sensible—"

"Tell me." We were still standing there in our large sitting room, coffee cups in hand, my coffee untasted.

"She's also a bit of a Puritan, I think you Americans would say. That's what led to her choicest bit of gossip. You see, Wolf has this yacht—"

"There was a large photo of it on the wall of his office."

"Yes, well, he keeps it a considerable distance from Germany—"

"Adriana, *please*—." I wondered whether my irritation sounded as strong as I felt it.

"—at a marina in Rhodestown—"

Off the coast of Turkey. My mind went racing in that direction.

"—in the eastern Mediterranean—Herta hinted darkly at the suspect morals of the Arabs or the Moslems, she spoke of them as identical—and on this yacht, which is a *huge* one as she described it—"

"It looked like a ketch or a yawl," I said, "perhaps a forty-two-footer—"

"Well, Herta made it out to be a truly immense floating palace, loaded with bedrooms, a Sultan-size bed in every one, mirrors on the ceilings, Ottomans literally on the floor, everyone smoking hashish, you get the picture."

"Wolf's floating harem?"

"Herta admitted not having any solid evidence of it, but that was the idea, yes. She had heard rumors, overheard fragments of conversation. One thing she *did* know for a fact is that Wolf's Munich house, near the English Garden, stands right next to a convent, and you can imagine what she makes of that."

"Something like the Boccaccio story about a male gardener

who takes a job in a convent and a few years later the nuns have to build on a kindergarten?"

"Something like that. She really makes him out to be a perfect lecher."

"How does that make you feel?" The question was out before I thought better of it. "I'm sorry. I should have asked whether that sounds like Wolf to you." That question was hardly much better.

Adriana looked at me coolly for a moment, then said, "I'm not an authority on Wolfgang Friedrich."

"That isn't his real name," I said, tasting the cold coffee and setting the cup down.

"That doesn't surprise me in the least," she said, thus preventing my winning this little skirmish. I might have considered provoking her a bit further had my mind not found itself gripped by the image of Wolf's yacht off the coast of Turkey.

"Herta also told me," Adriana added, "that Wolf has a gun in his office desk."

"I know about that," I said, "and there's a knife with it. Nothing menacing. Just mementoes of his days in Berlin."

"Michael!" he said, throwing his arms around my shoulders and squeezing hard. "You didn't wince," Massimo said happily, looking me over. "You must be recovering from that surgery nicely. And Marchesa," he said, turning to Adriana and embracing her more discreetly, "you look wonderful, as always!" We were standing at the reception desk, from which he had just phoned our room.

"Let's go into the coffee shop, shall we?" he said, taking each of us by the arm. "I know a waitress there. Bridget. She's Irish, but married to a Sicilian relative of mine. Both *gastarbeiter*. They like it in Germany and hope to stay."

Massimo must have tipped Bridget off that we were coming. The instant we had seated ourselves she appeared, bearing four cappuccinos. Massimo was already ingratiating himself with Adriana and me, or trying to do so.

Bridget greeted us as friends of her friend, but quickly vanished. "Her husband is more than simply a relative of mine,"

Massimo said, wiping a fleck of whipped milk from his lip, "he's also an informant."

"How so?" I asked.

"First let me tell you that on my way back to Rome from London this week, I stopped off in Palermo, partly on coin business but mainly to get any fresh word I could on what Brutto's up to. What I found out was he almost certainly had that courier murdered in Rome, the fellow who brought the decadrachm to Carlotta." I glanced at Adriana, who looked wide-eyed. "He may not have ordered the murder, it may simply have happened in the course of the torture. The torture was the point." I took Adriana's hand.

"It seems that before he died, the courier did tell Brutto's men something about the rest of the hoard—there's no way to know how much he knew or how much he told—and also that the hoard got to the mainland on the brother's little fishing boat. So it seems likely that for the last few days Brutto has been casting around for Luigi's brother."

"You learned something just now from Bridget's husband?"

"Yes, that a pair of bleeding mafia types looking very much like our old friends Pinocchio and Gravel-voice have turned up in Munich. If they *are* indeed here in the city, they're not likely to be looking for a fisherman who's almost certainly down South somewhere but, so to speak, for the fish themselves—"

"For the coins," Adriana said.

"Yes," said Massimo, "which is to say for whoever *has* the coins—Michael, Wolf, whoever—"

"Yourself," I said.

"Yes, me too."

"If Brutto did get hold of some of the coins," I said, "how would he market them?"

"There are a lot of Italian collectors with money, and Brutto could easily sell tetradrachms—at, say, twenty thousand dollars apiece—inside Italy. But for the decadrachms, he would need to hook into the international markets, where the truly big money is."

"Might he do that through Gilberto?"

Massimo considered that. "Gilberto could help. The most probable trading route in any case would be through the auctioneers here in Munich or over in Zurich, although Paris or London or New York wouldn't be out of the question."

"You're wondering," Adriana said to me, "whether there's about to be a river of hoard money flowing through Munich?"

I nodded, then gave Massimo his sister's information about Gilberto's reputed new wealth. "What I most feared may be coming upon us in full force," Massimo said gravely. "The hoard being thoroughly dispersed." He sat perfectly still, closed his eyes, put a hand to his forehead and began massaging it carefully.

The three of us stared ruefully at that prospect. Bridget cleared the cups, looked questioningly at us, left quietly.

"It just occurred to me," I said, "that our enemies may share our interest in keeping the hoard intact." I told Massimo of the corridor exchange Adriana had overheard between her husband and Brutto, and she filled in the details.

"Of course, of course," Massimo said, looking as though he had expected just such a collaboration.

"Well," Adriana said cheerfully, "at least there are the two new tetradrachms."

Massimo looked bewildered.

"You tell him," I said to Adriana, and she did. Her lively interest in the hoard was undisguised.

"Well, well," Massimo mused, "so Wolf told you about the tetradrachms." He thought that over. "There's another piece of information, or I should say a strong suspicion, that I brought north with me. After Palermo I went to Rome, talked with various individuals, including Carlotta. I *did* get that shocking message of yours, Michael, on my answering machine—did I tell you? You can imagine how long it took me to absorb *that* news." Like me, he plainly hadn't entirely absorbed it.

"Well, Carlotta's a conscientious woman, and she had thought obsessively about the theft of that decadrachm from her shop." Adriana stared at me as though offended or at the very least surprised at my not having told her about the theft before, let alone the courier's murder. "When I talked with her two days ago she had remembered a detail that seemed insignificant at the time. As Wolf was leaving her shop, the day you had taken him to see the coin, he said to Carlotta, 'You must work very long hours here.' Carlotta remembers telling him, 'Oh no, I come in about noon and almost always close up by eight o'clock.' It wasn't so much *what* Wolf said, Carlotta told me, as the rather excessive casualness with which he said it."

Adriana said, "It takes an Italian to bring off that sort of question with finesse. The Germans rarely manage it."

"So that you suspect Wolf of having burgled her shop?" I was stunned, the possibility never having occurred to me.

"Well, not in person," Massimo said. "But he could easily have hired it done."

Again we paused, thinking our own thoughts. "It occurs to me," Adriana said, "that Wolfgang may need to have a very large safe."

"For coins from Brutto and your husband, you mean," Massimo said, "possibly along with Carlotta's decadrachm."

"And the two recent tetradrachms," Adriana said.

"I owe you both an apology," Massimo said abruptly, "for not having advised you of my arrival in Munich. My intentions were honorable. I know all of the principal dealers here, and I thought I would just spend a day or two nosing around, picking up what rumors I could, looking for that stray nugget in the dross." He paused. "I confess to having thought of the two of you, moreover, as being on something of a honeymoon here, and I didn't want to—" He left it hanging.

I had decided some time ago that Massimo's explanations always left me a trifle unconvinced, and this one didn't change that. "What nugget did you have in mind?" I asked him.

"I came here, as I said, with suspicions of Wolf's having duped us in Rome. I was looking for some sign that Wolf was displaying a new aggressiveness—or a new self-confidence—in his business deal ings, or merely a rumor that something unusual was afoot in the Munich markets. We coin dealers are a secretive lot, I can tell you, and most of us develop a certain sensitivity to vibrations in the air — at hearing what is not quite said, or at noting what is not said at all—"

"Wolf has suggested several times," I said, "that Turks must have pulled off the decadrachm theft. And Gustav, his assistant, said that the two men bringing the tetradrachms to the office here were Turks."

"Did Gustav himself tell you that?" Adriana asked.

"Well no," I admitted. "Wolf reported that to me."

Massimo said, thinking it over, "It's not at all out of the question that the Turks might be involved. The only rival to our hoard is the Turkish hoard of 1984, and Turkish smugglers and dealers handled that one from the day of its discovery to its arrival in Munich."

"Turkish dealers who are here now?" Adriana asked.

"Who are here at this very minute," Massimo said, "the two foremost ones with offices just a few minutes' walk from Wolf's office."

"If their identities are known," Adriana said, "why aren't they in jail?"

"Well, it *is* illegal in Turkey to dig antiquities up without a license or to ship them out of the country, but nevertheless both the digging up and the shipping out are common practices. The 1984 hoard seems to have been smuggled by truck through Bulgaria to Germany, and there's a lot of evidence that most of the hoard coins were sold to the Munich Turks, who then sold them for immense profits to American dealers and investors. The Turkish government has been trying for several years to get the coins returned. But getting the American and German governments to co-operate with Turkish authorities in prosecuting the case hasn't worked thus far. The case has legal complexities of all sorts, and a large number of individuals of several nationalities are involved, some of them quite wealthy and influential."

"What do you mean," Adriana asked, "when you say that that hoard is a rival to ours?"

"Mainly in quality. The Turkish hoard is often called the decadrachm hoard. At last count it had fourteen decadrachms—all Greek, all silver, all early fifth-century—and all in mint condition."

I whistled. "That may even surpass ours."

"It's too early to tell. The unique features of our Sicilian hoard may be that it contains a duplicate pair of each coin type, and that it provides a complete collection of all the coins from a single, major mint over the span of three-quarters of a century. *The* major mint in Sicily, producing some of the very best coins in the entire Greek world. Hoards with uncirculated coins *are* found now and then, as I'm sure you know, although not often."

"How many coins in the Turkish hoard in all?" I asked.

"Nearly two thousand," Massimo said. I whistled again. "Ours can't be anywhere near that large, seeing that the quarry skeleton was holding only that one bag."

The phone rang. Adriana picked it up, listened, said "He's right here, I'll ask him." To me, with her hand over the receiver, "It's Wolf. He'd like us to have dinner with him this evening at his house."

I looked at Massimo, raised a questioning hand. "It's all right," he said, "tell him I'm here."

"Massimo's here too," Adriana told Wolf. "He breezed in just this minute and is dying to see you."

The evening arrangements made, Massimo said to both of us, "We can't confront Wolf with mere suspicions, but—"

"And yours may be unfounded," Adriana said. I looked at her sharply.

"Indeed," Massimo said, unperturbed. "But they're strong enough for me to want us to look at Wolf objectively tonight, to read him *very* carefully, to find out what we can, how much he really knows."

Which of us, I wondered, Adriana or I, did Massimo think might not be objective?

The sabreur who is drawn into a succession of parries against his will usually loses some of his control and accuracy of blade, and is apt to panic.

Massimo was staying at an inexpensive inn in the Schwabing district, not far from Wolf's place. He was going to walk directly from one to the other, would meet us there. The quality of his inn confirmed what he told me in a quick aside, that the robbery of his London shop *had* in fact cost him a bundle. I was sorry to hear that, but I was also gratified that he had in fact been robbed, that is that he had been truthful about it. Ever since learning of his initial deception that evening at Il Carretto, I had been skeptical of everything he told me.

Adriana and I left the Arabella early enough to walk from the Odeonsplatz subway station up the Ludwigstrasse to Wolf's place. It was a lovely early-September evening, and neither of us had yet seen much of the city on this trip. Adriana's music school lay only a few blocks to the west of this famous avenue, and though she had often gone north from the school to the cafes and bars of Schwabing, she told me, for some reason she had never actually walked on the Ludwigstrasse. "Just too grand," she said enigmatically.

I assumed that Wolf's house stood in a grand area, and the Ludwigstrasse looked like a preparation for it. It was a handsome six-lane avenue, with spacious sidewalks on either side, flanked by imposing stone buildings, their facades variously neo-Renaissance monumental. Most of the buildings looked remarkably new, a fact I attributed to the likelihood of their having been rebuilt after the war. That likelihood was confirmed by the condition of the stone facing on the huge Roman triple arch standing astride the avenue a few blocks along. "The *Siegestor*," Adriana said. "Another debt to Rome." Yes, the Arch of Constantine all right. As we came abreast of it we could see numerous pockmarks left by bullets and shells, the only memorial I had seen thus far in Munich of the destruction wrought by the war. Beyond the arch the street broadened, its sides now lined with statuesque poplars, adjoining the poplars a double sidewalk dotted with benches, beyond those more great trees shielding a variety of buildings behind. Despite the traffic it was quiet walking along here.

"I feel relaxed and free," I said to Adriana. "Isn't that odd? With all the tumult in our lives—" She smiled beautifully and snuggled closer as we slowed to a stroll, savoring the moment.

Now we passed one outdoor cafe after another, waiters carrying trays from the kitchens on one side of the broad sidewalk to the patrons swarming on the chairs and tables on the side abutting the street. This looked too commercial a section for Wolf's residence, but as we turned off onto the little side street of Nikolaistrasse some houses appeared, most of them a century older and in shabbier condition than I had expected. Another three short blocks, some corners turned, and we were standing before Wolf's building, a three-story nineteenth-century hodgepodge of stucco, dull-red brick, gray stone, window pediments, a Norman tower, a black dunce's-cap tower and other assorted features. So Victorian-cataleptic styles had hit Germany too—and Wolf had bought one of the products!

"There's the convent," Adriana said, pointing to a modern six-story concrete-and-glass structure next door. I would have expected the nuns to live in Wolf's building, or vice versa.

A few seconds after we pushed the doorbell, Wolf greeted us. "Come in, come in!" he exclaimed, kissing Adriana enthusiastically on both cheeks, hugging her tightly, shaking my hand heartily. He was dressed in a colorful silk smoking jacket over a white silk shirt, silken black trousers, shiny black soft-leather slippers. Wolfgang the expensively casual host.

The inside of his house, as I should have expected, had nothing to do stylistically with the outside. It also had nothing to do with his Spartan office. It was luxury, pure and simple, or rather impure and complex. At a glance, everything in it looked twentieth-century, much of it late twentieth-century at that, including the abstract tapestries and paintings covering most of the wall surfaces, the abstract statuary spaced artfully here and there, the modern Chinese rugs, the subdued lighting, the ficus trees and artificial plants and flowers, the chrome-and-glass coffee tables. Here was the affluent corporate setting I had expected to see at his office. It spoke of *success*. Thinking that, I realized how hostile to Wolf I had become. What had happened to my admiration of only yesterday? Smashed by the fist of deceit, that's what. But then we didn't actually *know* that he had deceived us.

Wolf was taking orders for drinks, filling the orders at a sculpted bar on one side of the living room, bringing the drinks to us on a lacquered Oriental tray. The glasses looked to be an original Finnish design, like nothing I had ever seen in a store. My Beck's tasted just like Beck's, though.

"It's a pity I can't show you the English Garden,'" Wolf was saying. "You must come again in the daytime. An entrance is only a hundred yards from this house. You must have heard of the Garden. It's immense, thousands of acres, wonderfully designed by Count von Rumford, formerly Sir Benjamin Thompson, originally an American, isn't that curious? Lovely canals, trees, bicycle paths, topless sunbathing, all the finer things." I glanced at Adriana, who appeared to be looking at Wolf afresh. Wolf invited us to sit down, began passing an hors d'oeuvres tray.

"I hear that you have a new piece of the hoard," Massimo said to him, helping himself to several large mushrooms stuffed with crabmeat and cheese. His tone was amiable, but Wolf seemed to hesitate a moment before replying.

"The tetradrachms, you mean," he said, refilling Massimo's wine glass. Massimo said nothing, merely sipped his wine, gazing steadily at Wolf's face. "What a piece of luck, eh? As I said to your friends here yesterday, the existence of this pair seems to confirm Luigi's story of duplicate coins."

Massimo persisted. "And so how many coins do you have now?" I was amazed at his daring, looked quickly at Wolf.

Again that minute hesitation. "Why, just the two. Why do you ask?"

"Well," Massimo said, still amiably enough, "given what my sister has just told me—"

"I don't know about that," Wolf said, seating himself next to Adriana. "What did she say?"

"Why, that the Marchesa's husband has suddenly been pouring money into Roman real estate. I thought that possibly he might have come across one of the coins, and might have approached you to put it on the market."

"No, he hasn't," Wolf said, not a muscle twitching. "I would certainly have informed you of it, if he had."

"We trust that you would, Wolfgang," Massimo said, carefully studying the mushrooms left on the tray before selecting one.

"As you're obviously a major coin dealer in Munich," I said, "possibly *the* major dealer, I suppose that you would hear about even any rumors of unusual coins coming into the market."

"Very likely, yes," Wolf said, "although the Turks usually operate along their own lines."

"You do lunch with them occasionally—?" Massimo said.

"Yes, and occasionally dine with them too," Wolf said, annoyance glimmering for the first time at the edges. "They're a sociable lot, always trying to prove they're as German as the rest of us, and conspicuously generous with their hospitality." That scar on his face seemed to flame brightly. That sign of his masculinity, honor.

"You sound the merest bit antagonistic," Adriana said, smiling as a good friend would smile at learning of one's peccadillo.

Wolf chose to accept her smile rather than her implied criticism. He put a hand over hers. "I'm fond of the Turks, I really am, as sociable creatures. They're lively and engaging at meal times, at all times day or night really do seem to enjoy being helpful in all sorts of ways—"

"These are all *men* you're speaking of," Adriana said. I wished that she would disengage her hand from his.

"Yes of course. Turkish men would never hear of their women going into business, the way some German women do."

"When you see the Turks socially," Massimo persisted, "you might detect signs of their having gotten wind of the hoard?"

"Never at dinner," Wolf said, "but possibly at lunch. We sometimes discuss business then, though almost always rather circumspectly. Something as major as the hoard would never get discussed."

"I don't know the first thing about the coin world," Adriana said, finally disengaging her hand, "but I've been wondering how a reputable dealer—like yourself, say—rationalizes dealing with smugglers."

Wolf paused for a few seconds, as though deciding which of the numerous explanations he must have devised over the years to advance on this occasion. "When you say 'smugglers'—by the way, we Germans seem to have invented the word, *schmuggeln*—you use it in a way to suggest illegal activity. Sometimes laws *are* broken. But it's hardly ever a clear-cut matter. When Greek coins of the fifth century B.C. are dug up on Sicilian soil in our century, whom do they belong to, would you say? The Italian government in Rome? The Sicilian government in Palermo? Sicilians themselves notoriously hate all governmental authority and would surely claim the coins as their own. But that effectively means whichever mafia chieftain gets control of them. Or do the coins minted in fifth-century Syracuse still belong to the Syracusans? Or to the Greeks back in Greece, whose designs were used and from whose mines the silver came with which the coins were made?"

If Wolf's aim was to obfuscate the issue, he was doing well. "So coins of any hoard are really up for grabs," Adriana said. "So nothing is illegal."

"That puts it a bit simply," Wolf said, "but in a way that's true, yes, practically speaking." We let that hang in the air.

Our silence was broken by the sound of dishes being stacked in a nearby room. "Ah, that's Marta," Wolf said cheerily, "let me introduce her. Marta!"

A slender and decidedly attractive black-haired woman in her thirties came quietly into the room. She was holding dinner plates and wearing an apron. "This is Marta," Wolf said with a sort of pride of ownership and without giving Marta our names. "She's from the Abruzzi and cooks like a dream." The others were doubtless thinking, as I was, that she had other talents too. Marta smiled shyly, gave what was probably an Abruzzi version of a curtsey, and left the room. "You should taste her pasta Marta!" Taste was indeed a question, I thought—Wolf's manners, that is, not his taste in women.

"That photograph of a lovely boat on the wall of your office," Adriana said, "is that your boat?" I sucked in my breath, ever so carefully. When Wolf nodded, his thoughts possibly still on Marta, Adriana asked, "Do you keep it somewhere near Munich?"

Wolf was beginning to look a trifle wary. "No, none of the lakes around here are suitable for it. It's a sea-going yacht. I keep it in the Mediterranean, here and there." Marta was bringing food to the dining-room table, lighting candles. "Ah, I see we're ready," Wolf exclaimed, rising. "Will you join me?" He offered an elbow to Adriana, who seemed destined to be attended by men with obtrusive elbows. We processed to the dining room, Wolf seating Adriana next to himself.

The antipasto was gorgeous, and while as a first course I had looked forward to pasta Marta, the *primo* turned out to be risotto Milanese, predictably delicious. Wolf was perhaps keeping pasta Marta for himself. The pink trout was fresh from some nearby mountain stream, the Italian reds and whites superb. The evening would have glistened, had it not been for the treachery we three suspected. We managed to observe the courtesies during the meal, though, and left off our questioning of the host.

After espresso and wonderful zabaglione on strawberries, we thanked Marta heartily, returned to the living room while she did the cleaning up. We were all a little tiddly, the three guests anyway, and my anger rose as Wolf seated himself again next to Adriana on the sofa, and took her hand. "You see why I prize Marta?" he said. We said we saw.

"May I ask," I said, "whether Gustav has had any luck tracking down those supposed Turkish couriers?"

"They were Turks all right," Wolf said, looking at me soberly, "and no, I haven't gotten a report from him yet. He's rather decrepit and can't physically do the investigation himself, of course. It may take him a few days to hear from the agents he's no doubt hired."

"You don't *know* that he has hired them?" Massimo asked.

Wolf affected a certain weariness. "I don't *know* it for a fact, Massimo, no. I trust Gustav completely. He'll get the job done."

"Doesn't it make a lot of difference," I persisted, "whether the couriers were Turks or not? What if they were Greeks, for instance, or Sicilians?"

"Well of course it makes *some* difference," Wolf said, dropping Adriana's hand and visibly clenching his own. "But it's not the crucial point, is it? Isn't the point that we have the coins in our possession—?"

"But they're not *your* coins," Massimo said with considerable force, "or ours—"

"Well, they belong to our hoard, do they not?" Wolf asked, his voice shimmering with innocence.

"Will the Turkish couriers or whoever they are see it that way," Adriana asked, "when they return?"

"Look," Wolf said, now sounding tense and weary, "I have a great deal of experience in these matters, more even than our friend Massimo. This sort of conflict of views—for that's what it is, at bottom, a difference between two notions of ownership—happens all the time, and I'm nothing if not skillful at resolving such conflicts."

"I dare say that's true," Massimo said, "but because Michael and I did after all discover the hoard in the first instance—"

"After Luigi," Wolf pointed out.

"—yes, after Luigi, and we brought it to you—"

"Placing its supervision in my hands," Wolf said.

"Well, we wanted you to guide its passage as only an expert could," Massimo said.

Wolf waved the distinction aside. "With you going back and forth to London, and Michael and Adriana essentially bystanders, if they'll excuse my putting it that way, I've pretty much had to take charge, wouldn't you agree?" Silently, we seemed to. "*Nehm' ich an*, and so I assumed from the beginning. If you see some other way of doing things—of coordinating information on the hoard, trying to gather its pieces together, placing it wisely on the market rather than as amateurs would—let me know."

Adriana tried tact. "I'm sure you understand, Wolf, that we've been feeling things getting a little out of our hands, for the very reasons you've suggested."

He looked at her, appraising the moment. "Yes, I can see that," he said calmly. "And now, what about a liqueur for everyone?"

We all declined, spoke of the late hour, rose, thanked him profusely for the magnificent evening, asked him to thank Marta again for us, and prepared to depart. As we shook his hand at the door—Wolf kissing Adriana thrice this time—Wolf said to me, "Michael, I would like to show you my favorite museum in Munich. It's the German Museum of Hunting and Fishing, not far from the *Neues Rathaus*, and has the most unusual collection of weapons and stuffed animals in all Germany." Despite his apparent amiability, Wolf's face seemed to me distinctly stern.

Outdoors, we began walking slowly away. "Munich is filled with great art museums," Massimo said as much to himself as to us, "and what does he recommend to a history professor? A hunting museum!" And then to us, "What was that about a yacht?"

"When I learned that he keeps it at Rhodestown," I said, "my first thought was smuggling off the Turkish coast. The distance is only a few miles. But then I realized that a yacht isn't a good smuggling vessel. Even with a strong Diesel, it's too slow."

"No," said Massimo, turning it over, "much too slow. But it *is* a curious geographical coincidence, isn't it."

"The boat is for orgies," Adriana said, eyeing the convent we were passing.

"You know," I said, "Wolf looks terribly fit, but he isn't a young man. I wonder what a lecher does when his sexual powers begin to fail."

Adriana chose to ignore any little barb flying toward her. "Becomes a dirty old man?" she said.

"Or exerts power in other directions," Massimo observed, "if he has the will and talent." Adriana and I said nothing, knowing that Wolf had plenty of both.

At Ludwigstrasse we parted, Massimo going off to his old

Schwabing inn. We promised to call one another first thing in the morning.

Back at the Arabella there was a message for me. Phil had phoned. "Arrived safely. College still here. Good to see pals. Giving film to physanthro friend. Love." Looks like he had kept well within his three minutes. But I was happy to hear from him. The desk clerk must have used up the rest of the three minutes trying to get the spelling of "physanthro" right.

We took the silent elevator, silently. "Wolfie is sleeping with that Marta," Adriana said, "he's not interested in me.'"

"That's what you think," I said, anger flashing.

"Don't you suppose I have some say in the matter?"

Back in our room, we undressed. Her nightgown dangling from one arm, Adriana came up to me. "Don't you think we should test whether *your* sexual powers have failed—or mine?"

With a memory like hers, how could I refuse?

The average fencer, thinking that he has recovered out of range, relaxes mentally and physically, and may be vulnerable to offensive actions which are then launched.

Hesitating to make a decision he may be late to parry.

I awoke the next morning determined to talk with a Turk. Several Turks, preferably. Turkish coin dealers, ideally. But if they were mostly crooks, or at worst smugglers? And would they talk to *me*? Not likely, but I felt an urgent need to get a grip on Munich, which meant learning things fast about the tight little coin world here, above all meant getting information and perspective on Wolf.

I decided to call Gustav. Massimo might have been able to set up a meeting with one of the Turkish dealers, but he hadn't appeared to be moving in that direction, and anyway I liked the idea of being independent of him and coming up with discoveries of my own.

Over breakfast at the Reform Haus I told Adriana of my

scheme. She didn't just applaud it, she insisted on coming along. The prospect of meeting an exotic Turk — and possibly a smuggler at that! — positively charmed her. Well, she could only be an asset in any such interview. In the clear light of a fresh Munich morning, both of us hung over not so much with unsettling memories of Wolf's party as with our peacemaking at the hotel, we felt confident of doing anything. The yoghurt and freshly baked rolls couldn't have tasted better.

Back at the Arabella, I phoned Wolf's office, got Gustav. Before I could broach my Turkish scheme he exclaimed, "It's Providential that you called!" He couldn't explain over the phone, he said quickly, speaking *sotto voce* as though in danger of being overheard. We agreed to meet in a half-hour at the Sculpture Gallery near the Konigsplatz. Adriana said she would wait in our room until she heard from me.

I had been waiting only a few minutes at the entrance to the Glyptothek when Gustav arrived in a taxi. He climbed stiffly out of the back seat, without his dachsund. I walked down the front steps to meet him, shook his outstretched hand.

"It's only a few short blocks from the office," he said, breathing heavily, taking my arm and steering me back into the building, "but I walk very slowly and wanted to talk with you without delay." There was urgency in his voice.

We entered the loveliest statuary museum imaginable, with capacious sunlit rooms, high vaulted ceilings, a floor of large blue slate, tan limestone walls pierced and enfolded and crossed by Roman arches of all sizes, the farther rooms visible through the receding arched doorways, the whole a cool, tranquil setting for Greek and Roman portrait busts, full-length statues, sarcophagi, wall mosaics, temple pediments. There were centuries and centuries of ancient art here, the marble busts rising on stone pedestals to shoulder height, as though the Greeks and Romans themselves who now lived only in these marble effigies would have spoken to us face to face if they could.

As soon as we passed beyond earshot of the ticket-sellers

Gustav said, "Wolf is planning some mischief against you." Towering over Gustav a few feet behind him stood the mutilated statue of a naked, bearded god with a child cradled in one arm. The hand on his other arm was missing, one leg ended in a stump at the knee. He looked down comfortingly at the child.

I stared at Gustav, his coat sleeve pinned up. "What harm could he do me?"

"What form it might take, I can't say. But he wields a lot of influence here. I came to the office a bit early this morning, saw the door ajar to Wolf's inner office and heard him bustling about in there. I sat down at my desk and heard him place a telephone call. I couldn't overhear everything he said, but I distinctly heard your name and Massimo's name mentioned and the word 'urgent.' That was enough to make me listen hard. Then he gave whoever he was talking to quite detailed *physical* descriptions of both you and Massimo. Wolf's voice was distinctly menacing, that's what got my attention in the first place."

"What could he do to us?" Even as I asked the question I remembered the beating Gilberto's thugs had given me in Rome.

"The first thought that occurred to me was that Wolf might accuse you of coin theft, but I don't see how he could make that stick. I can't think of a felony or even a misdemeanor that a German judge would consider seriously against either of you." He paused. "Did anything happen between the two of you and Wolf yesterday?"

"We must have threatened him last night," I said, "that is, *seemed* to threaten him. No, now that I think of it, we really did threaten him."

Gustav paused, forebore to ask questions. "I have no way of knowing his intentions, but it might be wise for you to stay out of sight. Perhaps even leave Munich."

Without the hoard? or even without seeing more of it? "Has he ever done this sort of thing before?"

"Never, so far as I know. But there's a great deal about him that I don't know. I *do* believe he's been growing more arrogant in recent years, and I suspect more unscrupulous."

"The arrogance of the rich?"

"No doubt," Gustav said. "He lives not only in the safe,

comfortable, self-enclosed world of the rich but also in the peculiarly insulated world of the successful coin dealer, with its own rules and parochialism and code of honor, if that's the right phrase." Gustav spoke with real vehemence.

"He also seems to me rather devoid of feelings," I said, reflecting that even his pursuit of Adriana might well have been carried out mainly at some rational level.

"Yes, and that's why you must get out of his way!"

I looked at Gustav, trying to fathom whether *he* had motives to fathom, whether Wolf might in fact have set him up to this conversation. I dismissed the notion as absurd. "I can't leave Munich—" I started to say.

"Why not?"

"—not after all we've gone through—." I raised a hand helplessly to the marble gods nearby. Gustav watched me keenly, not asking, perhaps not needing to ask, what I meant.

"Then you should drop out of sight," Gustav said. He was a much more decisive individual than I had realized. "Come stay at my apartment."

"But Adriana—"

"It's a double bed," he said simply. "And there's a spare bedroom. Small, but large enough for Massimo. I've seen Massimo a few times—did I tell you?—when he has come to Wolf's office on some business or other, so that I know what size of bed he requires. I have a friend nearby I can stay with for a few days." As I paused, still trying to sift it through, he said, "You have to decide at once."

I decided.

In fencing, the guiding principle must be to hit and not be hit.

Giddy if anything from the elation of fear, I phoned the Arabella from the Sculpture Gallery. After an irate "Wolf *what?*" Adriana calmed down enough to work out the details of the move from the hotel to Gustav's lodgings. She would handle it all, would bring our luggage by taxi, agreed that I should stay away from the hotel.

Gustav had an apartment in the Schwabing area, some blocks

away from Massimo's inn. I *had* to try to catch Massimo at his inn. If Wolf felt that I was a threat, Massimo might be even a greater one. Exactly what sort of threat either of us might be, I wasn't at all certain. The hoard was somehow involved, *that* seemed certain.

Following Gustav's hasty directions I walked from the Gallery, striking off north and east. I found myself feeling the anxiety of someone whose life has been menaced, the disorientation that comes from having one's routines however skeletal abruptly shattered, and yet a certain exhilaration from the adrenal pumping that secret agents must experience on the run. So *this* is what it's like to drop out of sight, go to ground as they call it. Looking around me at the gray facades of shops and dwellings I was passing, I realized how nearly invisible I really was to anyone inside who saw me. Luckily I wasn't wearing anything flamboyant or even markedly touristic that an observer might remember.

Turning left at a corner I noted idly that the street was named Turkenstrasse, then a few blocks farther on found Massimo's inn. He had told me it was unpretentious, but it was worse than that, not really an inn at all but a drab-looking place whose most prominent feature was the weatherbeaten sign, *Zimmer zu vermieten*. I knew a rooms-for-rent sign when I saw it. Had the robbery of Massimo's shop in London set him back that much?

Entering the dim foyer, I found myself face-to-face with a sour-looking elderly man behind the narrow registration desk. "Herr Massimo Bellini?" I said. He shook his head, jerked his thumb toward the entrance. "May I leave a message?" Another head shake. *"Vorrei lasciare un messaggio per il Signor Bellini,"* I tried, pointing with my ballpoint to a pile of papers on the desk.

He gave no sign of having understood that language either but grudgingly scrounged around in a drawer and handed me a small piece of blank paper. I wrote "Massimo—emergency—*caveat* Arabella—*caveat* Wolf—call 33-40-47 or G.(only!) at W's," and signed it M. Sourface wrote #4 on the note and laid it on a corner of the desk.

I said *"Danke,"* started to leave, thought that some insurance wouldn't hurt, put a five-mark bill on the desk next to my note. Sourface swiftly pocketed the bill, but his expression didn't change.

Gustav's address was only four blocks away. It was a walkup apartment building of a sort common in New York's Greenwich Village or London's Soho, but fronting on a clean street. I entered, using a key Gustav had given me, found a pleasant vestibule, walked up three flights, located his door, unlocked it, walked into a living room with the faint odor of burnt coffee. Quickly I went into the tiny kitchen to check the stove burners, but they were turned off. There sat the coffee pot, though, an old metal job that looked like Army issue. Had Gustav had it for fifty years? The kitchen was old but immaculate. In one corner stood a remarkable miniature Alpine chalet with a large entrance, the whole just the right size for a well-fed dachsund. The food and water bowls were brightly decorated to match the chalet.

I returned to the living room, whose furnishings were spare rather than Spartan, with simple knotty-pine chairs and a table. Pine bookcases lined all four sides of the room, floor to ceiling, even covering parts of two windows, and I could see at a glance that the books were in several languages and ran heavily to art, architecture and the ancient classics. Jammed along the sagging shelves in front of the books more or less at eye level were photographs of various sizes, mostly black-and-white, mostly framed. Many of them showed Gustav, usually with his arm looped around companions, some male, some female. Some photos showed Gustav as a young man, both arms intact, his craggy features recognizable and surprisingly handsome. Some showed him in Army uniform, one with the Eiffel Tower in the background and a laughing, blowzy woman on one of his arms, another with him perched in a Jeep against a backdrop of snowy fields.

Tucked halfway behind another photo was one I almost missed. Gustav one-armed and emaciated, a scrawny boy standing nearby but not touching Gustav. The boy stood with arms akimbo, a cocky look on his face. It was Wolf's face all right. Fritz's face. I was musing on the man that that boy had become when a bell squealed in the kitchen. I couldn't find an intercom phone or button and went down the stairs as quickly as I could to the front door. The taxi driver was helping Adriana deposit luggage on the stoop, his smile vanishing when he saw me, then reappearing when he saw how much Adriana tipped him. As he sped off, Adriana and I lugged the suitcases upstairs, she taking the heavier ones as I still couldn't lift much.

"It's generous of Gustav, isn't it," she said as we slowly toured the little apartment. I repeated to her what Gustav had told me of the overheard phone call, and the speculations he and I had had on it.

We paused at the door to the small bedroom. "I suppose there's no way to know," she said, "when Massimo might get your message." I shook my head, dread suddenly filling my soul.

"All we can do is wait here," I said, saying but the obvious.

And so we waited—into the afternoon and through it. Gustav's little boxlike refrigerator was stuffed with the prepared frozen foods that bachelors prefer, and I had eaten enough of those in the months after Susan died to come to detest them. There was also frozen bread, mustard and a supply of various German cheeses, and so we fixed sandwiches in the early afternoon and ate them in the living room.

I showed Adriana the photo of Gustav and Wolf the boy. She examined it attentively, silently. I explained that it would have been taken in Berlin, and told her what Gustav had told me about his own past, and about his relations with young Fritz. She listened to my account, said nothing.

Time stretched out before us indefinitely, and so we talked about what a sad and courageous man Gustav appeared to be, what a dreadful fate it was to have been born a German in the twentieth century. I told Adriana of my realization that night at the Olympic Park that I had been attracted to Wolf partly because I found myself identifying with him, might well have been born into the terrifying disruptions and confusions of his postwar era had my grandparents stayed in Germany rather than emigrating. She was visibly touched by the image of a German Michael Gardner who had escaped the brutalities of the war itself but suffered afterward as most Germans had suffered. Italy experienced such great convulsions immediately after the war, she said, that her parents had decided to leave for

Brazil, but even after their return to Italy in the late 'sixties, they found Italy still trembling from the shock of the Fascist era and the war. Italy had never fully recovered from either, she said with a sigh, right up to the present day.

"That's why you should move your piano into my living room," I said, knowing even as I said it that the piano she now had would never fit.

She smiled, for the first time that day, and was about to say something when the phone rang. I picked it up, with relief heard Massimo's voice. I gave him the gist of Gustav's warning, our decision, Gustav's address. He said he'd be here in twenty minutes.

He was. Adriana and I were fruitlessly speculating on our options in Munich when the bell in the kitchen cried out. This time Adriana went rapidly down the three flights to the front door. In a few minutes she returned with Massimo.

Panting from the climb, he sat down in the nearest chair to catch his breath. The suitcase he'd brought with him was of an expensive leather, well worn. "I very nearly went to Wolf's office this afternoon," he said, still wheezing, "but decided quite by chance to return to my *pensione* first. Give me the particulars, please."

Massimo listened gravely to my recital of events, saying nothing, simply gesturing enigmatically with both hands when I mentioned Gustav's disbelief that Wolf could have us arrested. "Do you trust Gustav?"

"Yes. Before today I'd had only one real conversation with him, but that was a long one. He struck me as the genuine article."

"And he *has* turned his apartment over to us," Adriana said.

"I still wonder what Wolf stands to gain by getting us out of the way," Massimo said, half to himself. "What skulduggery could he have in mind—?"

"That he couldn't carry out, "I said, "with us around."

"Exactly," Massimo said. "He knows his way around Munich, we don't. He knows the coin routes in and out of here. He must know the politics of the city."

"Suppose—" Adriana said tentatively, "suppose his aim isn't to get you both out of the way indefinitely but just for the next few days—"

"And maybe the *number* of days isn't the point—" I said.

"But a *particular* day is," Massimo said, racing ahead of us, "and Wolf doesn't yet know which one it is. Such as the exact day when a delivery might be made—"

"That's it!" I said, excited. "Let's say Wolf is expecting someone to bring him coins from the hoard—say, sometime this week—"

"That makes sense," Massimo said, "specially when a covert operation is involved, possibly with more than one agent along the line, or a considerable distance. Even if whatever coins from the hoard reached Rome and then were transshipped here, they wouldn't necessarily come by plane, they might travel overland, and not necessarily by the most direct route. So that the time of their arrival in Munich couldn't be calculated precisely."

Adriana said, "I'm thinking of the coin—let's say it's just one—that Gilberto may have come by. Supposing he *did* ask Wolf to sell it for him, how would he be likely to get it into Wolf's hands?"

"Unless Gilberto came to Munich himself—you could judge better than I how likely that is—he might entrust it to someone who could simply carry it in a moneybelt or pouch on his person on a regular commercial flight here. Or this agent could drive from Rome directly to Munich—"

"No problems at customs?" I asked.

"Not for anything so easily concealed. And a mere coin or two could easily be delivered to Wolf without anyone else learning of it. So that *if* his aim is to get us out of the way for some delivery, something *larger* than a coin or two must be involved."

"Or something different," Adriana said. "Perhaps he doesn't want one of us to see or meet the courier?"

"Because one of us might recognize him?" I said.

"Or her," Adriana said.

"Or," Massimo said, "because Wolf wouldn't want us to *meet* the courier—that is, be introduced to him—"

"Someone like Luigi's fisherman brother," I said, naming the first person to come to mind.

"Why would that matter?" Adriana said.

"Let's suppose it *is* the brother," I said. "Somehow Wolf has made contact with him, or vice versa—"

"Yes," Massimo said, "and Wolf has led him to believe that he is acting on *our* behalf, or just for *me*. I was after all as close to a friend of Luigi's as Luigi ever had—"

"So that the brother thinks he will be delivering the hoard—"

"Or what's left of it," Massimo said.

"—delivering it to Massimo, as Luigi may well have asked him to do." I paused. "Except that it's not likely to be the fisherman brother—"

"Why not?" Adriana asked.

"He'd almost certainly have had to go back to fishing," Massimo said, "once he delivered the hoard to someone on the mainland. But he'd have delivered it to another Sicilian, possibly *another* brother."

"Who might have looked in the leather bag," I said, "and decided to sell off a few of the coins—"

"My very thought," Massimo said, almost angrily, "just a few pairs, probably one coin at a time, thinking that no one would miss them. It might well have taken him a while to hear that Wolfgang the big Munich dealer is a friend of Massimo's—"

Adriana said, "You're assuming that this second brother feels an obligation to deliver the coins to Massimo."

"Yes," Massimo said, "and of course we don't know that to be the case. But a *Sicilian* might well feel that—might feel it as a family obligation, a matter of honor, specially after Luigi's death."

"Would it matter," I said, "whether he knew Luigi was dead?"

"It's impossible to say. But if he knew the mafiosi were involved in the death he might be eager to keep the hoard out of their hands and put it in mine, or even Wolf's."

Adriana said, "So if all this speculation has any truth to it—"

"Then the bulk of the hoard may be arriving at any moment in Munich," I said, tremendously stirred once again at the prospect of seeing it.

"We can't simply sit here, all mouth and trousers, waiting for that to happen," Massimo said, as though to illustrate the point laboring mightily to get up from his chair. "Even before I got Michael's message I had gotten in touch with the one Turkish dealer I trust. I'm to see him this evening. We desperately need help to find out what Wolf's up to."

"Is there any reason to think this Turk would know that?" I said.

"Or that he would help us?" Adriana said.

"Neither one for certain. I do know that he's strong in the Turkish community—he has real assets there is the way I've heard it described. And his German wife has connections in German Customs. In any case, if either of you has a *better* idea, tell me." An eruption lay close to the surface. "Do you realize," he said, giving each of his words equal weight, "that if we cannot manage to intercept Wolf's scheme at this point, whatever it is, we may never see another coin from the hoard again?"

And then he added, his voice sharp, "Except at the viewing prior to their being auctioned."

Neither Adriana nor I had a better idea than Massimo's.

The impression of having impaled himself on the point will be very demoralizing to the opponent, whose subsequent attacks will lose some of their conviction and fire.

The fencer who attacks into the attack is an aggravating type.

We could have walked to the Turkish dealer's office in a half-hour but decided that even after dark the three of us might be too conspicuous on the streets, particularly as that office lay only two or three short blocks from Wolf's. We took a taxi, instructing the driver to approach the office well to the west of Maximiliansplatz and to drop us off a block away from it.

Massimo led the way, explaining as we walked that Turgut Muduru of course had business dealings with the other Turks but had apparently managed over the years to keep aloof from their smuggling activities. Massimo didn't know him well, only through some business deals and by reputation, but had a strongly favorable impression of him. Muduru had come to Germany back in the 'sixties from a small village in Turkey, sardined in a freighter along with hundreds of other peasants, like them paying an exorbitant fare to the shipping agents. He had come directly to Munich, where the opportunities were, and soon went into importing, where the money was. "I met him not long after he started importing coins," Massimo said, "and I never knew a harder working individual. No pussyvanter he. One day, after I had gotten to know him a little, I asked him whether he ever did anything for pleasure. He looked at me almost scornfully and said, 'Our people didn't come here to enjoy themselves but to *work!*' "Massimo was about to tell us more when we arrived at the Muduru Gallery. At least this dealer goes by his own name, I thought.

"Not much chance of a confidential talk in there," I said as we stood gazing at the glass facade, through which we could see another glass wall fronting the adjacent street. The floor-to-ceiling Venetian blinds at both large windows were open, and enough ceiling lights were on to display the off-white walls and black-and-chrome furniture in the modern interior. The ceiling spots were aimed at marble busts and other artifacts mounted here and there in the gallery.

"There's an office in the back," Massimo said as he pushed a button near the glass door.

A smartly dressed, fair-haired woman entered the gallery from a door at the back and walked rapidly toward us, opening the door with some sort of electronic device and motioning us inside. "He will see you right away," she said with a rather tight smile, leading us to the rear door and standing aside as we passed through. She followed us into the room and closed the door behind her.

Though small, the office was much like the one I had expected Wolf to have, thick with tastefully expensive furnishings right down to the Oriental rug. Behind the desk, now rising to greet us, hand outstretched, was Turgut Muduru himself. I realized to my shame that a tiny, stereoplated part of my brain had expected him to be all flowing moustache and turban, a scimitar in one hand and a hookah tube in the other, with possibly a dancing bear in a corner of the room suffering the agony of a metal ring in his nose, or a gauzily clad concubine discreetly slipping out of the room as we entered. The man before us was clean shaven and dressed in a pinstriped business suit, not a scimitar, hookah, bear or concubine in sight.

He shook hands with each of us and introduced his wife, Frieda. "Would you like coffee?" he asked, and without waiting for an answer motioned to Frieda, who left the room and then reappeared immediately with a brightly polished brass tray of espresso cups and a brightly polished copper coffee pot. "Turkish coffee, of course," Turgut said, smiling, "for which the cup half filled with sugar is absolutely requisite," dumping sugar generously into his own cup by way of example. Frieda poured the thick black coffee over the sugar for each of us. The rich smell of cardamon rose in the air.

"And now, Signor Bellini," he said as we all sat down and started to sip the powerful mixture, "why have you come to see the Good Turk?"

Turgut's self-mockery surprised me, but Massimo appeared to take it for granted. "We have come on a serious matter," he said. "I realize that I may seem to presume on our business relations, and also that this is a delicate matter, involving as it does an important business colleague of yours in the city here." Massimo paused, perhaps to give Turgut a chance to respond, but Turgut only listened, motionless.

Massimo first of all laid out his own credentials as a reputable coin trader, then mine as an American university professor of ancient history with special knowledge of Sicilian coins, then Adriana's as a Roman Marchesa whose husband was a wealthy and knowledgeable collector. He then proceeded to give Turgut an emasculated version of the hoard tale, a version that he, Adriana and I had hastily concocted on the way over. The heart of his story was that the three of us had learned of a recent hoard discovery, that a few rare coins were involved, that we had become the owners of these coins and were having them shipped to us in Munich from

Rome, and that Wolf had almost certainly managed to have these coins intercepted somewhere en route. He then told Turgut something of Wolf's recent behavior, making a point of meticulously distinguishing what we knew from what we suspected. "Had my friend Professor Gardner not been told of Herr Friedrich's threat to both of us," he said, "we might well not have been able to come here tonight. There is no telling what might have happened to either of us." I feared Massimo's lurching over into some sentimental gesture, like mopping his brow with his handkerchief, but he skirted that. "As it is, the three of us have found it necessary to hide out in a dingy flat in Schwabing. Three perfectly reputable individuals, can you imagine that?

"And so we have come to you," he wound up, "hoping that you could help us."

"In what way?" Turgut's tone remained noncommittal.

"To begin with," Massimo now shifted gears smoothly, "We're hoping that you could shed light on channels that I may not know of by which a delivery might be made here in Germany to Herr Friedrich. We're also hoping that you may know of someone who could be hired to put Herr Friedrich under surveillance, so that we could be alerted to any delivery about to take place."

"Suppose you *are* alerted," Turgut said, "then what?"

Massimo drew a breath. "Well, we would also require help of some sort in confronting Wolfgang, perhaps some show of force—"

"I can see," said Turgut, "that you are still thinking the matter through." Something about Massimo's story—or about us?—seemed to amuse him. "Do you know what Herr Friedrich calls us immigrants when we're out of earshot? *Katzelmacher*. Of course we call him Wolf. Perhaps you do also."

He swiveled slightly in his chair toward Frieda. "What does my good German wife say?" She seemed accustomed to Turgut's ironic tone.

"There's little hope of picking up either the couriers or the coins at the border," she said to us. "Even a small bag of coins could be taken through customs without much difficulty. If you could give us a short list of names, what my friends there *could* do is tell us whether any of these names appear on the daily list of incomers. But of course that assumes that the couriers are traveling under names you know."

"So that the crucial question," Turgut said, "becomes that of delivery here in Munich, does it not."

"And the surveillance of Wolf himself," Massimo said.

"His office," Turgut said, appearing to think aloud, "his home, traveling about. Around the clock."

"That means a lot of manpower," Massimo said.

"Yes," Turgut said. "Which I do not command." He did, however, appear to have accepted the possibility of joining our side of the enterprise, or at least not to have ruled it out.

We all sat there, weighing the silence. "And you require this surveillance without delay," Turgut said, "if your intuitions are correct." If he was tightening the screws a little, that wasn't surprising.

"Yes," Massimo said.

"Needless to say, I don't keep a large crew of trained men on hand," Turgut said. "I don't run a private detective agency. But many of my fellow countrymen need work. I could possibly round up a small number of them quickly." We all waited.

Massimo asked it: "The price?"

"How many coins did you say there were?" Turgut said.

Massimo repeated our estimate.

"Rare," Turgut said, softly. "A private collection." He knew how to control a moment like this, the Good Turk.

Turgut looked at his wife. "Would you say three-quarters for us, my dear?" She appeared to think that over, but only for a few seconds, nodded.

"That's impossible!" Massimo exploded, rising from his chair. He stood there, arms dangling at his sides, as though uncertain whether to stand his ground or head for the door. I knew him well enough to sense the magnitude of his frustration.

"Well now, Signor Bellini," Turgut said, his voice still gentle, soothing. "Nothing is really impossible, is it. And you must recognize how expensive it would be for me to employ all those men.

We're talking about a minimum of six at a time, are we not, two at each of two locations and two to follow the Wolf. Eight-hour shifts, although six-hour shifts would be preferable, but let's say eight. Six men times three each day is eighteen men — and for how many days? We don't even know that. And then you want two or three armed men on hand — no, no, I realize you didn't specify armed but that would be necessary, would it not — two or three trained men to confront Wolf at the rendezvous. They don't come cheaply. And then the expense of cars, communications equipment —" He trailed off, with an expressive gesture toward the limitless world of surveillance costs.

"I must consult my friends" was the best Massimo could do, as Adriana and I rose to join him outside the room.

Our conference in the gallery outside was devoted not to the question of whether to accept Turgut's proposal but to various ways of shaving his commission down. Adriana was as incensed at Turgut's banditry as Massimo was. I felt so far out of my depth that I was simply resigned to whatever bargain Massimo could strike. In order to get Turgut's help we had had to tell him something about the hoard, and it was now coming home to us with a thud that having done that, we had introduced yet another party to the hoard pursuit. Although we were by no means ineluctably committed to Turgut, he now knew enough about the hoard to find it tempting. And without his help, the three of us stood almost no chance of winning the race ourselves.

We agreed to try to get him to accept half.

We returned to Turgut's office, stood before him, like petitioners before the Pope who believe that only he can intercede with the Deity on their behalf, who have placed themselves in his hands — but have already begun to perceive the ambiguous consequences of their having done so. In the few seconds we stood there before anyone spoke, I realized that even with the minimal knowledge of the hoard that we had given him, Turgut might well not need us *at all*. We were balanced on the knife edge of his generosity, whose precise dimensions we had very little notion of. So this Turk had a scimitar in his hand after all.

"Assuming that the delivery takes place in Wolf's office, as seems likely," Massimo said, "would your men have the skills to break in at the right moment?"

Adriana spoke up for the first time. "Wolf has small floodlights outside his office door and some sort of camera—"

Turgut said, "They can take care of those."

The negotiations were heated, but brief.

From his share of half the coins from the hoard, he should be able to hire agents who could not just deal with floodlights and cameras but could do *anything*.

The riposte is an offensive action which follows a successful parry. It can be direct, indirect or compound, and delivered immediately or after a delay.

And so that's how we left it, how we had to leave it—essentially in Turgut's hands. Turgut was to send word to us at least once a day on how his surveillance of Wolf was proceeding. He was to contact us *immediately* to report on suspect couriers arriving at German customs, or any behavior on Wolf's part that indicated an important delivery or rendezvous in prospect. As we had no reason to think that Gustav's apartment was being watched, Turgut's messengers were to report there.

Gustav himself had suggested his dropping by the apartment twice a day, on his way to the office and on his way back. So it was that at nine-fifteen the next morning he sounded the buzzer from the street and then, a few minutes later, knocked on the apartment door.

We had made coffee for all of us in his old tin coffee pot, and the four of us sat down in the tiny living room to share it. As Gustav had only a short time before going to work, we filled him in as expeditiously as we could on the events of the night before. "I'd be quite willing to let you into the office should there in fact be a delivery," he said, "and I could even turn off the burglar alarm, which Wolf would certainly connect for an occasion like that, but I think that for a delivery of that magnitude he'd never even let me into the office. I doubt that I could help you from the inside at all." But he was obviously intrigued by the whole scheme, smiling now and then as we unrolled it before him. "It's a re-enactment of a great historical drama, don't you see?" he said to me, "only reversed. This time it's the Trojans, which is to say the Turks, who are being surreptitiously let into the enemy's stronghold!" That idea appeared to please him enormously. Obviously he wanted to play the role of the Greek.

As he was about to leave I remembered a question I had wanted to put to him. "Turks?" he said with evident surprise. "Oh no, the men who brought the pair of tetradrachms that day were unmistakably Italian." With that he left, and Adriana, Massimo and I found ourselves with the first clear proof of Wolf's having lied.

It was Massimo who spoke. "It merely confirms what we've known for some time, wouldn't you say?"

We waited the rest of the day, at first restlessly, feeling cramped in the small apartment, tacitly taking turns in one room and another, somewhat as crew members on a small sailing vessel devise ways to avoid unrelenting confinement below decks with all the others and to secure occasional privacy. Adriana and I would hardly have felt we could pair up in one room leaving Massimo in another, so that to the awkwardness each of us felt under the circumstances was added, for me at least, the frustration of having no intimacy with the woman I loved. I rather hoped that Adriana felt that frustration too, but only a fleetingly affectionate look from her now and then fed that hope. What I had long thought of as Massimo's unquenchable sociability appeared quenched. Apart from a few amiable remarks to Adriana or me in the course of the day, he seemed sunk in upon himself, musing on God knows what. At one time or another each of us took a book from Gustav's choice little library and tried to read, but gave it up after a while.

Late in the afternoon Turgut's first emissary appeared. Massimo went down to meet him at the door and returned a few minutes later, shaking his head. "At least the man did show up," Adriana said.

Gustav arrived not long after, with nothing to report either, and after we exchanged friendly greetings and chatted for a while he excused himself, saying he had been invited to dine with the friend whose apartment he was sharing. We then explored the small refrigerator, which Gustav was obligingly filling for us each day with his favorite bachelor foods, and selected the most tolerable frozen packets to heat up for dinner. Not long after, bored and fidgety, we retired, Adriana and I to the double bed. Drawn particularly together as we had been by facing a common threat, nonetheless we found ourselves too distracted and weary for passion, and so we settled for hugging one another to sleep, front to back, curled foetally.

Another day passed in the same fashion, Gustav appearing in the early morning and late afternoon, large cold grocery bags in his arms. He was terribly upset, he told us, that he had been unable to devise a way of letting us into Wolf's office at the crucial hour. All he could think of, he said, digging into his wallet, was to give us his set of keys to the outer door of Wolf's office and the door to the building. We showered him with thanks. In the press of events we hadn't even thought of asking him for keys!

The hours in between Gustav's visits became harder and harder to bear, except for the afternoon, when Adriana found a biography of Paderewski that she soon buried herself in and I found a newly published history of ancient Greece written by an English historian with a lively style. I had read only a few pages, though, when my mind skipped to the Athenian Expedition, and I was soon agonizing over whether I would ever write my book on that Expedition, indeed have another opportunity in the foreseeable future to return to Sicily for the research that I had failed to do on this trip.

Finally in late afternoon Adriana put down her book, rose and said she had decided to make a quick trip over to the Arabella. Either of us could have a message languishing there, she said, and it might be important. Over Massimo's protest she went, saying she'd take a taxi and return in less than an hour. She promised us to slip in and out of the hotel inconspicuously, in return for our promise not to embark on any adventures without her, unless she was unconscionably late.

Turgut's emissary had still not shown up by early evening. Massimo and I were just sitting down to another defrosted dinner when the buzzer rang. Massimo went downstairs as quickly as his bulk allowed and in a few minutes came ponderously upstairs, holding on to the banister at the top of the stairs for a while to catch his breath while I stood there in the door, waiting.

"The Turk's message," Massimo said, still breathing hard but self-possessed enough to speak for effect, "was that two Sicilians with the name Crocefisso crossed the border into Germany late this afternoon, from the direction of Innsbruck, giving Munich as their destination. The customs chaps searched the car, but nothing turned up. They remembered that name, though."

"Crocefisso was Luigi's last name," I said.

"Yes," Massimo said. "It seems that his brothers are using their real names. Lucky for us."

My adrenalin had begun to spurt. "How long would it take them to get to Munich?"

"They could be here any minute now," Massimo said, checking his watch. "Turgut said we should sit tight and wait for the next messenger. He's to contact us just as soon as the Sicilians arrive at Wolf's office."

"*If* that happens," I said.

"If that happens," Massimo said. "Given the name Crocefisso, I'm certain it's going to happen. Let's finish this dreadful food."

An hour and a half after she'd left, Adriana had still not returned and I was getting worried. We were putting some food aside for her and clearing the dishes when the buzzer sounded. Quickly we turned out the lights, locked the door and went down to the street. Turgut's previous emissary had told Massimo that a black Mercedes would be sitting at the curb, a driver at the wheel, the engine running, and it was. Another Turk, as I took him to be, young and lean, opened the rear door for us. He was dressed entirely in black, from his thick cap to his blackened tennis shoes, and as he opened the door I saw the metal gleam on a gun sticking up from his belt. Massimo climbed in but I hung back, looking anxiously up and down the street for Adriana's taxi.

All of a sudden it appeared. Adriana had the rear door open

and was paying the driver before the taxi stopped. She almost fell onto the pavement. "I did cut it a bit close, didn't I," she said apologetically as we joined Massimo in the back seat of the Mercedes.

A direct attack is one which follows the most direct course towards the target and does not pass over, or under, the adversary's blade.

When the blade strikes the opponent, it must not be with a dead action, pushed and remaining on the target, as if the fencer were leaning on his opponent for support.

The Turk who had been impatiently standing by the rear car door got quickly in the front seat and we sped off to Maximilianplatz. On the way he gave us instructions. He spoke in a halting English heavily accented with German. We were to stay well behind him and his companion from the moment we left the car until they broke into Wolf's office. If Wolf—or his visitors—had a gun, it could be dangerous for us, whereas he and his companion were prepared to deal with that. They would go up to Wolf's floor, disconnect the floodlights and camera as quickly as possible, use the key Gustav had given us and rush into the office. We were to wait this whole time at the bottom of the stairs until their signal that it was safe to come up. "What about the burglar alarm?" Adriana asked. There was nothing they could about that, he said, except to get into the office as fast as possible to turn it off. Surprise was all on their side. So we all hoped.

Then we were there.

Both men rolled down their ski masks, sprang from the car, closed the doors noiselessly and crossed the sidewalk. One of them turned a key in the outer door to the building. The other man looked back at us and raised three fingers in an emphatic reminder. We sat still for exactly three minutes, then left the car as quietly as we could and followed the men into the building. They had wedged the outer door open for us.

Adriana and I held hands tightly but said nothing, all of us looking up the stairs, straining to catch any sounds at all. Then suddenly, "*Kommen Sie!*" We raced up the stairs. It seemed to take forever. The burglar alarm was clanging, louder and louder as we climbed. Abruptly, it stopped.

The outer door to Wolf's office was wide open. We entered in silence. One black-garbed Turk was disappearing into the inner office and as we came abreast of that door we saw that his companion was already inside, his gun trained on Wolf and two strangers. We entered Wolf's office.

It was a strange, powerful and disturbing moment. The others must have been as aware of that as I was. Even in the short time I had known him, Wolf had entered my life profoundly, and he had entered Adriana's life and Massimo's life in ways not likely to be soon forgotten. The four of us had once been friendly, after a fashion, if not exactly friends — and now those filaments between him and each of us had dissolved in a shower of suspicion and betrayal.

As though to give point to the betrayal, a dark, stained leather bag sat upright and open on Wolf's desk. It was about the size of a grapefruit. After Wolf and the two strangers, the bag was the first thing I saw. I glanced up at Wolf's face again and saw him watching mine. He said nothing, looked frozen. He also looked fearfully handsome and distinguished, the German would-be aristocrat at the peak of his career.

"We're grateful to you, Wolfgang," said Massimo with perfect equanimity, "for locating the hoard."

Wolf replied instantly, as though he had rehearsed just such a retort for some time, "Irony doesn't suit a Sicilian." His tone was urbane, a shade mocking.

"On the contrary," said Massimo, "every Sicilian is an ironist. He has to be, given the world he grows up in."

"Your ironic sense," Wolf said, "will be wonderfully reinforced by the condition of this so-called hoard." He inclined his head ever so slightly toward the bag on the desk.

Massimo moved quickly toward the desk, took the bag in

both hands, looked squarely at Wolf, then into the bag, holding it at an angle against a ceiling light. He set the bag down, looking distraught, glanced rapidly around the room, searching for something, saw a large glass ash tray on a shelf nearby, picked it up and laid it on the desk. He picked up the bag, tilted it carefully over the ash tray and began to pour out the contents.

Flowing slowly out in a thin stream were dull metal granules. Silver. Tarnished.

Massimo shook the bag gently and out slid metal fragments, pieces of coins, the same dull silver. Various sizes. About fifteen or twenty pieces altogether. What was left of magnificent coins.

Massimo finished emptying the bag, shook it gently several times to remove the last coin fragment, and with a studied restraint that spoke eloquently of his disappointment and surely his grief laid the bag gently down in the precise center of Wolf's desk.

For a long time no one said anything at all.

"There," Wolf said at last, speaking to Massimo, every word loaded with enormous disdain, "there goes your fortune."

Massimo reacted furiously. "My fortune! I suppose the thought of a fortune never crossed *your* mind!"

I tensed, ready to intervene should Massimo throw himself on Wolf, as he appeared ready to do. Then one of the strangers spoke, pulling a small, rough-hewn brown wooden box from his jacket pocket and laying it on the desk. His Italian was rough, barely intelligible. I thought he said "They're in there."

An astonished look on his face, Wolf suddenly reached out for the box, but the Turk standing near him behind the desk stepped swiftly to intercept him, brandishing his gun in Wolf's face. Wolf dropped his arm.

Massimo picked up the box, removed its lid—and smiled triumphantly. One by one he removed from the box and laid on the desk nine silver coins. Even as I moved to the desk I could tell there was one decadrachm and eight tetradrachms, shining darkly in all their silver splendor!

Massimo was rapidly sorting out the tetradrachms, looking for pairs. His face positively shone. Adriana joined us at the desk, looking over the treasure, putting her hand on mine, sharing our joy.

So absorbed were we that Wolf had struck the wrist of the Turk and opened the desk drawer partway before my brain registered what was happening, and Wolf had the pistol halfway to firing position when I brought my hand slicing in a stop-cut down on Wolf's wrist, his gun clattering to the floor. The Turk swooped up both Wolf's gun and his own, training his own once again on Wolf, jabbing him fiercely in the chest with it.

Wolf held his sore wrist to his chest, staring agonizingly at Massimo and me. It was the only time I had ever seen him speechless.

"We went through a lot to bring those coins to you," said one of the Sicilians. He had spoken to Massimo in dialect, and Massimo had translated it for us. All at once I perceived what had only been dim before, that both Sicilians strikingly resembled Luigi. They had rougher-cut versions of Luigi's face, as their speech was rougher than his. His brothers, no doubt of it. "That silver," said the one, gesturing toward the ash tray of particles and fragments, "is worth a lot."

Massimo, interrupted in his fury, looked with astonishment toward his fellow countryman, said something harsh to him in what must have been a Sicilian dialect.

The other brother then spoke. "We need the money," he said simply.

Adriana said, "Wolf must have cash on hand."

Wolf looked murderously at her, but then appeared to accept his defeat. "I have some in the desk," he said, pointing.

As Wolf raised his hand the Turkish guard jerked his revolver menacingly, then said *"Langsam, langsam."* Very very slowly Wolf reached down behind the desk, opened the top drawer, pulled out a thin packet of bills, threw it on the desk. Massimo picked it up, riffled through it. "There are only four hundred marks here," he said, tossing the packet onto the desk.

"Obviously I can't get more until the morning," Wolf said, as though having to deal with sheer idiocy.

"How much do you think they should get?" I said quietly to Massimo.

"It's impossible to know what any of those coins will bring at auction," Massimo said. "Small fortunes, very likely, but not certainly. I'd say we should pay them a lump sum—"

"A sizeable lump sum," I said, sensing in Massimo a certain tightfisted impulse.

"Yes, of course," Massimo said. "Sizeable for them."

Adriana motioned Massimo and me aside. "What about giving them the silver dust?" she asked quietly. "Would that be about right?"

"Or some of it," Massimo said, reluctance trembling in his voice.

"What would the whole pile of dust bring on the market?" I asked. "Not counting the coin fragments."

"I don't know," Massimo said, wearily. "We'd have to weigh it. Possibly a thousand pounds sterling. That's a very rough guess."

Massimo's face was sheer gloom. Had he expected not to pay the couriers at all? I couldn't believe that. He must simply be giving in to his sorrow or vexation at finding so much of the hoard turned to dust, trying to control what little there was left to control.

"Let's give them the whole little pile," I said, "and throw in the German marks."

"They've earned it," Adriana said emphatically.

Again Massimo hesitated, looking ruefully at the little cone of silver particles on the desk, at the small mound of coin fragments, at the handful of whole silver coins. "I understand your being sick at heart," I said. "I am too."

"Well, but *your* disappointment," he said, waving a hand as though to dismiss whatever different sort of disappointment I might be feeling. "All right," he finally said, sighing deeply. "*You* give it to them."

He had spoken indifferently to Adriana and me. Adriana stepped to the desk, picked up the leather bag, spoke distinctly to the Sicilians. "*Vogliamo che lo prendiate tutto.*" We want you to have it all.

She picked up a piece of paper from the desk to use as a scoop.

"Not into the bag," I cried out. "Don't give them the leather pouch. Use something else."

Adriana hastily put down the bag and began searching through the desk drawers. She then went into the outer office and soon returned with a large transparent plastic bag and an opaque manila envelope. With great care she began scooping up the silver grains into the plastic bag. Except for the Turks, who kept their eyes on Wolf, the rest of us watched Adriana's rhythmic motions, the little mound of silver in the glass tray gradually diminishing, the mound in the clear plastic bag increasing. I had never seen such a visible transfer of wealth. It was hypnotising.

And then she was finished, tying a knot neatly in the top of the plastic bag and placing the bag into the manila envelope, bending the metal clasps at the top. She handed the envelope to Massimo, saying "Why don't you give it to them." She was artful, that woman, or tactful, or both.

With a good enough grace, having apparently accepted the inevitability of the arrangement, Massimo stepped forward to hand the envelope to one of the couriers. As he was about to do so, one of the Turks stepped forward and laid the barrel of his gun on Massimo's hand. "Turgut, half," he said sternly.

Massimo glanced at Adriana and me, then said evenly to the Turk, "Half the *coins* for Turgut. That was our agreement. Nothing else." The Turk hesitated, uncertain.

Massimo then proceeded to hand over the envelope to the Sicilians. He even managed to make the act a little ceremonial, thanking both men in rather formal Italian on behalf of the Marchesa, the American Professor and himself, and also their deceased brother Luigi, then switching to their dialect for what I took to be farewells, as he shook their hands and saw them out the door into the outer office. I heard them all talking in low voices out there for a time and then heard the outer door close. Massimo returned to the inner office. Particularly in the face of the Turk's unexpected demand for half, Massimo had carried off the moment with admirable style.

I had begun scrutinizing the tetradrachms on the desk, saving the lone decadrachm for later. It looked like a Demareteion—possibly the one Luigi mentioned? Wonderful! I looked first for tetradrachm pairs, found none. At a glance all eight coins had familiar designs—except one. "Look at those twisted horses—," I said, beginning to grasp the unusual nature of what I was seeing on this singular tetradrachm.

"That means nothing at all," Wolf said, almost contemptuously.

"We can dispense with your expert opinion now," Massimo said, turning his back on Wolf and picking up another of the coins, only to put it down hastily. He turned round to Wolf. "We will however have those twin tetradrachms, if you please, and the decadrachm you relieved Carlotta of in Rome."

Wolf moved not a millimeter. It was a critical moment for him. His high-speed brain must have sped through numerous options on whether to surrender the coins or not, how to salvage *something* from the wreck sinking beneath him. "They're not here," he said.

"Then where are they?" Massimo asked, an aggressiveness in his voice that I had not heard before.

"Where you'll never get at them," Wolf said coldly.

Massimo paused. Then Adriana stepped over to Wolf's desk, moved behind it, forcing Wolf to stand somewhat aside. She bent down, running her hands over the drawers and panels of the desk, finally tapping at one panel repeatedly until it swung open. From where I was standing I could see the front of a small, inset metal safe. Adriana tugged at the dial. No luck.

Adriana was looking at Wolf tentatively, as though wondering whether he would cough up the combination, when the Turk close to Wolf took a step toward the desk, motioned Adriana back, aimed from a few feet away and shot the dial off the safe. Adriana quickly swung open the door and pulled out the lovely little inlaid wooden box she and I had seen before. Peering into the safe, she then pulled out another, smaller box, this one beautifully tooled deep-red Florentine leather, with a gilded filigree design on the cover. Still kneeling, she set both boxes on the desk.

I opened the inlaid box. The twin tetradrachms lay there

glimmering. Massimo opened the other box. There lay Carlotta's glorious decadrachm!

Wolf's little gambit had failed, and he stood there, not even deigning to shrug his shoulders.

Adriana was still exploring the interior of the safe. With a satisfied look she stood up straight, holding a bundle of papers in one hand and another tooled-leather box in the other. This box was a rich emerald green, also of Florentine design, and larger than either of the other boxes. Adriana set the papers on the desk. It was her turn and she took it, gently opening the green box. Massimo and I crowded near her.

Inside, laid out neatly on hunter-green velvet, was still another decadrachm, surrounded by possibly twenty tetradrachms, all of them mint condition, all of them fifth-century Syracusan, many of them obviously duplicates, all part of the hoard!

I turned to Wolf. "You may as well tell us where you got them," I said. It was the first I had spoken to him.

After wavering a very short while, to my surprise he told us. There were *exactly* seventeen tetradrachms, he said, in a manner suggesting that precise accounting was as important as any other features of the hoard. They had come from the Marchese, he said, who had refused to tell him where he had gotten them but was perfectly delighted to sell them to Wolf at much less than Wolf would later get at auction because he needed cash urgently.

"And the odd decadrachm?" Massimo asked.

This was a story Wolf was plainly more reluctant to tell. "They came to me through another collector" was all he was willing to say, despite our pressuring him in various ways to tell us more.

"Was this collector a Sicilian, perhaps?" Massimo asked. "Possibly with the name Brutto?"

But Wolf refused to say anything more, asserting his need as a reputable dealer to maintain client privacy. "If you ever have any more clients," Massimo snorted.

If that decadrachm had come from Brutto, I thought, it might well have been taken off the body of the murdered courier who had earlier brought the decadrachm to Carlotta's office.

"It's not the entire hoard," Adriana said, "but what a wonderful chunk of it!"

I went back to that singular tetradrachm on the desk. "This one has to be unique," I said to Massimo.

"The duplicate might have turned to dust," he said sourly.

"Yes, but its design is *quite* different from that of any of the others we've seen. Take a look."

As we bent over the desk one of the Turks moved quickly to our side. "Turgut's half," he said in his thick English. "I take *jetzt*."

"Yetst?" I said, puzzled, turning to Adriana.

"*Jetzt*," the Turk said more peremptorily, brandishing his pistol dangerously close to our faces, "*jetzt, sofort!*"

"He means right away," Adriana said quietly.

"Would you tell him," I said to her, "that we have every intention of carrying out our bargain, of giving him half of the coins, but that Massimo and I absolutely must look the coins over first."

"Tell him," Massimo added, "that we have to decide which ones to give to museums." As that was my idea, not Massimo's, I knew how ironic that remark was.

Adriana spoke in German to the Turk standing near us. He looked unhappy with the message, but stopped waving his pistol around. "*Zehn Minuten*," he said forcefully, glancing at his watch and turning his attention back to Wolf.

"*Zehn* is ten," Adriana said, standing close to Massimo and me at the desk.

"I could tell," I said, turning to sort through the coins. Massimo joined me in spreading them out on the desk. The impatient Turk was hovering near us, had replaced the pistol in his belt but kept his hand nervously near the handle.

It was dreadful having to make hurried decisions on which coins to keep, which to give to Turgut. Following the night of that fateful bargain with Turgut, Massimo and I had discussed how we might go about splitting whatever coins there were in the hoard with the Turkish dealer. As we knew definitely of only three coins, however—Carlotta's decadrachm and the twin tetradrachms—we found ourselves thrown back on such useless conclusions as that we would have to bargain with Turgut's men for coins we particularly wanted.

The one coin we had agreed we wanted was Carlotta's decadrachm, that remarkable design of Chol's. I wanted it for myself, first of all, to examine at leisure those skull and quarry designs for whatever light they might shed on the Athenian prisoners in the quarry. Then I wanted to give the coin to a major museum, for other scholars to examine and for the public to enjoy. After some gnashing of teeth, and with Adriana pitching in on my side, Massimo had finally consented.

That's where we started. For Carlotta's coin, we proposed giving Turgut the odd decadrachm—probably Brutto's, taken off the murdered courier's body. We trusted that Turgut's men wouldn't realize just how special Carlotta's coin was.

I had discovered something on that singular tetradrachm that led me to suspect its being still another design of Chol's, and so I prevailed upon Massimo to put that one aside too. Having surrendered the first one to me and to a museum, he gave in easily on this one. We decided to offer Turgut the twin tetradrachms in exchange.

And so it went. Massimo rapidly sorted through the coin fragments from the leather bag, and even he decided that he would rather see museum specialists reconstructing whatever whole coins that jumble might produce than turn them over to dealers. "The reconstruction might end up the same," he said, "but museum specialists might learn a lot for the history of numismatics." So Massimo had his non-commercial impulses too, I was happy to see. As the pile of fragments had yielded what looked to us like a broken Demareteion, we proposed trading the entire pile for the Demareteion from the brown box, quite likely the very coin Luigi had handled.

That left twenty-four tetradrachms. Eight matching pairs and the rest miscellaneous. That made it easy—four matching pairs and four single coins to Turgut, the same to us. Or rather to Massimo.

As I had gotten the prizes I wanted—if Turgut's men agreed—I was happy for Massimo to have the rest. He was nothing if not happy when I told him I had no desire to claim any of the twelve tetradrachms. "It's not really even a small fortune," he said rather ruefully, eyeing all the stunning coins laid aside for museums and for Turgut.

One of the Turks proved to be Turgut's negotiator, and our negotiations with him were as difficult as I expected. The Turk spoke English badly, but once Adriana had presented our explanation to him in German he appeared to grasp the point at once, merely taking a few minutes to look over the coins on the desk and make his own calculations of the money value of the two groups of coins. He made the calculations so fast, indeed, that I wondered whether he might not be something much more than a hired gun, possibly a numismatic assistant to Turgut. "He might be a son or a nephew," Massimo whispered to me.

Massimo and I held the line on our preferences, and in the end we won. Not that Turgut lost.

Adriana supplied plastic bags and manila envelopes for both parties, and what was left of the hoard thus vanished into two harmless-looking parcels. Except, that is, for the two coins of Chol's—one certainly his, the other possibly. I slipped these into the stiff leather bag, clutching the top of the bag tightly. Massimo took the envelope with the rest of our coins from Adriana's hands. He, Adriana and I had already decided to leave the office together with the Turks, none of us wanting to have what could only be a mutually painful exchange with Wolf, probably none of us able to think of anything not vituperative or melodramatic to say. Silently we filed out of the room, preceding the Turks, one of whom still kept his gun trained on the German.

As I left his office I took one last look at Wolf. He stood there, by his cleared desk, still nursing his hurt hand against his hurt chest, not looking at the three of us or at the Turks but out his office window, at whatever layer of Munich he could see, at whatever of Munich was left to him now.

COUNTER-RIPOSTES 281

At any weapon it is often necessary to have recourse to counter-ripostes to deal with an adversary whose defence is strong against attacks.

Climbing into the Mercedes, we were soon joined by our black-garbed companions, who delivered us back at Gustav's building. They left at once, without a word, no doubt to deliver their loot to an impatient Turgut.

Wheezing all the while, Massimo climbed the stairs to the apartment with a speed I wouldn't have thought possible, the manila envelope clutched tightly under his arm. As I was about to unlock the door, it opened, Gustav standing there before us. "I take it you've had an interesting evening," he said, his deep voice sounding at once celebratory and sepulchral. We hurried inside and as though by agreement over to the small table we had used for dining in one corner of the living room. Massimo tore open the envelope, took out the plastic bag and held it in the air in front of us in a gesture of triumph. The coins clinked faintly, glowed. "*Schön!*" Gustav said in a low voice. "Beautiful!" It was exactly what I felt once again.

With trembling hands Massimo lowered the bag to the table, untied the knot and carefully spilled out the coins. I added the two coins from the leather pouch. Adriana separated the various coins from one another, arranging them in a kind of rosette pattern, Carlotta's lovely decadrachm in the middle, the tetradrachms encircling it. From a separate little plastic bag she carefully shook out the coin fragments and arranged them in a crude ring around the tetradrachms. The rings of silver glowed darkly, luminous beyond belief.

I extracted the singular tetradrachm from the others and set it off to one side.

"May I?" Gustav asked politely, pointing to that coin. He lifted it almost delicately, holding it by the edge, bringing it up very close to his eyes, examining one side and then the other. I felt his excitement. "Let me get a magnifier," he said, setting the tetradrachm back down and going over to a small desk on one side of the room. In a moment he returned, offered the lens to me. I gave it to Massimo.

"Yes, let's look at that little beauty first," Massimo said, raising the quarter-size silver coin to within a few inches of his face and rotating the lens back and forth to focus on it. "It's perfectly done" was his first comment. "Late in the century—somewhere around 415 to 410, I'd say—about the same date as Carlotta's decadrachm. And there's the little quarry symbol—"

"Yes," I said, "that's what I noticed first of all. And so we're looking at a date of about 413."

"But even more striking—there's something more than simply energy in the horses—a contortion, almost a violence, as though the horses were in great pain—no, as though a bomb had just exploded near them and they were rearing up and recoiling from the shock—"

He flipped the coin over. "Arethusa's face—there's anguish in it. I've never seen anything like it. Usually her face is dignified, serene. But here—"

"May I look?" I said, taking the coin from his hand without waiting for an answer. Getting Arethusa's face in focus, I saw at once what he meant. "It *is* anguish," I said, "grief—or pain—or regret, something like that." I turned the coin over. "And the horses are suffering too—"

"Indeed," said Massimo, "he's expressed similar emotions in both."

"Do we know who the 'he' is?" Gustav asked.

I gave Gustav the coin and the magnifier. "Look at the ground line." I knew it would be there and I knew who it would be.

"C-H-O-L," Gustav spelled out, squinting hard. "It could be the prefix or an abbreviation for *cholos*. Lame."

"Of course!" I exploded, slapping my forehead. "Lame! I should have known."

"Ah well," Gustav said in the kindest manner imaginable, "you did tell me you always used a dictionary for classical Greek. Anyway"—here he gestured toward his missing arm—"I'm particularly aware of certain physical peculiarities."

"The lame skeleton—" Adriana said, catching her breath. She rushed over to the sofa, picked up her purse, scrambled around in it, came up with a crumpled piece of paper. "I'm so sorry, Michael," she said, coming over to hand me the paper. "I picked this up at the Arabella this afternoon—and then I was so late getting back here—it's from Phil."

"*Physanthro says bilateral clubfeet distinct in skeleton photos*," I read, my blood starting to race as I repeated the message aloud. "*Both feet bent inward, soles turned up. Talipes equinovarus. Hope this helps. Love, Phil.*" Chuckling over Phil's use of the Latin and driven nearly to tears by the welcome news, I told Gustav of Phil's anthropologist friend and the photographs Phil had taken of the quarry skeleton. I confessed how foolish I felt not to have seen the obvious connection between the lame skeleton and the engraver's name. I didn't mention not having noticed the skeleton's misshapen foot bones.

"It also helps account for all that emotion in the coin, don't you think," said Gustav, "I mean the engraver's own lameness."

"Well it could," I said, pointing to Carlotta's decadrachm on the table, "except that here is another coin of Chol's, and it doesn't at *all* have this riotous sort of emotion."

"It's expressionistic," said Adriana, who had been examining the smaller coin with a lens, "like the contorted emotion in a Munch or Nolde painting."

Massimo took another turn with the coin. He tried to get an arc of the reverse in focus but apparently failed. "Might you have a stronger lens?" he finally asked Gustav.

"I have one at the office," Gustav said, going over to his desk, "but I don't think I brought it home." He rummaged around in the drawers. "No, I did! Here."

Massimo returned to the task, finding the focus, rotating the coin slightly. "It has to be the war," he finally said, nodding his head as though having answered a question he had put to himself, setting the coin and magnifier slowly down on the table. "It has to have been engraved at the *end* of the war, after the Athenian defeat—413 or later."

"Because—?" I said.

"In the locks of Arethusa's wonderful, wild hair," he said, "wilder and denser and more precisely carved than usual, remarkable as that is on so small a coin, Chol managed to carve a tiny symbol filling out his identity. Almost invisible, even with a strong lens like this one—"

Sometimes Massimo's stage-managing was infuriating. "Just tell us," I said, barely controlling my impatience.

Massimo looked at each of us in turn. "He carved"—Massimo said, still drawing it out—"a tiny owl."

"Chol, the Athenian," Gustav murmured.

I knew instantly that Massimo was right. It *must* have been the war. That extraordinary anguish. Because lame, Chol would have been a non-combatant. But he would have shared his fellow Athenians' suffering at their defeat. And if he somehow learned of their having been thrown into the quarry, thousands of them, he could only have felt horror.

Massimo was right except in one detail. "Not *later* than 413," I said.

"Why not?" Massimo said.

"Because Chol was down there in the quarry with the other prisoners," I said. "That's where we found him. The soldiers were forced down there just as soon as the final battle was over."

"Couldn't Chol have been put down there much later on," Adriana said, "or even gone down voluntarily?"

"Not voluntarily, no," I said. I described the dimensions of the Cappuccini quarry and reminded her of the nighttime descent Phil and I had made there with Luigi. "Even with only invisible skeletons around us," I said, "that is, before we came on the one skeleton that had cradled the hoard—"

"Chol's skeleton," Adriana said.

"Yes, now we know it *was* Chol, don't we," I said, reflecting on that new certainty. "Well, even with no dying prisoners around us down there in the quarry, with orange trees and lovely flowers everywhere, and the most wonderful perfume in the air, the night perfectly still—even with all that it was a *haunting* experience. I can't imagine anyone at the end of that savage war standing on the edge of that quarry looking down into that living hell of dying men and not feeling wretched—"

"Unless he was a Syracusan," Massimo said.

"Yes, although the scene must have been so horrible that even the Syracusans must have found it impossible to gaze at the sufferings of those prisoners down there. No matter *how* vengeful they felt after their city had been under siege for so long. And after the first few days the dead ones would have begun to bloat and smell. No, that anyone who didn't *have* to go down there would even *consider* doing so voluntarily doesn't make sense. Unless he was suicidal. But Chol wasn't suicidal. These two coins are nothing if not exuberant, full of vitality—"

"Not this last coin of his," Gustav reminded me.

"Yes," I admitted, "there's the agony we've all seen in that coin." I thought about that. "But he *did* design it, don't you see? And managed to get it minted. That took energy and determination. What an act of affirmation that was!"

"How affirmative it was," Masssimo observed, "depends partly on what's on the coin, wouldn't you say?" He was looking at it once again, the powerful lens to his eye. "That quarry design—the lines of the rock face are much more irregular than on Carlotta's coin—"

"Engraved in a hurry, perhaps?" Gustav suggested.

"And next to that symbol in the exergue—almost in the quarry's shadow, so to speak, and so tiny as to be almost invisible—there's a curious figure—bearded—holding a hammer—his feet strangely shaped, curving outward—"

I asked, "May I see it?"

None too happily Massimo surrended the coin and lens. "What a lovely idea," I said, trembling enough to have difficulty getting the figure in focus. "It's Hephaestos."

"I should have seen that," Massimo said. "The volcanoes on my native island were his smithies."

"The god of metallic arts," Gustav said, "the great creator of beauty."

"Clearly meant as a self-portrait," Massimo said. "Except that the feet curve *outward*, not inward."

"You can put that down to artistic license, or necessity,"

Adriana said. "Isn't the main point that if he put that self-portrait next to the quarry symbol, he must have planned to join his fellow Athenians?"

"No, no," Massimo said, "he might simply have been suggesting his kinship with them, or his compassion for them."

"In any case," I said, "I still can't imagine his joining them in the quarry voluntarily."

"But he did end up with them, it seems," Gustav noted.

Adriana persisted. "Well if he didn't do it by choice, couldn't he have been forced down into the quarry long after the other Athenians were?"

"If my experience in Russia is any guide," Gustav said, "there would certainly have been soldiers assigned to guarding the rim of the quarry, on the remote chance that some prisoner might claw his way to the top. But even they would have stood farther and farther away from the dreadful stench with each passing day. I think they're not likely to have forced any new prisoner down into the quarry unless they absolutely had to. It would have meant their walking into that horrible smell themselves."

"Unless—" I started to say, uncertain. "You know, Adriana may be right. Suppose that Chol *did* deliberately slip down into the quarry one night, not with the idea of joining his countrymen in death but merely as a temporary hiding-place—"

"Despite the stench?" Adriana said.

"Yes," I said. "Out of sheer necessity. To elude pursuers. Think of him with a towel or scarf wrapped around his face, to reduce the smell." I was aware of speaking with a great rush, even a little hysterically, but couldn't stop. "This last coin strikes me as fascinating, not least because it makes the nature of his last days more definite.

"The one indisputable fact we know about Chol is that by the end of his life he was a brilliant engraver. These two coins show that. But where and when did he learn engraving?"

Adriana asked, "At the mint in Siracusa?"

"That's possible, but only if he had lived in Syracuse for many years. It must takes a great many years to become a master engraver." Gustav was nodding his head vigorously. "And we simply don't know where he had lived or for how long. But let's look at what's likely. As an Athenian, he might well have arrived in Syracuse with the troops—"

Massimo broke in. "There *were* thousands of merchants and other civilians in ships accompanying the troopships."

"It was amazing, was it not?" I said. "There were perhaps thirty thousand troops in the initial invasion, and some ten thousand civilians."

"The Athenians expected to win," said Massimo.

"To win easily, yes," I said. "But if we ask ourselves just *who* those civilians were likely to have been, then we realize that they must have included not just merchants and profiteers but a wide range of craftsmen and other skilled workers to take over Syracuse."

"Like coin engravers," Gustav said.

"*Senz 'altro*," I said. "Of course. And probably tool and die makers to set up their own mint, or take over and improve the Syracusans' mint. After all, it was from the Greeks earlier in the century that the Syracusans had learned how to design and produce their astonishing coins—"

"Most of the Syracusans *were* originally Greek," Massimo said, "from Corinth."

"—and the Athenians still controlled the great Laurion silver mines. And they not only had to pay all those soldiers and sailors but also would have wanted to set up their own coinage system as soon as they had taken over the city. Silver and gold coinage was one of their great achievements, as we know. Coins of their design and manufacture rivaled their famous painted vases. Minting their own coins *wouldn't* have been merely a practical necessity of the kind, say, that led the American government to establish a mint in San Francisco once enough Americans lived in the area. An Athenian mint would have made a major cultural statement as well."

"Hence Chol," said Massimo.

"Hence a master engraver like Chol," I said, "recruited as deliberately by the Athenians as any general or admiral—"

"Or a colonel anyway," Gustav suggested.

"Yes, I don't want to overstate the case," I said. "Let's just say he had become a master engraver somewhere in Greece."

"All right," Adriana said, "so Chol arrives in one of the merchant ships. Then what?"

"Well, you see, instead of the ten thousand civilians going ashore in a few days or weeks, as they apparently counted on doing, the war didn't go their way at all. They had to stay aboard their ships."

"Some of those merchant ships sailed up to Catana," Massimo said, "not far from where I grew up."

"Yes, and some of the naval vessels broke off contact with the enemy and retired there too. Warfare in those days was intermittent, given problems of supply and whatnot. And so the Athenians spent months now and then on such jobs as building fortifications on land to the north of Syracuse, and waiting for supplies and troops from mainland Greece. And then fitfully they went back into battle—"

"When Chol might have been captured," Adriana said.

"As a civilian," Gustav said, "he wouldn't have been a part of any military expedition."

"But there were Syracusan raiding parties on the Catana camps, as I recall," said Massimo, "and he could have been captured on one of those."

"My very thought," I said. "Let's say he was. And once his captors learned what his specialty was, what would they have done with him? Put him in *their* mint, of course. The Syracusan authorities prided themselves on their coinage too. Their coins were widely imitated elsewhere in Sicily and in Greek colonies on the Italian boot. They weren't likely to waste a talent like Chol's—"

"Especially after they discovered how very good he was," Adriana said.

"Right. And so let's say Chol goes to work in the mint, and settles in there, no doubt unhappy because he is after all a prisoner, but perhaps pleased too to be making use of his considerable talents."

"Possibly he even enjoyed learning what the Syracusan minters were up to," Gustav said.

"I dare say. And then one day a Syracusan aristocrat visits the mint. He's been visiting the mint regularly, let's say whenever the

Director of the mint notifies him confidentially that a new issue of coins is about to be produced. This aristocrat is following a routine that his father and his grandfather had followed before him, staying on good terms with the mint Director, probably inviting him once a year to one of their extravagant parties where philosophers or playwrights from Athens were the honored guests, making the Director feel an intimate member of that small circle of wealthy Syracusan aristocrats who educated their children in Greek ways, who trained racehorses for the Olympics back on the Peloponnesus every four years—"

"The family that built the coin collection," Massimo said.

"Yes, the remnants of which collection we're looking at on the table before us this very moment. Life-spans were short in those days, and so it might even have been the great-grandfather who was inspired to start the collection back in the 480s, when these brilliant coins began pouring from the local mint, working out some arrangement with the mint Director at the time to let him have not just a single coin from each new issue but a duplicate pair, only those in the very best condition of course."

"So that the collection would have been nearly complete," Adriana said, "when Chol went to work in the mint?"

"Yes, although to be sure the aristocrat grandson or great-grandson who visited the mint that fateful day wouldn't have realized that. On that day I can see him talking as usual with the Director, flattering him just enough and not too much, showing interest in some sturdy new bronze dies the Director has just had made, you can fill out the picture. Then the Director can't resist telling of his recent acquisition, this brilliant Athenian who shows as much genius for design and engraving as even the wonderful Kimon, and even more genius than Sosion or Eumenes—"

"Both of whom may have worked at the mint a few years earlier," Gustav said, "if I remember correctly."

I looked at him with fresh appreciation. "Yes, although they were probably replaced by Eukleidas and Euainetos. Now that I think of it, these two men were almost certainly working at the mint when Chol appeared there."

"And of course there was Phrygillos," Gustav said.

"Phrygillos indeed," I said. "I'd forgotten him. And Kimon himself may have been working there then. Amazing! To think of all these talented souls there together at the same time—"

"And so—" Adriana prompted.

"The aristocrat asks to meet him," I said, "and the Director hesitates, suddenly realizing the danger his boasting has led him into. But he can't refuse to introduce them, and so he does."

"And so Chol goes to work for the aristocrat," Massimo said.

"That's what I suspect," I said. "As Chol was a prisoner of war, in effect a type of slave, our aristocrat would probably have bought him."

"The idea being," Massimo said, "that instead of designing coins, Chol would now design silver bowls and trays for the aristocrat's villa, probably cut a few gemstones."

"Yes. As you know there are striking resemblances between the designs on certain coins and those on other artifacts like vases. Many artists must have worked in more than one medium."

"But I can imagine Chol's troubled spirit in that household," Adriana said, her eyes half-closed. "Not only was he a slave, but he might well *not* have wanted to design anything other than coins. And he might have left a wife or lover back in Athens, perhaps children too, and parents—"

"Troubled spirit indeed," I said, "or worse. His every day must have been loaded with anger, and remorse, and nostalgia, but above all resentment—against the Athenian authorities who had gotten him into this trap, but especially against the man who owned him." We were all silent, given over to our own imaginings. "Then one day the war was over. The great Athenians had been routed by land and on the sea. The aristocrat's villa must have been filled with the news, filled with rejoicing." I paused.

"And then gradually Chol heard particulars of the Athenian defeat. Their commanders Nicias and Demosthenes had been captured, probably tortured, then executed. After an agonizing, disorganized retreat northward, some seven thousand troops had been captured—and forced down into the quarry. We can only guess at Chol's feelings. In a careless moment he might have expressed them openly to the aristocrat or to one of the servants, who reported them. Or following the Athenian defeat the aristocrat might have become worried about this genius in his villa, quite possibly a mercurial or otherwise difficult man, might have worried about the man's buried anger. Or the two men might have clashed from the start, on any number of grounds. Whatever the cause, let's say Chol learns that his master wants to get rid of him."

"And so he decides to act first," Adriana said.

"But not before wounding his master," I said. "Perhaps in an unwise, prideful moment, the master had shown Chol his amazing collection of decadrachms and tetradrachms. After all, who could appreciate such a collection better than a master engraver? Chol would have remembered every coin in that collection, would have thought of it every single day thereafter. He must also have thought of a dozen different ways to deprive his master of that collection, so that when the day came for him to try escaping from the villa, he didn't even have to consider what act of revenge to carry out. The only question was how and when to do it.

"Somehow the occasion presented itself. Hastily Chol packed all those lovely silver coins into a sturdy leather bag. The very bag before us on the table. As a creator of beautiful artifacts exactly like those, he *hated* jamming them in all together, with all the risks of scratches and other damage, but he had no choice. All he could do was wrap each coin quickly in a soft piece of cloth or parchment. He then effected his escape from the villa."

"But where would he go?" Adriana asked.

"That's the question, isn't it," I said. "Athens would surely have been his destination, but to get there he would have to get passage aboard some ship—"

"He could have found his way along the coast northward toward Messina," Massimo said, "and then across the narrow straits to the mainland. But traveling by land would have carried its own risks for him."

"And now he was carrying this treasure on his person," I said, "and had to be infinitely more careful than usual of who he talked to."

"And so he thought of the quarry as a temporary hiding place," Gustav said, nodding his head as though that would have made good sense to a prisoner on the run.

"He *must* have," I said almost vehemently, as though fearful of a challenge to the tale I had spun. "The prospect of seeing his fellow Athenians in their dreadful captivity would have appalled him, but again he may have felt he had no choice. And if his escape had occurred within a day or two of the Athenians' imprisonment, there would not yet have been many corpses in the quarry—"

"Or the sickening odor of rotting corpses," Gustav said quietly, speaking as though remembering.

"And so he made his way to the quarry," I said, rushing on, "and probably at night managed to elude the guards around the rim—who after all would want to go down *into* that hell?—and drop over the edge into the depths."

"Wouldn't the drop have injured him?" Adriana asked.

"When Phil and I went with Luigi," I said, "there was at least one entry-point with a drop of only a few feet. We can only suppose that there may have been such points then too—"

"Remember that the ground level would have risen many feet over the centuries since then," Massimo pointed out.

"Yes, I know," I said. "There are lots of things like that we can't be sure about."

"Wait a minute," Adriana said. "If the chronology you've been working out is more or less true, when would Chol have had time to have that last special coin made?"

It was a staggering question. I looked around our small circle, feeling deflated. "The chronology may require a little stretching here and there," I said, trailing off.

"Given the quarry and Hephaestos figures on that coin," Massimo said, "it would have to have been designed sometime between the imprisonment of the Athenians and Chol's escape from the villa—"

"Not just designed," Gustav said, "but produced."

"Indeed," said Massimo. "I don't myself know enough about

ancient minting procedures to estimate the production time for a single coin, but—"

"I know a little about it," said Gustav. "I used to work as a metallurgist. Chol must have had enormous prestige at the mint. With an urgent request from him the coin might have been struck in—let's say—a day or two. If cold-struck, less than a day."

"But engraving the dies sometimes takes months," Massimo said.

"Sometimes it does," Gustav said, "and Chol might not have had even days this time—"

Another impasse.

"I don't know anything about engraving," Adriana said, "but could he have finished most of the work on this coin sometime *earlier* and then put in those little designs at the last minute?"

"You're inspired, my dear," Gustav said heartily, shaking Adriana's hand. "Yes, he could certainly have engraved the quarry and Hephaestos symbols in a day or so—"

"And the owl?" Massimo said.

"Another half-day for that, probably," Gustav said.

"Aren't we assuming," I said, "that Chol had perfect freedom to carry out his work without being spied on or interfered with?" Even I could spot problems in the narrative we were spinning.

"I don't see that as a difficulty," Gustav said. "Chol *must* have had workspace of his own, even if only in his bedroom at the villa. All he needed to engrave the bronze dies were a few tools. A small rotating vise, small chisels of various sizes, a hammer and a small anvil, a small amount of wax. Probably a small bow-drill. He might well have worked without a magnifier."

"He must always have been working at *something*," Massimo said, "so that even with a guard watching him he wouldn't appear to be doing anything different."

Yes, that's how it must have happened. I sensed the agreement passing through all of us.

"We do know in any case," Massimo said, "that Chol never left the quarry."

"Some mishap," I said speculatively, "some accident, some surprise—we'll never know what it was. Perhaps Adriana was right. Perhaps he was injured getting down over the quarry rim—he was after all lame—"

"It's not likely to have been violence from one of the prisoners or from a guard," Gustav said. "They would have lifted the leather bag right off him."

"And so it must have been some accidental injury," I said, "or something like a change in the guards' routine up on the rim, so that later on, when he wanted to escape, he found it impossible to climb out of the quarry—"

"And so he died a slow death," Adriana said quietly. "A slow, agonizing death—"

"Please don't," I said to her gently. "You're right but please don't."

Massimo said briskly, "We do have these rather unusual spoils to divide, do we not?" He rubbed his hands together like a gourmand faced with an eight-course dinner prepared for his very own tastes by the master-chef at the London Savoy.

There are few sabreurs who do not have to use false attacks in the course of a bout.

I awoke to the pounding of heavy rain on the roof above us. Gustav's apartment was on the top floor of the building and the roof could have been made of sheet metal, the rain fell with such a clamor. It was still dark, and I lay there befogged, unable to read my watch, without any clue whatever as to the time of night. All I knew was that I still felt dreadfully tired.

Adriana lay on her side facing away from me, sleeping heavily. Given the racket the rain was making on the roof, it looked as though she could sleep through anything. Now the gunfire of heavy pellets striking the roof. Hailstones! Adriana slept on. Incredible. I worked my way up to a sitting position, still couldn't read my watch, got to my feet, with the rain and hail no need to be quiet, and shuffled into the living room. There was a little more light there, must have faced east. It was six-ten, must be morning. I'd had maybe three hours' sleep.

I was about to return to bed when I noticed the door open to Massimo's little bedroom and saw him fumbling with the blanket, struggling to sit up. With all that weight, sitting up was real work. I had the impression that he had gotten heavier in the last few weeks. One eye open, he saw me and lifted a finger. He looked up at the ceiling, grimaced at the noise of the hailstones, got awkwardly to his feet and shambled out into the living room and on into the kitchen. Mindlessly, I followed him.

He poured water from the tap into Gustav's old percolator, put it on the stove, turned on the burner. He opened several of the small cupboards, located the coffee container, located a tablespoon, measured out the coffee into the metal basket in the pot, closed the lid.

"Two cups?" I said. He nodded, still half asleep.

My feelings were raw, I was just alert enough to sense that. Last evening had been nightmarish, with the masked gunmen and the race to Wolf's office and Wolf's treachery laid bare and the Sicilian messengers and the silver coins that were no longer coins but fragments and a mound of dust. And I was exhausted. And there was fat Massimo, standing in front of the old stove in his wrinkled underwear, staring stupidly at the coffee pot.

"It won't perk if you watch it," I said.

He ignored me.

Through the thickets of exhaustion my mind had begun to clear. "There are still some obscure points," I said, speaking to Massimo's back, "but I see some of the main lines plainly enough. The lines of dispersal, I mean, before the coins came together in Wolf's office."

Massimo might have been listening, or he might not.

"There's Carlotta's decadrachm, to begin with. Wolf had it stolen, and he probably brought it with him to Munich. That's simple enough. Then there were the twin tetradrachms delivered to Gustav by two Italians—"

"Luigi's brothers," Massimo muttered.

"Yes of course!" I said, wondering that I had not seen it before. "That makes sense. Wolf tried to pass them off to me as Turks. That would have had the double advantage for him of reinforcing the Turkish conspiracy he had planted in my mind and of drawing my attention *away* from the Sicilian connection." The links were cascading into place. "But why would they bring Wolf just that one pair of tetradrachms?"

"To test him," Massimo said, barely audible. "To size him up, to see whether he seemed trustworthy, to see whether he was in fact acting on my behalf, as Luigi's friend." Wryly, "The test failed them, obviously."

"They had the rest of the hoard stashed away somewhere, then — somewhere in Munich? or Rome?" The water boiled, rose in the metal stem, filtered through the coffee grounds. Massimo got out two crazed ceramic mugs from the cupboard, stood there watching the pot.

"Probably not in Munich," he said, still speaking almost grudgingly. "You remember that Wolf's rendezvous with the hoard couriers didn't seem to have a definite date, possibly because the bulk of the hoard had to be brought from somewhere else—"

"Well, and Luigi's brothers *did* cross the German border right before they showed up in his office. So the hoard must have been stored somewhere in Rome."

"Or in Reggio," he said, now turning ever so little toward me. "When I ushered the brothers out of Wolf's office last night, I asked them how the hoard happened to get dispersed. How a courier showed up at Carlotta's with a single decadrachm, and then a pair of couriers here in Munich with a pair of tetradrachms, and so on. That's when they told me *they* had brought the two coins—"

"So you weren't just speculating."

"No. I hadn't had time to tell you before. By the way, that murdered courier of Carlotta's was a cousin of theirs. Their big disclosure, though, was that from Reggio onward the *whole* hoard operation was — I was about to say masterminded but it was hardly that — it was crudely run by an uncle of theirs down in Reggio."

"An uncle of Luigi's," I said.

"Yes. This uncle, may his soul be damned, took over the leather pouch from the fisherman brother who brought it ashore. He then got the advice of some other relative who was a local coin dealer in Reggio—some provincial son of a bitch who knew enough about hoards to know that not too many coins should be put on the market at one time, but who hadn't the faintest idea what the extraordinary features were of this *particular* hoard—"

Coffee grounds splattered out of the pot, stank on the burner. "Damn!" he said, moving the pot hastily to another burner, turning down the heat. He got a sponge from the sink, mopped up the mess on the stove, moved the pot back onto the first burner.

I said, "So that the uncle started to ship the coins to Rome one or two at a time—?"

"Or in somewhat larger bunches, yes. We still don't know how many coins that murdered courier had on him besides the decadrachm he took to Carlotta."

"I have an idea about that," I said. I reminded him of the corridor exchange between Gilberto and Brutto that Adriana had overheard. "Those two already had *some* of the coins in their possession, that was Adriana's distinct impression. But where would they have gotten the coins?"

"Various possibilities," Massimo said, "but I suppose off the murdered courier would be most likely."

"I think so too. And that explanation also helps us understand how Gilberto could be conspiring with a snake like Brutto."

"Brutto had come to him with the coins," Massimo said, flatly.

"Exactly. You pointed out to me the evening I met both of them that a mafioso like Brutto often has great social ambitions. What could be more natural than Brutto's bringing to Gilberto at least some of the coins his thugs had taken off the courier's body—?"

"Giving Gilberto a few as a gift—"

"Yes. Fiorella phoned us with the news that Gilberto had been investing heavily in Rome real estate—did I tell you about that?—and Adriana said that was surprising because he had big debts."

"Those seventeen tetradrachms we took off Wolf," Massimo mused. "At—say—a minimum of twenty thousand dollars apiece—even with Wolf's commission—"

"There was also that odd decadrachm."

"Well, but Brutto wouldn't be likely to have given *that* to Gilberto, no matter how lusty his social ambitions."

"No, but he might have asked Wolf to sell it for him, as Gilberto might well have asked Wolf to sell the seventeen tetradrachms."

"Opportunity?" The coffee smelled burnt. Massimo turned off the burner.

"You ask the very question that I've just now come up with the answer to. I hope." I sketched in the Caligulas episode at the villino that jampacked afternoon. "Adriana thought that Wolf had arrived there *after* her husband and Brutto had left the house, but I've just realized that he could certainly have arrived shortly *before* they left—"

"So that the three of them could have transacted some business, coins passing from Brutto's and Gilberto's hands to Wolf's—"

"If they were quick about it, yes. Maybe the two thieves had even contacted Wolf earlier, before they met at the villino—"

"That's probable. You don't conclude a major coin transaction in just a few minutes, let me tell you."

I was still working it out. "So that even as Wolfgang Friedrich was pretending to join me in the pursuit of the thieves who'd stolen Carlotta's decadrachm, he was deceiving me about his relations with Gilberto and Brutto." What a chump I was.

"A master con man, yes," Massimo said, apparently impressed as well as censorious. "I have to tell you I had no idea he was so dodgy."

He poured two mugs of the steaming black coffee. His hand was shaking. We carried the mugs into the living room.

Massimo settled ponderously onto the sofa. He set the hot mug on the floor, then just sat there, staring off at some invisible object. I sat down on a chair opposite him, hastily putting my hot mug on an end table nearby. On the little dining table a few feet away the leather pouch stood solitary and slightly crumpled. I got up, went over to pick it up, sat back down in the chair, kneaded the bag in my hands, feeling the millennial folds, feeling Chol's touch.

Massimo looked toward and past me, with a look somewhere between irritable and hostile. I had seen that look of his fleetingly before, had wondered what it meant, what I had done to inspire it. Or maybe I was being grandiose in thinking that I had inspired it. Or maybe I wasn't. I felt raw, vulnerable. "You look at me as though I'm your enemy," I said.

The glare went out of his eyes. He pursed his lips, sighed deeply, as though uncertain what to say.

"It's not you" was finally all he said, turning back to some indefinite point in space.

Something in me wouldn't let it go. "Then what is it?"

Again he looked at me, only a dull, searching stare in his eyes now. For a while he said nothing. Then "Your father."

In the silence that fell between us I became aware of the silence outdoors. The hail had stopped. Not even rain was falling. Everything seemed listening.

"I would have told you sooner or later," he said, appearing to grope for words. I had never before felt that he groped for words. "In a way that's what the whole enterprise was really about. On my side. Not simply the coins. Oh I wanted *those* all right. Wanted them exceedingly."

"Enough to send my son and me to Sicily," I said.

"Oh yes, although you were going anyway, remember? And I've explained my impresario impulses." Not all that convincingly, I thought. "But there was more to it."

I waited. He raised the mug to his lips, began to sip.

"This whole enterprise was really about what?"

He took his time, measuring everything. "Not solely about your father," he finally said. "About us too, you and me. But behind us, behind it all, was your father."

Feelings swirled up, inchoate and unsettling. "Explain that," I said.

The hot coffee seemed to have started his juices flowing. "You know what a hero Kurt was in our family. I've told you about it more than once, I told your son in London, I've often told others, relatives of mine or even strangers I've had to spend time with on business trips. His was a truly heroic action, of the sort one reads about in great literature, the rescue of a helpless virgin by a valiant warrior."

"Only of course she wasn't a virgin. She had already had me." He paused, sipping his coffee, appeared unwilling to continue.

"Go on," I said.

"At the time my father was off in the godforsaken African desert defending Mussolini's empire. Actually my father had already been taken prisoner by the Brits and there wasn't any more empire. The point was that he hadn't been home for three or four years." Some long-damped coals in Massimo blazed up. "However much we despised the Fascists, what the war really came down to for my mother and me was that my father—her husband—had been away all that time and we had all the farm chores to do."

He finished the coffee, set the mug down on the floor. "I was seven years old when your father rescued my mother from the German soldier that memorable day. As you know, everything I saw that day fixed itself inerasably in my memory." He stopped, appeared to scroll that memory before his mind's eye. "What was *not* fixed in my memory, of course, was what I did *not* see. What I learned about later." Another long pause.

Massimo continued staring everywhere in the room but at me. "A seven-year-old's idea of time isn't to be relied on, but I now know it was several months later that I noticed my mother's belly getting swollen. And then she had a baby. My sister. Fiorella."

I knew before he said it what was coming.

He read my face. "Yes, it was Kurt's child. There could have been no other father."

I still held myself in. "When did you decide that?"

"I pieced it together, years afterward," he said heavily, as though at last utterly tired of all the emotions his pondering the whole episode must have cost him over the years. "The chronology, the looks of nostalgia and regret I sometimes saw on my mother's face when your father was mentioned, that sort of thing."

A part of me felt struck by a heavy blow, but another part felt utterly untouched, as though the tale Massimo had unfolded had taken place on another planet. Only faintly did the notion begin to take hold that I now had a sister, or a half-sister. And that I had had her for a long time.

Questions swarmed in my brain. As usual, Massimo anticipated some of them. "I loved little Fiorella, I felt protective toward her, particularly in the year or so before my father came home from the war. Finally my father did come home, gaunt and shattered. That's how I remember him, gaunt and shattered. I had absolutely no idea what he had gone through in all those years away, of course, and as I hadn't seen him for over three years I had only a dim memory of what he looked like. But I still remember how *sorry* I felt for him when he returned, how gentle he seemed, how my heart went out to him. He seemed to need protecting as much as my baby sister did.

"Later I realized that he must have needed protecting much much more than I could possibly have known. First of all, the shock he must have experienced at finding an infant at home. Then the anguish—for my mother too, of course—of whatever recriminations and weeping must have transpired between them out of my hearing. And then the villagers must have laughed at him and scorned his adulterous wife, perhaps even threatened her. How he must have suffered through years of all that."

"How did he treat Fiorella?"

"I don't remember his treating her badly, although I can't imagine his not feeling some sort of distress every time he looked at her, wondering who her father was, remembering his wife's betrayal. Luckily, he had always been a kind man, given to forgiveness. And the war had broken whatever aggressive spirit he might otherwise have shown."

I was trying to visualize the individuals in Massimo's family those years, but even their ghosts eluded me. I was feeling very strange, heartsick and yet somehow elated.

"As I grew up my relations with him changed, naturally, but I never lost that tender feeling toward him, almost a paternal feeling. So that when I began to realize that *he* couldn't have fathered Fiorella, that it must have been Kurt, I began to hate Kurt. To hate your father. On behalf of mine."

"And eventually to hate me," I said.

"I regret to say that's true." Now he looked squarely at me, perhaps wondering how I would take it. "That was by no means my only feeling toward you. Surely you know that. But hatred was there all right, all the time, mixed in with all the rest. No, hatred is too strong. Something more like a smoldering hostility. Oddly enough, it got stronger once your father died."

"You must have hoped for some sort of revenge."

"Yes, I did. It was childish, but—." He gestured hopelessly.

"That evening at Il Carretto," I began.

"When I told you about the hoard? Yes, I confess to tempting you deliberately. I wanted to get you involved—"

"To make me run risks and suffer."

He inclined his head, pursed his lips. "I wanted to get the hoard out of Luigi's hands. That above all. You looked like the most promising instrument for doing that. If it caused you some pain along the way, well—." Again that gesture off toward the indefinite. "And you were going to Sicily anyway," he said again.

"But not to run afoul of the Mafia," I retorted.

"Or to meet Gilberto," he said. "Or Gilberto's wife." He let that sink in. "Are you sorry for that? Or sorry to have met Wolf?"

"No," I said, thinking it over, "no, I'm not sorry. And in most respects—"

"You're actually glad," he said, a fraction too hastily.

"The way it turned out, yes. But it *could* have turned out quite differently, down there in Sicily, and for my son too."

"But it didn't," he persisted. "And I know you felt—well, invigorated tracking down the hoard—and eventually finding what was left of it—"

"Well, but—"

"And now there's the Marchesa—"

"Stop dangling her before me," I said angrily. "We were talking about *your* motives, remember? Your revenge against my father."

"Your father, please remember," he said, "is also Fiorella's father." He had switched tactics, but I couldn't deny their relevance. I sat silently.

"Michael," he said in a suddenly conciliatory voice, "I've gotten to know you fairly well in this adventure together—we've gotten to know one another, have we not?—and one of your more endearing qualities is that you still, at your age, want everyone's motives to be pure."

I chose to ignore the condescending side of that remark. "I know that," I said stiffly, knowing that I had in fact come to recognize my innocence rather late in life, indeed recently, indeed through this very enterprise in Massimo's company, and partly because of knowing him. But I didn't like his pointing it out.

"Well, *my* motives have never been pure," he said, "any more than yours or—anyone's." He appeared to wait for me to challenge that. "Of course I recognize that my motives or impulses are a good deal more flamboyant than those of most people, existing on a grander scale—"

"Like Mussolini's," I said.

He smiled. "Yes, like Mussolini's." Resisting, I nonetheless warmed to his smile. It *was* a magnificent smile. It seemed to warm him too. "Mussolini was slimmer," he said, patting his gut.

We sat there in silence, he very likely as exhausted as I, no doubt trying as I was to absorb the new texture of our battered friendship, no doubt wondering too whether either of us *could* absorb it, whether our friendship could survive the battering.

I was already feeling that swift descent into lethargy that follows the release from prolonged exertion. Massimo must have been feeling that, and Adriana too. The labor, the abrupt release, the deadness. After living with such intensity for weeks, the terrifying descent into the ordinary.

He may not be quite so sound in defense if he has to take two or more parries in succession. . . .

"I was jealous of Wolf, you know." This admission carried no pain at all now, although the jealousy itself had been painful in the extreme as it erupted.

"Has it occurred to you," she said, "that the reverse might also have been true. That Wolf might have been jealous of *you*."

Somehow that thought hadn't crossed my mind. Wolf had seemed to have—well, everything, including some vestige of Adriana's affection, if only nostalgia.

We were strolling in the morning sunshine in the spacious English Garden, both of us beginning to recover. Massimo had left Gustav's apartment soon after Adriana arose, saying he wanted to get a decent breakfast out somewhere and then phone his wife and his London office, in that order.

"If Wolf was jealous, as I suspect," she said, "that would help explain his wanting to get you out of the way a few days ago, to have someone follow you and then—who knows what?"

"We worked that out, the three of us, remember? And it wasn't just me. Wolf wanted Massimo out of the way too so that he could deal with the Sicilian couriers on his own."

"But the point I'm making is that he may well have had *other* reasons too, or at least this one other reason. Out of his foolish, unrealistic hope that he might renew my interest in him—out of his competitiveness with you, once he had actually seen us together, and yes out of his jealousy too—on more than one level he *wanted you out of the way*."

"Maybe," I said. I was coming to think that I had been incredibly dense about motives, my own included. I moved to safer ground. "It seems Wolf's yacht off the Turkish coast was just for pleasure after all."

"So it seems," she said. "I shall always treasure Herta's fantasy of huge orgies on that boat, with ceiling mirrors and hashish and all the trimmings."

We contemplated that image. "We'll never know the whole truth about Wolf," I said.

"Would you like to?"

"No," I admitted. "But then *yes*. Massimo kept speaking of him as 'extraordinary,' and he is."

Adriana looked as though she were about to say something, and then didn't.

Last night's hailstones must have formed somewhere way up in the stratosphere, because at ground level this morning it was remarkably warm, the glowing warmth of early September. Idle young men and women were spreading blankets on the great expanses of grass, some were starting to strip for sunbathing. We stood and watched them for a while, tan flesh against pine-green grass. The sight was restorative.

"Shall we return to the Arabella?" I asked. "Until we decide what's next."

"Let's *do* that," she said, pretending to be pleasantly surprised. "For tonight, anyway. I'm really tired of that cramped apartment, aren't you. Gustav was sweet to put us up there, but—"

We turned back to the woods bordering the Garden. On a broad path through the woods joggers and bicyclists were now out in such numbers that crossing the path was like crossing a busy city street. More woods, then a small stone bridge over a swift clear brook, then the intersection of a narrow street with the street where Wolf lived.

As though by tacit agreement, we turned left, avoiding Wolf's street.

"Those naked sunbathers," she said, taking my hand as we walked along, "seemed to feel completely at home in their bodies."

"Yes," I said.

"Have I ever told you that one of your great gifts to me has been to make me feel at home in mine—to *enjoy* our passion together—?"

"Tell me again," I said. I quickened our pace. "Better still—"

"Almost nothing has worked out the way I anticipated," I said, quickly putting away my few garments in the closet, setting the leather pouch next to them. "Here in Europe, I mean." Then hastily, "Some things for the better, of course."

Adriana sat near the window, her back to the Munich landscape, her body framed in the glowing aura of the afternoon sun. She was ever so slowly taking off one garment after another, a lovely smile on her lips. "Does it bother you very much, having your expectations frustrated?"

"Sure," I said, going over to sit on the floor at her feet. "But I'm trying *very* very hard to be more flexible." I clenched my fists and bared my teeth to illustrate the point.

"You *have* changed, you know," she said, taking my hand, unfolding the fist, "even in the short time I've known you."

I had begun to learn to embrace life, that's all.

"Well, I *have* recovered from my surgery," I said, fondling her knee with my free hand. "I would like to think I've improved your life one-tenth as much as you've improved mine."

The phone jangled just as she was about to say something. She rose from the chair to answer it.

I was admiring her graceful posture at the phone when a look of pain cut across her face. "That's horrible," she said quietly to the caller, listening intently. After a while, "Yes of course I'll tell him. He's right here." She put down the receiver, looking stunned. I scrambled to my feet, went over to put my arm around her.

"Let's sit down," she said. We sat on the edge of the bed, close together.

"That was Gustav," she finally said. "Massimo had told him we might be here. He was—he was calling from his office. Wolf's office. When he came in to work about noon he found the inner door to Wolf's office ajar, and when he knocked on the door to say good morning he—" She faltered. "The door swung open enough for him to see Wolf lying curled up on the floor—"

"Dead?"

She nodded, tightening her grip on my hand. "He had apparently been—beaten up. Badly. Bruises all over his face. Other marks elsewhere on his body—"

"Any idea how he died?"

"Gustav had called the police right away, and when they examined the body they said he had been stabbed repeatedly—" She was sobbing now on my shoulder.

It could only have been Brutto's thugs, I thought. My body felt rigid, but from what causes exactly I couldn't at all be sure. They might well have followed us last night to Wolf's office, waited till all of us left. Maybe we had left the doors unlocked. Maybe they couldn't believe what Wolf would have told them, that the hoard had come and gone, had passed right through his office without their getting a glimpse of it. Their surprise and frustration, if that's what it was, could easily have turned to rage, all in Brutto's name, all in the name of honor. *Well, you didn't kill him* Phil had said to me of Luigi. No, but I felt myself to be an accomplice in his death, as I did now in Wolf's.

It is quite a common fault to allow the point to lag behind the hand.

In each other's arms now, the shock muted, sensations sorting out, consolation, affection, all the grief of the world still out there, but for the moment out there.

"You're not alone in coming late to love, you know," she said, gently stroking my shoulder.

"Did it really have to take all *this* time?" I said, knowing how foolish the question was. I had begun to tell Adriana of my growing awareness of how locked into the past I had been for years, in fact for most of the twenty years after the Olympics, when I had inexplicably turned away from the exhilaration and physicality of fencing to the world of books, history, the remote.

"Has it occurred to you," she said, her fingers moving down my arm, "that your—let's say—preoccupation with those Athenian prisoners in the quarry somehow mirrored fears of your own—"

"Yes, but that thought struck me only recently. Fears of abandonment, entrapment, god knows what all. Only after meeting you—and, well, chasing the coins with Massimo, and with Wolf too—did I begin to realize how caged-in my life had become." I paused. "And how I hated that. Feared it."

She hesitated, then said ever so delicately, "So you'll be giving up on those Athenians?"

"Oh, I couldn't do *that*," I said explosively, sitting up. Adriana lay there on her side, propped up on one arm, watching me. "I could never give them up," I said, trying for a conciliatory tone. "Well, I shouldn't say never. Not until I've done them some justice, seen that their fate is told—"

"And Chol?"

"Yes, Chol has to be the center of whatever I say now about the seven thousand."

"And so your weeks in Europe haven't been entirely wasted," she said, drawing me down to her side.

The words I struggled to speak remained somewhere deep in my throat. Of how I now had a sister, and how comforting that was beginning to feel. Of how my son and I had grown closer. Of how she and I seemed to be learning to rescue one another. Of how her grand piano would never fit in my living room.

But then Adriana could, if she would.

ACKNOWLEDGMENTS

I acknowledge with great pleasure the aid given me by these individuals in interviews and correspondence:

- in London: Dr. Andrew Burnett, Keeper, Department of Coins and Medals, the British Museum;
- in Rome: Judith Green and Piero Greci;
- in Berlin: Dr. Alfred and Gisela Weber;
- in Munich: Dr. Hubert Lanz.

Every one of these individuals was wonderfully generous and helpful in guiding me through the mysteries of coins and cities.

In London too, David G. Sellwood, former President of the Royal Numismatic Society, Tom Eden of Sotheby's Ltd., Robert Johnson, and Joseph Cribb and others at the British Museum all made indispensable contributions to this book, as did various coin specialists in Munich who requested anonymity.

John Aiello introduced me to the world of ancient coins and often pointed me toward persons and books I needed to know. Dr. Arnold R. Saslow launched my numismatic education by setting trays of Greek coins before me and patiently explaining what to look for on obverses and reverses, and he also responded promptly to subsequent inquiries of mine.

A friend of many years, Laurence Fleming, disclosed areas of expertise even beyond those I had already known he possessed when he furnished details of Renaissance music and costume, and he also was kind enough to help tune my American ear to British locutions. Not least, he designed the wonderful cover and the Colossus logo.

Adriana Greci Green cheerfully carried out photographic and other research for me in Rome, and read the Sicily and Rome portions of the manuscript, saving me from linguistic and cultural errors, and providing crucial information besides.

Both Dr. Roland Werres and Kurt Wiedenhaupt took time from their crowded schedules to tell me in detail of their boyhood years in Germany during and after World War Two.

Help of various kinds was also munificently given me by Paul Arnold, Dr. Simona Balzer, Penny and Robin Bryant, Dr. Jane Buttars, Steve Freeman, Professor John von der Heide, Miriam Lefkowitz, Dr. Paul Lewinter, Dr. Leslie Myers, David E. Myers, Beverly Parker, C. Robert Paul, Jr. of the U. S. Olympic Committee, Professor Barry Qualls, Dr. Sally Rackley, Dr. Kim Sommer, Professor Rebecca Story, Brit Weimer, Mark Weimer and Dr. Donald Weinstein.

Nearly all of our information on the Athenian Expedition comes from Thucydides' *The Peloponnesian War*. Other material is presented in Peter Green's scholarly *Armada from Athens: the Failure of the Sicilian Expedition, 415–413 B.C.* (London, 1971).

David E. Myers gave me indispensable counsel in publishing matters and so made the Colossus Press and this book possible.

Robert Tebbenhoff eased me into his typesetting world skillfully and painlessly.

As the dedication only faintly suggests, Joan Weimer aided and encouraged me in the writing of this book from beginning to end, not least by her editorial astuteness. Noelle Roso also read the complete manuscript and proved a really discerning critic. Portions were also read and helpful suggestions made by Dr. Ilona Coombs and Professor Nadine Ollman. To all of these readers I am most grateful.

D.W.